Tiger
Blood

by Penny Grubb

Tiger Blood

by
Penny Grubb

Cover design by Heather Murphy

First Published in 2016 by Fantastic Books Publishing

ISBN: 978-1-909163-95-9

To George – natch

acknowledgements

With thanks to the editors and copy editors at Fantastic Books Publishing for all their hard work.

Thanks also to the Hornsea Writers for their unflagging critical energy.

Special thanks to Kevin Fitzgerald for an amazing tour of the historic Travellers Club.

prologue

York: Little green men

The couple sit in their car and wait. She looks away from the red signal – a watched traffic light never changes. Across the junction a mother and child wait on foot. All waiting for green lights … green arrows … little green men.

His fingers tap-tap-tap on the steering wheel as he watches for the signal that will allow them to filter through. She feels irritation that his tapping breaches the silence. She's tired. He's tired.

It isn't silent anyway. The roar of traffic is all around them; grey November air presses down. Dusk pushes in and the rush hour isn't even at its height.

Tap-tap-tap. His stare is on the blank face that will show the green arrow. She glances up at the main light showing red – stop – to the main carriageway and left lane filter. They'll both be allowed to set off when that light turns green. But she can look further into the future by checking the side road. It has its own green light allowing the vehicles from the minor road to cross the main artery. Its turn will soon be over. She can't see its traffic signals full face, but she can see the ghostly green glow. She knows that a couple of seconds after the glow disappears their own green arrow will pop up. It's only seconds but she's tired … even this tiny wait gets boring, frustrating. Her attention wanders from the signal to an approaching van. Ha! It slows. It's too late. It won't get through. Her eye catches the amber glow and then red. The side road has had its turn.

No, she's wrong ... trick of the light. The van picks up speed ... the green glow is as strong as ever.

She feels the roar of the engine under her, turns to berate him. Not yet, don't jump the gun.

But the arrow's there. The car is moving. Their counterparts on the main artery surge forward, their lights shining green ... green ... green.

Her thoughts race ... body won't move ... brain says 'No!' ... mouth can't open to frame a shout. For a fraction of a second there's nothing but the roaring in her ears and the ghostly glow of green traffic lights.

And in her line of sight the mother and child across the junction ... the woman grabbing the girl, hauling her up in an arc, turning to run, supermarket bags flying, thumping to the ground, spreading their contents.

The screech of tyres ...

The clash of metal on metal ... a shocking grinding crash.

The squeal of rubber on tarmac goes on and on through the deafening smash. A lone horn blares out a mournful note.

A moment of paralysis. White faces, mouths hanging open. Cars melded ... concertinaed ... pools of dark liquid spreading out from the point of impact as steam billows.

'I saw it,' she says. Her words are shaking like her hands, like her whole body. 'It flipped red to green ... both lights were green.'

prologue

....

Holderness: retired Capt. Donald Farrar's unexpected visitor

Donald glanced at the figure opposite, framed by the silky magenta-patterned cushions of the settee, and winced at being asked to recall the specifics from six months ago.

'I go every year in May, on the 19th.'

He'd told the tale already. Exhausted after the 12-hour round trip, he'd been on the phone as soon as he'd come through the door, while it was still fresh in his mind. That should have put the responsibility for recording the details fair and square on official shoulders.

He'd always known that the trip six months ago was going to be the last time he climbed that magnificent staircase. No point trying to explain to this surly wooden top his son had sent along. He gave a huge sigh and did his best to run through it again.

'I sat in the Morning Room for ten minutes, then I went upstairs.'

He'd had to stop to rest on the landing, the halfway point where the staircase paused to show off its grandeur, splitting to curve right and left to the first floor. He saw himself pausing there, turning his face towards the portraits that had looked down for decades on ascending dignitaries, but massive as they were, the pictures had blurred into the marbled walls, indistinguishable from the stars that had danced at the edge of his vision. The halfway point. His last ever ascent of the big stairway.

He'd thought back to other bivouacs, ice fields, rocky outcrops. He had a sudden temptation to tell the wooden top, to pass on some of his wisdom. You think you'll sleep a few more hours and wake refreshed, but you'll never wake again. Your brain will asphyxiate in the thin air. At his age, simply standing still threatened to rob his legs of enough strength to make the final half flight. Hesitate and you're lost. He'd pulled in a breath and grasped the hand rail. The air felt thin, but he'd known it was just old lungs labouring. And he'd made it to the top.

'Someone said, "Good afternoon, Captain," at the door of the coffee room. A member of staff. And before you ask, I haven't a clue which one, not with my eyesight as it is. The club'll have a record of who was there that day, if it matters.'

He'd stepped inside the room and glanced down its length. The cascading diamonds of the chandeliers were as vibrant in his memory today as they'd been six months ago, but it had only been memory that had given him a clear picture. The room had seemed awash with tiny scattered jewels that glinted from every surface, an upmarket camouflage blanket removing the clarity from polished wood corners, chairs and tables. The splashes of colour overlain with the low hum of a dozen conversations had made an artist's impression of a room full of diners. The consciousness of movement had told him people sat at the club table, but for all he'd been able to see of them, they could have been ghosts.

'Then a young chap spoke. Reckoned to know me.'

Behind the words he relived the turmoil all around him, the hand slapping his back. 'Donald! Wonderful to see you. It must be years.' And how he hadn't been able to focus on the young man's beaming face until the commotion had settled. He'd taken the proffered hand.

'I didn't know him. I'd an idea I'd seen him somewhere but I couldn't put a name to him.'

He didn't have the words to articulate that hint of unease with which he'd half remembered the face.

'He introduced me to a young lady.'

A tiny slip of a thing she'd been, hair scraped back in a ponytail, handshake limp, her skin cool against his.

'He didn't mention his own name. Assumed I knew him, you see. Her? I remember her as Dr China, but I might have misheard. It was noisy.'

The wooden top murmured, 'Ah, Dr China,' but he ignored him. The young man had invited him to lunch and he'd thought, why not? If they turned out to be bores, he'd head for the smoking room after lunch where she couldn't follow. They'd been seated at a table for three.

His vision had robbed her features of clarity. All he could say was that there'd been nothing familiar about Dr China. And yes, he'd known they had an agenda of their own, but youth attached importance to trivia. His aim had been to keep the custom, enjoy the feel of the place he could no longer appreciate with his eyes.

Dr China had spoken to him while the young man delved in his rucksack. Fidgety. Not the sort they encouraged.

'She said she understood my son was a Chief Constable in Yorkshire. I told her he wasn't so exalted. Not yet.'

He heard irritation in his voice at the memory of Dr China scraping the superb dressing from a piece of lettuce before she ate it.

'She looked like one of those waifs. Never had a square meal in her life.'

And that was a daft thing to say. In all the bustle and glitter of the room, he'd barely seen her at all. He was describing an impression, nothing more.

She hadn't troubled him with conversation again until the meal was all but over. He remembered watching her cut a neat incision with a fork down the length of her meringue. In his memory the food was so much more solid than either of his companions. He couldn't be bothered with the detail. Let the wooden top think the conversation was all of a piece. What did it matter?

'She told me she'd ... that her friend had died.'

The memory of the crunchy meringue was sharp, dissolving on his tongue. Her words had been, 'I lost a friend,' and he'd said, 'Mislaid or died?' which had annoyed her. She'd snapped, 'Died.'

'She told me the coroner had said suicide but the note had been unsigned.'

He let out a sigh, weary now, just as he'd been then. He hadn't needed the rest of the story from her and surely the wooden top wouldn't need it from him. She hadn't gone to this trouble for nothing to tell her tale to a stranger. She wanted the information to find its way back to his son. His memory was of running his fork down the snowy peak, and watching the meringue shatter. But even in the memory he could hear the sour note in his voice as he'd asked how she knew John. It had been the first time anyone had run him to earth to get to his son. Even this long after retirement he expected it to be the other way round.

Her head had shot up at his question. 'John who?'

'My son. I'm assuming you want me to tell him that your friend's death needs to be looked into.'

'Oh … Yes, I see. That's right. You will, won't you? Her name …' He smiled. It had stayed clear in his memory.

'Pamela Morgan. She died on October 21st 2001, almost a decade and a half ago.'

He'd told Dr China to contact John herself. 'Ring him up. Send him an email.' He'd regretted his failing eyesight that hadn't allowed him to read her discomfort as he'd said, 'What are you scared of? Did you kill her?'

'I asked if she'd killed the woman herself. She said she hadn't.'

The denial had come loud and fast. 'No!' Then she'd seemed to deflate and the young man had been at his elbow saying sorry, but there was a phone call.

'Then I was told there was a phone call for me …'

Dr China had muttered something as he'd pushed himself up out of his seat. Of course the young man had had no idea of the impossibility of that staircase. He'd gone down in the lift.

Downstairs at the lodge, they'd been very apologetic and hadn't known anything about a call, had helped him back to the mahogany panelled elevator and eased back the metallic grid door.

Upstairs, the chandeliers threw out their great blanket across the room, woven from luminous stars, sewn with shadows and sunlight. Dr China and the young man were gone.

'… and that's the last I saw of them.'

The wooden top scribbled in his notebook, then said, 'But something about the young woman touched you. What was it?'

A lifetime's training suppressed Donald's instinctive start of surprise. He took the time to reach for his glasses, took the trouble to look properly. Ah, not a wooden top, after all. Someone had decided to take this seriously. He wondered why. *Touched you …?* He allowed his lips to curve to a smile. Even in his full account six months ago he'd given away nothing like that.

He paused as her voice echoed across half a year, the tone more memorable than the words. Quiet, sad, spoken almost to herself.

'She spoke as I left the table. I think she said, "Poor Quinny." '

chapter one

The vehicle sat on ramps, its front end a rusty shell but the rest surprisingly well preserved. Detective Superintendent Martyn Webber remarked on it as he watched, glad to be at the other end of a video link and not in the huge draughty garage space where the car was under examination. The bare concrete walls behind the equipment would be no protection from the hard cold of mid-November.

A tall woman in a blue coverall moved into shot. Her gloved hand held a closed evidence bag. 'Deep mud at the bottom of the gravel pit,' she told him. 'It probably sunk into it as soon as it was dumped. The rear end anyway. The front's stripped bare, but stuff in the back might have survived. Given what could be in there, we've been going carefully with the boot space, getting a camera in first. Something's sealed it tight over the years. I didn't want to lose anything in a rush of muddy water.'

He nodded. 'And it's definitely the car matching the licence plate?'

'Oh yes. It's a 1984 Ford Tempo. The VIN matches. You have the details.'

'And the boot?'

She let out a sigh, tipping her head in a yes-no gesture. 'The camera isn't giving us anything dramatic. A lot of plastic sheeting but it's not clear if there's anything inside it. I'll have more when we get it out, but your Chief Super wanted a heads-up.' As she spoke, she peered at the screen.

'We'll let him know,' said Webber.

'Are you at HQ?' she asked.

'No, we're in York.'

'Oh right, not so far from where it was found, then.'

'The original crime scene's on our patch, too. Can you get back to me when you've got that stuff out? I need to know if we have a case here.'

The woman nodded and turned away as someone spoke behind her. The video link blanked.

Webber looked at the man and woman beside him. 'Let's have the stills up on the board,' he said, adding to himself, even if we're taking them down again in half an hour. He flicked through the old case file that lay open in front of him.

The woman spoke as she thumbed through the pictures. 'Guv, what sort of car did she say it is?'

'A Ford Tempo.'

'What the hell's one of those?' from the man.

'Not one of Ford's better ideas,' Webber said. 'I think they only made them in the 80s. That model was discontinued after three or four years. And that particular car was bought new by its first and only owner in 1984, then stolen two years later.'

He glanced towards the door at the far end of the wide space. He'd been pulled from his morning briefing and brought across here, couldn't shake the insecure feeling of having left a station rudderless behind him. The disintegrated front end of the Tempo chimed with the tangled wreckage at the junction last night where every witness claimed their light was green. Someone might have died. He should be working on that current case, not this ancient one.

What had happened yesterday was no random accident, he was sure of it. The anomalies in the witness statements had run a shudder of unease through him. He could feel the flutter of it in his gut right now. Someone messing about with traffic lights this time, a level of sophistication above an incident just a week earlier. That had originally been put down to kids messing about, blocking the road. A different location, different type of traffic chaos, but something about it resonated with last night's carnage. They'd just got in the CCTV and started to explore links when the order came to hotfoot it across the city. He'd tried to protest, to have the time at least to tie some loose ends, but the command had come from the Chief Super in tones that brooked no argument. At the very least, he'd expected Farrar to be here to tell him what this thing was all about. He'd dug out the old case file, found himself a makeshift corner to work, and had been through it from cover to cover without unearthing a hint to propel it to these levels of urgency.

'It was found by divers a couple of weeks ago,' he told the two DCs as they picked through the old photos and clicked them to the board under magnets. 'Edge of that site.' He pointed to where the woman had written the address next to a picture of the carcass of the car. 'Fishing lakes. They're expanding into the old gravel pits. They brought us the licence plate. They did the right thing but they weren't expecting much interest in such an old car. Be warned they'll be after anyone and everyone for intel on what we're doing with it. They want to get on with the work.'

He looked up at them, making sure their eyes met his. 'If you're offered money, bear in mind it'll have to cover you for a lifetime's earnings and a few years inside.' He didn't suppose either of them were fool enough to fall for an approach, but nor did he underestimate the growing desperation of a company losing money every day while their development site lay fallow.

'Unluckily for them, it's a car we have on record from a robbery on a post office in 1986. It was reported stolen the morning of the crime and clocked as the getaway car later that day.'

'So it's been in that gravel pit for close on 30 years.'

'It was last seen almost 30 years ago,' corrected Webber. 'Forensics will tell us how long it was in there, but yes, chances are it was dumped straight away. Tell me about the crime,' he said to the woman who was flicking through the old notes.

'Uh … Two brothers were arrested just a few days after the robbery. They were convicted and gaoled. Eight years.'

'Complete incompetents,' Webber said. 'A post office raid in 1986 wasn't the cleverest of crimes to go for. Why?' He fixed his gaze on the man at the board, knowing he was only playing tutor with them because the Chief Super had unsettled him.

'Big push on safety in post offices in the early 80s,' the man told him, unfazed. 'Most of them had security screens and so on by then.'

Webber nodded and relaxed. He liked it that they were on the ball. He turned to the woman. 'Witnesses to the crime? Why are we still interested?'

'Yes, all the witnesses talked about three masked men,' she said. 'There were three brothers, so it was assumed they'd worked together.'

Webber raised his hand to stop her further exploration of the file. 'You won't find the elder brother in there. No one ever had a sniff at him, nor at most of the money. It was assumed he'd skipped the country with the cash.'

He thought about the car, its boot sealed tight, decades under the mud. How much of a body would survive in those circumstances or a stash of bank notes?

'How much did they take?' she asked.

'About ten grand, equivalent to probably double that today, and some recorded delivery mail. There was a theory they were after something specific in the mail but it came to nothing.'

'Not enough to start a new life on, even back then. Do we know where they are now? Can we re-interview them?'

Webber gave her a wintry smile. 'Not without a Ouija board. There might be some family still around, but it looks like the brothers acted on their own and some godforsaken idea of family solidarity kept them quiet about the eldest. We can't really do anything until we see what comes out of the car. As it stands, there's nothing here.'

'Is it right that the Chief Super was involved in the original case?'

Webber nodded. He looked at the file remembering what he'd read. Police Constable John Farrar, as he was then, had had quite a spat with the car's owner who'd resented being put under the spotlight. Maybe this was at the root of Farrar's interest, though it seemed a pitifully inadequate reason to have pulled him away from his live cases.

'The Ford Tempo was owned by a Mr Brad Tippet,' he told them. 'And it seems there was reason to think he knew the car had been stolen the night before he reported it.'

'He might have been involved, you mean?'

'They couldn't link him to it at the time, but I want his statement under the microscope and let's find out if he's still with us. If he is, I want someone out to talk to him pronto. See how he takes the news that his car's resurfaced largely intact. Do we have any recent intel on him?'

As the man moved to access a terminal, Webber saw him lean towards his colleague and heard the murmured question, 'Is this case why the Chief Super's in such a mood today?' It was a quiet aside, not meant for Webber's ears. He carried on riffling through the papers as though he hadn't heard, curious to know if she would answer. Women sometimes had a direct line to these sorts of things, and he too had been hearing rumours that Farrar was seriously on the warpath. The woman didn't speak, just gave a brief shake of her head.

Webber looked up at the whiteboard where the major players now hung from their magnets next to a photograph of the skeletal front end of the Tempo and a peaceful shot of the fishing lakes.

'Tippet was watched for a while,' he said. 'For untoward spending and so on, but nothing. Depending on what forensics turn up in that car, we might take another look, but ten grand could sink without trace over three decades.'

'What if big brother post office turns up in the boot?'

Webber looked again at the board. Decades-old pictures for the most part, sitting alongside recent ones of the decades-old car. 'Well,' he said. 'What would it mean?'

'Murdered him for the money ...?'

'Why? And where did the money go ...?'

'What if the money's in the boot ...?'

'Why would you rob a post office and dump the money ...?'

'... but if the money and the body ...'

Webber let them bounce ideas back and forth as he looked at the photographs. If there was a case to run here, where would he start? He'd have Tippet interviewed if he was still around and compos mentis. Had it been a live case, he'd have him in and see the whites of his eyes when he heard about the car. But if forensics found nothing, it was hard to see what was left to investigate. Evidence of a murder would release resources for a bit of a second look at the family and the witnesses, but to what purpose this long after the event with all the players dead? Maybe it would be the money that turned up, not the brother. Had they accidentally dumped their getaway car with the loot still inside? It would confirm their incompetence.

His best guess was that Farrar's involvement in the original case had pushed it up the priority list but that unless the car held any surprises, it would soon sink again. The forensic cost would be considerable and, other than Tippet, he had no intention of authorising any action. But it wasn't the detail of the case that made him uneasy, it was the case itself. Why had Farrar dumped it on him when there were live cases backing up?

His mind turned to the traffic chaos they'd experienced the other side of the city. The theory of kids playing about, chancing their arms, looked thin now. Last night's incident had taken rather too organised a turn and almost killed someone. He wanted to know what they'd found, to be hearing reports of modern-day cars, live suspects and theories that might do more than unravel a decades-old crime.

The computer screen in front of him beeped a request for a video link to the lab. He opened the call and signalled the DCs round to watch.

It was the same woman, now in a white coat. The background had changed to a more conventional laboratory and her expression told Webber she'd found something.

'The boot was stuffed full with a single large sheet of plastic,' she opened without preamble. 'And it was … well, not exactly dry, but not inundated. The mud had sealed it from the worst of the water. The car must have sunk quickly. Nothing obvious in the sheet but it's been used to wrap something. We're getting samples from the boot space but it's the inside of the plastic that's giving up its secrets. We haven't analysed anything yet, of course, but take a look down the microscope.' She reached to fiddle with something outside Webber's line of sight. '40 times magnification,' she said.

The screen blurred and then refocused on a circular landscape of pitted brownish-yellow, black spiders pressed into it at intervals, some whole, most in bits. A bath sponge that had spent 30 years at the bottom of a gravel pit was his best guess.

'What am I looking at?' he asked.

There was a hint of triumph in her voice as she replied. 'Brain tissue. There's a lot of it. Someone was bashed over the head and wrapped up in that plastic.'

And there, finally, was the reason for the brothers' non-cooperation. Not family solidarity. Quite the opposite. 'Could the body have been in there when the car was dumped? Rotted away or whatever?'

'Not a chance.'

Webber sat back. 'Body tipped in first and the car on top of it?'

'Forensics on the car can't tell us that. We'd have to dredge the rest of the pit.'

'That's what I was afraid of.' He sighed. 'Can we do anything cheaper with geo-phys?'

She shrugged. 'I can look into it. And obviously we'll do the DNA on the brain matter. Do you want it fast-tracked?'

'Are we definitely talking about a body?' he asked. 'Could it have been a survivable head injury? Could the guy have walked away?'

'Not a chance.'

Webber looked up at the two DCs to see what they made of this development. 'Not a chance,' he repeated the woman's words. 'Phrase of the day. Well, do we fast-track the DNA tests?'

He saw from the man's expression that he was heading towards a knee-jerk, yes of course, but he hesitated as he looked at Webber. 'Uh … I guess … maybe not.'

'No,' Webber confirmed across the video link. 'Let me know what else you come up with.' And he closed the call.

'What would we gain?' He turned to his two colleagues. 'Confirmation that a couple of dead guys killed their brother. Our prime suspects aren't going anywhere.' Nor is this case, he added to himself, wondering what Farrar would do about the gravel pit. They could hardly hand it back for development if there was a body down there.

The door banged open at the far end of the space. Webber felt the tension before he looked up. Chief Superintendent John Farrar stood there, expression like flint. Another man stood behind him. After a pause that might have been for dramatic effect, Farrar strode in, his companion scurrying behind him.

'This is DI Davis,' snapped Farrar. Such was the fury behind his words that no one made a move to acknowledge the man and Farrar didn't leave time for pleasantries before pointing at the pictures on the board. 'That the Tippet case?'

'Yes,' said Webber, surprised at the label. Had they thought of it as the Tippet case all those years ago? 'We were just discussing …'

'You!' Farrar barked, ignoring Webber and pointing at the DC next to him. 'Bring DI Davis up to speed. He'll be running this case. And you ...' His finger swung round to Webber as scorn overlay the anger in his tone. 'Come with me.'

He turned on his heel and marched out. Webber felt the weight of his bottom jaw, and saw the two DCs exchange a bewildered glance. Davis kept his head down. Webber had no idea what he'd done, but there was no sin greater than keeping Farrar waiting. He leapt up to follow.

chapter two

Farrar marched down the centre of the corridor, the tension in his shoulders radiating rage. He slammed through the door to his office. Webber had to put out his hand to stop it rebounding into his face. Farrar threw himself into the chair, grabbed a notepad and scrawled on it, before looking up.

'Well …' his tone hard but neutral.

Webber couldn't read whether it was a question or a statement. Knowing it was nothing to do with the cold case, he said anyway, 'It's definitely Tippet's car. The lab …' His voice faded. He had to make a determined effort not to back away from Farrar's anger.

'What you do in your private life, Detective Superintendent, is entirely your own affair.' Farrar's voice remained quiet, measured, but as Webber struggled for context, Farrar's fist banged down on the desk making a wire tray jump and Webber's heels snap to attention. 'Until it impacts on the job,' Farrar bawled. 'What were you thinking? Are you after throwing your career down the pan as well your marriage?'

With a terrible sense of injustice Webber felt the pieces fall into place. That's not fair, he wanted to say. I got away with that. I ended the affair, no harm done. Of course he shouldn't have gone anywhere near the woman. He'd been infatuated, mesmerised. Not only was she a private investigator, she'd been a whisker from becoming a material witness in a big case. He remembered her couldn't-care-less attitude to his abrupt ending of their liaison. Must have misread that. What had the vindictive cow done?

'It was nothing, John. It was stupid of me. I put a stop to it before …' Again his voice died away under the glare from across the desk.

Farrar barked out an incredulous laugh. 'Before any damage was done? Is that what you're going to tell me? It's too bloody late for that. If I could, I'd strip you of your rank right now and have you directing traffic in some seaside town for the rest of your career. As it is …'

A sudden vision blanked out Farrar's wrath. Webber saw his wife as he'd left her this morning, smiling, Sam on her hip, waving his chubby fists. 'What do you mean?' he interrupted. 'Throwing my marriage down the pan. Mel doesn't know anything about this.'

'You can hardly keep it from her.' Again that scornful incredulity. 'And if I'm not much mistaken, she'll be hearing all about it right now from the woman herself.'

'What!' A kaleidoscope of images played in Webber's head. He barely heard Farrar's bellowed, 'Where do you think you're going!' as he dived out into the corridor and raced for the exit.

Uppermost in his mind was the picture of Mel, the first time he'd seen her. No, not the first time … he'd originally known her as a press officer in East Yorkshire … but the first time he'd *really* seen her. A God-awful mess of a drugs raid … bad intel. The big targets had been there all right, too many of them, and with their own hired muscle. It could have been a rout, a debacle. In the melee the image was imprinted on his brain. PC Melinda Bryant ducking under a flying fist, taking out the would-be assailant with an efficient right hook and back elbowing another in a smooth continuation of the same move. It was a memory he'd often replayed fondly, but not now.

He sprinted across the road, randomly pleased he hadn't found a space in the car park. No chance of Farrar stopping him. In his head he saw the willowy form of the private investigator on her way to confront his wife. She would sashay into their house with an infuriating air of indolence, taunting Mel until Mel snapped.

She knew all about winding people up. She'd revelled in provoking him to a white heat of anger, and without the surcease of sex he'd probably have killed her himself.

As he reached the car, he grabbed his phone from his pocket and turned it off, relieved he'd remembered it before Farrar had thought to call. If he didn't get home in time, Mel was going to kill the woman; hit her so hard she'd never get up again. The blare of a car horn followed him as he carved his way into too small a gap in the traffic. Mel on a murder charge, Mel convicted ... in prison. He couldn't bear that, couldn't let that happen. But what if he was too late? He'd find a way to take the rap for her. Or they'd get rid of the body ... who'd miss a woman like that? They'd find a way through this.

The back end of the car fishtailed as he took the corner too fast. And there was his house ahead of him. His heart plummeted, hollowing out everything inside him. Too late. It had already happened. There was a patrol car at the gate.

The bricks in the low wall glittered from the remains of a night frost. The light was harsh, the sun still low. He pulled up and climbed out, senses tingling with the need to read and react instantly to whatever had happened.

An officer was coming out through the front door. He was aware of movement from the living room, but didn't look directly at the window. Where was Mel? Who was in there?

'You're a pervert, Martyn.'

He stared at this upstart of a sergeant who'd stepped into his path. Who the hell did she think she was that he might have the least interest in her ramblings at a time like this?

'Fuck off, Suzie.' He bundled her aside and pushed through the door, down the hallway and into the living room to face Melinda.

'Mel! Are you OK? Where's Sam?'

Within arm's reach, her expression stopped him. He looked into her eyes, not daring to let his gaze drop. There might be a bloodied body breathing its last on the carpet beside him, but Mel had been about to do something and his sudden appearance had stopped her. Nothing else mattered.

'Sam's at play group.' She answered one of his questions, her tone hard.

'Are you all right?'

She stared at him, then her glance flicked briefly towards the window. He couldn't read her expression. He could feel her hostility but nothing showed in her face. 'I'll be honest with you, Martyn, even if you can't be honest with me. My first thought was to pack my bags.'

'Mel ...'

'But I got past that in about half a second,' she spoke over him. 'My second thought was to pack *your* bags.' She stared into his eyes as though daring him to interrupt. He held still, almost held his breath. 'I've decided not to,' she said. 'Yet. But the only reason me and Sam are staying here, the *only* reason, is that this way I look like less of a fool while I get my head together. But don't think I've closed off any options.'

'Mel, I ...'

'Oh, for fuck's sake, don't start spouting garbage at me. You didn't want to ... She made all the running ... yeah, yeah ... Don't insult me any further by making me listen to it.'

That wasn't what he'd been going to say. He didn't want to talk about anyone or anything except him and Mel. He wanted to tell her he wouldn't lie to her ever again, but if he said it now, it would be an admission that he had wanted it, that he'd been the one making the running. He prayed she wouldn't make him say it. He daren't lie to her from this knife edge.

'There's one thing I want to know, Martyn, and I want the truth.'

He nodded. She could have the truth about whatever she wanted. He couldn't deny her that. The phone rang from the table by the window. As Melinda moved towards it, she turned back to him with a smile that didn't reach her eyes. 'How many times did you have sex with that woman?'

'How ...?' He stopped as she picked up the handset. How could he answer? The truth was he hadn't kept a tally, but he couldn't say that.

'Yes, of course he's here, John.'

Webber heard the laugh in her voice. She was talking to the Chief Super. Her relaxed tone astounded him. 'Don't be daft, John. It's mainly your fault, you know.'

Disorientated. It was the wrong conversation. Was it John Farrar at the other end of the line? What was she talking about?

'... going on about him like you do. You put the idea in her head, set him up ... Me? Oh well, when he told me she'd come on to him, I laughed ... No, you won't, John,' Webber heard steel in her voice. Was she threatening Farrar?

From outside a car engine revved and Webber caught a glimpse of the patrol car as it vanished up the road.

Melinda's face lost all trace of good humour, but her tone remained level as she said into the phone, 'Yes, he's on his way back. I'll tell him ...' and replaced the handset. She spun to face him and yelled, 'I said how many times did you do it with that sanctimonious little cow?'

As she strode back towards him, her face was blotched with all the anger she'd suppressed. It hit him. She'd been waiting for that car to leave so she could drop the pretence. Everything came at him at once. Farrar's rage. Nothing to do with material witnesses ... *you didn't want to ... she made all the running* ... But it's true, he wanted to say. I *didn't* want to. She *did* make all the running. It was nothing ... really nothing. I'd forgotten about it. This was nothing to do with the private investigator. It was Sergeant Suzie Harmer who'd just driven off.

'How many!'

'Once,' he said and had to look away. It was the truth but he couldn't meet her eye.

Unexpectedly, she chuckled. He stared at her. 'I guessed she wouldn't stomach it twice. I told her we'd laughed about it.'

Even from the knife edge, he wasn't having Suzie Harmer take the credit. 'I was drunk,' he said. 'Almost too drunk to … After that, I told her to piss off. I never went near her again, Mel, I swear. And she backed off.'

'Backed off once she was sure she had what she wanted. You're a fool, Martyn, but you're not making a fool out of me. I'll play charades with this marriage to make the Harmer bitch as uncomfortable as I can, and I'll do it to keep John Farrar from getting you demoted because I'm not having Sam suffer financially for your stupidity.'

'Sam's not …'

'Listen to me, Martyn.' She jabbed her finger painfully into his chest. 'If I leave, Sam comes with me. And if you leave, you leave without him.' He flinched and had to brace himself not to lose his footing. Her finger dug in harder with each jab. Her voice rose. 'I'm too bloody angry to think it through right now.' And suddenly her eyes were wet, tears were falling down her cheeks. She shrieked a torrent of abuse at him through gulped back sobs.

He tried to put his hands on to her arms, desperate to pull her close, to start to repair the damage he'd inflicted. She would calm down. It was only Suzie Harmer. No one had told her about anyone else. He'd play whatever part Mel asked of him. For a moment, it seemed that she might let him hold her. Then she pulled away.

'You've to go back to work. I've to get Sam from play group. And we're going to act round him like nothing's wrong.'

'Yes, of course. I'll stay now, Mel. I'll come with you.'

'You bloody won't. You need to keep that job. John Farrar can't kick you out for impregnating his favourite girl, and once he's cooled down he'll probably come round, but you'd better tread on egg shells until he does.'

The astonishment must have been plain on his face. 'You hadn't got it, had you?' She spat the words into his face. 'You stupid shit!

What did you think she was after, for fuck's sake? She's gay. And you're almost old enough to be her father.'

He felt shell-shocked, stunned like some stupid adolescent. Nothing lasting could have come from that sordid alcohol-fuelled episode.

'I didn't know she was gay. So Fiona …? The flatmate?'

'Yes, Martyn. They're a couple. They've been together for ages. You weren't even first in line,' Melinda mocked him, then paused. 'That's kid's getting DNA tested before she gets a cent of our money.'

'But why …?' He didn't know which question he was trying to ask.

'They've been wanting a kid for ages. You know what a selfish bitch she is. Fiona's no better. They wouldn't settle for IVF or whatever, not when they could find some idiot to get good money out of. And you're the one they hit the jackpot with. You're the sperm donor. Congratulations, sucker.' For a moment he thought she was going to laugh at him. If something would break the brittle shell, they'd be all right. They'd get past this.

'I'm staying home today,' he said. 'I'm not leaving you on your own after this.'

She laughed, but it had a chill edge. 'Yes, you are. You're going right now to face a station full of gossips, people sniggering behind your back, and most of all you're not going to give John Farrar any excuse to kick you out. He'll cool off, but until he does, you lick all the boots you have to. If we have to shell out for bloody Harmer's bastard kid, it's going to be out of a Superintendent's salary. You're not going to short-change Sam.'

He nodded, holding on to a serious expression but inside he felt elation bubble up. She was talking about facing this thing together, about the long term. She was going to stay. It was going to be rocky but it was going to be OK. And, as she was being business-like, he would be too. 'On the phone just now you told John you'd tell me something.'

'Oh … yes. He said he wanted the Tippet case sorted and you'd better be back to see to it.'

Webber nodded, surprised. So Farrar was going to punish him by leaving him on the cold case. He had a fleeting moment of anxiety about the loose ends he'd left back at his own station, then he thought about Suzie Harmer, always one of Farrar's favourites, though he'd never known why. He'd saved her life once after a knife attack. The invitation to a meal at her flat had supposedly been her thank you. He hadn't wanted to go. It was Mel who'd said he should. The drink had flowed. Fiona, the monosyllabic flatmate, had looked daggers at him. No bloody wonder. But then she'd melted away.

'She's an ungrateful little cow,' he burst out.

Melinda drew in a breath. 'Be that as it may,' she said. 'But she's pregnant, so don't go pushing her around like you did when you got here.'

It was only with difficulty he recalled the rough gesture with which he'd shoved her aside. His focus had been to get to Mel. 'She called me a pervert,' he remembered.

'That's for coming home from her bed and telling me all about it.'

'Why did you say that?'

'Because it makes a fool of her and less of a fool of me.'

It was a weird conversation but at least they were talking. 'What about me?' he asked.

And suddenly she was yelling again, calling him all kinds of fool, telling him he deserved it, that if it weren't for Sam … Again he tried to catch her arms, to pull her to him, to let her pummel him if that's what she needed to do. He saw the strike coming, but was half-hearted in raising his arm to fend her off. She had every right to want to hurt him. Cheap at the price if it was the way to save his marriage.

Realisation came too late. His mind had separated Mrs Melinda Webber, who he desperately wanted to keep close, from PC Melinda

Bryant who knew how to use her fists. He tried to duck out at the last moment, saw stars as her fist smacked into him. He fought to keep his feet, to keep his face turned away, to ward off a follow-up blow.

And before he'd regained his equilibrium, she was gone, the door banging behind her. He knew better than to try to follow. His task now was to get his head together enough to drive back to the station, withstand whatever shit Farrar planned to throw at him, and pick up the loose ends of the Tippet case. Automatic anger at hours of unproductive boredom died as it was born. He realised it was exactly what he needed and hoped Farrar wouldn't think it through too far. If he were pitched into a live investigation with all this in his head, Farrar would have him on capability grounds within five minutes. But as for using a few lab results to prove that two dead guys had killed another dead guy thirty years ago, he'd write all the reports that were asked of him. For once in his life he actively hoped that none of his enquiries would turn up anything of interest.

chapter three

With Mel's words echoing in his head, Webber hurried back, half wondering if Farrar would be waiting to kick him out. He imagined having to face Mel with suspension or worse. If he were to say the wrong thing to Mel now – and the wrong thing might be anything at all – that would be the end of everything. He'd left her talking of the longer term. He had to consolidate this gently, step-by-step, until leaving him was no longer an option. It wasn't so different from gradually pulling the rug from under a suspect. But key to his strategy was to avoid any mess-up at work that Farrar could bring to his door.

He parked away from the station and took his phone from his pocket. With no idea how long Farrar intended to keep him locked down over here, he had to know what had happened to his own team after he'd been whipped away, if they'd unravelled that smash at the traffic lights.

'Yes, we're getting somewhere now.' The voice was upbeat. 'Wait till you see it. We ... uh ... Will you be back this morning?'

Webber sighed. 'No idea. Lap of the gods at present.'

'Um ... OK. Yeah, we've ID'd a guy from the CCTV.' The ghost of a pause told Webber that there would be no more questions about his absence. The grapevine had done its work. 'Tom Jenkinson,' the voice went on. 'Young guy from Scarborough. First year university student here in York. Not the brains behind it, but I'm thinking he's been using his talents to supplement his student loan.'

'A first year student?' Webber didn't like the idea of someone so young being able to manipulate traffic light systems. Once the pattern had begun to emerge, two theories vied for top spot; a rehearsal for something big or teenage testosterone getting out of hand. Last night, clearly before Suzie had broken her news, Webber had talked it through with Farrar.

'What are we looking at, Martyn? Some bloody *Italian Job* setup?'

He'd favoured the gang warfare theory himself. Youngsters earning their spurs by gridlocking the city streets. It fitted with that flare up of trouble a week ago. Reports were now being reassessed and collated to see what links emerged. Pattern or no pattern, he had no sense of a level of organisation underneath it to point to anything really big, nor could he think of a viable target.

'When did you ID Jenkinson?' he asked.

'Just after you left.'

'What have you got out of him?'

'Nothing. We haven't brought him in yet.'

'Why not!' Webber fought an urge to swear. His eye had barely left the ball and they were making decisions that made no sense.

'We know where he is. He's not going anywhere. Thing is, this boy's had more cautions and interviews than most students get Big Macs. Record as long as your arm up to two years ago. All juvenile stuff. Kept his nose clean since then. But he knows how to keep his mouth shut and we need him talking. This isn't his scam. It's a million miles away from anything he's ever been involved in.'

'What turned him round?' Webber asked, thinking of Jenkinson's two-year clean record. 'Or did he get clever and just stop getting caught?'

'That's the thing. You know that "Kids with Potential" initiative? Intensive mentoring took Jenkinson from no-hoper to university place. He was one of its success stories.' There was a moment's silence. Webber saw the images of chaotically angled vehicles, the distorted wreckage, the shock that overlay the aftermath as every witness swore blind their own lights had been green; and the miracle of the drivers who'd climbed out shaking but with only minor injuries. 'Apparent success story,' the voice amended. 'Do you know Ayaan Ahmed, DC from Scarborough?'

'Yes, I've worked with him.'

'Well, he's the one credited with turning Jenkinson round. We're getting him over later today. See if he can guilt-trip Jenkinson into telling us everything.'

Webber slowed his pace, keeping a row of houses between him and the station building. Once in sight of those windows, he mustn't show any hesitation in his step.

'How was it done? How sophisticated a scheme are we up against?'

'No sign of any systems compromised that we can find. It's looking more like sleight of hand than clever hacking.'

Sleight of hand was teenage bravado, Webber thought, but if it turned out to be tampering smart enough to leave no trace, that would bolster Farrar's worries about an *Italian Job* style felony in the making.

He closed the call, took in a breath and lengthened his stride as he came within sight of the red brick and glass building. Farrar had said he'd to come back and sort out the Tippet case. It would be an effort to swallow his rising irritation. His mind should be on what was happening the other side of the city, not on some 30-year-old vehicle hauled from a lake, but with luck he'd wrap the thing up and be back with his team by lunchtime.

The reception area was busy, no one reacted to his reappearance. Even upstairs in the big office his entrance caused no more than a couple of glances his way. Davis sat where Webber had last seen him, hunched over a stack of papers, alone.

'What's new?' Webber asked as he pulled up a chair.

Davis jumped slightly. Webber had the impression he'd been nodding off over the case file.

'Oh … uh … yes. Mr Tippet's still around. Works down the road. I've sent someone out to see him.'

Webber nodded. 'You on your own?' he asked, and wasn't surprised to hear that one of the DCs had already been grabbed for another job and the other would follow as soon as she returned from interviewing Tippet.

'Have you come up with a way of checking for a body in that pit that won't break the bank?'

Davis shook his head. 'Shame the commercial outfit didn't do a more thorough job while it was down there. I bet they wish they had now. At least we'd know.'

'Would they have had to take the car out before they stocked the lake?'

'No idea. I don't know anything about fishing.'

Webber glanced at the man. 'Well, look it up,' he snapped, tipping his thumb at the computer terminal inches from Davis's nose. 'Or get on to the development company.' He knew this wasn't the time to make enemies of anyone, but Davis must have had the best part of half an hour with nothing to do. He could easily have mugged up on fishing lakes and old cars. Instead he'd chosen to take forty winks in the middle of a busy station.

As Davis scrabbled through the paperwork and picked up the phone, a cold draught told Webber the door had opened behind him. It was the DC returning from her interview with Tippet. She looked briefly startled to see Webber sitting there. 'Anything interesting?' he asked her.

'No, not a flicker. It took him a while to figure out what car I was talking about. Then he just said it wasn't his. It's the insurance company's. He showed no concern at all.'

'No big surprise there, but we need to ...'

The rush of air from the door slamming open made Davis juggle the handset and slap his palm flat on the file as the pages took flight. Farrar towered over them. 'What the hell do you think you're doing?' His glare bored into Webber.

Farrar's sudden appearance had made him jump, but as he

looked up, Webber knew this was staged. Farrar had waited for the DC to return to give him a bigger audience in front of whom to bawl the reprimand. Farrar hadn't been able to maintain his anger at white heat, no matter that he'd probably wanted to. His rational self had moved on. Webber kept his expression neutral as he got to his feet to meet Farrar's stare on the level.

'You wanted the Tippet case sorting out,' he said. He watched Farrar as he spoke. *The Tippet case.* It wasn't the Tippet case. It had never been the Tippet case. But that was what Farrar had called it, once in his hearing and once to Mel.

Farrar stared as though Webber had gone temporarily insane. 'Yes, the Tippet case. Not this one. What's this case to do with Tippet? Just because the man had his car stolen. I want a preliminary report in my inbox when I get back from lunch today.'

Farrar turned on his heel and was gone.

The DC stared intently at her shoes as though she'd spotted a poisonous snake coiled there. Davis eased his shoulders round and spoke too loudly and with studied nonchalance into the phone. Farrar's raised voice had caused a sudden lull into which heads turned from the far end of the big office.

Webber kept his voice level. 'Find out what else they got out of that pit before work stopped. No one's talked to the divers who went down. If the car landed on the body, it's unlikely they'll have seen any sign of it, but check what they saw. Other than that, wait for the forensics.'

'Yes, Guv.' Her gaze shot up, met his and immediately dropped again.

Farrar might have lost the white heat of anger, but he was still smarting over the upset to whatever plans he'd had. And he would have to account for his deployment of resources. All this garbage about old cases had to be more than a means to administer a good kicking. *Another* Tippet case? What were the chances? Farrar clearly didn't like the guy, but Tippet had a clean slate. However, he'd promised Mel that he'd jump through whatever hoops Farrar put in front of him so he'd have to ask round and find out what other case Farrar had been nibbling at. The records guys would know. He turned his back on the two of them and headed for the door.

◉ ◉ ◉

'He must mean this one. He asked about it this morning. That's why I have it out.'

Webber's gaze rested on the slender file. 'Did he look at anything in particular ... say anything about it?'

'He didn't look at it all, just said he might need it later. I got it out after he'd gone. No one's touched it in six months.'

Webber took the folder with a word of thanks. It was thinner than the one he'd left with Davis. He was making for the door, when a familiar voice caught his ear and he ducked back inside to avoid Suzie Harmer who marched past oblivious to him, intent on berating the man scurrying behind her. He felt a surge of anger that he'd been reduced to ducking behind doors while she strode through the place as though she owned it. Not that she should be here at all; probably she'd been called across for her share in Farrar's reprimand. They'd have to talk sometime soon, but he couldn't face it today.

In his mind's eye he saw Mel standing tall by the window, the phone to her ear, all that pent-up distress concealed behind a couldn't-t-care-less façade put on for Suzie Harmer in the car outside. His anger crumbled. He deserved everything Farrar could throw, not for the Harmer bitch whose predicament he didn't see as his fault, but for the other woman about whom Mel must never hear a whisper.

Farrar had done the worst he could do by failing to prevent Harmer's visit to Mel. And if he'd felt the need to administer a

32

public dressing down to complete the humiliation, he could have used any one of a hundred excuses without wasting scant resources on non-cases.

He looked down at the thin file in his hand which must hold the key to Farrar's real agenda.

chapter four

Mid-morning sun streamed through the big windows. Webber chose a corner where he could read comfortably without lights, but it was hard to give his attention to the file. He was aware of the bustle all around that didn't encompass him, the feel that he was being carefully ostracised. No one wanted to get on the wrong side of him, but even less did they want to get on the wrong side of Farrar.

He paused for a deep breath, laid the folder on the desk in front of him and flipped it open. The first thing he saw was Farrar's handwriting at the top of the page. The words *Brad Tippet* were scrawled between two question marks. He flicked through the few pages looking for the name in the official prose, but it didn't crop up again. There was a summary report from a coroner's office. It gave the outline of a 2001 suicide of a woman called Pamela Morgan. With it was a brief page of notes that had been written in May, almost six months ago.

Had Farrar picked a non-case at random and scribbled Tippet's name at the top? Webber shook his head in disbelief. Nothing was worth this level of time wasting, no matter how angry Farrar might be. He flicked through to identify the report's author and picked up the phone.

'Martyn Webber here. Some months ago, you wrote up a report for John Farrar on a woman called Pamela Morgan. Suicide. What was it about?'

'Morgan?' There was a pause into which Webber read memory

being searched for something that had made no dent. 'Oh yes ... vaguely. Has something come up? I thought there was nothing to it.'

'You're probably right, but tell me what you know.'

'John wanted me to look into it. It'd be ...' Again a pause. Webber heard the clatter of a keyboard. 'Yes, here it is. Wanted me to check if there was anything iffy about it. Woman in her 40s. Took an overdose. It was straightforward, she left a note ... oh, that's right, there was a minor question over the note because it wasn't signed, but there was no doubt that she'd written it.'

'Why did John want it looked at?'

'I can't remember. Hang on ... Lana, didn't you take the original call on ...?' Webber heard bits of a one-sided exchange before the voice was back in his ear. 'That's right. It was his father, Farrar's father, who called it in. Said he'd been told there was something iffy about the death. Farrar said to have a look.'

'He's written a name on the file. Brad Tippet. That mean anything to you?'

'Yeah, they've just pulled his car out of ...'

'No, not that. I mean to do with this Pamela Morgan. Anything from six months ago?'

Again the background rumble of voices, from which Webber picked out a slightly indignant, '... never mentioned that name to me ...'

His finger tracked the words through the brief report. Pamela Morgan had killed herself because she couldn't live with what had happened to her husband, who'd died in an accident. No details.

'No,' said the voice in his ear. 'Tippet wasn't mentioned.'

It occurred to Webber that Farrar hadn't had his hands on the file, not this morning. 'So when did John write Tippet's name on it?'

'Probably before it was filed six months back. He was the last person to look at it.'

'What happened to Pamela Morgan's husband? How did he die?'

'I didn't get as far as that. Robert Morgan, wasn't it? Not the easiest name to trace from cold. I got some stuff faxed from the coroner's office and that was about it.'

Webber's gaze scanned the pages as he listened. Pamela Morgan had left a note addressed to a friend. It was referred to as 'long and detailed, but unsigned'. There were a few extracts ... *the way it happened ... plays out in front of me ...*

'It says here the husband died in an accident, but that ...' He turned the page. 'There's a reference to perpetrators ...'

... we'd quarrelled, never made up ... it won't get better ...

'Yeah, it's coming back to me, but I didn't have time to chase it. 2001, wasn't it? I wondered if he'd been a 9/11 victim? Not that I found anything to say he was working in the States or anything, but ...'

Webber flipped through the pages to find the date of Pamela Morgan's suicide. It fitted. 'Yes,' he said. 'Could be.'

There was another name on the file that hung at random like Tippet's, bracketed by question-marks, but this time not written by Farrar. 'How about Dr China? Where does he fit into it?'

'I think that was Lana ... Hang on ...'

After a pause, a different voice came on the line. 'As far as I can remember, Guv, Dr China was the person who told Mr Farrar ... uh ... Chief Superintendent Farrar's father, I mean, about the woman who committed suicide, but he wasn't sure about the name.'

'How do you mean not sure?'

'He said it was noisy. I think he's quite old.'

After he'd ended the call, Webber pulled forward his keyboard then hesitated. Someone called Dr China had talked to John Farrar's father six months ago and told him that a woman called Pamela Morgan who had died 15 years earlier might not have been the suicide of the official record. He started with a search for Pamela and Robert Morgan. The information wasn't there, but the databases he trawled through weren't designed to track blameless people who went through life never stepping out of line. He fired a brief email to the coroner's court that had provided information last May, asking for Pamela Morgan's full file.

A clatter from across the room snapped his attention to his immediate surroundings. A minor fracas erupted as fallen boxes were retrieved. He smelt fresh coffee, saw someone tugging the wrapper from a sandwich. He blinked and stretched his arms, astonished to see the clock show it was after midday, surprised at how engrossed he'd been. But what had he found? Nothing. And Farrar needed a report.

Robert Morgan. The name began to feel familiar, but he supposed he'd encountered a few Robert Morgans over the years. His hand hovered over the phone handset. Farrar would jump down his throat if he found resources expended. Who could he trust to do a bit of digging without making a song and dance of it? Lana, who'd taken Farrar senior's call in May, knew her stuff, but in the circumstances he'd better not use a female officer. And of course, it needn't be anyone stationed in York. He thought back to an earlier conversation and picked up the phone.

'DC Ayaan Ahmed,' said a familiar voice.

'Hello Ayaan. Martyn Webber here. How are you?'

'Oh … I'm fine, thanks. Uh … how are you?' The slight hesitation told Webber all he needed to know about how far the rumours about him and Suzie had spread. 'I'm coming over to York later,' Ahmed went on. 'Tom Jenkinson. I'll kill the little sod if he's gone off the rails after all we've done for him.'

Webber laughed. 'Get the information out of him first, but that's not why I'm ringing. Tell me, how busy are you on a scale of 1 to 10?'

'Tennish without a trip to York. Off the scale really.'

'Good, then you can do something for me. Married couple, Pamela and Robert Morgan. The wife committed suicide in 2001 after the husband was killed, possibly a 9/11 victim, never formally verified, something like that. He doesn't crop up on any of the obvious lists. I want to find the detail of his death, but I don't want a big drama made out of it.'

He heard the ghost of a sigh, as Ahmed said, 'OK, give me what you've got.'

After he'd ended the call, Webber realised he hadn't congratulated Ahmed on his forthcoming marriage. At least that was what he'd heard on the grapevine. He'd say something when they next spoke.

His phone beeped a request for a video call. The woman from the lab. He looked around for Davis but couldn't see him anywhere. Probably off stuffing his face. He accepted the call and the woman, still in her white lab coat, came into view on the small screen.

'Ah, tracked you down,' she said. 'We're done with the car.'

He should stop her and say he'd get Davis to call, but was curious to know what they'd found.

'There was a book of some sort in a pocket at the side of the boot space. Owner's manual probably. We'll have a go at it. Other than that ...'

He listened as she told him they'd had nothing from the plastic sheeting, just the evidence of a fatal head injury. 'No sign of anything else,' she said. 'And I'd guess the whole body was in there.' She talked about blunt trauma to the back of the head as opposed to the debris that might accumulate from a severed neck.

'When will we get the DNA results?'

'Tomorrow morning.' His surprise must have shown, because she said, 'Your Chief Super wanted it fast-tracked. Didn't you know? Said he wanted it out of the way.'

'That's going to cost–' He swallowed the phrase, an arm and a leg, and let the sentence hang.

A smile of satisfaction spread across the woman's face. 'Given the circs,' she told him. 'We're going to give it a spin with a new toy. Lab-on-a-chip technique, you've heard of it?'

Webber nodded. He'd heard the phrase. With geekish enthusiasm she began to explain hydrodynamic pumping, whatever that was. He wondered if this stuff would be admissible in court. '… it's the electrophoretic movement …' Her voice washed over him. It didn't matter. Two dead guys had killed another dead guy 30 years ago. This wasn't going to court. They just needed to confirm the ID. He let his hand rest on the Pamela Morgan file, gently pushing the pages aside so he could skim them whilst the accolade to science washed over him.

'That reminds me,' he said into a pause. 'DI Davis has taken this over. I'll pass this on but you should contact him when you have the DNA result.'

She laughed, hint taken. 'Conductive polymers remind you of Davis, do they? Yes fine, I'll report back to him. So what are you working on? Anything else that's going to come my way?'

'No, it's nothing much. It's …' He paused on a sudden impulse. She would have easy access to a different type of information, including 9/11 databases that went beyond the official lists. 'There is something, but only if it's at your fingertips. I don't want you spending time on it.' He told her what little he had on Robert Morgan. 'Some kind of an accident is all I actually have in front of me.'

'But you think it might have been 9/11?'

'The timing fits.'

It was no more than a shot in the dark, but Webber felt a stab of unease as he cut the call. Perhaps he'd get back to her in a while, tell her he didn't need the information after all.

Constructing a substantial report out of the thin data on Pamela Morgan wasn't easy. The only new information he had was that it was Farrar's father's call that had initiated the thing in the first place. Not something that would be news to Farrar.

A movement caught his eye. Davis had returned and was heading for his desk. Webber felt his eyes narrow. He supposed the man was looking forward to a post-prandial nap. Since he had no intention of allowing Farrar to catch him anywhere other than hard at work for the rest of the day, he called Davis across, updated him on the lab results, and sent him off with an order for a sandwich and coffee.

It was as he finished his report and was about to send it that an email popped up from the coroner's office. Webber hesitated. He hadn't expected them to be as quick. He didn't want to risk being late – when I get back from lunch had been Farrar's order – but nor did he want to miss anything significant. He clicked on the new email and opened the attached file.

Speed-reading the pages gave him a blurred, whistle-stop tour of the events surrounding the end of Pamela Morgan's life. There were more extracts from the note she'd left.

... the horror multiplied ... can't stop seeing it ... we'd quarrelled ...

A pall of despair, a woman without hope. In losing her husband, she'd lost everything that mattered to her, and in the end she'd lost her life. Despite skimming it at speed, he absorbed the picture of a placid sensible woman. *Cheerful, loved by everyone.* Even allowing for the tendency to speak well of the dead, the picture seemed sincere.

He paused to pull in a breath. Suppose something terrible happened to Mel, could he find himself in Pamela Morgan's shoes? No, because there was Sam. There'd always be Sam. The Morgans couldn't have had children or she wouldn't have done what she'd done. He caught references to friends, but not family. In the end he supposed, friends couldn't bridge the gap.

The document gave him nothing substantive to add to his report, and with the mood Farrar was in, he wouldn't chance his arm making nebulous comments. Nonetheless, the weird events of the morning had forced him to take a step back, to see things differently. The new angle somehow shone a spotlight on the gravel pit as though it had played the role of catalyst. Two weeks ago they'd found a car down there. Then a few days later and quite unrelated some kids had rampaged about the city like a chaotic virus, flaring and dying away, only to re-erupt in yesterday's near carnage at a junction showing green traffic lights in all directions.

Pamela Morgan's suicide sat there as another unrelated curiosity. Not that he could put his finger on what was odd about it, except maybe that it was on his desk at all, and it had Brad Tippet's name on it. *The Tippet case.* The handle Farrar had given to each file in turn. Tippet was linked to a 30-year-old crime by being the victim of a theft. His only link to Pamela Morgan was his name scribbled on a page.

Webber looked across to where Davis suddenly became busy at his keyboard, perhaps conscious of his stare. Few of the people catalogued inside either his or Davis's files were still alive, and of all the deaths recorded, maybe only Pamela Morgan's was unrelated to any crime. Six months ago, someone had tried to throw doubt on that.

His report said none of this. He had no way to articulate it that Farrar would engage with. Turning back to his email, he pressed the send button.

chapter five

Farrar's name popped up so quickly in his inbox that Webber thought their emails had crossed. Then he saw it was the automatic read receipt for the report he'd just sent.

Deleted unread.

When the phone sprang to life a second later, it wasn't hard to guess who it would be.

'Well, was it a suicide?' Farrar's voice rapped out.

'Yes.' As he answered, Webber saw his mobile buzz a call, Ayaan Ahmed's name on the screen. He let it go to voicemail.

'Any doubts?'

'No.'

'Car in the gravel pit, what are you doing with that?'

Wait a minute, Webber wanted to say, you took that one off me; go and ask Davis. 'I told them to check out Tippet's original statement and to have a word with the divers who found the car.' He chose his words carefully. 'But not to set any hares running before we have the forensics back.'

'It'll be the third brother, will it, the one who disappeared after the post office raid?'

Big brother post office, thought Webber. 'Yes,' he said. 'The question is whether or not he's still down there.'

'The other one, Pamela Morgan, the suicide, anything to follow up?'

'I'd like to get chapter and verse on the husband's death. Find out why she did it.'

'You've had hours. What's your investigation there?'

Webber wanted to ask why Farrar had written Tippet's name, but said only, 'Nothing. I just wanted a full picture.'

'There's no time for that sort of indulgence. Not with things stacking up the way they are. What's the latest on that traffic lights scam?'

Irritated, Webber said, 'I don't know. I've been busy on this.'

'For God's sake, man, get a grip! Someone could have died yesterday. Get it sorted.'

Permission to resume ordinary life. Webber felt a weight lift.

There was a pause, then Farrar said, 'Tippet knew the older brother. They were at school together. Now get to the bottom of that bloody traffic chaos.' And the line went dead.

Webber sat with the phone in his hand, listening to the drone of the dialling tone. What was he to make of that? Farrar had told him to get back to work, back to his own team. And he intended doing just that, but what was the crack about Tippet? Was he saying Tippet had been involved all those years ago but they hadn't been able to prove it?

He stood up, grabbed his jacket from the back of the chair and marched across to Davis. He pointed at the file. 'Ring me in the morning. Keep me up to date.'

'Sure.' Davis smiled up at him. 'I'll get on to you as soon as I've heard back from the lab.'

'No,' said Webber. 'You'll ring me first thing. *And* you'll let me know when you hear from the lab.'

He pulled out his mobile as he made for the exit. Ahmed had left a text and a voicemail. The text read,

Found your guy. All over the papers. Article here.

Webber looked at the link but didn't want to stop to decipher a newspaper website on a tiny screen. He'd check later. Reliable officer, Ahmed. He'd be over here now to deal with Jenkinson. With luck he might get across town in time to see how it panned out, and catch a word with Ahmed before he returned to Scarborough.

He put in a call to the lab. The woman wasn't there, so he gave the message to one of her colleagues. 'Tell her not to bother about Mr Morgan. I've found him.' And he read out the URL Ahmed had given him.

Sunlight speared through the line of trees, bouncing from every reflective surface, making bright jewels of a pair of discarded drinks cans. Webber shaded his eyes and pulled his jacket tight around him. He strode away from the building imagining Farrar's stare following.

What was the deal with Brad Tippet, the man who'd ruffled Farrar's feathers back when he was a lowly constable? Bloody Farrar! Bloody Suzie bloody Harmer! The best part of a day lost chasing some silly suicidal woman. No, that wasn't fair. Pamela Morgan hadn't come across as silly, just desperate. Ahmed might have left more detail on his voicemail.

'Found your man, Guv,' said Ayaan Ahmed's voice. 'I'll text you a link. It was horrible, but nothing to do with 9/11. Robert Morgan died in 1986.'

1986? Webber tried to fit this to his image of Pamela Morgan. Sensible people did senseless things on the spur of the moment. They didn't wait fifteen years. It was a common enough name. As he wondered whether Ahmed had found the right Robert Morgan, he felt again that glimmer of something reaching out from his own past. 1986. He'd have been at school, in his O Level year. What had Ahmed said? It was in all the papers. Yes, by attaching it to a year, the sense of familiarity was heightened.

His phone pinged a new email as he climbed into his car. The woman from the lab. The subject said, *Robert Morgan*. Opening it, Webber read,

re Mr M. Got your link. Nasty business. Here's the PM report if you want it. Grim reading though.

Webber hurried in and over to where two colleagues sat watching the screen that showed Tom Jenkinson in the interview room. He leant across them to take a look at the boy who'd caused all the trouble. *Had more cautions and interviews than most students get Big Macs.* Certainly Jenkinson looked relaxed. He wore a battered hi-vis jacket, garish orange with black lettering Webber didn't recognise. Its ripped collar hung lopsided as Jenkinson leant back in the chair, eyes at half-mast.

'How long's he been in there?' Webber asked.

'Half an hour. Ayaan Ahmed suggested we let him stew 30 or 40 minutes.'

'Is Ayaan here yet?'

'Yes, he's chasing something from Jenkinson's record.'

Webber looked again at the relaxed young man in the interview room. 'I thought this was outside Jenkinson's MO. What have we got?'

'The systems aren't showing any tampering and they've had time to have a good look.'

'So, is it sleight of hand or something sophisticated enough to escape detection?'

'Sleight of hand. I'd put money on it.'

It was what Webber wanted to hear, but he wasn't going to be convinced just because it was the easiest answer. 'Tell me more.'

'The statements. It was quick, chaotic. Most people were too shocked to be sure what had happened, but when you boil it down, we have the couple waiting for the filter. She saw it go green. Said it just flipped red to green like on the continent. And the driver approaching from the north. He's slowing for the red light when he realises it's changed and he speeds up. And bang. And the woman at the crossing. She swears it was showing both red and green, but for a split second the green was much brighter. They're the three who had reason to notice.'

'What's Ayaan looking for?'

As he spoke, he saw Ahmed come through the far door, a look of satisfaction playing about his features. 'I'm sure that's it,' he was saying. 'It's on the footage where he …' Ahmed pointed towards a screen that was replaying the CCTV images from last night.

'Ayaan.' Webber acknowledged him with a nod. They turned to the frozen image of a junction at dusk, Jenkinson in profile. 'Show me what you've found.'

Ahmed hurried across and reached for the mouse to set the film running. 'This is the bit, here.' He clicked an icon and Jenkinson's moves slowed until he was wading through treacle. 'See how he looks across the junction, then glances back at the traffic coming through behind him. Now … there … he's looking directly at those lights.'

Even through the artificial sluggishness of the image, Webber saw Jenkinson cringe, his face puckering as though he'd bitten into a lemon. 'He knows exactly what's going to happen,' Ahmed said, his voice heavy with censure.

On the image Webber saw Jenkinson screw his eyes tightly shut, saw his fists clench before he spun on his heel and made to run. 'Didn't look like he was over pleased about it,' he commented.

Ahmed ran the film backwards. 'Now look again. The bit before he turns. He looks at the traffic and then up towards … whatever's up there at the far side of the road.'

'Trees … gardens,' someone said.

'Way back,' Ahmed went on. 'He'd have been eight or nine and it wasn't put down to him, but a gang of them started messing with traffic signals. All sorts, chucking paint, taking the lights out with air rifles. And flashlights. No damage done, but it's surprisingly effective in the right light.'

'Flashlights?' Webber said. Surely they hadn't caused that near carnage with flashlights.

'Or a handheld laser. Split second stuff,' said Ahmed. 'A powerful enough beam, the right time of day, tired drivers.'

Webber turned. 'Read me what the guy in the VW said. And the woman at the crossing.'

He let his gaze lose focus as he listened to the two accounts.

'... *slowing down, lights red ... just flipped like one of those French lights ... suddenly saw ... speeded up again ...*'

'Does this fit with anything else?' he asked, and turned to Ahmed adding, 'We had some anonymous intel 10 days ago. Someone wanting to gridlock the streets during the rush hour. And we had some kids try to blockade a junction last week.'

'They weren't messing with lights,' someone put in.

'And it wasn't Tom Jenkinson. He was back in Scarborough that day.'

Webber fought down a surge of frustration. They'd picked up some of the pieces but not the pattern. On the other hand, if all they were talking about was kids messing about, nothing high-tech, then he would allow himself to relax a bit.

'OK,' he said, pointing again at the image of Jenkinson. 'How come he doesn't have a flashlight with him?'

'I think that's what he was looking back at,' said Ahmed. 'Either some kind of fixed light, set to go off at a particular time. Or maybe he had an accomplice. But why? He's grown out of stupid pranks, turned his life round. Why would he do something so idiotic?'

'Have you got enough to get the story out of him?'

Ahmed nodded. 'More than enough.'

'Then let's find out, shall we?' Webber nodded Ahmed towards the interview room and moved to watch on the screen.

◉ ◉ ◉

Webber looked at Jenkinson, lying back in the chair semi-dozing. He hoped this idea of bringing Ahmed across was going to work. He didn't want to have to chip the story out over hours. On the screen he saw the door begin to open, saw Jenkinson's bored glance flare into a start of alarm as Ahmed entered.

Webber felt his mouth curve to a smile. Jenkinson shot upright in his chair, mouth agape, and stammered out, 'M ... Mr Ahmed. What are you doing here?' It would be OK. Jenkinson had surrendered at the first hurdle.

Ahmed gave Jenkinson a hard stare, then took his time pulling out a chair to sit facing the youth. Eventually he said, 'Someone could have been seriously hurt yesterday, Tom.'

Webber, expecting the boy's eyes to drop, saw he'd misjudged the situation. Tom Jenkinson launched at once into a detailed account of the walk across the city that had brought him to those lights at the key moment, of how he'd seen a young lad with a flashlight and known just what was going to happen. '... from that business when I were a kid, Mr Ahmed. You've seen my file. We've talked about it. I saw what were going to happen, but I were too late to do owt. Just a young kid, like I was. I only got a glimpse. Up in a tree the other side of that fence. I couldn't see him properly. I were looking into the light. Probably I should have got on to one of your lot, but what with my record ...'

Jenkinson spread his hands in a gesture of supplication and gave Ahmed a pleading look. Ahmed maintained his relaxed bearing, sitting back, hands in his lap, fingers interlaced, his expression neutral as he watched Jenkinson in silence.

Webber cursed under his breath and heard someone spit out an expletive behind him. Jenkinson's story was way too prepared and detailed to hold an iota of credibility. But it was good. They hadn't a shred of evidence to contradict him. He hoped their faith in Ahmed was justified. Today of all days, he didn't need to be late home.

Ahmed maintained his silence. Jenkinson fidgeted in his seat, his hand shot up to loosen his already loose collar. 'Honest, Mr Ahmed, I wouldn't want to see some kid go the way I did, would I?'

Webber watched with interest as Ahmed's apparent indifference seemed to rack up Jenkinson's tension. At last, Ahmed made a move. His hand rose to his mouth to cover a yawn. He let out a sigh before fixing Jenkinson with a benevolent gaze. His tone was mild as he said, 'You gave the kid the flashlight, Tom, and you showed him how to do it, didn't you?'

Jenkinson's demeanour took on a level of desperation. He ran his hand through his hair. Then his gaze dropped to the floor and he said, 'Yes, Mr Ahmed. I did.'

Webber felt his mouth stretch to a grin that he saw mirrored on his colleagues' faces. Ahmed had been on a wing and a prayer, but he'd held his nerve and Jenkinson had blinked.

'Good work,' he murmured into the microphone. 'Now get the detail.' As he spoke, he glanced at the clock. It was nearing the time of day it had all kicked off yesterday.

Having crumpled, Jenkinson couldn't have been more anxious to tell everything he knew.

'It were the money, Mr Ahmed. I had to give me mam fifty quid last week.'

'Tom, your mother has to manage her money. You don't have enough to keep bailing her out. How many times have we been through this …?' Webber heard Ahmed make a conscious effort to rein in his exasperation. 'Look, I'll go and have a word with her. Now tell me about yesterday. How did that come about?'

Jenkinson told of hearing a rumour about money on offer for someone with particular software skills. 'I know nowt about that stuff, Mr Ahmed, but I put out me feelers. I needed the cash. I thought maybe I could go in with someone.'

Webber was interested to learn that Jenkinson knew about the gang of children who'd tried to block the traffic a week before.

'They weren't going to get no dosh for that. Whoever it was, wanted something better. And I thought about that thing with the lights and I thought, well, if I can convince him I'm doing something clever, maybe he'll shell out. And he's not going to report me, is he, when I don't deliver?'

'Who is he, Tom?'

Jenkinson shrugged. 'I don't know, Mr Ahmed. Honest. I never met him, never saw him. I tried once … we had a go. Wouldn't have gone that far if we'd thought he were streetwise, but …'

Bit by bit, Ahmed chipped out the information.

'See, I just put out feelers, talked things up, waited to see if he'd bite and he did. First time he rang me I told him straight, said I could wire him up a mobile to interfere with the traffic lights. For a cost, of course.'

'And could you do that, Tom?'

'Nah, 'course not. But I thought they use them to set off bombs and that, so he'll likely believe me. Then I said he'd have to get me a special phone. I thought if he doesn't fall for it, the thing with the lights, then at least I'll get a good mobile out of him. And if he falls for it, then I'll have cash in advance before I agree to do more. Only I never knew if he'd be watching, so I got this kid, young lass called Emmett. She's right good, on the ball. So I stand at the junction, with my phone, so if he's watching it'll look like it's me doing it, but I've already said to him this is a test 'cos I don't know what sort of systems I'm dealing with, so it's like a one-off and if it works then I'll be able to sort him out properly.'

Ahmed's glance briefly flashed towards the camera lens as he said, 'And what did he think of that little charade yesterday?'

Jenkinson shook his head. 'I never meant for that to happen, Mr Ahmed. If you do it right, the cars set off then they stop and you get all the shouting and swearing. That's all I wanted. A load of action with car horns, drivers cursing and that. Only Emmett, she didn't have the right view of the road and … Anyway, if he saw what happened, he'll be back for more.'

'How will he contact you, Tom?'

'He'll ring. He might be ringing me now. Your lot have got my phone. One of you answers it, that's goodbye to my cash.'

Webber spoke to Ahmed through the mic. 'Push him on how he

talked to the mystery man, whether he ever saw him, I want to be clear whether this character exists outside his head.'

'Tom, you told me you'd never seen this man, but that you'd "had a go". What did you mean?'

'I thought I'd seen him ... Well, not seen him, but I knew he was watching me. It were spooky, Mr Ahmed, like a ghost. It was after he'd first been on to me, like he was checking me out. So I thought if I can get my mate to bring his wheels round and I can clock him when he thinks I'm all tucked up in bed, then maybe we can just turn the tables, follow him home. I don't like people following me, not when I don't know who they are.'

Webber felt a touch on his shoulder. 'Jenkinson's phone, Guv,' said the woman at his side. 'The number that's been calling him. We've not tied it down yet, but there's a message, a voicemail from that same number. Yesterday just before the traffic thing kicked off.'

'Hang on.' Webber spoke to Ahmed. 'Ayaan, ask if he's ever had voicemail from this guy.'

They both watched Jenkinson shake his head. 'No, Mr Ahmed, it were always ... Oh, hang on, yeah, there were one. Yesterday. I didn't hear it ring with all the traffic and that. But it were just saying get on with it, nowt really.'

'Go on about when you followed him, Tom.'

Webber looked the question at the woman beside him. 'Just a single word. *Go.* We need to analyse it, but it doesn't sound like a man's voice to me.'

Webber looked back at Jenkinson. Was his mystery man a mystery woman? Did she exist after all?

'... tried to clock him,' Jenkinson was saying, 'but we weren't sure and we ended up following the wrong car. I think we had him.' Jenkinson sounded uncertain. 'We're a few cars back from this fella we think is him and you know how it gets all twisty round town down there. And he gets well ahead of us and we think we've lost him. Then we spot him heading out of town so we get back on his tail. Only when we get near enough to see, there's two of them, and it's a woman driving. So we know we've lost him back in town and we go back.'

'What can you give me on the cars you followed, registration, make, colour?'

Jenkinson squirmed in his seat. 'I'm right sorry, Mr Ahmed. We were that busy keeping out of his way, I didn't really think to clock owt like that. Not till later. I said to me mate, I said, we're gonna look like right Charlies if anyone asks us. We was kinda hoping no one would. It were silver. They were both silver cars. But we must have lost him right down in town and there were no point going and looking for him. We'd been led a right dance, way outa town.'

'Just for the record, where did you end up before you stopped following the car?'

As Jenkinson answered, Webber felt his eyes open wide.

'Right out by them old gravel pits,' said Jenkinson. 'Where they're doing up the fishing lakes. That's where we turned back.'

chapter six

Webber eased his way down the stairs, treading carefully to avoid waking his son. Melinda sat at the computer in the living room. Her back was to him but he could see she was reading his emails and making no attempt to hide it. Two days ago, last night even, he'd have demanded to know what the hell she thought she was doing. It didn't seem to matter now. He wondered how long she'd known his password.

Sam had been uncharacteristically amenable to his father doing the bedtime routine and had fallen asleep before page three of Dr Seuss. Maybe Melinda had counted on him taking longer to settle the boy, but she could hardly be unaware of him, now standing behind her, reading over her shoulder.

Then he saw his phone lying beside her on the desk and looked again at the programmes open on the PC. It was her own email, not his. She'd forwarded things from his phone. He reached across her to pick it up. It might or might not have occurred to her that emails forwarded from his police account to his wife's personal email might get him in deep water. His inbox was sorted by sender. She'd checked for other communications from the woman at the lab. He deleted the forwarded mails from the sent box and hoped for the best.

She'd checked his texts, too. A copy of the article Ahmed had found was lying by the printer.

When he'd arrived home, she'd been very matter-of-fact, almost cheerful, but he supposed that was put on for Sam. She'd told him she'd contacted Harmer's partner, Fiona, and that all future negotiations over paternity, alimony, access and everything else would be conducted by her and Fiona. The reference to access threw him. Was he expected to play a role in this child's life? How was that going to work?

'There's no reason for you to have any contact with Harmer that isn't strictly necessary for work,' she'd said, and he'd agreed.

'You won't like not being in control,' she'd added, 'but that's your look-out.'

Was she right? Being in control was part of his job. He'd never thought about it spilling over into home life. He didn't like the idea of her and Fiona becoming close, but that wasn't something to make a fuss about yet.

'The guy wasn't involved at all, was he? He was just in the wrong place.'

For a second he didn't understand what she was saying, then realised it was the article about Robert Morgan's death. He'd only skimmed it. Morgan had fallen victim to a group of animal rights protesters trying to make a name for themselves.

'Was he? I can't remember. Poor sod. I haven't had a chance to look at it in detail.'

'They should have thrown away the bloody key! Some of them were no more than children but the ring-leader should never have been let out.'

The pictures in his head were from his brief reading of the article along with the 30-year-old memories that had surfaced. He'd been right about remembering the name. The protest group had released circus animals in a stunt that became too big for them to handle. Robert Morgan had been killed by the tigers they'd freed.

'It was a big story at the time. Everyone was talking about it. Do you remember?'

She threw him a withering glance. 'I was barely six.'

'I was doing O levels. I think we were the last class to do them, it was GCSEs after that.'

'I can imagine adolescent boys revelling in a story like that.'

There was disapproval in her tone and he felt ashamed of his 16-year-old self. She was right. They'd delighted in the exotic nature of the crime, the gruesome outcome, full of self-righteousness about people who played with fire. Most of the perpetrators had been their age which had given a glimpse into an alien world. In other circumstances, it could have been him and his friends fired up by one irresponsible adult. As with all these things, a series of half-truths that made good copy had been splashed across the headlines. But yes, it had all come out in the end. No element of just desserts. Wrong place, wrong time. She was right, Robert Morgan had been an innocent bystander and his wife Pamela had suffered for 15 years then killed herself because of what had happened.

He pulled up a chair and sat down. Close to her but not too close. Farrar's cold cases gave them neutral ground. These were details he couldn't share with anyone outside the team without compromising his integrity, but he told himself that Pamela Morgan's suicide wasn't even a cold case. It wasn't a case at all. He told her all he'd found out about her.

'Poor woman,' she said, her forehead creased to a frown. 'What a dreadful thing to have to live with. Especially after the people who did it came out.'

Webber stared at her; couldn't believe he hadn't thought of it. 'When?' he asked. 'When did they come out?' Could there be a link between Pamela Morgan's suicide and the release of the people who'd caused her husband's death?

'How should I know? Who's the bloody detective here, Martyn?'

He acknowledged her point as he glanced through the paperwork. Ten years, he estimated, for the ring-leader; considerably less for the young kids he'd roped in. He'd get the detail later.

'What puzzles me,' he said. 'Is this Brad Tippet guy. What's he doing all over everything today?' He told her about Farrar's scrawled note. Then he crossed another line and told her about the real cold case, the car in the gravel pit and Farrar's throwaway comment about Tippet and the missing third brother.

'Big brother post office,' he said. 'John told me Tippet would have known him at school.'

His thoughts stalled for a moment on Tom Jenkinson, the car he and his mate had followed to the gravel pits. A link there made no sense at all, but he hated unexplained coincidence.

'And it's the missing brother who's at the bottom of that lake, is it?' Melinda said. She didn't sound very interested.

'Probably, but I doubt there's much left to find.'

She turned to look at him. The blank indifference in her eyes chilled him. He would work through her anger and upset, but he had nothing with which to battle indifference. She was putting it on, she had to be. She knew how to unsettle him, how to give him a rough ride. He had to keep his nerve.

She said, 'You haven't made any plans for tomorrow, have you?'

He wasn't sure what she was getting at but replied with the negative that was clearly the answer she needed to hear.

'You hadn't forgotten it's Saturday and you're not working?'

'No … 'course not.' Of course he had. He thought about his instruction to Davis to call him first thing. It would be easier all round if he were working and Davis wasn't, but clearly Melinda had plans and his only option was to fall in with them.

'Tell me about John Farrar's father,' she said. 'He must be knocking on. How would he know Pamela Morgan?'

'He didn't. Someone told him about her.'

'And you don't know where the Brad Tippet man fits in?'

He shook his head and she angled her thumb towards the article about Robert Morgan. 'Surely big cats have been banned from circuses for decades. How could it happen?'

'I don't think so,' he said. 'They went out of fashion, so to speak, but no outright ban until pretty recently, the last year or so. In the 1980s the protesters were out in force.'

'So was Brad Tippet involved in animal rights stuff?'

'Not as far as I know. Other than John scribbling his name on a piece of paper, he has no link to Pamela Morgan. And anyway, it happened in Dorset, not round here.'

'What was Robert Morgan doing in Dorset?'

'I don't know. I expect it's in the case files somewhere.'

'Is it just John Farrar holding a grudge, then?'

Webber gave her a half shrug. Which grudge did she mean? Farrar and Tippet or him and Harmer? Neither were ideas to which he wanted to give currency, yet Farrar's behaviour hadn't been entirely rational today.

'Everything I've read,' he told her, 'says Tippet was just a bystander caught up in someone else's crime. Like Robert Morgan. Tippet had his car stolen and used in a post office raid. Morgan ran into the middle of some insane scheme to release big cats from a circus.'

'What did they do, Martyn? How did it happen?'

'How long's that PM report?' He pointed to the screen where her inbox showed the forwarded email. 'Can you print it?'

It was more than a post-mortem report. It was a detailed reconstruction of the protesters' plans and of Robert Morgan's last moments built from the forensic examination of the scene and the expert witnesses at the time of the court case.

'They had inside help,' he told Melinda as he read. 'They drove the lorry with the tiger cage to a derelict warehouse. Maximum hassle to recapture the animals, but without putting anyone in danger.' He felt the curl in his lip as he recited what had been the protest group's attempt to rationalise what they'd done.

'Morgan was found, what was left of him, when the authorities went to recapture the animals. The group got their publicity. Quite a panic in the local area.'

'Why didn't they do them for murder?' Webber heard the anger in Melinda's voice and felt pleased it should be diverted away from him.

'It was pretty clear that they didn't know he was in there. The moment it came to light someone had been killed, they all came forward.'

'I'd have done the bastards for murder,' she spat out. 'But why was he there?'

Webber read on, turning the page. 'It doesn't look like they ever found out. The place was supposed to be deserted. They claimed they'd checked it out earlier in the day.'

'You said his wife's suicide note said they'd rowed, never made up?'

'I haven't seen the full note, but yes, one of the extracts said something like that.'

'So he'd gone and got drunk and staggered into that place to sleep it off.'

Webber gave her a tight smile and pulled himself to his feet, the papers clasped in his hand. Yorkshire to Dorset was a long stagger. Grim reading, the woman at the lab had said. It was that all right. He walked across to the window, gazed out on to a road lit only by streetlights and pulled the curtains across. 'Let's hope so,' he said.

He didn't want to look into her eyes as he spoke. He'd read through enough of the reconstruction, the painstaking work done by the various forensic experts. Later, after she'd gone to bed, he would delete it from her email so she'd never get to read it for herself. Robert Morgan hadn't been sleeping anything off. Webber suppressed a shudder. The evidence showed that Robert Morgan had been chased from one end of the big space to the other. With his lower leg ripped to shreds, he'd managed an almost impossible climb up a heap of rusted equipment in his desperation to reach a tiny window that would have been too small for him to get through. The tigers would have had no trouble bounding up to grab him down again.

As he yanked the curtains fully closed, shutting out the night, Webber imagined a man finding the strength to pull himself up a makeshift mountain, trailing a semi-amputated leg. Had he heard them loping easily towards him or had they moved silently, invisible until the agonising burn of claws stabbed into his flesh to drag him down? He squeezed shut his eyes, trying to block out the picture. Melinda was right. He'd have wanted the bastards done for murder, too.

chapter seven

At one minute to eight the following morning Webber's mobile sprang to life. He was in the bathroom; heard it cut out as Melinda answered it. There'd been an air of recklessness about her since she'd faced down Harmer. It left him uneasy, scared she was about to do something rash.

'DI Davis,' she told him. 'Said you'd instructed him to call first thing.'

'Sorry, I did ask him to call. He's a lazy sod, I wanted to make sure he was on top of things. What did he say?'

For a moment she just looked at him. Webber had the impression she was spoiling for a fight and the least little thing would spark it. Then she seemed to rein back. 'No change,' she said. 'He's waiting to hear from the lab. Will you nip down to the shop? We're out of cereal.'

'Sure. Do we need anything else?'

He savoured the crisp morning air as he strode down the street, relieved to be away from the tension, annoyed at being on eggshells around her. Early days, he told himself ... he had to remember that. She'd accepted that there was no emotional attachment between him and Suzie; never had been. It was just the blasted child that was going to be solid evidence of his infidelity forever. He'd checked the wall calendar in the kitchen to work out how far on this pregnancy was. Barely three months. Not too late for her to lose it, not that he wished the woman any harm, not really. He just wished he and Mel could be left alone to lead a normal life. Mel would blow up at him if he voiced thoughts about miscarriage. Women were odd like that. Look at all this joining forces with Fiona stuff. He'd bet the Harmer bitch was no more pleased about it than he was.

He and Mel had always planned to have two children. The decision was whether to have the second before Sam was two, or whether to wait until Sam was about five and going to school. The latter option would allow Mel to go back to work, pick up her career. He'd even floated the idea of him being the one to take leave for the second baby; still hadn't worked out whether that was a daft idea or not. Where were those plans now? Early days, he told himself again. Get over these first few weeks, establish that his marriage would survive and then ... Then of course, there would be an imminent birth overhanging everything. Then there'd be a child and all manner of complications.

The street was waking up as he returned to the house. He swapped brief hellos with his neighbours, knowing he'd never get on to the same easy footing as Mel had with them.

Sam was in his high chair, at work with an outsize spoon on a bowl of the cereal they'd supposedly run out of. Melinda greeted him with, 'I found a box at the back of the cupboard,' but didn't meet his eye. He was pleased but kept his expression neutral. Her slightly defensive stance said she knew she was being childish sending him on fool's errands. Fine by him if she snapped herself out of it and he didn't have to. He'd been planning on giving her a few days' leeway before he made a stand.

'So what do you want to do today?' he asked pleasantly.

'We'll go to Spurn Point,' she said. 'Sam and I will enjoy watching the birds.' She still avoided his eye.

'Spurn? In this weather?' He stared at her. It was the last thing he'd expected.

'We'll wrap up. It's not wet. Just cold.'

She insisted on taking the wheel. He knew there was an agenda, but wasn't worried. Her recklessness wasn't going to affect her driving, not with Sam in his seat in the back. If he'd been driving, he'd have skirted Hull to get to Spurn. She chose to head for Beverley and fight her way through the Saturday morning traffic. She didn't say much, and when she spoke it was to quiz him on Pamela Morgan, the woman whose husband had been killed by tigers.

'Why would anyone go out of their way to suggest it wasn't a suicide?'

'Hard to guess without finding out who it was and talking to them directly.'

Sounds from the back seat. Webber turned to see Sam fast asleep, his lips working as he mumbled to himself. He smiled as he studied the tiny features and fought down an urge to reach out to stroke the smooth skin. Best to let him doze.

'John Farrar didn't do much when it was first reported, did he?' As she spoke, Melinda clicked on the car lights. The greyness of the day intensified. It would have turned to a proper fog by the time they reached the coast.

'He had someone look into it,' he said. 'She left a note. There were no doubts.'

'No one dug deep though, did they? What if it was to do with her husband's death?'

'It was. That's why she did it. But if you mean maybe one of the original perpetrators turned up again, reminded her, opened old wounds ... well, there's no crime there. She chose to take her own life.' He was aware that her lips tightened. 'I'm not defending them,' he said. 'I'd have locked up the stupid bastards and thrown away the key. I'm just saying that John probably did all he could by having someone look into it.'

'So why get you to look into it again now?'

He opened his mouth to reply then closed it again. Farrar had done it for much the same reason Mel had clobbered him, but he wasn't going to say so. Any discussion that touched on Harmer and her pregnancy had to be initiated by Mel if he was to stay out of trouble. 'It'll be foggy at the coast,' he said.

He thought she'd taken the hint about the weather when she turned off the road before Patrington and headed for Withernsea. He didn't know what Withernsea offered out of season, but hopefully more shelter than Spurn. They bumped along the narrow lane, grey clouds a dark arrowhead leading the way towards the sea. A muddy lay-by opened to one side, bordered by skeletal hedgerows, a line of coloured plastic recycling bins standing bedraggled as its only occupants. Melinda slowed as they reached a small village. High walls and hedges lined their route as they wound past a conclave of prosperous dwellings. The road ahead forked. She looked unsure. Webber thought about saying, 'Go right,' but didn't want his head snapped off so kept quiet, even as she eased the car the wrong way. She'd find out soon enough. There was no way through. The narrow track ended in the tall pillars of a gateway, the entrance to another of the big houses.

She manoeuvred the car in the small space, turning it round and then reversing a short way into the drive, where she stopped, put on the handbrake and turned to him. 'We'll go and have a look at the sea,' she said. 'Me and Sam. We'll be back in about an hour. Well, go on, don't wait till Sam wakes up.'

He looked into her eyes, saw a tiny spark of triumph under an expression she fought to keep neutral. 'Where the f ...?' He swallowed the curse for Sam's sake not hers. 'Where are we, Mel?'

'Donald Farrar's house,' she told him. She looked at the clock. 'Dead on time. You know what these ex-military types are like on punctuality. I rang this morning. He's expecting you.'

He held her gaze as anger bubbled up inside him. Thoughts churned in his head. If she'd done this a week after Harmer's revelation and not a day, he'd have already been wresting control of the car from her and they'd be in the middle of a shouting match. He would make allowances. Clearly she didn't think Farrar had done enough and was making sure he was back in the firing line. There was a tiny voice deep down that wanted to grab the chance to talk to Farrar senior about his call last May, but he suppressed it. It wouldn't even be a legitimate interview. It wasn't a case, and if it had been, Farrar had taken him off it.

He would be perfectly calm about this. He would get out of the car, go round to Mel's side and help her out. Then he'd drive them all to somewhere where it might be sensible for a family to spend a grey Saturday in November. And he'd check whether she'd genuinely rung to make an appointment with Farrar senior. If so, he'd ring back and smooth over the cracks.

'OK, Mel, you've made your point.' He kept his tone soft. Her gaze dropped. He put his hand on her arm. 'I understand what I've put you through, and I'm truly sorry. But enough of this nonsense. OK?' She gave a half nod. 'Now, let me take you somewhere for the day where Sam can have a good time.'

She unclipped her seatbelt and reached for the door handle. He climbed out, leaving the door open, glancing into the back where Sam was beginning to stir.

The rev of the engine took him unawares. He leapt back as gravel sprayed across him, felt his jaw drop as the car lurched forward, its passenger door swinging wide. In a second he was sprinting after them, flinching as Mel threw the car into an abrupt swerve that slammed shut the open door, and then, with tyres squealing they'd vanished round the corner leaving just the receding whine of the engine. He stopped, his heart hammering hard in his chest. The stupid cow! She'd unclipped her seatbelt to make him think she would do as he asked.

He couldn't even phone her, his mobile was in the car, and it would do no good if he could. An hour, she'd said. And this godforsaken place didn't boast a shop, never mind a pub or anywhere he could get shelter from the persistent drizzle. She'd led him by the nose and left him with no sensible option but to do her bidding.

As Webber sank into the silky magenta-patterned cushions of the settee and accepted a wafer-thin bone-china cup of fierce tea, he felt that he'd walked through a time warp, not just up a driveway and into a house. The unsmiling elderly woman who'd let him in could have come straight from a 1950s film set, just like the room into which she ushered him. He'd offered his ID but it had barely been given a glance and now lay on the table. He placed his teacup carefully beside it and looked across at the elderly man in the chair opposite. Farrar's father. He only knew the headlines; ex-military, ex-Foreign Office, ex-mountaineer. It must have been Davis's call that had tipped Melinda over the edge. She'd catapulted him into a situation that would be a red rag to Farrar the moment he found out about it.

Farrar's father was distant, as if he couldn't be bothered. His housekeeper, if that's who the woman was – there were no introductions – fired genteel resentment at him as she gave him his tea. Farrar senior assumed his son had sent Webber. He didn't contradict the idea.

'I go every year in May, on the 19th,' the old man said, but without much interest. He seemed more resigned to answering questions than keen to do so.

It was when the story was over that the timbre of the interview changed. Webber thought about Donald Farrar's insubstantial answers, his talk of the young chap he'd half recognised, of the young woman he'd never seen before, the Dr China of Lana's note, and he tried to see behind the words. 'Something about the young woman touched you,' he ventured. 'What was it?'

At that point he'd seen a glimmer of surprise in the old man's face. He watched as Donald Farrar reached for his glasses and held out his hand for Webber's ID. Having inspected it, he scrutinised Webber, then his eyes narrowed in a speculative look. After a moment, his lips curved to a smile. 'She spoke as I left the table,' he said. 'I think she said, "Poor Quinny."'

'Quinny?' Webber queried. 'Do you know what she meant?'

Donald Farrar shook his head. 'I don't know *what* she meant, but I know she meant it. It came from the heart. If I'm honest, I didn't listen to much of what they said to each other. Wasn't interested. The young have their agendas. If I'd known ...' His voice tailed off.

'Known that she was going to tell you about Pamela Morgan?' Webber prompted.

'Was it a suicide?'

A movement caught Webber's attention. The woman who'd let him in was in the garden beyond the French windows. It still drizzled out there. He wondered what she was doing. 'Yes,' he said. 'She left a note.' He thought about the note being unsigned. It had been long and hand-written. There were no doubts that she'd authored it. He told Donald Farrar about Robert Morgan, about the animal rights stunt gone wrong.

'Nasty way to go,' Farrar commented. 'But odd she should wait 15 years.'

'Yes, I thought so. It might be to do with the perpetrators being released. I don't know.'

'And the friend she addressed the note to?'

Webber spread his hands in a gesture of helplessness. 'I haven't even found out who it was. John asked me to have a quick look, but we're too stretched to do much. We don't have the resources to dig deep.' Webber hesitated. Commenting on resources sounded silly when he'd come all this way. 'I have the weekend off.' That too, sounded daft.

'I said I didn't listen to much of what they said to each other, but I heard some of it. I think that's why that last comment stuck. It wasn't just the way she said it. I remember thinking at the time that their talk was full of Qs.'

'Qs?'

'Quinny ... quintets ... Quintina ... Now, I only heard her say Quinny that once, but he mentioned quintets a time or two. She just brushed it off. And Quintina was mentioned by them both. He was … I don't really know … resentful I think gets closest. She was awkward. But assuming Quintina and Quinny are one and the same, she spoke quite differently when she thought the young man wasn't listening.'

Webber wrote the words, tracing his pen around the capital Q of Quintina. He didn't doubt that Farrar's father had plucked the significant exchanges from the words he'd overheard. Even if he hadn't been interested at the time, his decades of experience would have kicked in to log the key points. One of the things Farrar senior was unable to give him was much of a physical description.

'I struggle with my eyes in that sort of place. Too many lights everywhere.'

'Do you know a man called Brad Tippet?'

Donald Farrar sat up with a start. 'That's it!' He gave Webber a grin. 'I knew I knew him. That's who the young man reminded me of. Tippet. Must have been a relation, his son maybe. Does Tippet have a son?'

Webber could only shrug a don't-know. He'd never been so badly prepared to interview a witness.

When he sauntered back down the drive just an hour after he'd arrived, he felt buoyed up. Farrar's father had made a huge effort to delve into his memory, and John Farrar must have considered the possibility six months ago of it being Tippet. Why else had he written the name? A bigger puzzle was why he'd never talked to his father about it, but clearly he hadn't.

The car was parked by the gates. Melinda climbed out as he approached. He saw from the defensiveness of her stance that she was expecting a row, but his head was full of the things Farrar senior had told him.

'Quite a set-up he has here,' he told her as he climbed into the driving seat. 'I don't think John and his father get on, but I've found out why he wrote Tippet's name on the file. Looks like it was

Tippet's son who approached Farrar senior back in May. I wonder how he guessed. What have you two been doing?' He turned see Sam clutching a plastic toy.

'Called in on a friend,' Melinda said. 'So it was worth seeing him, was it?'

He laughed as he nodded. 'But if you drive off like that again without your seat belt, I'll book you.'

She didn't react, but he had an idea she was holding back a smile. 'You've had a couple of calls,' she told him. 'Davis again. Wants you to ring back. And Ayaan Ahmed. Ditto.'

He glanced at his phone in the tray under the handbrake. He blew out a sigh as he set off down the narrow lane. 'Davis will have heard from the lab. He can email me. I wonder what Ayaan wants.'

'Davis was quite insistent, sounded upset when I said you weren't available.'

Upset? 'OK,' he said. 'Call him back.'

She clicked in the number and switched it to speakerphone. 'Martyn Webber,' he said as Davis answered. 'What have you got?'

'I've had the lab results back.'

He wouldn't have used the term 'upset' but Mel was right, this wasn't Davis's normal laid back tone. He sounded on edge. 'And?'

'It's not big brother post office in the back of that car. It's not any relation, and we've no match. We don't know who it is.'

Webber sighed inwardly. This was going to end up in a full underwater search, he could feel it. And that wouldn't do anything to appease Farrar's temper. He listened as Davis told him what he'd initiated, the trawl of missing persons reported around the time the car was known to have disappeared, the interrogation of the original dive team. He felt surprise to learn that Davis could shift himself when he had to. He supposed he'd had Farrar on his case. This wasn't the sort of loose end anyone wanted. He wondered if he'd be able to have a coherent conversation with Farrar by next week.

'Are you going to have that pit dragged?' Mel asked as he ended the call to Davis.

'Probably have to. We can't leave it with some poor sod rotting at the bottom of it.'

When she offered to call Ayaan Ahmed back, he knew her motive was to keep herself up to date on the detail he might otherwise not tell her, but that was fine. They were going to need neutral ground over the next few months if they were to keep talking at all.

He wondered about Ahmed. It must be something about Jenkinson. Maybe he'd got a name. But then why ring Webber and not one of the team who were on duty today. It wasn't like Ahmed to pester anyone on a day off.

'Did you tell him I'm not at work today?'

'Yes. He said sorry, but he needed to talk to you. He said it's about Jenkinson.'

He felt a frown crease his brow. The more he thought about it, the less sense it made that Ahmed should call him and not the team back at the station. 'Yes,' he said. 'Call him back.'

chapter eight

'Thanks for getting back to me, Martyn. I'm sorry, I know you're off today but I can't let this lie. There's more to it than they think.'

Webber slowed the car as they left the hamlet behind and headed out into open country. What had been a mist was now a steady drizzle. Hard to know where they could go that wouldn't be every bit as miserable as sitting in silence at home. Sam, now wide awake, began to intone, 'Oy oy oy,' and Webber felt the rhythmic thump of his son's shoes in the back of the seat. It didn't happen to Mel. She had the seat further forward, out of his reach. He saw her now in his peripheral vision as she turned to crinkle her eyes at Sam. He needed to see her smiling at him like that again.

'Hang on, Ayaan, you're losing me. What's happened? Last I knew was that you had Jenkinson coming in this morning to look through some photos.'

'He didn't turn up. It looks like he's done a runner. I got the warden to let me into his room. He's cleared his stuff. There was just a stack of drugs paraphernalia.' Webber heard a level of disgust in Ahmed's voice. He imagined the upset of seeing his successful mentoring going full circle and heading towards Hull gaol. 'They think it was all an act from start to finish, but I wouldn't have missed that. I know Tom. There's more to it.'

Webber blew out a sigh. Mel was still leaning into the back playing some game that made Sam giggle, but she was listening to every word.

'He was pretty well prepared for you, Ayaan. I mean he seemed

shocked to see you, but he had a story all ready when it was needed.'
Not only that, thought Webber, but when he appeared to give up altogether the story had been incomplete, giving them nothing to go on, unless the gravel pit was anything, but that too could have been a carefully prepared diversion which did nothing to lessen the unease of the coincidence. 'You said there's more to it. What do you mean?'

'I think there's the promise of money behind it. He'd go to ground for that. Either he was holding something back about his dealings with the mystery man ...'

'Or woman,' murmured Webber, thinking about the anomalies in Jenkinson's tale. He was aware that Mel shot him a curious glance.

'... or he's trying something stupid. But there's more to it than they think.'

Webber replayed Jenkinson's carefully crafted tale, with all its layers. The most likely explanation, though Ahmed wouldn't like it, was that it had been honed with Ahmed in mind. Maybe there was no third party involved at all. They were chasing the supposed child accomplice, Emmett, and the CCTV from the night Jenkinson said he and his mate had followed the silver cars, but if Jenkinson's story was made up, he wouldn't want to risk another face to face to have it pulled to pieces. His record said he was the type to act first and think later. Ahmed's professional pride had taken a knock with the assumption of Jenkinson holed up somewhere laughing at how he'd been duped.

'What sort of stupid?' he asked.

'If he told me the truth, he was after rooking that man for some setup with the traffic lights. Maybe he doesn't want to give that up ... maybe he's going to use police involvement to see what he can get. Money for keeping quiet, something like that.'

'What are you suggesting we do about it, Ayaan?'

'You need to up the urgency on finding him. Find out what it's really about. There's more to it. This isn't the Tom Jenkinson I've known for the past two years.'

Webber turned his attention to the junction that took them back on to the main road. 'I'll see where we are on Monday morning, Ayaan. But you need to keep an eye out for him in Scarborough. If he wants to keep out of our way, he'll probably head for home.'

After she'd cut the call, Melinda put down his phone and said, 'What was so urgent about that, that it couldn't wait till next week?'

'Just wanted to get his side in first,' Webber said. 'If the lad's gone to ground, it looks like he had Ayaan round his little finger. Bruised pride.'

'Could he be right? Is there more to it?'

Webber shrugged. His goal was to focus this weekend on Mel and Sam, emphasise how strong they were as a family, start to draw Mel out of her angry bubble. 'Maybe,' he said. 'I'm happy to keep an open mind on it. Ayaan knows his stuff, but he's emotionally wrapped up in this one. Tom Jenkinson was a big success story for him. Whatever the truth of it, it'll keep till Monday.'

The following afternoon, the weather had lifted. It was as though they'd swapped countries. Clear skies made for a hard, cold day; the bright autumn sun making a warm cocoon of the car. Webber was behind the wheel again, Mel at his side, Sam in the back. They shouldn't be with him, but Mel had been too determined and he was supposed to have the weekend off. He hadn't found a way to say no. The words echoed in his head. *It'll keep till Monday*. Talk about tempting fate.

After a sham of a family Sunday lunch, with both of them talking to Sam and around each other, the phone had rung. Instinct told Webber what sort of call it would be so it hadn't come as a surprise to hear Davis's apologetic voice at the end of the line. And something in his expression had alerted Mel. She made no secret of picking up the extension to listen in.

Webber brushed aside Davis's apologies for another disturbance to his weekend. 'The ... uh ... the Chief Super said to call you. I'm on my way up to the gravel pits. We've had an emergency call. The site owners, they've sent their divers down again. They've found something else.'

'What the hell are they doing there at all? The site's supposed to be closed off.' He heard the rebuke in his tone, knowing it wasn't fair. Keeping that open site secure would have taken a battalion. He tried to soften his voice as he asked, 'What have they got?'

'I don't know. I just had the call from John Farrar to get on to you and to hot-foot it up there.'

As he put back the handset, Webber glanced at Melinda expecting to be the target of an unsheathed-daggers glare. But no, she wasn't looking at him. She was lost in thought, eyes unfocussed. 'How would they get a dive team on to the site?' she asked. 'And why risk it?'

'It's taped off,' Webber told her, 'but we can't keep it secure 24/7. They're only a small group, the ones who own the site. We've told them to stay clear of that gravel pit but it's their livelihood we're threatening all the time we're keeping them from it. It'll have been those interviews.'

'How d'you mean? Come on, Sam, let's have you changed.' She picked up the boy as she looked at Webber. Her expression was interested, open. It might be fleeting but he could see that for a moment she'd forgotten the hostility that had underlain every interaction since she'd found out about Suzie Harmer. She was right of course, the site owners had been cowed into acquiescence to start with. The interviews were the only things that had happened that could have made a difference.

As she saw to Sam, he allowed himself to think aloud. 'Davis got them interviewing the divers who'd found the car. It's a small outfit. I think there are only five of them, and they *are* the dive team. They've pooled their resources to make a go of this venture. We hadn't talked to the two who'd actually found it. I told Davis to get the detail from them on what they'd seen. No one knew at that point that we weren't going to match the DNA with the third brother of the post office trio.'

'So these people could lose everything if this delay goes on too long?' Her concentration was on Sam's arm and getting it to mesh with the sleeve of a pullover, but her tone was still all focused on the case. It occurred to him that she must miss being part of the dialogue, batting theories back and forth, easing out the answers from the remnants of crime. She'd always been good at it.

'Yes, they're probably kicking themselves for not keeping shtum about the car in the first place. But they must have pushed for answers. How long? How serious? All that stuff.'

She sat Sam up and battled the chubby fists that tried to join in getting buttons and buttonholes together. Webber thought the outfit a bit on the warm side.

'Someone's told them more than they should, d'you think?'

He tipped his head in a yes-no gesture. 'Probably nothing concrete, but they'll have got the idea. The papers got on to the car pretty quickly so they could easily have researched the post office raid.'

'You can see their point. Go and get your boots, Sam.' She stood the child on his feet and he toddled towards the footwear. Webber didn't think he needed boots, but wasn't going to comment. 'You won't hand back the site,' she went on, 'because there might be a 30-year-old corpse. But you're not going to go down and look because it costs too much.'

'And they have a dive team ready and able,' he finished. 'And if they could pull out whatever's down there they could get things moving. Probably thought it well worth whatever rebuke they were going to get.'

'Well, it looks like they've found it.'

'Found something anyway. Does Sam need his jacket on? Won't he be too hot?'

'No, it'll be cold up by those gravel pits.'

Webber showed his ID, asking questions of the two uniformed constables as he ducked under the replenished stretch of tape that flapped by the side of the tattered original. Something had been found, they weren't sure what, but focus was on a half-built walkway as well as the pit. The Chief Super was on the site somewhere with DI Davis.

He looked around. The main fishing lake spread out ahead, still open for business. He could see figures crouched under giant umbrellas at intervals along the shore. The gravel pit was hidden behind a copse. People milled about by the battered shack that served as a reception point and equipment store. He was fairly sure he spotted Mel and Sam in amongst them. He quizzed the two constables on exactly who was about, who had been here earlier. He had a feeling it would be one of those occasions where there would be no shortage of witnesses who'd been close but not close enough, but if Farrar had turned up then the whole thing was climbing the priority list.

'Get some PCSOs up here to secure the site,' he told them. 'Then get on with rounding up witnesses and taking statements.'

As he pushed through the undergrowth, bypassing the direct path, the dark expanse of the gravel pit lay before him, flat, grey and uninviting. A police dinghy floated a few metres out from where a huddle of people watched from the shore. He recognized Farrar and Davis. A man and woman both in wetsuits with blankets round their shoulders huddled on a makeshift seat. As he approached, he heard Davis telling someone to take them back to the hut, get them warm and dry.

Farrar spoke into a radio, talking to the team in the dinghy, then turned to Davis. 'Go with them,' he said, nodding his head at the shivering divers. 'I don't want them spreading stories until we've collared any witnesses.'

Webber broke into the exchange to tell Davis the officers on the tape would be his once the PCSOs arrived. Farrar nodded approval and said, 'Whatever's down there, they'll have it out before long. Come and see this.'

Webber could detect no trace of hostility in Farrar's tone; he seemed focussed entirely on what was happening around him. 'What is it?'

As he followed Farrar away from the gravel pit, down an uneven path that snaked through the scrub, Webber took in a summary of the events of the past hour. The theory he'd voiced to Mel was right. The site's owners had picked up on the lack of urgency that might sink their new venture and had taken matters into their own hands.

'It's possible they've disturbed a 30-year-old corpse down there,' Farrar told him. 'But unlikely. I had a devil of a job getting hold of anyone who could give me an opinion. You'd think the world stops on a Sunday. Thought it might have been a body buried in the mud, well-preserved, trapped by the car. Car gets pulled out, the body pops up. Visibility's not good at that depth. The idiots who went down thought it was trapped clothing, a green jacket, but when they went to pull it free apparently it bled.'

'Bled? But ...'

'Yes, a 30-year-old corpse doesn't bleed. The woman said she tried to pull it free and it leaked some kind of greenish goo. Whether it was blood or not, it freaked them. They're adamant that the clothing wasn't there when they found the car.'

'But if it was trapped under the car, they wouldn't have seen it anyway.' He stopped to look out over the dark water. There was a single figure in the dinghy now, leaning over one side staring into the depths. It had been a good while since he'd had a case that had needed an underwater search unit. 'Green? How deep do you have to be for blood to look green?'

'20 odd metres, I believe.'

'Christ! Is it really that deep?'

Farrar nodded, then turned away from the water and scrambled up the slope. 'But forget the water. Come and look at this. They plan to build a walkway across this stretch. It's barely started, just foundations for this one end.'

Webber stood at the top of the slope at Farrar's side. Behind him was the gravel pit where Tippet's car had been pulled out. Ahead he looked down on a boggy reed bed with an untidy construction half-built at one side. It too had been taped off. Farrar made his way across. Webber followed, trying to avoid the deeper mud but there was no dry path and he felt moisture squelch over and into his shoes. He supposed common sense should have told him to bring wellingtons, but it hadn't, he'd been focussed on the issue of having Mel and Sam in the car with him.

'This is your case, now,' Farrar said as he stopped short of the metal framework of the half-finished structure. 'You can have Davis as well.'

Webber bit back on a sarcastic, 'Thanks,' and winced inwardly at the hit his budget would take. He had a feeling the underwater unit was just the start. He recognised Lana standing beside the newly taped off area.

'Footings to hold this end of the walkway,' Farrar said as the three of them stood looking down at a smooth concrete base. Further comment was interrupted by the buzz of his radio. 'Update Superintendent Webber,' Farrar said to Lana before turning away.

'They're extending that path,' she said, pointing back towards the thicket that hid the working section of the site. 'And there'll be a walkway held up by two towers, one here and one at the other end. Only they swore blind they'd stopped work on it a few weeks ago, before they found anything in the pit. Money was getting tight. They decided the walkway would be stage two and the main thing was to get the pit ready for customers.'

Webber looked again at the smooth concrete. 'It looks fresh,' he said.

She nodded. 'The one who made the emergency call earlier, she said she came across here. It's the quickest route from the gravel pit to the hut and the phone. She said it didn't dawn on her until they were back by the water waiting for us to arrive. She asked who'd organised to have the concrete base laid and how they were paying for it. None of them knew anything about it.'

Webber pulled in a breath and closed his eyes for a moment. 'When? When was it laid?'

'There was no concrete in there a fortnight ago, that's all they're clear about.'

He looked back towards the slope that hid the pit from view. He'd known the underwater team was the least of it. 'What kind of idiot hides stuff on a site with us crawling all over it?' he muttered.

'It could have been done before they found the car – just.'

Farrar marched back towards them, beckoning Webber with a jerk of his head. 'No body,' he said. 'It's a jacket. It was weighted down. They've got it out.'

Webber trudged behind Farrar, not bothering where he trod. His feet were sodden, the cloying mud pulled at his shoes. As they topped the hill, he saw the dinghy now at the water's edge, a sodden heavyweight orange jacket lying on the grass. As they approached, he felt a weight descend on to his shoulders, a weight he wanted to duck away from. Farrar had said green, but at that depth all colours from the short end of the spectrum would have appeared green.

'What are you looking so gloomy about?' Farrar snapped with a trace of his previous rancour. 'Can't you cope with another case?'

Webber hurried forward and called out, 'Let me see that coat.' They lifted it for his inspection. He took in the lopsided rip at the collar, the black lettering. A couple of days ago he'd spent time watching that jacket with its owner inside it.

'I'm not sure you've given me another case,' he answered Farrar. 'That belongs to Tom Jenkinson.'

chapter nine

Webber strode down the pavement, his feet splashing through the puddles that gathered on the uneven tarmac surface. The early sun was all light, no warmth. He'd worn his heavy overcoat and found himself huddling into it as he pushed through the doors.

His 'What's new?' to the desk sergeant was a routine greeting, rarely met with anything other than 'It's quiet enough,' or 'It's all through there waiting for you.' This morning, the man flicked the corner of a newspaper and said with grim satisfaction, 'Fatal RTA last night. Makes you wonder about that business with the lights and those kids the other week.'

Webber stopped in his tracks. 'Where? Who? The same time?'

'Could have been; no one knows. No witnesses. Arthur Trent. Mid-50s. It's made the early editions.' He held up the local newspaper. Webber took it and looked at the photograph. A single car concertinaed into a tree. He skimmed the article. The time of the collision was estimated in the small hours, a long time from the height of the rush hour, the window for the recent traffic disruption, and anyway there was no rush hour on a Sunday, no traffic lights nearby and it wasn't a well enough used stretch of road to have caused gridlock at any time of day.

'It looks like Trent died at the wheel. Heart attack probably. We'll get more from the post mortem but no other vehicles involved.'

Webber relaxed a little. Death, accidental and natural, carried on regardless of what went on around it. He looked again at the crushed front end of the vehicle. 'He was doing quite a speed.'

'Yeah, he's not been coasting. Looks like he had his foot hard on the pedal.'

'Deliberate?' Webber murmured, his mind conjuring an image of Pamela Morgan. She'd killed herself with pills – a tidier end than Arthur Trent in his smashed car.

He had a briefing to run, that business at the gravel pit to unravel. He stopped, looked back. 'I suppose the local press have been all over the crash site?'

He saw the sergeant bristle. 'Not until we'd done what we needed to do.'

◉ ◉ ◉

Something had animated Davis. Maybe he had just bowed to the inevitable. Under Webber's eye he wouldn't get away with doing half a job. He'd called the team together. There wasn't room for Webber at the table so he leant on one of the filing cabinets and listened as Davis mapped out the situation.

'The jacket is with the lab. Don't know what we'll get with it having been underwater. Ayaan Ahmed's chasing up Jenkinson in Scarborough. There's no sign of him in York. We had someone out to his known haunts last night and we've some more to check this morning.'

'No sign of him down there with the coat, then?'

'Not yet.' Davis's glance flicked briefly to Webber. 'We had a bit of a break with the shape of the pit at the bottom there. It's deep and it's steep. Funnels down. Makes for an enclosed search area. Full of muck and junk that'll take some sifting but it's doable.'

Not as expensive as it might have been, thought Webber, but any surplus would be swallowed up chipping out that concrete, the embryo of a foundation for a walkway between the gravel pit and the working section of the site.

As though plucking the thought from his head, Davis switched tack. 'There's fresh concrete in the foundation for the far end of the walkway.' He pointed to one of the photographs on the table. People reached forward to swivel it their way for a better look. 'It wasn't there a fortnight ago, but it was there yesterday. Initial signs are that it's at the recent end of that window. We had a builder take a quick look. What I want is to pin down who delivered it and when.'

'Could it have been mixed on site?' Webber asked.

Davis shook his head. 'There'd have been signs if it'd been mixed nearby and it's too good a mix to have been done in situ. Apparently it would show round the edges. But more than that, there are tyre tracks. There's a lorry of some sort been down there. A wagon's backed down there and poured concrete directly in.'

'Do we know what depth?'

The officer nearest him looked round at Webber, giving an exasperated shake of her head. 'They each say something different. All they agree on is that a hole was dug for the foundations before they left it and turned their efforts on to the gravel pit. So no one's been near it – so they say – since work was suspended on the walkway a couple of weeks ago, except that a couple of them said the hole was used to dispose of hard-core. The more they could fill it, the less concrete they'd need and it'd be cheaper. There was definite friction about it in the group. Two of them wanted to keep on with it, thought the walkway would be the bigger attraction than making the gravel pit useable. So a couple of them are saying there was no more than a foot, eighteen inches on top of the rubble. The others are saying between two and four foot deep.'

'What extra facilities?' asked Webber. 'It's just more fishing, isn't it?'

'No, no. Water sports. The gravel pit's deep enough for scuba training, that sort of thing.'

'So has one of them organised that concrete on the quiet just to keep the walkway job moving?'

'It's possible. Certainly they weren't all aware of the plan to dump rubble down there. But if so, I'm surprised we haven't had an admission. We put the pressure on.'

Worst case, thought Webber, four feet of concrete to chip out.

'Do you have the schedules for all the concrete firms in the area?' Davis was saying.

Webber watched as the papers were laid out for inspection. 'I've got everything local for the last fortnight. Nothing was dispatched to that site.'

'In the grand scheme of things,' said Davis, 'It's not a huge amount. It could be skimmed off a bigger load without anyone noticing.'

'How does that work?'

'Bent driver takes a detour and a backhander. It's not unknown.'

'So we can assume it came off one of the bigger loads.'

'We can cut it down further than that,' Davis said. 'It's set but it's not fully dried. Definitely no more than seven days, possibly no more than three. But we're probably looking at a mix with a low slump index, the sort of mix that's the least workable, sets the quickest, typically used in wet foundations.'

Webber was surprised at the level to which Davis had mugged up on concrete mixes. Maybe his admonition the other day had done some good.

'OK,' said Davis, 'we're looking for large loads. Start with the most recent and work back. Take note of the mix, but no assumptions. It might have been anything.'

When Davis had dispatched his team to chase concrete deliveries and Jenkinson, Webber asked about Ahmed. 'I spoke to him last night,' said Davis. 'No sign of the boy as yet, there or here, but he's supposed to be in classes this morning. I was going to see if we turn anything up at the University before I get on to Scarborough again.'

'I'll give Ayaan a ring,' said Webber. 'I want to speak to him anyway.'

Davis looked curious but Webber didn't elaborate. He felt an ill-defined unease about Ahmed. He was a promising officer who should have a glittering career ahead of him. He'd got his sergeant's exams and needed to be pushing for promotion, not stagnating in an east coast backwater. Jenkinson had been a real feather in his cap and if the boy had gone bad it would be a blow. He wanted to know that Ahmed was keeping things in proportion. He pulled his phone from his pocket and flicked through for Ahmed's number.

'Ayaan? Martyn here. How are you doing with Jenkinson? Any luck?'

'I caught up with his mother,' said Ahmed with what sounded like a sigh of resignation. 'I was on my way round to theirs and I spotted her on Queen's Parade. She bit my head off, reckons Tom's gone off the rails again and it's all down to us.'

Webber did a quick recap in his head of events since last Friday. 'So she's seen him.'

'I think so. I know she's spoken to him. She won't admit he's been back over but I think he has. And I know what it means when she gets defensive like that. He's told her something that she's keeping quiet about.'

Ahmed's annoyance was clear but Webber felt a smile curve his mouth. 'You'll save us some time if you can get her to talk, Ayaan.'

'Any ideas? Tom's a doddle in an interview room compared to his mother.'

Webber took time to question Ahmed about Jenkinson's mother, to suggest a few tricks he might try. It was almost a rehearsal for his own strategy to get round Melinda. Despite the turmoil of the various cases he felt more relaxed than he'd done in days. Jenkinson had been back to Scarborough, he'd confided in his waster of a mother. He'd done what Ahmed had feared and gone off the rails. Webber wouldn't voice the thought right now but far better that than have him turn up under a foot of concrete.

As he ended the call, he saw one of Davis's team coming back with a look that said he had something. If his luck held and both Jenkinson and a credible explanation for the concrete delivery turned up, he might salvage something from the tatters of his budget on these cases.

'What have you got?'

The man glanced towards Davis, on a phone at the far end of the room, then turned to Webber. 'I'm pretty sure this is the delivery. They sent two lorry loads out. Foundations for wind turbines. Here's the thing. I've spoken to one of the drivers. He'd tipped his load and was on his way off the site when he saw the second batch arriving. He didn't think anything of it, but according to these dockets, it was the other batch that left the depot first, a good forty minutes earlier. I'm just waiting to hear back from someone who can point me at the driver.'

Webber pointed at the page in the man's hand. 'Which one is it?' he asked. 'When was it delivered?'

'That one.' The man ran his finger down the list pinpointing the date and time. 'Yesterday morning early. The first batch was out of the depot before six am.'

Webber felt his forehead crease to a frown. Could that concrete bed have been as new as that? He too looked across to where Davis was still hunched over the phone, caught his eye and beckoned with a nod. Davis gave him a hunted glance, then spoke into the handset before ending the call. He hurried across.

'That concrete base we saw yesterday,' Webber said. 'Could it have been as little as seven or eight hours old?'

Davis nodded. 'Yes, with something like calcium chloride in the mix. Why, what have you got?' They showed him the paperwork. He nodded again. 'I know that area. The foundations for those turbines are practically under water. The mix has to dry fast before it's compromised. I suppose it's not that different from the reed bed behind the gravel pit.'

A voice called out to Webber. 'Guv, the Chief Super's on the phone.'

Webber suppressed a sigh. 'Talk to that driver,' he said, 'and let me know what he says.'

'Tell me about the fishing lakes,' Farrar opened.

'A bit of luck with the underwater search,' Webber told him, explaining about the funnel effect at the bottom of the pit that would reduce the search area. 'Another thing, it might mean that the jacket was thrown in well away from the place the car was found, off the far side for instance, and with the weights, it would have slid right round.' He envisaged it as he talked. Someone, maybe Jenkinson himself, wanting to get rid of the brightly coloured jacket. Instinct would say to throw it out away from the edge, and it would have been caught by the anomaly in the underwater terrain. They'd have done better just to drop it where they stood.

'What about the walkway? Are you going to have that concrete out?' Farrar asked, then interrupted his own question before Webber could answer. 'Just by the way, Brad Tippet … what have you found out about him?'

With a mental change of gear, Webber's mind raced through the pros and cons of discussing his off-piste interview with Farrar's father. 'Am I right in thinking Tippet has a son?'

'Yes, he does. Why?'

'It's likely it was Tippet's son who approached your father back in May about the suicide. Well, it was some woman with him who mentioned Pamela Morgan, not Tippet himself.'

There was a pause. 'Is there anything worth following up there?'

'Not that I can see.' As he spoke, Webber became aware of Davis and the DC who'd been discussing the lorry schedules. The DC had just put down the phone. Both men were staring his way. Webber walked towards them as he spoke into the handset. 'That fifteen-year gap is a bit odd, but …' His voice tailed off as he looked at the paper being held up for his inspection. The driver who was assumed to have taken an unscheduled detour to the gravel pit.

'Get a team out there,' he barked at Davis who sprang to the nearest phone.

Farrar's voice in his ear. 'What's happened?'

The words snaked in front of his eyes. Some sick kind of mirror of the traffic chaos that had plagued the city for the past two weeks. The paper held the identity of the driver who'd filled that hole with concrete barely twenty-four hours ago. A driver whose body lay in the mortuary, his car concertinaed against a tree on a quiet road. Mr Arthur Trent, mid-50s.

'Yes,' Webber replied to Farrar. 'We're having those foundations out.'

chapter ten

Webber pulled his coat collar tight against the driving rain as he paced a line from the footpath to the sapling hedge that bordered the metal stanchions of the embryo walkway. The concrete slab was now hidden behind flapping canvas. He'd chosen to keep at a distance rather than getting togged up in overalls, but couldn't help thinking of the added warmth an extra layer would have provided. Ayaan Ahmed stood at the far side, motionless, his gaze fixed on the barrier from which the clatter of drills and scrape of metal on concrete jarred the peace of the surrounding woodland. He'd been there when Webber arrived and when he'd asked how Ahmed had squared his absence from his base in Scarborough, Ahmed had said, 'I told them you wanted me here.'

His voice had been dull, no hint of apology in the admission of the lie. Webber had bitten back a reprimand. He'd wait until they discovered what had been hidden before sending Ahmed away with a flea in his ear. It wouldn't be Jenkinson; it couldn't be. Jenkinson had been back to Scarborough whether his mother would admit it or not.

A drill suddenly screamed a higher pitch, a cloud of dust erupted from beneath the canvass. It jerked his attention to the present. He saw Ahmed jump slightly and stare with increased intensity as muffled curses floated out with the clang of metal tools.

What was the link? Why here? Traffic chaos … a rotting vehicle from a 30-year-old crime … Jenkinson and his tale of a silver car … flashlights confusing tired drivers … and a middle-aged man dead at the wheel. Webber stamped his feet to keep his own blood circulating as he thought over what had come from the initial examination of Arthur Trent. Already dead when the car hit the tree. Nothing yet to suggest it wasn't natural causes, but nothing to say it was. The car's cruise control had been engaged which might explain the speed of the impact, but also raised questions such as why would anyone use cruise control on that stretch of road?

Why did everything lead to the gravel pit? It made no sense. He glanced again at Ahmed who stood as though cast in stone. Enquiries at the university had revealed a completely different Jenkinson. There he was diffident, quiet and considered a hard working but average student; same story from his fellow students. Everyone said he wasn't a drug taker. Not that Webber would have expected Jenkinson's friends to say anything else, but Ahmed had said the same. *How could I ever have thought it? He saw what it did to his mother. He's never touched anything. It was planted.* But whatever the truth about the drug-taking, Webber's gut told him not to trust Jenkinson's elevation to model citizen.

'We have Jenkinson's flat under wraps,' Webber had reassured him. 'If that place has anything to give us, we'll find it.' So far, nothing. It was forensically clean. Too clean. Webber was inclined to go with Ahmed's conclusion. The layers of Jenkinson's story weren't simple to unwind. No sniff of the mate he'd talked about, the one whose car they'd used to follow the mystery man. No trace of the child accomplice, Emmett.

It was a reaction from Ahmed that alerted him. Someone was pushing their way from the enclosed area. Encased head to toe in white, eyes showing over a face mask, a small woman looked around, caught sight of Webber and beckoned. The mud squelched beneath his boots as he made his way over. Her voice was muffled by the mask and the crackle of the breeze against the canvass, but he caught the sense of the message. They'd found something. 'We're trying to get underneath from the side where the concrete's not so thick. Might be a tailor's dummy, of course. Looks like part of a limb between the bottom of the concrete and the rubble. It must have set before it settled. We got a camera in.'

Webber peered at the screen she held up in front of him. Alabaster skin. He couldn't have guessed whether it was flesh or plastic, arm or leg, but the tattoo was clear. He hesitated a moment and then called out to Ahmed.

Ahmed sprang into action and raced across the slippery ground. 'What is it?' Webber could hear the effort he made to keep his voice level.

He put out his hands in a calming gesture. 'Don't know yet. Look at this. Do you recognise it?'

The gasp from Ahmed collapsed into a whispered, 'Oh no ...' and told Webber everything he didn't want to hear. Ahmed had turned his back and was doing his best to stride away from them, his feet slipping on the mud and grass. The woman stared after him. Webber bit back a curse and said, 'Do what you can to keep the body intact. We're going to need everything we can get from it.' He thought about Jenkinson's room and didn't hold out much hope for useful forensics, but then no one had expected this body to be found for decades. They might get lucky.

He hurried after Ahmed, almost losing his footing up the incline. Ahmed had stopped, his back to Webber, his hand clutching a tree branch as he stared out across the deep water of the gravel pit.

As Webber came up behind him, he spoke without turning round. 'I have to get back to Scarborough.' The words were barely audible, strangled under the emotion he fought to suppress.

Webber glanced around, wanting to see someone he could call across to take care of Ahmed until he'd composed himself. One thing he was sure of was that Ahmed wasn't getting behind the wheel of a car just yet.

'Give me your keys.'

'I'm all right. I'm ...'

'I said, give me your keys, Ayaan.'

Ahmed's hand pulled the keys from his pocket and thrust them backwards towards Webber. 'Don't move,' Webber told him as he turned away, tensing as he heard a convulsive sob. It was Davis he needed, with his laid back avuncular manner, but Davis wasn't here. He jogged down the path to the car park, calling one of the PCSOs over. 'DC Ahmed's car's in here somewhere.'

'Yes, it's that one.' The man pointed it out.

Webber handed him the keys. 'When you get a minute take it to Fulford Road and leave these in reception. Tell them he'll collect it later.' A movement from up by the entranceway caught his attention. 'Oh shit! The bloody grapevine's on overtime. No one goes through here, OK? If you have problems, call in. I'll deal with this lot for now.' Pulling in a breath, Webber ran his hand through his hair and strode forward to meet the group making their way down, nodding a greeting to the woman he recognised as a local TV reporter.

Retracing his steps to the crime scene, Webber was conscious there could be a camera lens following him and didn't relax until he was into the cover of the trees. He was relieved to see that Ahmed had composed himself though his face was tear-streaked.

'You're coming back with me,' Webber said. 'We'll talk about this later.'

Ahmed followed him in silence and didn't speak until they were driving away from the fishing lakes. 'I must get back to Scarborough. Can't let strangers break it to Tom's mother.' His voice held a scratchy undertone.

'All in good time,' Webber murmured pulling up at the junction that would take them back to the heart of the city. He paused for a moment, didn't want to take Ahmed back to the station or to some busy coffee shop. He'd take him home, couldn't think of anything else. He wondered if Mel would be there and wasn't sure if that would be a good thing or not. 'We'll get a hot drink before we do anything else. All we have so far is a photograph.'

'Don't,' snapped Ahmed. 'Don't tell me it's a tailor's dummy with Tom's tattoo. We both know it's Tom. He'd worked so hard to ...' Abruptly he stopped and turned his head to look out of the side window.

'I wasn't going to tell you anything,' said Webber. 'Though with the twists these cases have taken over the past few days, anything's possible.' He was aware that Ahmed shot him a glance. 'But yes,' he added, not wanting to give false hope. 'I'm afraid it's going to be Tom Jenkinson down there.'

◉ ◉ ◉

The house was empty, though as he ushered Ahmed inside, Webber saw the tell-tale signs of visitors. Melinda had had friends in. 'Go through,' he said. 'I'll put the kettle on.'

'Thanks.' Ahmed was subdued now, his voice quiet but controlled. 'Can I use your bathroom?'

'Top of the stairs.' Webber listened to footsteps ascending as he went to the kitchen. Two cups in the sink, the ones with the brown and gold dragon-tail pattern that didn't see everyday use; two plates alongside Sam's plastic one; bacon rind; the remains of toast and scrambled egg. This was more than the usual friend in for coffee. He wondered who had been here. Where was Mel? On her way to fetch Sam from playgroup, he supposed, though it was a little early for that.

It occurred to him that the living room might be knee-deep in Sam's toys, but he wouldn't worry over that on Ahmed's account. It was the sort of family chaos he would have to get used to. Mentally he gave himself a kick. He still hadn't congratulated him on his engagement. It was hardly appropriate just now. He'd see where the conversation went.

As he carried the drinks through, he heard the sound of the flush from upstairs, followed by water running. There was a heap of soft toys in a corner and Sam's blackboard and easel were propped in front of the TV alongside a mirror that had been taken from the wall. He registered the marker-pen scribbles, the photograph flapping from a length of Sellotape as he listened to Ahmed's steps descending the stairs. What on earth had they been doing ...?

With a start, he made sense of the words.

He banged the cups down on the table slopping coffee on to the polished surface, and dived across to flip the mirror to face the wall. As Ahmed entered, he tipped the blackboard and easel so they clattered face down on to the floor.

Ignoring Ahmed's puzzled glance at the fallen toys, he indicated the cups. 'Get that down you, thaw out a bit.' He grabbed a handful of tissues from a box on the settee and dabbed at the spillage on the table.

Ahmed sat down cradling his cup, his gaze on the surface of the hot liquid. 'I'm sorry, Martyn,' he began. 'I know I shouldn't have ... Well ... It's just that Tom ...'

Webber looked across at him, pulled in a breath and kept his tone mild. 'Tell me about Tom Jenkinson.'

As Ahmed began to talk, Webber sat back, giving him an occasional nod and trying to keep track of the general sense of what he was saying, but all the time he could feel his heart thumping with the shock of what he'd seen. Across the blackboard, Mel had written two lists, one headed Suicide and the other Murder. He hadn't had time to read the detail but it was clear she'd listed things to be checked in order to rule out one or the other possibility. All he could recall was *Previous attempts?* from the suicide list and a name inscribed under the photograph sellotaped to the mirror. The lists were in Mel's handwriting, the name wasn't.

But where had Mel found a photograph of Pamela Morgan and who had been here with her discussing the case?

chapter eleven

That evening Webber stood listening to the sounds of Melinda settling Sam in the room above him, then strode to the window and yanked the curtains closed, feeling something give. One of the hooks had slipped from the rail. He fought an urge to pull down the whole lot to vent the frustration he'd kept under wraps throughout the evening. Melinda must have known he'd been back during the day because he'd forgotten to put away the coffee cups, which still stood on the chair arms, but she'd stacked the blackboard and easel out of sight.

He'd got them out again, propped them accusingly against the TV. He didn't want any ambiguity. They would have this out once Sam was asleep. But the toys had been an added irritation because Mel had ignored them, focusing on Sam while Webber had tried to watch the local news around the intrusive corners of the boards and their lists.

His voice emerging from the TV had caught Sam's attention. Melinda had looked across, sniffed and said, 'You could have combed your hair.'

'It was blowing a bloody gale up there.' He had defended himself as he watched the impromptu interview. He'd been careful to say nothing, to promise more information in the morning. They hadn't known the worst then, not for sure, but it hadn't taken long. Tom Jenkinson's mother would have had the knock at her door that no parent should ever hear. He tried to blank out thoughts of tomorrow. How much would they release to the press? How much would the press have already found out for themselves? Getting rid of Tom Jenkinson and then the lorry driver felt like opportunistic acts, and worse they felt like panic. Were there other victims being lined up?

Hearing footsteps on the stairs, he pushed the thoughts aside. 'You can't do this,' he shot at Melinda, pointing at her marker-pen lists, his voice angry, but low volume in deference to Sam.

She tossed her head, snatched up the cups he and Ahmed had used and marched through to clatter them into the sink.

Her voice from the kitchen was quiet but matched his in ferocity. 'Why the hell not?'

'You can't just conduct your own enquiry.' Webber injected incredulity into his tone. She wasn't stupid. This was to get at him. 'How much trouble do you want to get into?'

'Who else is going to do it?' She marched in, stared hard at him, then pointed at the blackboard and easel.

Suicide: the means (drugs) ... the note ... how specific ... final arrangements??

Murder: drugs administered by someone else ... the note unsigned ... family ... intentions ...

'Who else is going to fight for justice for this woman, Martyn? You're not going to, are you?'

'There's nothing to fight for, Mel. She killed herself.'

'Says who? You haven't even read her suicide note.'

'Have you?' His anger melted into amazement.

She tossed her head again, a gesture of irritation. 'No. How would I get hold of it? You have the means and you didn't even try.'

'It was looked at by a coroner. She sounds like she was a nice woman and it's awful what happened to her husband. It's sad that she felt she had to do it, but she did it herself. No one raised any doubts.'

'Yes, they did!' Her tone was triumphant. 'What about China Kowalski?'

He saw the sudden move with which she tensed as she heard the slip-up. There was a pause. He didn't know if he was angry or impressed. It might have been sudden fear for her that made him stride forward and grasp her arms. 'What have you found? Who have you been talking to?'

'Why should you care?' She tried to shake him off.

He wanted to pull her close, and it was nothing to do with her stupid lists and off-beat enquiries. He felt again the recklessness that was his fault. It scared him. 'Mel, you can't go off on your own like this. You have to tell me what you've found. I'll … I'll help you, but you've got to tell me.'

'You're hurting my arms.' Underlying her words was a threat that she would fight back if he didn't comply. He let his hands drop. 'I haven't been talking to anyone,' she said, looking him in the eye. 'I've just been following up the paperwork.'

She was lying but he wouldn't get the truth by making an issue of it. And anyway there was a lie behind his own words. He wouldn't help her investigate Pamela Morgan, but had every intention of helping to get her out of this rash frame of mind where she felt obliged to throw herself into something like this. And the first step would be to find out who had been here discussing it with her, which he intended to do tomorrow morning when this person, whoever it was, was scheduled to arrive soon after he left for work. No secrets when you're married to a detective, he thought, but then he shouldn't have had secrets of his own. That's where all this had started.

'So you've found Dr China,' he said. 'I'm impressed. Who is she?'

The next morning, Sam was fractious. It seemed to Webber that he and Melinda were as bright and friendly with each other as they'd been since before Suzie Harmer's revelation, but Sam seemed to see through the act.

'Come on, Sam, have your cereal.' He rested his palm against the boy's forehead, wondering if he were sickening for something. If he stayed off playgroup, Mel would cancel her meeting and he'd have to wait to find out who she'd been talking to. It crossed his mind it might be Harmer's partner, Fiona.

'Sam!' Webber leapt back as the cereal bowl flew from the table, cascading milk down the front of his shirt. He saw Melinda grin as Sam banged his fists into a pool of soggy Weetabix and laughed.

'That's the way to get Daddy's attention, Sam. He could see you were miles away. Serves you right.'

Webber pulled off the wet garment, checking that the spillage hadn't spread to his trousers. 'Hell, I'm running late as it is.'

Melinda jumped to her feet, reaching to take the shirt from him. 'Keep an eye on Sam. I'll get you a clean one.'

He watched her march through to the kitchen, where she clicked on the iron, tossed the wet shirt down and pulled a clean one from a tangle in the dryer. If she was prepared to iron his shirt, she was keen to have him out of the house which meant her meeting was earlier than he'd assumed. He'd planned to call in to work and come back again, but maybe he'd just park up at the top of the road and keep watch.

As he drove off, Webber clicked his phone to speaker and called in to get an update. 'Don't wait for me,' he said. 'I'll be late. Any developments overnight?'

When he heard that Tom Jenkinson's mother had been over to ID her son's body the previous evening, he was tempted to leave

Melinda to her own devices. It seemed petty to be spying on his own wife when other people were dealing with death in these circumstances. 'How was she?' he asked.

'Holding things together. Nothing like I imagined her to be, if I'm honest. Small, neat, full of talk about Tom and what he'd achieved. It's a crying shame.'

'Yes,' Webber agreed. 'I suppose she didn't come clean about whatever contact she'd had with him after we let him go.'

'Well, no one was pushing her, not in the circs, but no. She was careful to talk as though she'd seen and heard nothing of him for about a week. Lying, of course, but there's a time and a place for putting the pressure on.'

'It'll have to be soon. She might have the key to this. And we have to find out what the hell happened.'

'Are you thinking blackmail?'

'Yes.' Webber eased the car to the side of the road, parking between two other vehicles. Mel wouldn't spot him from here and he had an unimpeded view of the front of the house. 'He's gone back to his mystery man, probably asked for hush money. And they've got him up to those lakes.'

'Why there?'

'Probably thought we'd lost interest. As far as anyone knows, it was just an old car pulled out.'

'Why the jacket in the lake?'

'The way I'm seeing it,' Webber began, then stopped. 'Hang on a moment.'

A car had pulled up outside his house. A tall blonde woman sat behind the wheel and he could see a small child in the back. He knew the face. Jo ... Jess ...? The house door opened and Melinda appeared with Sam. It was one of the mothers from playgroup, but it occurred to him that they must all have had other personas before motherhood took over. Maybe she'd been one of Mel's colleagues in the job. Then he sat back. She hadn't come to talk investigations with Mel, she was here to collect Sam. Mel was strapping the boy in the back with the other child. He watched her as she waved the car off, saw her look up the road. He shrank back in his seat, but she wasn't looking for him. She was expecting a visitor.

'The way I'm seeing it,' he repeated as Melinda disappeared indoors, 'is that he … they … whoever … got Tom Jenkinson to the edge of that foundation pit and hit him on the head so he fell in. No sign of a struggle anywhere nearby. They rearranged the rubble on top of him, but it wouldn't have been deep enough to cover him completely. You'd disguise a body in bad light, but not that jacket. I think they pulled it off him, bunged some bricks in the pockets and went and hurled it into the gravel pit off that bit of a bridge, never realising it would end up where the car had been. It could well have been blood the diver saw, trapped in the hood. Then they went back to guide the concrete lorry in.'

'You're talking like there's more than one of them.'

Webber blew out a sigh. 'Yeah, maybe. I don't know.'

'And surely he went into the concrete after it was laid, not the other way round.'

'It's speculation until we get the official report.' Webber conceded the point. 'But I don't think there was enough depth for his body to have sunk into it, not that thick a mix. I think it went in on top of him, but he was still alive.' He shivered as he thought of the pathologist's informal first impressions. *I'm pretty sure there's concrete mix in his airways.*

'Unconscious, I hope, but alive.' He closed his eyes and felt thankful that nothing Melinda was dabbling in had any involvement with anyone who would do that to another human being. 'Let me know if there's anything new,' he said. 'I won't be long.'

He cut the call. Another car had drawn up outside his house. Webber watched intently. Again a lone woman driver, this time no child with her. This wasn't one of Mel's playgroup friends. The woman's hair was neatly styled and silver-grey. He judged her to be in her sixties. The right age for Dr China if Mel was right. She'd told him Pamela Morgan had had a school friend called China Kowalski who surely must be the Dr China who had spoken to Farrar senior. Webber hadn't contradicted her but the 'young woman' of Farrar senior's account didn't fit with someone in her sixties. If Farrar's father was right about the man being Brad Tippet's son, then maybe the woman had been China Kowalski's daughter. It was an unusual name and Mel had dug out a link with Pamela Morgan.

He watched as the woman in the car climbed out, straightening her coat. She looked unassuming and harmless enough but Tom Jenkinson's words played in Webber's head.

When we get near enough to see, there's two of them, and it's a woman driving.

He watched her walk up to the door and ring the bell. After a moment, Mel was there, smiling and letting her in. He realised his fingernails were digging into his palms. He was desperate to race down, to burst back in, to shout at Mel not to trust her, whoever she was.

Who was she? The car registration was clearly visible and he made sure he noted it accurately before he called it in. If he was questioned, he wasn't sure he could justify it, certainly not if Farrar wouldn't back him. And if Farrar wanted an excuse to have him directing traffic for the rest of his career, he was handing it to him on a plate, but he had to know.

The name that came back meant nothing. Mrs Joyce Yeatman, 63 years old. Nothing of any interest attached to the car's details. He reached for the keys and started the engine, pulling out to coast down the road. As he cruised past his house, he peered in through the front window. The tableau was clear. Joyce Yeatman, assuming it was her, sat on the settee cradling a cup. Mel stood by the TV. It wasn't possible to see anything more but he'd lay bets that Sam's easel and blackboard were centre stage along with the mirror and its photographs.

He didn't want to leave Mel alone with this stranger but she'd go off pop if he walked back in on her. His phone rang.

'I'm on my way,' he said. 'What's happened?'

'Jenkinson's mother's on the warpath now. She's gone to the local press, the ones who did features on the "Kids with Potential" initiative. We've killed her son, all that stuff.'

Webber pursed his lips as he listened to the detail of the alcohol-fuelled tirade that had been unleashed. He couldn't blame her but it probably meant that the press would get chapter and verse on whatever Tom had confided to his mother before it came to them. 'Local press,' he said. 'They'll come to us before they go into print, but we need to get her in.'

'But that's not why I rang. I took a call from the Chief Super's office. He wants to see you. Now.'

'Oh, for fuck's sake!' Webber couldn't hold back his annoyance. With all that was unfolding, couldn't Farrar get past Suzie Harmer? 'What now?'

'Afraid he didn't say. I … uh … I didn't say you hadn't been in, just said I'd pass on the message.'

'Thanks.' Webber ended the call and blew out a sigh. The only bright spot was that from here, he wasn't far away and would have appeared to answer Farrar's summons very promptly. He turned the car and drove past the house again. Mel had her back to the window. The woman sitting on the sofa looked benign. Again his fists clenched as every instinct screamed at him not to leave Mel on her own with this stranger. With a sick feeling in the pit of his stomach, he drove away.

Webber walked towards the familiar entrance way, wondering if Farrar's gaze was on him from an upstairs window. Inside, he listened to the swell of conversation as he closed on the big office, trying to work out if Suzie Harmer's tones were in amongst the throng. He walked through, gathering a handful of absent nods of recognition.

Farrar's office door was ajar. Voices. Farrar's and a female whose tone was familiar but not Suzie. He knocked and stepped inside.

Farrar's expression was hard but Webber didn't think he was the focus. 'Ah, Martyn. Come in.' Yes, the tone was normal. Farrar waved his arm in an indeterminate gesture. 'You know each other.'

Webber looked at the woman in the chair. It took a second to recognise her. He'd only ever seen her as an image on a screen. Out of context here, outside her lab, she looked different. She wore a tailored suit not a white coat or overalls. He had no idea of her name and couldn't remember if he was supposed to know so didn't ask.

Farrar moved behind his desk and slumped into his chair, waving Webber to sit down and then pointing at the woman. 'Tell him,' he said.

Webber stared from one to the other of them. Farrar's tone was almost despairing.

'I've ID'd your body,' the woman said. 'From the boot of the car.'

'A bit of lateral thinking apparently,' Farrar said. Webber felt something like disapproval coming at him.

'Who is it?' Lateral thinking's good, he wanted to add, especially if it's got us an ID. He looked back at the woman. Here was someone who dealt in facts, who savoured the solidity of hard evidence. But she wasn't happy now. He read uncertainty in her face, and could see that uncertainty was uncomfortable territory for her.

'I've checked and double checked,' she said to Farrar.

'So you say.' His tone was dry.

'Who is it?' Webber asked again.

She pulled in a deep breath. 'The DNA we took from the plastic sheeting ... And bear in mind that it was a body that was wrapped up, no severed head, no survivable injury nonsense.'

Webber nodded. She spoke as though he'd asked the question. He wanted to give her a shake and say, get on with it.

'The DNA ...' She spread her hands in a gesture of helplessness. 'It's an exact match for your guy who was killed by tigers, Mr Robert Morgan.'

chapter twelve

···

'It can't be,' said Webber. His mind ran over the exchanges he'd had with this woman; her devotion to forensic science. She'd been trying out some new toy and it wasn't as good as she thought it was. He recalled the reports she'd sent him on Robert Morgan. 'What are you comparing against? They cremated what was left of him.'

'Histology slides,' she said. 'I used to work for the man who did the analyses at the time. That's where I got the report I sent you. I don't know why I thought of it. Well, to be honest, I didn't. I was pleased with what we got from that plastic, that material was pretty well degraded, and I wanted to try again with something as old. It just occurred to me your tiger guy died at about the same time, so I asked if I could have some samples.'

'Degraded material,' Webber said. 'We know it can't be an exact match. Are you saying it's a relative?'

She gave him a hard stare. 'I'm saying it's a match. I got full profiles from both sets of samples near enough. The mud had preserved the ones from the car and the slides had been properly stored. If it's a relative, we're talking identical twins.'

The connection sparked in Webber's head. 'Quintets!' He sat upright, looking expectantly at Farrar. 'Is that what that quintets business was about?'

'Quintets?' Farrar returned his stare blankly. 'Do you mean quintuplets? Why would you think that?'

Tripping mentally on his error, Webber ran through a lightning reconstruction. Farrar had no idea he'd interviewed his father. The quintets comment didn't exist in the paperwork. He would have to come clean about his trip to the wilds of East Yorkshire. Or would he? He'd sent Farrar a written report on Pamela Morgan. Farrar had deleted it unread. 'Uh … the word she used was quintets. The woman who originally approached your father. Apparently that's what she said; something about quintets. It didn't make any sense at the time, but …'

'It's not making much sense now, Martyn.'

'The warehouse where Morgan died is still there.' The lab woman broke in.

'You won't get forensics from the scene after all this time.' Farrar's tone was dismissive.

'No, no, of course not. It was in use as some sort of commercial garage for years, then for storage, but it hasn't been pulled down or anything. It's probably pretty much the same as it was 30 years ago.'

Webber sat back. She'd already started making enquiries and wanted to go racing down south to check out the crime scene; chase the mystery. Shades of Mel and her surreptitious investigation, only this woman wanted to do it on his budget. 'There'll be nothing left to find after 30 years,' he said, knowing that whilst it was probably true, if the investigation were to be reopened officially, then walking the scene would be top of the list. 'Nothing you can't get from photographs. If there's anything to uncover, it'll be in the case files or it won't be anywhere.'

'But I can go back to the original forensics and check them out, can I?' Her voice was eager.

'I didn't say that.' Webber closed his eyes for a second, trying to make sense out of this development. If Robert Morgan were one of quintuplets, he couldn't believe the news reports had failed to mention it. Twins weren't so newsworthy, but why had Dr China talked about quintets? It had to be identical twins or the forensics were at fault. The former was easily checked. He caught Farrar's eye. 'We're going to have to take a look at this. That blasted gravel pit! It's been like a magnet for bad news these last few weeks.'

He saw Farrar glance at the woman, who now sat, eyes unfocussed. Planning her hyper expensive retesting of a 30-year-old crime, Webber supposed. He felt trapped by this turn of events. Whatever had happened to Robert Morgan or to any identical sibling, it had happened 30 years ago. He wanted to see a way to leave it dead and buried, but it had begun to resonate with recent events. He could see no option but to allow the woman to review the original forensics. He knew she must be wrong, but he was going to have to pay for her to prove it.

'I'll get Davis on to Robert Morgan,' he said. 'Find out about his family. I'd like you to recheck that match. I know, I know ...' He forestalled the objection she began to make. 'You've done all that, but do it again before you take a look at anything else. Someone's wrong somewhere along the way.'

After she had left, Farrar turned to Webber. 'What are you thinking, Martyn?'

'I'm thinking I want this mess unravelled as soon as possible. There's enough going on without diverting resources into 30-year-old crimes. I want to talk to Brad Tippet's son. And while I'm at it, I'd like a word with the woman who spoke to your father last May.'

'Do you know who it was?'

'Possibly the daughter of one of Pamela Morgan's old school friends, a woman called China Kowalski.' He watched for any sign of recognition from Farrar. Nothing.

'Anyone else?'

Webber thought about Joyce Yeatman sitting on the settee in his own living room, but he shook his head. 'Not for now.'

'This stays under wraps, Martyn,' said Farrar. 'If we're dealing with mix and match bodies, let's get some answers before the press scrum starts.'

Back home that night, Webber found all Melinda's focus on Sam who had returned from playgroup with a streaming nose and mild temperature. It took Webber a while to identify the cause of his own unease as he sat with the boy on his knee. It was only a minor virus from which he was already looking brighter. But as Melinda bustled through from the kitchen with Sam's favourite juice, he realised that it wasn't his son's illness that was worrying him. Quite the reverse. His and Melinda's united front had been genuine, their differences buried in the uncharacteristic whining of their child. His unease was guilt at finding an upside to Sam's discomfort.

Sam had never been much of a crier. He rubbed the boy's back, watching as he reached forward and closed his fists round the plastic handles of the cup Mel held out to tempt him.

'I'll give him another dose of Calpol,' she said.

Webber nodded, catching her eye and smiling. 'He's looking better than he was.'

She smiled back, just as though nothing was wrong between them, as she lifted Sam from his knee. He saw her pause. It was momentary. He wouldn't have noticed if he hadn't been watching for it. For a while, there had been no Suzie Harmer between them. As they disappeared upstairs, Webber moved to clear the plates and pick up Sam's toys before clicking on the kettle and preparing coffee. He wanted information from Melinda and didn't want any routine household chores in the way as an excuse for her to avoid him.

There hadn't been time for Robert Morgan after sending the lab woman back to her forensic lair and giving Davis the brief to look for siblings. The major effort was focussed on Tom Jenkinson, but leads into his final hours were thin on the ground and the official verdict on Arthur Trent still inconclusive. The best Davis had come back with by the end of the day was that Morgan had been born in Canada and there were no records of brothers or sisters.

What Webber wanted from Melinda was an open admission about Joyce Yeatman, to know who she was and where she fitted in; and he wanted her to have found out more about China Kowalski so he could shortcut his own search for the Dr China who might be her daughter. For the moment, he was leaving the Tippet family well alone. He needed a better feel for whether he was dealing with witnesses or suspects before he had them face to face.

Melinda took her time upstairs, but Sam had a cold and would not be his usual amenable self. Webber looked around the kitchen. Everything looked tidy enough. He returned to the living room and pulled out the two boards to see if Mel had written anything new. Lying them flat on the coffee table, he stood looking down on them. The words *final arrangements* were crossed off the left hand list. Was that a point for or against suicide?

The word *School* had been added in a corner of its own and a new name, *Gary*, linked to *Pamela* with a double-headed arrow. Webber wrote *China Kowalski* underneath it, creating his own link from China to Pamela, but with a broken line. He straightened as he heard Melinda's footsteps on the stairs.

'How is he?' he asked as she came in, handing her a cup of coffee.

'Thanks.' She sank into a chair and blew out a sigh. 'He's gone down, but I doubt we'll get an unbroken night.'

'We'll cope.' He smiled at her and thought she almost smiled back, before turning her attention to her drink. Don't push it, he told himself, and waved his hand at the boards. 'Who's Gary?'

'They were friends at school. Gary Yeatman.'

Webber made a pretence of studying the words. He didn't want Mel hiding stuff from him. How had she found Pamela Morgan's old school friends? Presumably Gary and Joyce were related. Husband and wife ... brother and sister? Mel had been at his emails. She'd seen the coroner's report.

'Mel?' He watched her closely. He was taking a leap based

as much on gut reaction as evidence. 'Have you been on to the coroner's office about Pamela Morgan?'

He saw her instinctive move to deny it, and knew he was right. She settled for a shrug and looked part surprised, part irritated.

'Mel, please don't keep me in the dark.' He tried to strip his voice of any hint of censure. 'What if I'd been back to them for the same information? What if John Farrar got to know what you're doing? He'll blame me for sure and God knows where it'd end.'

'If you were going to do anything, you'd have done it by now.'

A part of him wanted to say that things had changed, but he didn't want to go anywhere near the lab woman's forensic mix-up. He couldn't talk to Mel about that and if she knew he was keeping secrets, he'd get nothing out of her. He looked again at the words on the board. 'Why Gary and not Joyce?'

This time she made no attempt to hide her surprise. 'Oh, so you know ... Joyce wasn't at school with them. You didn't tell me you'd found out ... So, have you seen Pamela's note?'

'No. You know I haven't have time to dig.' He kept his gaze on the chalk board, tracing his finger around the names as his mind connected the pieces. What had she had from the coroner? It was obvious. The name of the recipient of Pamela Morgan's suicide note. Joyce Yeatman, who if she hadn't been at school with them, must be Gary Yeatman's wife not his sister. 'So ... uh ... have you seen it?'

She shook her head.

'You could track Joyce Yeatman and ask her. She might still be in the area.' He reached for the marker pens, not having anything to write but needing to avoid her eye, to distract himself while she weighed up whether or not to come clean.

'She is. She never read all the note.'

'What? But the inquest said it was long and detailed.'

'And unsigned. Joyce Yeatman found it, read the start and rang the emergency services. It was too late.'

'Didn't she read it later?'

'The police took it. She got it back eventually, but by then she didn't want to read it.'

'Does she still have it?'

Melinda sighed and looked into her cup. 'Yes, I think she does. It'll be locked away somewhere and she won't want to get it out. Too many bad memories. I'm reluctant to push her. She might destroy it. Martyn, would they have kept a copy, whoever dealt with it in the first place?'

'I doubt it. It was never classed as a crime. It shouldn't have been kept. I can probably check. What about Gary Yeatman? Where's he in all this?'

'He died twenty years ago.'

'Why did she address the note to Joyce Yeatman? Had she stayed in touch with her husband from school? Is that how she knew them?'

She looked up at him. Webber read in her face that she'd harboured the same questions. 'From what I've found so far, Gary didn't have much to do with anyone from school beyond the occasional reunion. It wasn't until after he died that Joyce and Pamela became close.' She paused and looked across at the window. 'I've spoken to Joyce Yeatman. I've met her. But you already know that, don't you?'

'I'd guessed,' he said, hoping she'd take that at face value and not want to dig for detail. 'Was there ... I mean did you get the idea that there could have been animosity between Joyce Yeatman and Pamela Morgan?'

She shook her head. 'Quite the opposite. Joyce said it was Pamela who kept her going after Gary's death; said she knew what it was like to lose someone stupidly.'

'How did he die?' Webber asked.

'Car accident. He had some sort of seizure at the wheel. She was devastated, but she said Pamela pulled her through.'

'So how did she take it when Pamela died?'

'She didn't ... doesn't want to believe it's suicide, said she couldn't think of any reason why Pamela would do it after all that time. I think that's why she agreed to talk to me.'

'If she read the note, she might know why. Was it her who told you about China Kowalski? Does she know much about her, where she is, if she has family?'

She gave him a hard stare. 'If I pass on what she gave me, will you chase it up?'

He nodded. 'Yes, I will. I wouldn't mind getting a word with her.'

'It's an email address. That's all she has. She didn't really know China Kowalski. She said Gary had known her but China had never kept in touch. She was surprised it was China raising doubts.'

Webber bit back on vocalising his thoughts about Mel passing information to Joyce Yeatman. 'What did you mean, to lose someone stupidly?'

'It's the expression she used. Pamela had lost Robert because of his stupidity of going into that warehouse that night.'

'Why did he go in there?'

'No one knew.'

'Why was he even in Dorset? They lived round here.'

'No one knew that either.'

It fitted with what he'd read of Morgan's death. Wrong place, wrong time but no one knew why. 'What stupid thing did Gary Yeatman do?'

'Something with the car so it crashed at speed when he collapsed. He might have survived otherwise.' Her attention snapped away from him at the sound of a half-cry from upstairs.

They both froze and listened. After the initial wail, it remained quiet, but Melinda stood up. 'I'll just nip up and see. 'On the day Gary Yeatman died,' she added, pausing in the doorway, 'he was using the cruise control. Joyce told me she'd never known him use it at all. The one time he did, it killed him.'

Webber gaped after her as she left to check on Sam.

chapter thirteen

It was late morning before Webber got as far as his own desk. He'd hung around the team that was chasing Jenkinson's connections. Several promising lines had ebbed, but left a hint that Tom's contacts might have been wider and more sophisticated than anyone had guessed, as though his persona as a petty criminal was just a front. They'd failed to find the mate with the car, and the theory was gaining ground that he had been no more than a mirage designed to mislead. But where did that leave the mystery man or woman? The body encased in concrete was no mirage.

After sending for the details of Gary Yeatman's death, he'd relegated the lab and the DNA conundrum to background noise. Davis had had a look at Robert Morgan's family. It was pretty certain now there were no twins involved, though Webber had asked him to double check Morgan's history. One glimmer of interest had been a call from Brad Tippet. He'd been on the defensive, Webber was told, and wanted to know why an officer had been sent out to talk to him. The woman who took the call had suggested he drop in later in the day and Tippet had agreed.

Webber picked up the phone and called Davis into his office. 'Brad Tippet,' he said. 'You spoke to the officer who interviewed him. What were your impressions?'

'Bit of a nonentity, apparently huffy we'd sent a junior out to talk to him. Small man. Self-important.'

Webber narrowed his eyes. There were things he'd like to know from Tippet that might have no bearing on anything relevant, but he'd like to know them anyway. And if Tippet could be impressed by rank maybe he could use that. 'Rumour says he might still be holding a grudge against the Chief Super for treating him as a suspect in that post office raid 30 years ago. What do you think?'

Davis spread his hands in a who-knows gesture. 'Is that what you want out of him when he comes in? He'll be wary of going anywhere near anything like that.'

'Let me know when he arrives,' Webber said. 'I think I'll have a chat with him myself. And I want you watching closely. We'll see what's still sensitive after all this time.'

As Davis left, Webber looked at his computer, exasperation rising as dozens of new emails scrolled on to the screen. His glance ran down the list. Where the hell was the information on Gary Yeatman's death? How long did it take to dig out old records? Early incarnations of cruise control systems such as Yeatman must have been using had had their problems. It would have been nothing like the cruise control that was engaged when the lorry driver, Arthur Trent's car hit that tree. But coincidence never sat easy. It might not be pertinent to the current cases but he needed to know because Melinda had got herself involved with Gary Yeatman's widow. And until he could clear away the dead wood, he couldn't get a handle on what was relevant and what wasn't. So far, not a hint of a link between Jenkinson and Trent, but Webber was convinced he had a double murder on his hands and wanted the confirmation that would justify the resource to start chasing it.

Researching Jenkinson was like dealing with two people. They'd been all over his university contacts and provisionally eliminated them all from involvement. As to the rest of his network, it was beginning to look like they'd barely scratched the surface.

A knock at the open door. Webber looked up. 'Initial report on Trent, guv. You said to let you know. They've just emailed it.'

The machine pinged a new mail as the words were spoken.

Webber clicked open the document and skimmed the words. Trent had had a heart condition for which he was on medication. No sign that it had killed him. Injuries from the crash were consistent with him having died at the wheel before impact. Blood alcohol borderline. Further toxicology to come. Inconclusive.

He sat back and ran his hand through his hair. Inconclusive wasn't what he wanted to hear.

A throat-clearing pulled his attention to the doorway where Davis had reappeared with a file. 'The extras you wanted on Robert Morgan. No male siblings. I could dig deeper but it'll take time.'

Webber held out his hand for the sheaf of papers. 'Give me the headlines.'

'Born in Ontario. One elder sister. His parents split up when he was ten. His mother remarried and had three more children. He and his sister stayed with the father. He first came to the UK when he was eighteen on some sort of youth scheme visa, married Pamela Quinliven a year later and stayed.'

'Quinliven?' It was the first time he'd heard her maiden name. Was she Dr China's poor Quinny? 'Are you saying his marriage might have been more convenience than love match?'

Davis shrugged. 'As far as I can tell, the Morgan family weren't close. No sign that either of his parents attended when he married Pamela. His father died when Morgan was in his late twenties, then of course Morgan himself had that unfortunate encounter with wild animals when he was thirty. Doesn't look like his mother came over, if she was still around.'

Someone called Davis's name. He gave Webber an interrogative glance.

Webber nodded him out and looked at the file, opening it and flicking through the pages until he found Robert Morgan's marriage. Pamela Quinliven ... Quinny ... It seemed to make sense with the rest of Dr China's agenda in contacting Farrar senior.

He looked up. Davis was framed in the doorway again. 'Brad

Tippet's just arrived. Prickly as a hedgehog. Shall I go and do the cup of tea thing, soften him up?'

Webber felt surprise. It wasn't like Davis to volunteer to do anything. 'OK,' he said. 'I'll be along in a minute.'

After Davis left, Webber sat with his elbows on the desk, chin in his hands wondering what secrets Tippet could have held on to after all this time. He'd like to hear Tippet's version of the feud with John Farrar. He pushed the Morgan papers to one side and flicked through the old file again. Tippet had reported the car stolen the morning of the raid, the same morning, he now knew, that Robert Morgan's remains were being found in that warehouse hundreds of miles away. Tippet's initial report had come with the caveat that his car might have disappeared the previous evening. It was a caveat that hadn't convinced the officers who took his statement. He skim-read the notes to remind himself of the details of the anomaly. The car appeared to have been driven off fast in a spray of gravel, spattering an otherwise neat border, yet neither Tippet nor his wife had heard it go. It was nebulous, they might have been at the back of the house, though both sitting room and bedroom looked out over the front. It had meant close scrutiny of Tippet and his movements, and that had exonerated him from involvement in the crime.

What had Davis said? He'd seen Tippet as self-important, impressed by rank. Webber hoped that meant credulous, someone who might be coerced into a confidential chat in the right circumstances. After a moment, he stood up and went to rummage in the bottom drawer of the filing cabinet, giving a huff of satisfaction as he pulled out an old Dictaphone. He weighed it in his hand wondering if he would find Mr Tippet credulous enough to fall for a very old trick.

It was as he turned to leave the room that his computer beeped a new email.

At last, Gary Yeatman's PM report. He was tempted to open it at once, but that would stretch his new-found confidence in Davis. It could wait.

◉ ◉ ◉

Tippet was a small man with wiry hair that held traces of ginger. Webber knew from the record that Tippet was 58. It occurred to him the man was five years younger than Joyce Yeatman but going on appearance alone he'd have reversed their ages. Tippet was the sort who had been born middle-aged. Davis seemed to have lulled him into some kind of cosy chat about politics. More mouse than hedgehog Webber thought as he approached, though the moment he made them aware of his presence, a shutter came down. Tippet's lips pursed and his eyes hardened.

'Mr Tippet? I'm Detective Superintendent Webber.' As he introduced himself he noted that the rank seemed to mollify Tippet whose handshake went from limp to firm.

He guided Tippet towards an interview room, nodding Davis to observe.

'I'm grateful to you for agreeing to come in, Mr Tippet. You're one of the few people left who can iron out some discrepancies in a very old case.'

'Well, it's an imposition, Superintendent, I won't say it isn't.' Tippet seemed mildly intimidated by the more formal atmosphere. 'I've never been in trouble in my life. The nearest I've come to a crime is having my car stolen.'

Webber gave him a smile and said the things that would be needed on the official record should Tippet jump down the complaints route later on. He reiterated that his presence was voluntary and that he was free to go at any time. Seeing the change in Tippet's expression, as though he regretted his decision to come here and was trying to summon the courage to act, Webber wondered if the man would walk. He gave him a moment then reached into his pocket and pulled out the Dictaphone. 'Do you mind? Only I'm hopeless at taking notes when I'm talking.'

Tippet shot the machine a suspicious glance but nodded his assent. Webber clicked the on switch. It whirred gently, but hadn't worked in years. He took Tippet through the 30-year-old reporting of the stolen car, mentioning in passing the query over the time of the theft.

'I've never been one for gadding about at night, Superintendent. I'm not now and I wasn't then. I parked the car as usual when I got home from work. In the morning it was gone and I reported it. I've no way of knowing when it was taken.'

Webber thought back to the notes he'd read. 'You didn't hear it being driven away?'

The spike in tension was palpable. He must have been asked at the time, but clearly hadn't anticipated the question again. It seemed to Webber he'd administered an unexpected shock that Tippet fought to hide. So he *had* heard the car being driven away. Even after all these years, Tippet could provide the time of the theft if he chose to. What kept him quiet?

But this wasn't the time to push him into walking out. 'It's all a long time ago,' Webber said easily. 'I doubt you can remember much.'

'No, no. I can't. It's thirty years.' There was a hint of gratitude behind the words.

Davis, watching from behind the scenes, probably thought Webber was losing it, letting Tippet off the hook, but it wasn't the car he was interested in. It was the aftermath. He leant forward, met Tippet's eye and injected puzzlement into his tone. 'It's not the car theft that's important to me after all this time, it's the robbery. And there's one thing I'm struggling with, Mr Tippet … Uh …' He stopped as though unsure whether or not to go on.

Tippet sat upright. 'I'm a law-abiding citizen, Superintendent. I don't know what I can tell you that you don't already know. My car was used in the robbery, of course, but that was after it was stolen.'

'Didn't you know one of the men involved?'

'I did not!' Tippet's indignation was real.

Webber reached out and pulled the Dictaphone towards him, deliberately clicking the switch to turn it off. Tippet watched and gave him a questioning glance.

'Something that puzzles me,' Webber murmured. 'Why would Chief Superintendent Farrar have told me you knew one of the brothers?'

Tippet glanced again at the machine on the table. Webber lowered his voice further. 'Something you might not be aware of, Mr Tippet. Last May your son contacted John Farrar's father.' Tippet gasped. Webber saw the blood drain from his face. 'He's not in any trouble,' Webber reassured him, 'but he's rather put the cat amongst the pigeons. I'd like to know what's behind it if I'm to damp things down.'

Tippet pulled in a breath. 'It's nothing to do with Bradley,' he whispered. 'It's my fault for things I've said in front of him. I thought this was all behind us.'

'What's all behind you? What happened?'

'I won't say this on the record.' Tippet glanced at the Dictaphone then fixed Webber with a hard stare, 'but I caught Mr Farrar out early in his career and he's never forgiven me. He was determined to involve me in that robbery.'

Webber tried and failed to envisage circumstances in which Tippet got the best of Farrar. OK, he would pursue that in a moment. Let the man stew for a while. 'So you didn't know any of the perpetrators?'

'Three brothers, wasn't it? The eldest went to the same school I did, but no, I never knew him. He was two years ahead of me. I wish I'd never known anyone from that lot, but I never knew *him* at all.'

'Who did you know that you wished you didn't?' Webber felt his way carefully. *That lot*? Was Tippet about to disclose some kind of relationship with another of the brothers?

'One of them married Tina, my older sister,' he said. 'I knew it was a disaster from the off. He married her for money and two years later she was dead.'

'Your sister? I'm sorry ... Who did she marry?' The original enquiry couldn't have missed the marriage of Tippet's sibling to one of the robbers. And what was that about money? The proceeds of the raid had never resurfaced.

'A man called Michael Drake.' Distaste suffused Tippet's face as he spoke the name.

'And who was he in relation to the men who stole your car?'

'He was in the same year as the eldest brother. Like I said, I wish we'd never had dealings with anyone from that lot. Not that Drake and his ilk would have had anything to do with that family, far too lah-di-dah. Or so he liked to think. The obsessive type. Idolised Charlie Sheen, can you imagine? That's how he drew my sister in.'

'When did they marry?'

'1974.'

Webber shelved his embryo theory of a link between Tina Tippet's money and the proceeds from the crime. The robbery had taken place twelve years later. And the Tippet family finances had been under the spotlight. There wasn't any money. This sounded more like a manufactured grudge.

'That would have been a bit before Charlie Sheen's era, wouldn't it?' he said.

'They married the year Sheen first appeared on the big screen in *The Execution of Private Slovik*.'

Webber nodded, no idea if this was accurate. He'd never heard of the film. It was Tippet who came across as the trivia-collecting obsessive. 'You say Drake married your sister for money. Was she very wealthy?'

Tippet gave an irritable shrug. 'Of course not, but why else would he marry her?' Tippet's disapproval of his sister's suitor shone brightly and irrationally from across the decades. Webber knew he was heading into a dead end.

'Apparently your son mentioned quintets. What would he have meant by that?'

'I've no idea!'

Webber wondered if the denial had come too quickly, but Tippet was still tight-lipped over his ex-brother-in-law. He mustn't start to read reactions that weren't there. Farrar senior hadn't been certain who had made the quintets comments.

He lowered his voice again to emphasise the charade of a confidential exchange. 'What did Farrar do? You said you'd caught him out.'

Tippet's glance shot left and right as though to check for eavesdroppers. Webber had an idea he was relieved at the change of subject. 'I told him everything,' he hissed. 'Everything. Drake, Tina. He was there to take my statement about the car and I told him about the murder of my sister. What's more important, Superintendent, a car or a person's life?'

Webber nodded sympathetically.

'He did nothing,' Tippet went on, his words laden with venom. 'Nothing! He chased after a car and abandoned a murdered woman. I've never forgotten and he knew I'd never forget. I could drag his name through the mud anytime I wanted to. If it weren't that Tina isn't here to defend herself I'd do it tomorrow.'

In Tippet's voice, Webber heard the seam of irrationality with which he'd talked about his brother-in-law. It was nothing. Mountains from molehills. Old grudges gone bitter over the years. The only thing of any interest was the time of the car theft and Tippet pretending not to know. And now in order to cover all the bases, he would have to chase up yet another decades-old death, Tina Tippet / Drake. He looked at the man opposite, took in the spiteful gleam. Tippet thought he'd reeled in an ally against his long-time foe. Even if he'd had anything on Farrar, he would never have made a move. He was the sort who manufactured the bullets for others to fire while he watched from a safe distance. Webber didn't like him, but if Tippet had reached the age of 58 and still believed in 'off-the-record' inside a police interview room he was probably the innocent he purported to be. He pocketed the Dictaphone and stood up. 'Inspector Davis will come and take some details. Thank you for your cooperation, Mr Tippet.'

'My pleasure, Superintendent.' Tippet gave him a conspiratorial smile as he proffered his hand.

Davis entered almost at once, flicking open a notebook highlighting the lie that no one had been listening. Tippet didn't seem to notice. 'Let's start with your sister's details, Mr Tippet. What's her full name?'

As Webber left, he heard Tippet say, 'Quintina Tippet. Well, Drake when she died, of course. We always called her Tina.'

Quintina? Webber thought back to the puzzlement in Donald Farrar's tone as he'd repeated the overheard comment. *Poor Quinny.* Maybe Quinny wasn't Pamela Morgan but Tina Tippet.

Back in his office he pulled out the email address Mel had given him for China Kowalski. Using it, and the name, a simple search found her. Dr China Kowalski BSc MBA PhD worked in the science and technology cluster of the Mara University of Technology in Selangor, Malaysia. He found a brief professional bio that said nothing about her family or personal life.

What did he want to ask her? He framed a careful question around her daughter's approach to John Farrar's father last May. Being deliberately vague on substance he implied that he knew more than he did; he mentioned Quintina Tippet and Pamela Morgan. Then with some careful rewording, he managed to tag on, 'and the quintets of course,' leaving the reference ambiguous.

If it weren't for the official signature, it was an enquiry that invited unthinking deletion as spam, and that might be its fate. But if any of the phrases chimed with her, she'd surely check with her daughter. Though it might be her niece or some other relation. He hesitated and then wove a little more ambiguity into his queries. The only clear message he wanted to convey was that he knew everything there was to know, so there was no point in hiding anything. If she responded saying she hadn't a clue what he was talking about, there'd be little he could do about it, but if she swallowed the lie he hoped she'd chase up the detail and unwittingly leak it back to him. He read through what he'd written, felt some misgivings, but sent it on its way.

That done, he opened the report on Gary Yeatman's death and began to read. When he'd finished he leant back in his chair wondering what to make of it. Joyce Yeatman had lied to Melinda. Her husband's death was recorded as suicide.

chapter fourteen

As Webber pulled up outside home he could see Melinda quarter profile towards the back of the living room. She hadn't seen him. Her focus was on something out of sight and he saw her lips move as she spoke. Her demeanour told him it was Sam who was the target of whatever she was saying. As he watched, he saw her laugh, and felt his brow crease as though at a sudden pain. He'd been weighing up how honest he could be about the Yeatman woman and everything else that was going on. He desperately wanted to tell her everything; to trust her unconditionally and rely on her discretion not to get him into trouble. How else would he win back her trust? He'd promised to help with her informal enquiry about Pamela Morgan, and though he hadn't meant it at the time, it was something he could do wholeheartedly, something that might help them find a way past the stupid Harmer bitch.

She ducked out of sight as he climbed from the car. When he looked again, she'd seen him. Sam was in her arms grinning and flapping one chubby fist. As he waved back, he felt oddly as though on the verge of tears. Shaking the sensation out of his head he went in to greet them, taking advantage of her holding Sam to embrace them both.

'Had a good day?' He aimed the question at his son, but realised he was anxious to hear her answer.

Sam chattered back at him. 'Da boy ... oy ... oy ...' stringing out the word, as though stretching elastic. 'Da book ...' He tipped himself over Melinda's arm to point down at the heap of toys on the carpet.

Webber bent to retrieve the picture book. No, *your* day, he wanted to say to Melinda. I want to know what *you've* been doing. She wouldn't believe him if he said it. What Mel got up to while he was at work had always felt intangible and to do with babies and mothers at playgroup. Suddenly it had become real. Life hadn't stopped for her when Sam came along. It had just changed.

'Da book!' Sam pushed away the offering with such a fierce stare that Webber couldn't hold back a laugh.

Mel smiled, too, and said dryly, 'Wrong one. Try *Thomas the Tank Engine.*'

'gine ... gine ... gine ...' Sam confirmed, snatching the book from Webber's hand.

'Gently, Sam,' said Melinda.

Out of nowhere Webber remembered an overheard snippet, Mel and one of the women who'd become part of her new world.

... no, the wife's usually the only grown-up in the family ... laughter ...

He couldn't remember if it had been Mel speaking, but if so it hadn't occurred to him she might have included their own relationship. And now they were poised at the lip of a precipice, held by a flimsy glass barrier that might shatter in an instant. He wanted to tell her he'd turned a corner ... grown up ... realised how stupid he'd been, it would all be different from now on, but to say that would be to admit to past sins in the hope of forgiveness and at least he was grown up enough to know that wasn't the way it worked.

Thank heavens for Pamela Morgan. Thank heavens for China Kowalski's daughter and her bizarre approach to Donald Farrar. At the moment it was all he had to hold a solid link between him and Mel. Telling her about Gary Yeatman wasn't just a matter of showing trust; he was scared for her. She was being reckless to prove a point. He wanted her to be cautious. Joyce Yeatman might look harmless but who could say what secrets she held.

He tipped his thumb towards the stacked boards. 'Anything new?'

She glanced up meeting his gaze for a second before turning back to Sam. All he could read was that everything remained in the balance. After an uncomfortable pause, she said, 'John's father ... you said he'd talked about quintets. What was that about?'

'It was just the word, quintets. I don't know why he picked up on it, and nor did he. Why do you ask?' He thought back to his talk with Tippet, his momentary certainty that the word quintets had sparked a reaction.

'Mentioned by Tippet's son or by China Kowalski?' she asked.

'He wasn't sure. And ... uh ...'

'What?' She set Sam on the floor amongst his toys, where he slammed the book down and grabbed Webber's trouser leg pulling himself to his feet and holding out his arms, his lower lip beginning to wobble.

'I don't think it can have been China Kowalski,' he said as he crouched down with Sam and pulled building bricks at random from the pile, stacking them to half a dozen high before Sam lunged to topple them with a delighted shriek. 'I think it's more likely it was her daughter. John's father described her as a young woman. Kowalski would be in her 60s by now.'

'I didn't know she had a daughter.' He saw Melinda frown as she took this in.

'I don't know for certain, but it's an unusual first name and there's some kind of link. I think it's likely.'

'Have you found out anything about her?'

'I've emailed her, but I haven't heard back. I didn't get to it till late in the day and it turns out she works in Malaysia. She's about six hours ahead of us. Hopefully there'll be a reply in the morning.'

'So you don't have anything new for me?'

'I didn't say that.' He concentrated on stacking a new tower for Sam to demolish. He'd heard the hint of a challenge in her tone. She'd found something and hadn't decided whether or not to tell him. She was going to trade information. But Joyce Yeatman could have ulterior motives. He had to regain her trust. She needed to be telling him her plans in advance, not keeping him guessing. 'I checked on Gary Yeatman,' he said. 'I was going to wait until Sam's down.'

One hand gripping a tower of coloured blocks, protecting it from Sam's determined fists, he looked up at her. Her gaze rested on Sam for a moment before she met his eye, her glance speculative. 'OK,' she said and turned on her heel to head for the kitchen.

After they'd eaten, Webber carried his son upstairs. Mel had said nothing about what she might have uncovered, but he assumed it was to do with the quintets comment. As he lowered Sam into the shallow bath water, his mind created words from the floating letters of the waterproof alphabet. *Dread* and *peril* swirled around before Webber swept his hands through the rubber squares creating a mini tsunami that Sam slapped down with his palms. It wasn't until he carried the boy, warm, dry and encased in thick pyjamas, through to his bedroom that Sam began to grizzle. In the aftermath of his cold he was clingy for Melinda. Webber half turned towards the stairs to call out to her, then stopped. It was his job to read people, to keep a step ahead, to wheedle them to his way of thinking. If a boy Sam's age could outpace him, he'd have no chance with Mel. It was all a matter of trust. Trust and concentration. He picked up the bedtime book and emptied his mind of everything except the rhythm of the rhymes as he paced back and forth. Sam's head lolled against his shoulder as sleep crept up, then snapped upright to twist round looking for Mel. Webber traced his finger round the pictures intoning the hypnotic words again and again as Sam fought to stay awake.

It took half an hour and as he made his way down, stretching the cramp from his right arm, it occurred to Webber that Sam had proved a harder nut to crack than Brad Tippet.

Melinda had made coffee. He sank into the chair and picked up his cup. 'Why did you ask about the quintets thing?' he said.

'Nothing much.' A pause. 'You said you'd looked up something about Gary Yeatman.'

He could tell from her tone that she expected a stand-off. Him to refuse the information until she told him what she'd found. But that wasn't the way to get her talking to him properly. 'Yes, I got the reports on his accident. The thing is, Mel, it's not recorded as an accident.' That caught her attention; he saw her gaze snap to his face. 'It's recorded as a suicide.'

She stared at him open-mouthed then turned to the window, her brow furrowed in thought. 'It was a car accident. Why suicide?'

'He was in some kind of financial difficulty. There was a reference to a note. And yes, I've sent for the full file.' He raised his crossed fingers. 'Let's hope no one wants to know why I want it.'

'But that's ... Why would she lie to me?'

He didn't answer. She knew as well as he did that people were secretive about suicide for a whole range of reasons, guilt, shame, religion ...

'So we've an accident that's a suicide and a suicide that's a murder,' she said.

'We don't know that. Your best bet would be to get Joyce Yeatman to show you Pamela Morgan's note. Could you persuade her?'

She blew out a sigh. 'She's cagey. Sort of wants to know but doesn't, if you know what I mean. I don't want to push her or she'll just back off.'

'How often have you met her? Do you have another meeting planned?' As he spoke, he found himself tracing his finger around the dragon-tail pattern on his coffee cup. These were the cups he'd found out that time he'd brought Ahmed back here.

He became aware that Melinda's gaze was following the movement of his hand. 'She's never been here when Sam's around. Only when he's been at playgroup.'

The defensiveness in her tone came as a surprise, but at the same time it reassured him. She'd sensed enough of a potential threat to keep Sam out of the way. He smiled. 'I'm impressed that you found her at all, that you've got as far as you have. But I've not seen anything yet that says it wasn't as straightforward as the coroner said it was.'

'Where do I go from here? You said you'd help me, Martyn. What do I do next? You're the detective. I've never been near a cold case before. I can list reasons in favour of one or the other.' She pointed to the board with its suicide/murder lists. 'But I'm not managing to rule stuff in or out, well, not enough to make any headway.'

'You need that note,' he said again. He wished that Joyce Yeatman would hand it over. Mel might not have thought it through this way, but if the note had convinced a coroner, it would probably convince her.

'I know, but she's being precious about it. I'm in no position to make demands.'

'Reel her in slowly, Mel. You know how to get round a witness. Chip away at her. You'll get there.'

'Martyn, suppose it was shown not to be suicide ...' She held up her hand to forestall an objection he hadn't been going to make. 'Just bear with me. Just say it looks like murder after all. What's your next move?'

'I'd probably go and see if Davis had fallen asleep on the job again.'

'Why?' She looked at him blankly.

'Because I'd want an excuse to swear at someone. It's a 15-year-old case, Mel. It wasn't treated as suspicious at the time so no one was out gathering evidence. No photos, no statements worth anything. Certainly no forensic after all this time.' His train of thought stalled for a moment on the image of the woman from the lab. *I'm saying it's a match!* Not a peep out of her since yesterday morning. He wondered if she'd turn up in person to tell them she'd got it wrong. No, that message would come by email. If she came in person it would be because she was right. 'Suspects,' he said to

Melinda. 'I'd be looking for suspects, anyone who was around at the time.' He pulled forward the second board and wrote the word *Suspects* in the middle.

'For starters, the bastards who killed her husband,' she said. 'When did they get out?'

He wrote *Tiger guys* on to the diagram. 'I haven't checked up on their release dates. Be fair, Mel ...' He reacted to a tightening of her lips. 'We just pulled a lad's body out at those gravel pits. I haven't had a lot of time. I'll try, but there ought to be a paper trail in the public domain. Who else?' He wrote *Known associates*, and added Joyce Yeatman's name.

'How's she a suspect?' Mel said. 'Why would she have agreed to talk to me if she'd done it?'

'How better to find out exactly how close you'd got to the truth?' He watched her take in his words, pleased to have given her a solid reason to be wary of the woman. 'China Kowalski and her daughter,' he went on. 'That gives you links to the old school network, Gary Yeatman and whoever else.'

'Gary Yeatman died twelve years before Pamela,' Melinda said. 'I think even you'll allow that as a watertight alibi. But doesn't China Kowalski's daughter provide a link to Brad Tippet?'

He nodded and added Brad and Bradley, encircling their names and drawing a line to where he'd written *Suspects*, then enclosing Kowalski's daughter and Bradley Tippet's names in square brackets. 'Probably too young to be viable suspects 15 years ago,' he explained. 'But they give us the links.' He added a final bubble labelled *Other*, and sat back. 'Person or persons unknown. Could be anyone. And none of this means anything if the coroner got it right. We're back with the note.'

'How would you find out about these people after all this time?'

'Work out who was around when she died. We know Joyce Yeatman was. Maybe Kowalski, too, back then. Tippet never moved from the area.' He thought it through. He'd be out looking for friends of friends, the people this lot had been close to at the time. People invariably incriminated themselves somewhere along the way and when it was something big like a murder it was their friends and lovers who were the key, and it was usually all that was left to work with at this distance. But he didn't want Mel out chasing those sorts of leads. 'If it had been a murder enquiry,' he said, 'there'd be statements and alibis to recheck, but it wasn't. Your best bet is still the note.' She nodded, her gaze fixed on the spider diagram he'd created. 'Mel ...?'

She looked up.

'Why did you ask me about the quintets comment?'

'Yes, that was odd. I let the word drop out when I was talking to Joyce ... What?'

He hadn't intended to react visibly but her comment had brought a clash of emotions, partly relief that she was telling him openly, but ... 'Mel, please be careful what you say to her. If this were to turn into anything and she pops up knowing stuff she shouldn't ...' He didn't need to spell it out, hoped she wouldn't clam up again.

She looked mildly annoyed; he couldn't guess whether at herself or him. 'Yeah, OK.' She bit off the words and took in a breath. 'Anyway, Joyce repeated it. Quintets. Asked me what I meant. I didn't tell her anything, I played dumb, but she said it rang a bell with something Gary had said. He'd had a row with someone once and the word had stuck in her mind, but it was all a long time ago. She said she had no idea what it was about.'

Webber worked it backwards. Gary Yeatman had died 20 years ago. It was a long time for an unconnected word to stick in someone's mind. He was about to say so when Melinda stood up and clacked the boards together, carrying them to their corner. 'By the way,' her voice had hardened, 'I spoke to Fiona today.'

His insides hollowed out. They'd been relaxed and talking for ... he glanced at the clock ... way longer than he'd realised. She'd trusted him with her snippet of information from the Yeatman woman. And in that one phrase the bridge between them had collapsed like the unstable towers he'd been building for Sam.

'She said they don't want your name on the birth certificate.' Her expression was hard, closed.

He suppressed a sudden hope that they'd decided the child wasn't his; not wanting to show emotion until he knew what emotion Mel wanted him to show.

'I told her no admission of paternity, no support. And if they want to fight through the courts fine, but that's how it is. She told me they didn't want us to have any involvement with the child, bar financial.'

'Well ... let's not rule that one out.' Webber tested the waters. Not to be involved suited him just fine.

'That'll be our decision, not theirs,' she snapped, turning her back and marching through to the kitchen.

At least she'd said ours, thought Webber, though he knew she meant it would be her decision and not Suzie's. He imagined the result of the negotiation carried back to Suzie who would be livid, but Melinda had manoeuvred both biological parents out of the equation. He felt an unexpected fellow feeling with the dour Fiona. She'd have a hard time with Suzie.

He stood up and crossed the room to put his phone on charge. As he clicked in the lead, it beeped a new email. For the second time that evening he sent up a silent prayer of thanks for the existence of a woman he'd never met.

'Email from China Kowalski,' he called out.

Melinda hurried through, drying her hands on a tea towel. 'What does she say?' The sour note was gone from her tone. She was bright, interested again.

'Haven't looked yet.' He clicked the icons to open the mail, holding the phone where she could see it, showing that he wasn't trying to check before showing her. 'She's up and about early,' he commented. 'It can't be 5 a.m. where she is.'

China Kowalski declared herself surprised to receive his mail, saying it had arrived just in time as she was setting out on a research trip where she would have no internet connection. She was pleased the matter had been taken seriously, adding, *I couldn't have spoken out sooner, I didn't know about her.*

'Know about who?' said Melinda. 'Pamela Morgan?'

Webber shrugged and shook his head.

I'm sorry if it's caused you any trouble, Kowalski wrote. *I wasn't expecting you to identify me. The policeman's father must have been sharper than he looked. But there's nothing more I can tell you. And Brad's son doesn't know anything. I simply used him because of the history. It was the best I could think of at the time.*

'Does this make any sense to you?' Melinda asked.

'Not really.' He scrolled to the next paragraph.

I don't know whose daughter you mean. Neither Pamela nor I had children.

'If she doesn't have a daughter, was it her who met John's father?'

'That seems to be what she's saying.'

He checked that Melinda had read to the bottom of the small screen, then scrolled down again. There were just two more sentences before China Kowalski's formal signature.

It's nothing to do with the quintets. They were dead and buried a long time ago.

chapter fifteen

The next morning, Webber watched as Davis called his team together. He leant back against the narrow window ledge, early morning light streaming through behind him, showing the figures around the table in stark relief, and making him all but invisible to them in the glare of the low winter sun. The dynamics of the group interested him. He wanted to see them engaged and working together. It was a weird tangle of cases that needed sharp minds and no shortcuts. His misgivings about Davis had largely eased. The man looked haggard but then he probably hadn't worked this hard in years. He was on the ball though, and keeping his team up to scratch which was all Webber asked. Almost all. He wanted positives on the case as well, and was pleased to hear progress being reported.

Persistent pursuit of every lead had finally set them on the track of the elusive mate of Jenkinson's. He existed after all. An old Scarborough connection, but not the sort they'd expected. A young man who'd been plucked out of hopeless circumstances in Hull and dropped into the 'Kids with Potential' initiative a few months before Jenkinson. He'd seemed a perfect candidate at the time but his Hull address had had to be dealt with because the grants were rigidly postcode dependent. He'd moved in with an aunt in Scarborough, though he hadn't spent much time there as far as anyone knew. Like Jenkinson, he'd hit adolescence and been expected to use low level crime to become the family breadwinner. Getting hapless parents to stand on their own feet had all been part of the support network. Somewhere along the way he'd met Jenkinson but the only evidence for that was that they'd been together in York. It didn't nullify the theory that Jenkinson had had higher level dealings with an organised crime ring, but Webber hoped it was a step along the way.

'We just had the lass from downstairs at the flats to start with,' Davis said. 'She's identifying him as having been a regular visitor those last few weeks. We wanted independent corroboration,' He glanced towards Webber, 'because it seems that Jenkinson and the lass'd had some sort of relationship. She says it was nothing, but there's always the worry of payback when you're dealing with exes. Anyway, we have our corroboration. CCTV from the end of the road.'

'Which is interesting in itself,' someone else put in, 'because of the times and the route. Coming to Jenkinson's flat from that way is pretty tortuous, but it avoids the main cameras.'

'And once we had photos to tout about, we got a tutor who saw the guy hook up with Jenkinson outside a lecture.'

'That's not all we had from that camera,' Davis said. 'We might have a sniff at the mystery man too. We've a witness who saw Jenkinson with a second guy, no detail but he clocked a distinctive walk, and we have similar on one stretch of footage. The stills are crap and we're trying to get the pictures enhanced.'

Webber heard the phone ring from his office and let out a sigh, pretty sure it would be a conversation he'd rather not have. Not only was Tom Jenkinson's mother raising Cain, but Arthur Trent's family too. Understandably, they wanted his body for burial, but despite nothing untoward having shown up at the post-mortem, Webber would not authorise the release before he had comprehensive toxicology results.

He pushed himself away from the window and went to answer it.

By mid-morning the day was developing into a series of frustrations and annoyances. The only bright spot had been Davis putting his head round the door to report that Jenkinson's mate had been picked up in Hull. Webber, who was on the phone, had given him a thumbs up but missed the detail. A later call had brought a report from Scarborough. Ahmed losing his rag, having to be pulled up by the sergeant there. That was a genuine worry. Ahmed had been in some sticky situations in his career, but he'd never lost the plot. The whole Jenkinson business was getting to him and if things weren't calmed down this was the sort of path that could lead to disaster for a promising career. He'd hate to see Ahmed throw everything away and wondered if he could find an excuse to bring him to York.

Hanging over him was the forceful warning he'd felt obliged to dole out that morning before he'd left home.

'Steer clear of the Tippets. Don't go near them. They're potentially involved in another case.'

To have revealed the forensic detail about the car would have been a step too far, but in terms of the cat and mouse game between them, it had become a huge step backwards because he was openly withholding information. Her rational self wouldn't have asked him to do it differently, but it didn't stop her milking it, and it didn't stop him feeling bad about it.

When he finally escaped his desk and went to look for more detail on Jenkinson's mate, he found the place all but deserted. As they were out chasing the various leads from this morning's briefing, he couldn't complain, but felt frustration at the number of loose ends that flapped without order or promise of closure. Leafing idly through a heap of files, he caught Suzie Harmer's name on a list. His lips tightened. The sooner she was gone on her maternity leave, the better.

He paused. Who was going to cover for her? He thought of

Ahmed in Scarborough. The perfect opportunity. Ahmed to step up to acting sergeant and come to York for however many weeks ... months it would be. He would have to float the idea in a way that Farrar wouldn't veto.

He turned back to his office. He could call Farrar ostensibly to brief him on the latest developments, to test the water and see if things had settled enough for normal interaction.

He hadn't quite made up his mind when the phone rang an internal call.

'Martyn, there's a woman just come in. Says she's Arthur Trent's sister-in-law. She wants to speak to someone.'

'What state's she in?'

'Quiet ... Calm.'

He cast around for an excuse. He didn't want to do this, not now, but in the circumstances, he shouldn't palm her off on someone else. 'OK, I'll come down.'

A coffee would be welcome. If she didn't look the sort of blow up and create mayhem, he'd take her up the road to the café.

◉ ◉ ◉

The woman cradled her tea as Webber sat down opposite her. He'd chosen a table in the window, away from the other customers who had huddled into the back of the shop away from the draught by the door. All she'd said was, 'I want a word about Arthur,' and had agreed to his suggestion of a chat over a hot drink.

'They're very upset,' she said now. 'They can't understand why they can't have him back.'

This woman wasn't a blood relation to Arthur Trent but she'd known him well. He intended taking this chance to do a bit of digging.

'He had a car accident,' she went on. 'It's tragic but it's not uncommon. What's the delay?'

'I'm just waiting for the final lab reports. Some of these tests take time.'

She looked him in the eye. 'What's the problem? Are you saying it wasn't an accident?'

'No, I'm not saying that.' Webber chose his words carefully. 'But I want to be sure. If there was more to it, you'd want to know, wouldn't you?'

'Of course.' She nodded.

'Tell me about Arthur. What was he like? How long had you known him?'

She gave a small laugh. 'I married his brother almost twenty years ago. Arthur was … a good man. A good family man. Nothing out of the ordinary to most people, but …'

'He'd been in that job a good many years, I believe.'

'That's right. It suited him. He liked to be out and about, not stuck indoors.'

'One of his last deliveries …' Webber watched her as he spoke. 'He took concrete to a site where they're putting up wind turbines.'

She nodded, accepting his assertion.

'Would he have had reason to take a detour on the way to the delivery? I mean, if he did, why would that be?'

'No, of course not. He was a good man. He'd done that job for a long time. He'd never have done anything like that. I mean if he was going to call at home or something, it'd be for an emergency, that's all. Not that there was any emergency that I heard about.'

Webber kept his expression neutral, uninterested, as she replied with far too many words, trying to shield her relative's reputation, unsure where the attack was aimed. So Arthur Trent was not averse to diverting a yard or so of concrete here and there. He'd probably get an interesting analysis of the family's driveways if he chose to. But he wasn't sure she knew anything specific.

'I thought tests could be done within minutes these days.' She returned to the first topic. 'You test people at the side of the road.'

'That's for alcohol,' he said. 'That one can be done quickly. Arthur wasn't over the limit.'

'Of course he wasn't!' Her vehemence came as a surprise. She glared at him across the table.

He tipped his head. 'He wasn't that far under. Alcohol might have been a factor.'

'What!' She stared, mouth agape, her expression horrified. 'Arthur didn't drink. He was teetotal. He hadn't touched alcohol in decades.'

Webber stared back. There was no dissembling here. She wasn't trying to protect anyone's reputation now. This was the truth.

◉ ◉ ◉

Webber deliberately turned away from the station, crossing the main road as a gust rose to spit raindrops in his face. He hadn't brought his coat. He'd be soaked in seconds if this storm got going. He could hear Mel's voice in his head, *If you must traipse about in the rain, go and get your coat; it's a two minute detour, for heaven's sake.*

But he needed to think.

Why do you have to be wet to think?

He didn't have an answer for that, not one that would have satisfied Mel. If he went in, he'd be caught by someone or something. He'd never get out.

But her voice in his head and the thought of sitting in damp clothes all afternoon made him turn back. He broke into a run. Having decided to beat the breaking storm, it would be annoying to end up wet anyway.

He'd liked Trent's sister-in-law. She was a sensible type. But he didn't much like what she'd had to say. Trent's blood alcohol had been high. Not high enough to prosecute, but high enough to have generated a stern talking-to in different circumstances. Had Trent been a secret drinker? Had he had alcohol without realising what he was drinking? Those levels in his blood, if he genuinely wasn't used to it, could have been enough to cause him to lose control. Or was it one of those anomalous readings, the results of some post-mortem process? He didn't know but he would find out. He felt the rumblings of anger at the idea of slipshod lab procedures. There was too much at stake to have people being careless, not doing their jobs properly. Hell, if Davis could raise his game, they all could. But still, he had no evidence yet to point to where this anomaly lay. It might even be that Trent's sister-in-law was a liar.

He reached his office without anyone stopping him. The rain rattled against the window panes, coming down in sheets now. No light blinked from the phone, so no new messages. He knocked the mouse to bring his computer to life. A dozen new emails but nothing that couldn't wait. His coat wouldn't keep him dry in this lot, but he grabbed it anyway. He would head for the shopping mall where he could get undercover; try to walk these puzzles out of his head and into some kind of sense, grab a sandwich. If nothing else, he could think out the best way to tackle Farrar about Ahmed.

When he scurried back inside later, he was one of a crowd shaking out wet coats, rubbing hands to generate warmth. He felt better for thirty minutes brisk exercise although he'd returned with nothing resolved.

A voice called out, 'Martyn, you had a call from the lab. On your desk.'

Trent or Morgan, he wondered as he went through to check.

Morgan. It was the woman with the tiger theories. She wanted to know if he was available for a video call later. That was good. It meant she'd got it wrong. She wasn't coming to see him in person.

And he could use this. He picked up the phone and called through to Farrar's office. 'I'm organising a video call on that DNA anomaly. John'll want to be patched in if he's around. Does he have any time this afternoon?'

'He should be back in an hour, then he'll have twenty minutes before he's due to meet ...'

'I'll fix it for an hour's time,' Webber interrupted. 'See if you can get a message to him. I think he'll want to be in on this one.'

He typed out an email to the lab woman, telling her one hour, that he'd call her. She'd go through whatever she'd found, he would get rid of her as soon as he could. He and Farrar would stay on to debrief. He ran through scenarios in his head, reasons for bringing Ahmed on board as Harmer's replacement.

An hour later, Webber opened the call. The rain no longer pounded on the windows. A fine drizzle blurred the outside world as the light faded on a drab day. The lab woman's icon showed as live. Farrar's didn't. OK, he'd get what he could out of her and patch in Farrar as soon as he showed up.

She was on her mobile phone. He watched her pull off a face mask and cap as she walked. The building behind her was unfamiliar. Not the lab. She must be out on a job. And in better weather than here.

'Hi,' he said. 'You've sorted out this DNA anomaly, I gather.'

She nodded, looking tired. 'Pretty much. It's always hard this long after the event.'

'Someone got things wrong, then?' He couldn't resist needling her a bit.

'Oh yes,' she said. 'Someone got things very wrong.'

A shaft of sunlight speared down behind her and Webber realised she wasn't out in the open at all, but in some kind of big barn. A sudden suspicion hit him. 'Where are you?'

'This is the warehouse where it happened.'

The bloody woman had gone all the way to Dorset after he'd specifically said not to. He held back the reprimand. That could wait.

'What are you all togged up for?' he snapped. 'What are you expecting to find after thirty years?'

'It's more as a protection from the dust and stuff. This place was used to store chemicals for years.'

'And was it worth the trip?'

She had the grace to look sheepish as she met his eye. 'I couldn't figure it just from the photos. The crime scene tells the story of the crime. I had to see the place. And yes, I ...'

'Hang on.' Webber stopped her as he saw Farrar come online. He patched in the Chief Super and gave him a brief outline.

Farrar looked annoyed. Webber hoped it was the Dorset trip. 'OK,' he said. 'Spit it out. What have you found?'

'You remember the report,' she said, as she turned and walked towards the edge of the large space. 'They worked out that Robert Morgan had been about here to start with. They said he must have heard the kerfuffle and tried to keep out of the way, not realising what was happening. So he'd have been through here – there was a doorway back then – and partway up the staircase. That's gone too, but it went up from ...'

Webber stopped her. 'Move back where you were, your signal's breaking up. We've read the report. Just tell us. We don't need to see every inch.'

She shrugged and retraced her steps. 'OK. Well, you remember how they tracked where he'd run; his injuries, all that?'

'Uh huh.'

'And they had him end up this other side, trying to get to that window.' The view tipped as she angled her phone upwards. 'Old crates piled high back then, so there was something to climb.'

The scene tipped again as her face reappeared.

'Psychology's not my thing,' she said, 'but the animal rights lobby had had some really bad press round then ... round here ... They weren't exactly treated sympathetically.'

'Your point being?' Webber tried to suppress his impatience.

'I think it was one of those trial-by-tabloid mass hysteria things. Make it look as bad as it could be so they could crucify the ones who'd done it. And I think the CSIs at the time must have been caught up in it. I don't think they did a great job.'

Webber took a glance at Farrar. He was watching intently.

'Go on,' Webber said.

'Robert Morgan couldn't have climbed up there.' She pointed towards the window. 'Crates or no crates, not with the injuries he had at that stage. I don't think he even tried to hide in the first place.'

Webber felt the crawl of something over his skin, something nasty. 'The crime scene tells the story of the crime,' he murmured, repeating the woman's words from earlier. 'You're telling us this isn't the crime scene.'

'What are you saying?' Farrar broke in.

'I'm saying it was all the work of the tigers,' the woman said. 'The patterns fit big cats fighting over his body. It doesn't fit him making any attempt to get away. Robert Morgan was dead when the tigers found him.'

'The DNA?' snapped Farrar's voice.

'Oh, I rechecked that,' she said casually. 'I told you, it's a match. No doubts. Not a relative. Not an error. It's him.'

Something inside Webber wanted to grab the phone to Mel, to tell her Robert Morgan hadn't died that awful death pursued by big cats and ripped to pieces. He wanted to be able to say it to Pamela, to tell her there was no need to do what she'd done. But of course it was too late for that. Years too late.

It was Farrar who spoke into the silence. 'Solves the mystery of why Morgan should have walked into that warehouse in the first place. He didn't.'

Webber nodded. Robert Morgan had been brought there, already dead, his body dumped. If that made it one of the animal rights lot, it had to have been the ring-leader; the rest were no more than kids going along for the ride. And if it hadn't been the animal rights lot, it must have been someone who knew about the planned release of the tigers, used them as cover for the killing.

He glanced again at Farrar, wondered if he was thinking the same thing. Thirty years ago, Robert Morgan's body had been driven to Dorset in a car that Brad Tippet had waited over twelve hours to report stolen.

chapter sixteen

Webber put his phone on speaker and clicked in his home number as he waited in a queue of building Friday traffic. The answerphone cut straight in, the line in use. He wondered who she was talking to.

'Mel, it's me. I have to call in and see John. It shouldn't take long but you know what he's like. Don't wait to eat if I'm not back. If I'm really late I'll pick up a take-away.' He paused. He'd overheard Davis making a similar call, which he'd ended quite casually by telling his wife he loved her, then he'd turned back to the briefing and carried on as though it was nothing out of the ordinary. That's what he should say to Mel now. There was no audience to worry about, no one else would hear the message.

The traffic ahead began to move. 'Bye,' he said and clicked off the phone.

Farrar had had to leave the video call to get to his meeting. Webber had stayed on and quizzed the lab woman for all the forensic detail she could give him, probably more than she could give him. They'd been talking for half an hour. She was getting ratty, telling him she was a scientist not a psychic when Farrar's icon popped up again and he re-joined the call. The woman had taken the opportunity to duck out saying she'd given them all she could for now. Farrar had been in a hurry, issuing the summons to Webber to get across to see him, and to bring anything and everything he could find on Tippet. Webber could imagine the worry. This was a case Farrar had been involved in decades ago. Tippet's involvement had been minor. Farrar had no reason to remember details at this distance,

143

but a concern hung over the latest revelations. Forensics had made a balls-up of it, but had someone closer to home missed something?

There had been no obvious opening to bring up Suzie Harmer's maternity leave or Ahmed's situation, but encouraged by the normality of the exchange, when they'd agreed next steps, he'd said, 'John, while you're on, there was something I wanted …'

Farrar had interrupted him. A raised hand, a steady stare from out of the screen that had made Webber think his thoughts were etched on his forehead. 'Best you don't say anything, Martyn. Get that info for me and we'll talk later.'

He wondered about it now. Had Farrar known what he was going to raise? That's how it had felt. After all, Farrar kept his eye on the ball and must have had word of what had been happening over in Scarborough. The tone hadn't been discouraging. It was almost as if Farrar was warning him not to make the request explicit, that that would stymie it.

Beside him on the seat, he had a set of files; some fat, some thin, everything they'd dug out for him that had any relevance to the events thirty years ago: Tippet's car, the post office raid and subsequent arrest of two of the three brothers. And the Morgans. There was next to nothing on the latter. The crime scene had been a long way away. He'd contacted who he could, asked for records to be searched out.

Farrar's glance ran across the heap of papers Webber slapped down on the desk. 'If you're thinking of lobbying me about Suzie's maternity leave,' he opened. 'Don't.'

Webber nodded and felt pleased. Ahmed's situation must have come to Farrar's notice. He and Farrar had been thinking along exactly the same lines, but for whatever reason, Farrar didn't want the suggestion to come from Webber. That was fine. It was the outcome that mattered.

Farrar tapped his finger on the file. 'You interviewed Tippet the other day. What's bugging you?'

'Two things,' said Webber. 'One's the car theft. He knew it had been taken that night, I'd put money on it, though what we can prove now, God knows. Any brief worth his salt will tell Tippet to stick with not remembering.'

'Knew it had been taken or drove it off himself?'

Webber pulled a face to match the frustration of insubstantial information. 'I haven't had the chance to get at this lot yet, but I went through the post office stuff when they first pulled the car out. Tippet was looked at. It was his car after all. Not that anyone was thinking of a trip to Dorset, but there was a neighbour who'd called round or phoned or something. I guess that ambivalence over when the car disappeared must have been obvious at the time.'

Farrar nodded. 'I'm hoping something in here will jog my memory, but he must have been checked out. He was at school with one of the brothers who did the post office. I wonder if the neighbour's still alive. You said two things. What's the other?'

'He's holding one hell of a grudge against you.'

'Yes, I remember that. It was a big deal at the time. First complaint I'd had against me. I thought he'd wrecked my career.' Farrar gave a wintry laugh. 'If I'd known then what I'd have to weather over the years, I'd not have given it a thought. It came to nothing. I can't even remember what it was about.'

'He says his sister was murdered by her husband. He told me he gave you the gen and you did nothing about it.'

Farrar blew out a sigh. 'It's ringing a vague bell. I'd have taken it back to my inspector, an accusation like that. I must have done.'

'Tippet remembers it all like it was yesterday.'

'OK,' Farrar poked at the files. 'Let's take a look.'

They spread out the papers in front of them. Farrar ran his finger down one of the older ones. 'Any of this lot digitised?' he asked, reaching for his keyboard.

Webber thought of the time that had elapsed, of all the people who must have been involved. Put the tiger incident in the mix and the cases crossed boundaries. Getting everything together wouldn't be easy, might not be possible. 'Anything immediately accessible is here,' he said. 'I've put out feelers for the obvious gaps, mainly Robert Morgan of course.'

'Was Morgan's body in the boot of that car when it left Tippet's? Was he killed in Tippet's garage? Does he have a garage?'

'I don't know,' Webber said. 'The car was taken off the drive. But from the original forensics, we can say the body probably wasn't in the boot at the time.'

He'd quizzed the lab woman on exactly this. She'd told him that although she thought Robert Morgan had been dead when the tigers found him, the original results suggested that he hadn't been dead long. 'I can see where they might have concluded he was alive,' she'd said. 'It's the chase hypothesis that holds no water at all.'

'People have been known to do incredible things in extremis,' Webber had pointed out.

'They don't defy the laws of physics,' she'd countered. 'And anyway, he was dead when he was wrapped in that plastic. I told you before, that wasn't a survivable head injury.'

'But could he have died in that warehouse?' He'd pushed the scenario as hard as he could, needing to reach the extremes of what was and wasn't possible, wanting her to convince him. And she had. Morgan's body had been wrapped in that plastic sheet; the sheet had been in the car boot.

He summarised this for Farrar, ending, 'Best guess, he was killed nearby, bundled in the boot and driven to the warehouse. The sheet was to keep the car clean.'

'Any chance we can place the car down there?'

'Unlikely after all this time, but you never know,' Webber said. 'When the circus found the tiger cage gone, the animal rights people were in the frame straight away. They'd held protests, majored on lax security as well as cruelty. They'd arranged for an anonymous statement to arrive at the local press the next morning. Then Robert Morgan was found and they turned themselves in. The investigation went to town with the case against them, tracked their movements, took statements from all and sundry, didn't want to leave them with any loopholes.'

Webber was silent for a moment as he thought about the avalanche of reports and statements heading his way.

'Ah, here's Tippet.' Farrar pulled a sheaf of papers free and studied them. 'Yes, a neighbour,' he said as he read through. 'Mrs Bell, friend of Mrs Tippet. She called round mid-evening, stayed nearly three hours. They sat in the kitchen. Tippet was in the front room watching TV. There was a rugby match on. It pans out, and anyway,' Farrar frowned as he flipped the pages, 'I went there. I interviewed him at his house. I remember it as of a piece, small, through lounge-diner, straight on to the kitchen. Unlikely you could pretend someone was there for hours if they weren't. And she talks about him coming through to get a drink.'

'The car,' said Webber. 'For it to have travelled to Dorset and be back in time for the post office raid, it had to have been gone by the time she left, even if it was still there when she arrived.'

'Back door,' said Farrar, still reading. 'She came and went through the kitchen, gap in the hedge. It was a regular thing. Unless she's in on it, it looks like Tippet was at home.'

Webber opened another of the files. 'Here we are, John. Tippet's allegations against Michael Drake, the brother-in-law.'

Webber skimmed the pages, passing them one by one across to Farrar. He was interested to see that Tippet had originally provided detail on the financial angle, saying that Michael Drake had taken out a large life insurance policy on Quintina before poisoning her. Farrar had been right. He'd reported the matter upstairs, but after that, hadn't been involved. An investigation had concluded there was nothing in it.

'It was given to a DI,' Webber said, showing the page to Farrar.

Farrar nodded. 'Yes, I remember him. He'll have done a good job. No longer with us sadly. What did he find?'

'There was an insurance policy,' Webber summarised from the report. 'But it was Quintina Drake who'd taken it out, not Michael. In fact she'd insured both herself and her husband,' he said as he read further. 'They both had life insurance but the policies were too new to pay out. She did it through a broker, a family friend. According to this, it wasn't clear the husband even knew about it before she died.'

'So this broker was a family friend of Tippet's sister, not Michael Drake?'

'Yes, must have been,' Webber said reading on. 'In fact he did insurance for Brad Tippet and his wife as well at the same time.'

'That policy'll be worth a bit now if it's still running,' Farrar commented.

'Ah, here's something,' said Webber. 'Tippet senior, Brad and Tina's father, weighed in on Michael Drake's side, said he'd been a devoted husband; that Brad had always been jealous. Drake worked for Tippet senior. Looks like he pushed Brad Tippet's nose seriously out of joint. That feels to me like the origins of the grudge against Drake.'

Webber sat back and ran his hand through his hair. Other than the original forensic team falling prey to melodramatics, it looked as though a thorough job had been done on all the various cases and angles, although the bulk of the information on Robert Morgan's death was still to land. 'It's hard to know how much resource we can give this,' he said. 'Trace and interview everyone from the original case or cherry pick?'

'It's thirty years, Martyn. Mother Nature will have done the cherry-picking.'

'I suppose we'll have to see who's still around and then take it from there, but I don't want to pull anyone off looking for

Jenkinson's killer. There are too many loose strands on that one as it is.'

'Anything come of that link to something more organised, major drug trafficking?'

'Nothing solid, but it looks like there was something. Davis raised it with Ayaan Ahmed. He couldn't rule out Jenkinson keeping some irons in the fire and well below the radar. He had family circumstances pushing him into petty crime but he was a bright lad. Ayaan reckoned that if he was going to choose a life of crime, he'd go for the big time.'

Farrar gave him a speculative look. 'On Morgan there shouldn't be much urgency. It's been thirty years. If anyone was inclined to destroy evidence, they'll have done it a long time ago. All the same ...'

Webber nodded. Farrar was hinting at some kind of clock ticking in the background. He could feel it himself, not sure what it was. Whoever had killed Robert Morgan might get wind of the new developments. What might they do? As Farrar said, evidence would have been destroyed or simply vanished over the past three decades.

'My original interview with Tippet,' said Farrar suddenly. 'Where is it?'

Webber raked through the papers and passed them over. He watched Farrar's stare run across the words. 'What are you looking for?'

'I'm seeing myself back in that room. Tippet perched on the end of the chair, all uptight.' He gave a tut of annoyance. 'It's not here but I'm sure he said it. Quintets. I can hear him saying something about quintets.'

... their talk was full of Qs ...

Webber's mind went back to the day he'd sat with Farrar's father, drinking tea watching the rain.

... Quinny ... quintets ... Quintina ... she spoke quite differently when she thought the young man wasn't listening ...

'Whatever it was, I didn't note it down.' As he spoke, Farrar looked up and met Webber's eye. 'What is it? What are you thinking, Martyn?'

'A woman called China Kowalski,' he said. 'She's the one who approached your father back in May. She works in Malaysia now but she knew them all thirty years ago. It would be good if we could talk to her.'

chapter seventeen

He was late home. Farrar had insisted they try to chase up Kowalski at once. Webber had pointed out that it would be late evening for her, heading for midnight, and anyway she'd said she was going on a trip. Farrar had brushed that aside and picked up the phone himself. Half an hour chasing leads and pulling strings netted the contact details for Kowalski's boss who wasn't answering the phone, and a mobile number for Kowalski herself. When Webber tried the latter it went straight to voicemail. 'If she's out of internet range, there's probably no mobile coverage either.' He'd left a message anyway.

As he came through the door, Melinda was coming downstairs. She raised her finger to her lips. Webber could hear his son's voice, a low crooning that would be aimed at one of the toys that crowded the cot. He wondered, not for the first time, why Melinda could leave Sam before he was properly asleep and he couldn't.

Once in the living room, he said, 'I rang but you were on the phone.'

'Yes, it was John. He said you were on your way to see him.'

'John?' He was puzzled. Why would Farrar chase him at home when he knew he wouldn't be there?

Melinda looked at him. He couldn't read her expression. It was as though she was puzzled too. 'He was just asking if I was OK.'

'Oh, right … good of him.' Webber tried to keep his tone neutral. He didn't like the idea that Farrar had been talking to Mel behind his back. He didn't need Farrar butting in causing more trouble, though her demeanour seemed somehow warmer than he was used to since Harmer's visit. What had Farrar said? Was it to do with Farrar? Was he imagining it? No, because there she was putting out the meal she'd saved for him.

'Thanks.' He smiled at her and she sort of smiled back, before turning abruptly and heading to the kitchen. He certainly hadn't expected her to keep food warm for him. It seemed to signal that they'd reached some kind of understanding, or rather that she had. He hadn't a handle on any of it. And he couldn't ask her, didn't know what he wanted to vocalise.

He glanced towards the TV where Sam's blackboards were stacked. They'd been moved. She hadn't given up her quest for the truth about Pamela Morgan. If he tried to lay down the law, he might jeopardise what felt like a fragile reconciliation, but he had to say something. The live enquiries edged closer. Robert Morgan's death was under the spotlight. How could he tell her to stop and still sound like he trusted her?

'Problems?'

He jumped; hadn't noticed her come back into the room. 'Sorry, it was … just this bloody case.' He paused, then amended, 'these bloody cases.' He had to trust her with the truth even if it cost him his job, because otherwise he'd lose her. As he ate, he told her about Trent's sister-in-law.

'And you don't think Arthur Trent was a secret drinker.'

'That would be too much of a coincidence. He was given something, but who knows if it'll show up.'

'But it's not just that, is it?'

He wondered if she meant something specific or if she was just guessing from his manner. 'No, it's everything really. Some bastard killed that lad Jenkinson in cold blood and not a sniff at a suspect yet. It's been almost a week.'

'Three days,' she corrected.

'Three days since we found him. It's close on a week since he was seen alive.'

'John told me ...' He looked up as she paused. Her glance met his briefly, then shied away. 'He ... uh ... said what you'd ... well, anyway, it was a nice thing to do.'

So that's what it was about, his aborted request to get Ahmed out of trouble. He wasn't sure what astonished him the most, that Farrar had told her at all or that she'd taken it this way.

'I ... uh ... gather Ayaan Ahmed was over here,' she went on.

He thought back to that day at the gravel pit; couldn't remember what he'd told her. Things had been pretty strained. 'Yes, I brought him back to the house. He was there when they found Jenkinson. Didn't know where else to take him really.' Maybe she'd spotted the tell-tale signs of a visitor the way he had. It had been the day he'd first found her behind-the-scenes investigation. It was hard to think it was only three days ago.

'It's been tough on him,' she said.

He nodded. 'Another reason it'd be good to get this case tied up.'

'John's bringing him over here to cover *her* maternity leave.'

Shock rippled through him. He knew he was staring at her open-mouthed.

'Didn't you know?' She was laughing at his expression. He couldn't believe that Farrar would have told Melinda and not told him.

'Well, no. I knew he was thinking about ... He didn't say anything to me.' It came out with a touch of petulance.

'It's good,' she said. 'Don't look so shocked. It's what he needs right now.' He felt so far out of the loop that he wasn't entirely sure if she was referring to Farrar or Ahmed.

'OK.' She became suddenly business-like and strode across to pull out the makeshift evidence boards and prop them against the TV. He saw a new list and an unfamiliar photograph. 'I made some unexpected progress with Joyce today. Or rather she made some headway with old memories. Some more of Gary's school friends. Martyn, is it OK if Joyce contacts China Kowalski? She never really knew her but ...'

He watched her run-down as she looked into his face. But thank God she was checking with him. 'No Mel, you need to keep clear. We've had some unexpected developments, too.'

Finishing his meal, he picked up the plate and headed for the kitchen, talking to her over his shoulder, beginning the tale of the lab woman's trip to Dorset. He came back with coffee for them both and sat on the settee as he told her about Robert Morgan and the over-dramatic conclusions that the original forensic team had drawn. As the story unfolded, she backed away from the blank face of the TV and sank into a chair. 'But, that's awful … she spent all those years thinking … so, when …? Who?'

She came out with all the questions that had been thrown around the video call. He told her everything he knew, half hoping a new angle might emerge as they talked.

'So this Brad Tippet …?' she began.

He shook his head. 'Morgan was killed within minutes of being dumped. Tippet was at home all evening. His alibi looks solid.'

'You're going to check, though?'

'Oh yes.' Webber thought about Ahmed. Checking out old alibis would be something safe to divert him into. He didn't want him anywhere near the Jenkinson enquiry. 'Brad Tippet was at school with one of the brothers who did the post office, the eldest, the one who disappeared. You said something about Gary Yeatman's old school friends.'

'Oh yes, the quintets thing.' Melinda pointed to the photograph. 'Joyce remembered something and went delving around for old photos. But Martyn, that's awful. How could it have happened? That means it wasn't an accident.'

'No, probably not. And you mustn't say anything to Joyce. Not yet.'

She nodded absently. 'I know, but you'll keep me in the loop, won't you?'

'Yes, I will.' He wanted to add that he really meant it this time. 'You won't mention anything to John, will you?'

'Of course not,' she snapped, giving him a who-do-you-take-me-for look.

'So Joyce has worked out the quintets thing?'

'Not sure, but Gary went round with a gang at school and apparently there were five of them. They were a tight knit group. That might have been what the quintets thing was about.'

She reached forward to pull the photograph free of its Sellotape mooring. Webber took it from her and tipped it towards the light. She sat beside him as she pointed to the group. He saw a laughing carefree gang, arms lightly round each other's shoulders, each kicking one leg in the air for the camera, hair flying, huge grins.

'That's Gary,' Melinda's arm brushed his as she leant across to point. 'And that's China Kowalski.'

He took in the small dark-haired girl at the end of the line, then ran his gaze to the woman in the centre. 'Pamela Morgan,' he said and paused. She looked so vibrant, full of life, more so than any of them. Yet she'd been dead for 15 years.

'Michael Drake,' said Melinda, her finger resting on the smiling young man next to Pamela.

Webber studied his face. 'Brad Tippet's ex brother-in-law,' he said.

'No, really?' Mel had turned to face him, close enough that he felt her breath on his cheek. He held on to the intimacy of the moment, the lives of strangers bringing them close. He told her about Tippet's sister, Quintina; the resentment that burnt bright in brother Brad.

'Who's the fifth one, the other woman?'

'Joyce said she's Edith Stevenson,' said Mel. 'There was a list of names on the back of the original. That's a copy.'

'Did you see the original?'

'Yes, why?' He sensed a hint of sharpness as though he was questioning her ability.

'I wondered if the list might have had more than five names on it.'

Her brow furrowed. 'No. No, I don't think so. Why would there have been more than five? What is it, Martyn? Come on, what are you thinking? Tell me and I'll see what I can find out from Joyce.'

He ran his finger along the faces in the photograph. China Kowalski, a doll at the end of the line, dwarfed by her contemporaries. Physically dwarfed at any rate. He suspected she'd outstripped them academically from an early stage. Gary Yeatman grinned out of the picture beside her, his arm hugging her off-balance. His other arm encircled Pamela Morgan, her face the most carefree of all, laughing from between Gary Yeatman and Michael Drake, their three heads tipped together like an inner-circle within the group. And Michael Drake's other arm was around the third woman, the one new face and name in Melinda's latest find. She was smaller than Michael, but not by much. Her other arm was mostly out of shot. It might have been a badly framed photograph, but he didn't think so.

'It's been cut,' he said to Melinda. 'There's someone else the other side of Edith Stevenson.'

chapter eighteen

Ayaan Ahmed tried to curb his impatience as he approached the tiny bungalow, one in a network of low buildings, interspersed with narrow flower beds constructed with emphasis on neat corners rather than botanical expertise. Old food wrappers gave more colour to the displays than the few plants that straggled limply in poor soil. He would be offered tea, possibly biscuits, and he'd have to accept because this interview needed the trappings of an informal chat. He wanted more than her recollections of an evening thirty years ago. He wanted her insight into the Tippets, the couple who'd been her close neighbours. The whole of his Monday morning looked set to comprise tea and biscuits with York's old and infirm. If this was the best the job had to offer, he had to do some serious thinking about his future.

There was a long gap after his knock until the door swung open. The woman standing there didn't look as old as he'd expected, but she hobbled awkwardly bent over two sticks. 'Mrs Bell,' he greeted her. 'We spoke on the phone ...'

'Yes, you're Inspector Ahmed, aren't you?' She didn't spare a glance for the warrant card he held out, but began to turn away to lead him into the house; the curve in her spine not allowing her to look up to meet his eye. 'Come in, come in. I've just made tea.'

'You ought to have checked my identity before you invited me in,' he admonished gently, letting the misplaced promotion slide past. It wasn't the first time a member of the public had erroneously accorded him inspector rank, and she'd hit a nerve. The Chief Super had brought him across here to work with Suzie Harmer because they'd be short-handed once she went on maternity leave. He felt resentful there'd been no hint he'd be doing the actual cover as acting sergeant. Just another dogsbody on the cheap. Not only that, but he suspected he might be kept around for a couple of months and then sent back so someone else could step in. Melinda Webber, for instance. She was due back from her maternity leave soon. If she was given the role, he'd take a bet she'd have the temporary promotion, too. He was on a loser either way. If Farrar had chosen him over Melinda, he'd have Webber's resentment to deal with. Something else to be pissed off about because he'd always got on fine with Martyn Webber.

'We've a warden on site,' Mrs Bell said and laughed. 'If you start any funny business, I'll go for my panic button.'

'Let me help you.' He followed her to the cubby hole that held the kitchen, marvelling that he could hear nothing but cool tranquillity in his tone. Inside, he boiled with impatience, wanting this interview over and done with so he could hurry back to the station. He'd learnt that from Webber; that ability to flick the switch when stepping across the threshold into the interview space. He noted the cups, saucers and milk jug balanced precariously on a tray with a plate of biscuits. Mrs Bell leant against the work surface for balance as she tipped the kettle. He reached forward to re-stack the tray, then lifted the steaming teapot from in front of her and gave her a big smile. 'I'll take these through. Those biscuits look good.' He couldn't imagine how she'd have manoeuvred a single cup from kitchen to living room, let alone a heavy teapot and a tray of crockery, but it would have taken far too long. He had everything on the table, cups back in their saucers, biscuits re-ordered from where he'd shoved them aside to fit the teapot, and she hadn't even made it into the room.

'Why on earth are you going back over it?' The words arrived before she did. 'It was only a car theft and it's such a long time ago.

I wasn't sure I'd remember much when you first rang, but do you know, it's all quite clear. I suppose it's because of the fuss at the time, making a statement to the police. It fixed it in my mind.'

She propped her sticks in a corner and eased herself into a chair. Ahmed sat opposite her.

'Some new evidence has come to light, Mrs Bell. We're checking everything to do with Mr Tippet's car.'

'Oh, I never thought much of Brad,' she said easily. 'Very prissy and uptight. Quite the opposite of his father who was a good man, strong, decisive. Brad's son took after his grandfather. Every good trait in that family seemed to skip a generation with Brad. I can't say I was that close to his wife either, but we lived next-door to each other. We shared an evening together now and again, but really I was old enough to be her mother.'

'In your original statement, you told us ...'

Told us ... As Ahmed listened to his own voice, he reflected that the theft of Tippet's Ford Tempo pre-dated his birth.

⊙ ⊙ ⊙

By the time he was striding away from the tiny bungalow Ahmed's spirits had lifted. It had taken less time than he'd expected and she'd been clear about what she could and couldn't remember. A useful witness. He flipped back through his notebook as he walked. Brad Tippet was the closest they had to a viable suspect at this end of the country. It was the animal rights gang who were more likely to bear fruit but none of them had been traced to this area; some hadn't been traced at all yet.

Mrs Bell had been his second call; should have been his third but he'd been stonewalled by Edith Stevenson who had sounded like a grumpy old woman on the phone. It didn't bother him. As far as he could tell she was on the list for being an old school friend of Robert Morgan's wife. She was hardly a key witness. She would be in the paperwork somewhere. All the old friends had been interviewed at the time, but he had a mountain yet to dig through.

His first call had been to more of the Morgans' old school friends, Michael and Tiffany Drake. Michael had known them, anyway. Tiffany had greeted him with a glare and a petulant toss of her head.

'Tiff's not too well just now,' Michael had said.

Ahmed had made no comment, but had noted it was Michael who was the unwell one. Shades of Mrs Bell, he too walked with a stick and with a certain fixity of expression that revealed pain in every step. A nice enough guy, open about his strained relationship with Brad Tippet. Ahmed thought about Webber's notes of his interview with Tippet as his gaze had rested on a stack of DVDs by the television; Charlie Sheen. According to Tippet both Drake and his first wife had been Sheen fans. Maybe it was something he had in common with the second Mrs Drake too.

However, it wasn't rocket science to know that it was more than a 30-year-old car theft that had brought Ahmed to their door. Michael Drake was no fool.

'Oh God, it's nothing to do with Pamela, is it?' he'd said, his expression troubled.

'Pamela who?' Ahmed had asked, hiding his surprise. 'How do you mean?'

'Pamela Morgan. Someone's been saying that the police were looking into poor Pammy's death. I just wondered if there was a link. You said you're interested in Brad's car, the one that was stolen, only that was round the time Robert died. Pammy's husband, Robert.'

'Where did you hear we were looking at Pamela Morgan's death?'

Ahmed had watched Michael Drake closely. His eyes scrunched in reflection as his gaze lost focus. 'Where was it? Tiff? Who was it mentioned Pammy the other week?'

It was at that point she'd stood up, squinting against a shaft of sharp winter sun, and given Ahmed a look of contempt. 'I never met Saint bloody Pamela, so how the fuck would I know?' And she'd stormed out.

Ahmed had seen her husband's gaze, part distress, part embarrassment, as it tracked her departure. Glancing at the disappearing woman, he'd seen she was younger than he'd first realised. Michael, with his shaky health, probably leant on her a lot. It couldn't be easy for either of them, but his sympathies were with the man who'd offered a shamefaced apology as Ahmed had turned the conversation back to Brad Tippet's car.

Thinking over the encounter, he wondered how long the Drakes had been married, how old she was, what were their circumstances? He should have had all this at his fingertips before he'd been in touch. He'd been cutting corners. And why not, he thought sourly. Fat lot of good it had done him playing it straight all these years. Tom Jenkinson's mother hadn't turned it into an official complaint yet, but some bent lawyer would find her, go after him to see what they could get, turn Tom's death into a compensation circus.

At least from over here he'd be on hand to learn the latest on the enquiry, even though not officially in the loop, which was why he wanted to get back. No one was going to wait around to debrief him. He would have to rely on his own eyes and ears. He'd talked to the Drakes, had the brush off from Stevenson, and seen Mrs Bell. He checked the time. DI Davis would be debriefing his team in about twenty minutes. Perfect timing. He'd be back and discreetly tucked into a corner of the office ostensibly intent on his own paperwork.

As he reached for the key to start the car, his phone rang. The screen told him it was Sergeant Suzie Harmer. 'Ayaan, whereabouts are you? How's it going?'

'Just about to set off back.' He gave his location and a summary of his two calls. 'Tippet's neighbour pans out,' he told her. 'His alibi's solid. He didn't go to Dorset with his car that night.'

'How about the other one, Drake? The guy Tippet fingered. What did he have to say?'

'He was frank about bad blood between them. He told me his first wife, Tina, used to borrow Tippet's car. Apparently it was never an issue until she started seeing Drake, then Tippet made a huge fuss over it, constant digs about them taking advantage.'

'Is that new?'

'I don't remember it from the original statements but I'll double check. Drake told me they didn't have much to do with Tippet after they married, but they couldn't keep completely out of his way. They both worked for Tippet's father. He said it came as no surprise that Tippet should accuse him of stealing the car, but at that time he hadn't had anything to do with Tippet for about ten years. That pans out. The first wife, Tippet's sister, died in …' Ahmed raked through his notes. 'In … uh … 1976. A decade before all this kicked off.'

'What about Stevenson?'

'She wouldn't see me. Why was she on the list? I didn't find her in the initial enquiry.'

'She wasn't. She's one of Superintendent Webber's ideas. Probably a waste of time, but he insisted we add her. You know what he's like.' She chuckled. Ahmed laughed uneasily.

'Um … Another old friend of the Morgans, isn't she?'

'It's like Martyn says,' she went on. 'When a case is this cold, you're not going to find a fresh crime scene. You need all you can get on how your suspects were acting at the time.'

Everyone said Suzie was easy to work for as long as she got her own way, and so far Ahmed had no complaints, but he hated to hear her talk about Martyn Webber. She unbalanced him by her switch from formal to informal address and he was terrified she'd pull him into a conversation he didn't want to go anywhere near. He snatched at the topic of suspects. 'I don't think we have any suspects this end of the country. Brad Tippet's not looking good.'

'That's where you're wrong and that's why I'm ringing you. Just heard that one of the animal rights group headed back this way when he was released. The ring-leader Will Jones. Did you see a note about a hitchhiker in that first batch of files from Dorset? A walk-in witness, after the publicity about Robert Morgan. Some guy had picked up a man near the warehouse.'

'Vaguely,' said Ahmed, something sparking in his memory from his initial skim of the old notes. 'It didn't go anywhere, did it?'

'No, it wasn't followed up. They didn't need to. They all turned themselves in. I'm thinking of Will Jones dumping the body in the warehouse then going back to join the rest of them. Does that mean he was acting alone?'

'Well, hang on. How did he get the body there? Why was he hitching? What …?'

'I didn't say I'd thought it through. This hitchhiker thing might never have been relevant but you bear it in mind when you talk to him.'

'When I talk to him? Where is he?'

'I have a last known that's not far from where you're sitting.'

Ahmed suppressed a sigh and flipped his notebook to a new page. 'OK, go ahead.'

'I'll email it.'

The phone pinged as he listened. He clicked on to it to check.

'Yes, I have it. How about a phone number?'

'Couldn't find one. Call round there. You never know.'

'When did he get out of prison?'

'July 1996.'

As he ended the call, Ahmed looked at the time. No chance of getting back for Davis's briefing now, even if the guy wasn't in. Unless he were to cut another corner, head straight back and simply pretend there'd been no one there.

He pulled himself up. This had to stop. He'd had a setback. He hadn't done anything wrong. If he threw away his career, his future in-laws would put a block on the marriage plans. He felt his mouth curve to a smile as Cari's face shimmered in his mind, returning his smile with that sparkle that melted his heart. She'd said herself that this relocation to York could be the start of something good. They'd been talking with her parents, her father running away with things as usual, her mother promoting him to inspector in a trice. Smiles … laughter … He saw the quick glance she'd shot at him. He'd had to duck his head to hide a grin. She hadn't been talking about the York move in terms of career progression, she'd been thinking distance. Too far for her mother to be popping in every five minutes. Yes, that suited him just fine. Stifling family or no, Cari was the best thing that had ever happened to him.

Time to get his head together. If the animal rights brigade had been involved, this Will Jones was a prime suspect for Robert Morgan's murder. He took the keys from the ignition and climbed out of the car. All that tea had given him indigestion. He craved a strong coffee and there was a café at the end of the road. No point rushing, so he awarded himself a ten minute break, strode down the pavement, arms swinging, feeling suddenly better than he'd felt at any time since the awful moment he'd known it was Tom under that concrete.

He went through the door turning to hold it open for a woman coming in behind him, and found himself face to face with Melinda Webber.

chapter nineteen

Ahmed's relaxed mood vanished. Every muscle tensed. His hope that she wouldn't recognise him died as it was born.

'Hi,' she said. 'Ayaan Ahmed, isn't it? How are you?'

Thoughts kaleidoscoped through his head. She must know why he was in the area, that he reported to Suzie Harmer, that he might be her rival for the upcoming acting sergeant cover. Her greeting was friendly and open. Was it a little too friendly, a bit forced perhaps? He battled an urge to loosen his collar as he replied.

'Uh ... Hello, Mrs Webber. Thanks, I'm fine. How ... um ... how are you?' The question seemed a gross impertinence, as though he were asking outright, what's the story with your husband and Sergeant Harmer?

She laughed as though she was aware of his discomfort and found it amusing. 'Melinda, please. If you're staying over here we might be colleagues in a few weeks.'

He didn't want to move inside the café. He wanted to change his mind and leave, but it would mean pushing past her, and there was someone else waiting to come in, waiting for him to get out of the way. 'Just grabbing a quick coffee before my next call,' he gabbled as he headed for the counter.

'Me too,' she said pleasantly. 'I'm doing a stint at Sam's play school. There's nothing more exhausting than a roomful of toddlers. It'll make the Saturday night drunks a piece of cake when I get back.'

He reached the head of the queue and felt he had to offer to get her drink, too. She smiled her thanks and signalled to the man behind the counter that they would be drinking in. It was a natural assumption. He wasn't quick enough to contradict her before the fat china cups were under the machine. Of course, she wasn't deliberately cornering him into sharing a mid-morning coffee with her. Why would she? His imagination ran riot as it conjured up answers. She wanted to check up on Harmer ... she wanted to check up on Webber ... she wanted a confidante on the spot ... she wanted to get back at Webber and sharing coffee was just the start ...

'I heard you're getting married,' she said, as she took a seat at a table by the window. 'Congratulations. Have you set a date?'

She looked interested and the words came out so naturally that he relaxed. No one else had bothered to ask properly. If they mentioned it at all, it was laced with inadequately disguised curiosity about whether the nuptials had really been arranged by the two sets of parents. 'If it were up to us, we'd nip down the registry office and just get it over with,' he said and then laughed at a sudden image of a set of four faces; his parents and Cari's. That would unite them. There'd be no polite bickering over minutiae if they had something like that to talk about.

She asked about Cari, about their plans, and he found himself talking openly. She was the first person outside the family to show interest in the things that mattered. Inside the family it was all stress and strain over details that simply weren't important.

A wedding doesn't organise itself ... you'd soon complain if it wasn't done properly ...

'Oh, and sorry if I've caused you any extra work.' She dropped the words into a pause.

Puzzled, he looked the question at her.

'Edith Stevenson,' she said. 'She was an old friend of the Morgans. It was me who mentioned her to Martyn.'

'Oh ... right ... How ...?' It sounded to him as though his voice had risen half an octave. She didn't seem to notice.

'I know someone who knew them years ago. Just coincidence, that's all.' She gave him a sudden sharp stare. 'I hope you're not thinking Martyn's been telling me things he shouldn't. You know him better than that.'

He had to bite back an urge to say, I know he's been *doing* things he shouldn't.

'We were on a trip the other week with Sam,' she went on. 'Martyn was called out and we had to go with him, so I probably know a bit more than I should, but anyway, maybe this Stevenson woman will have something useful to say.'

Ah ha! That was it. Ahmed felt the satisfaction of an anomaly ironed out. He hadn't given it much thought but yes, she'd been one in the crowd up by the public areas that Sunday when they'd found Tom's jacket in the lake. He'd seen her name on the witness list. It had been a bleak Sunday for a family day out, but maybe they'd been at the cinema or something.

She gave him a sympathetic smile. 'I'm really sorry about that boy you mentored. That was awful. All that potential just cut down. I'm sure they'll get whoever did it. I just hope it's soon.'

He returned her smile. She was very understanding, and she was right about Tom. He'd been on the verge of making something of his life. Of course, she would know the frustration he felt, being so close to the enquiry but not a part of it.

'But this whole Morgan thing's a bit of a nightmare, isn't it?' she went on. 'It's such a long time ago. I mean where do you start? I shall never complain about the futility of going after petty car crime again. A thirty-year-old car theft, for heaven's sake!'

Of course he shouldn't talk to her about any of this, but he reflected that she was Webber's wife and pretty close to being back in the job. He wasn't giving her any information, not really, nothing she didn't already seem to know. And he learnt a thing or two from her. Not least that the Webbers' marriage appeared as strong as ever which he was glad about, although mystified.

'Oh no!' Her exclamation cut through his thoughts. She was raking through her handbag.

'What's the matter?'

'I've left my phone in the car. Hell, I've parked miles away. I'll be late now. Oh, unless …' He saw hope dawn in her eyes as she looked at him. 'Could I use yours? Just a quick call. I promised Martyn I'd ring and if he tries to call me and doesn't get through he'll panic, you know what he's like.' Her mouth curved to a grin. 'He'll mobilise a full search and rescue, but I just can't be late at nursery.'

Ahmed laughed and pulled out his phone. 'Yes, of course.' He was amused at the thought of Webber freaking over a missed call from his wife. Webber liked to project a persona that rarely got ruffled, let alone panicked.

She gave him a grateful smile as she punched in the number.

'Hi, it's Mel. I … uh … No, it's Ayaan Ahmed's phone. I bumped into him, thank God because I've left my phone in the car. I know, I know … Uh …' She lowered her voice and turned towards the window.

Ahmed realised he was staring at her, openly eavesdropping. He jumped to his feet. 'I'll take the cups.'

Fortified by the coffee and a pleasant chat about his wedding plans, Ahmed didn't bother to go back for the car. Will Jones' last known address was just a couple of streets away. He checked his email to be sure it was the right place before walking up to the door and pressing the bell. Footsteps sounded from inside and the door swung open. A tall elderly woman faced him. Older than Mrs Bell he judged, but in far better health. He held out his warrant card as he introduced himself.

She read it through then looked him in the eye. 'What can I do for you, Detective?'

'I'm looking for a Mr Will Jones. I have this address as–'

Her expression froze as her words cut across his. 'Oh, for

heaven's sake! No! Mr Jones lived here for less than a month 20 years ago then cleared out owing me rent. I've had callers for him ever since. He made a credit black spot of this address.'

'Would you have the dates? And did he leave anything behind?'

She glared at him. 'July 1996. You'll find the exact dates on your own records. I reported him as a thief. And yes, he left a heap of garbage in his room. I paid a man with a van to take it all to the tip. Whatever he's done now, I hope you find him soon and throw away the key, but I never want to hear his name again. Goodbye.'

With that, she shut the door.

Ahmed shrugged and turned away, pulling out his phone. It had grown colder while he'd been inside the café and now the wind was getting up. He could feel damp in the air. It was going to rain. Quickening his pace, he pressed the button and listened to the ring tone as he wondered whether this made it more or less likely that the animal rights group was involved. Will Jones had been the ring-leader; the rest of them had been little more than kids, barely old enough to feel the full force of the law. He'd decided less likely, when he was jerked to a stop by Melinda Webber's voice in his ear.

'Sorry, there's no one here to take your call ...'

Of course. He clicked it off. The last call had been Melinda to her husband. He was glad Webber hadn't answered. That would have been an awkward conversation.

He clicked in the correct number but Suzie Harmer was on another call. He outlined what he'd found, adding, 'Can we check up on that theft report? I'm surprised we don't have anything more recent on him.'

'You on your way back?'

'Yes, I'll be ten minutes. By the way ...' He paused. Melinda Webber's voice played in his head ... the friendly chat ... the clipped tones of the answerphone. 'Has Martyn Webber been anywhere this morning?'

'No, he's not been out of his office. Why?'

'Nothing.'

She'd called Webber at home. He'd heard her speak to him …
speak to someone … before he'd taken himself out of earshot. As he
ended the call, Ahmed turned to glance in the direction he'd seen
Melinda take after they'd said goodbye outside the café.

chapter twenty

Webber arrived home to the sound of laughter, Mel and Sam. He walked into the living room. They were too engrossed in their game to see him at first. Toys were scattered everywhere. Sam's laughter ebbed as he stared expectantly at his mother who made a sudden move that bounced a set of plastic cars across the carpet. It was clearly the move Sam was waiting for. His shrill peals of laughter set Melinda off again, to the extent she reached for a tissue to wipe the tears from her eyes. The move brought Webber into her line of sight. She paused, laughter stilled, but a broad smile remained on her face as she looked at him. He grinned back, couldn't help himself. There was nothing so infectious as Sam's laugh.

''gain ... 'gain ...' Sam waved his arms in excitement demanding more.

Melinda got to her feet. 'OK, Sam, enough for now.'

Webber saw his son's face crumple as he watched his mother stand up, but before the ear-splitting wail could form, he was on his knees beside the boy, ruffling his hair and picking up a handful of the scattered toys. 'Daddy's turn,' he declared.

'Don't overexcite him. He won't sleep.'

He glanced up. Mel looked down at them, a smile still playing around her eyes. The laughter that had bubbled up inside him seemed to set into a hard pain. He had to look away. You can't leave me, he wanted to say, we can't lose all this, it's too important. He wanted to plead with her, but it was too soon.

The boards behind the TV looked undisturbed from the previous night. It occurred to him she might have heard that Suzie Harmer was now on the cold case. Would that make her drop her informal enquiries or make her all the more determined to carry on? It was a conversation they had to have at some level. The cold case nestled too close to more recent anomalies. He didn't want to be chasing after Harmer for progress reports, but he'd do it if that's what Mel wanted him to.

'Martyn! You're getting chalk dust on your trousers. Go and change before you wreck that suit altogether.'

She took Sam from him as he stood up. He heard her mutter something about dry-cleaning bills as she headed for the kitchen. He slipped out of his jacket, glancing again at the corner by the TV. Had those boards been moved? He stepped closer, reaching out his hand to tip the closest to one side, and saw at once there was a new name on the list.

Will Jones

It rang no bells with him. Maybe Mel had beaten the official enquiry to yet another name. But he hadn't heard anything about the cold case since early morning, so wasn't sure where they'd got to. Had the boards just fallen back this way or had Mel gone to some trouble to make them look undisturbed?

'Have you spoken to Joyce Yeatman today?' he called through.

'No, I'm hoping she'll ring. I left her a message. Something I want to run past her but she hasn't been back to me.'

'Weren't you doing a stint at play school this morning?'

'Yes ... Oh, and I bumped into Ayaan Ahmed on my way there.'

Webber paused. Ahmed had been sent out to interview the Tippet's ex-neighbour and some of Morgan's old friends. He knew that much from the morning briefing. In his head a map appeared with pins locating the various addresses and Sam's play school. *On my way there?*

'Take these up, will you?' She was at his elbow with a pile of clean laundry. He took it from her.

'How did Ayaan end up anywhere near play school?'

'No, I was just getting …' As she spoke, she hunched down with Sam and began clearing a way through the fallen toys. He caught the words, 'shop … those crayon things …'

'Who's Will Jones?'

Her head shot round as she gave him a sharp stare. 'What do you mean?'

He pointed to the boards. 'I saw you have a new name on there. I wondered who he was.'

'Oh … Yes, that. I was hoping you could tell me.'

He shook his head. 'Sorry, I've been all out on the Jenkinson case. I've had no time to catch up on anything else.'

Her eyes narrowed, 'Martyn, I know that Ayaan's reporting to the Harmer bitch. Poor sod. You don't need to pussyfoot around it.'

'I'm not. I haven't been anywhere near the Morgan case all day. So where did you get Will Jones from? Where does he fit in?'

Webber couldn't imagine Ahmed discussing case details with Melinda and even if he had, no one had mentioned a Will Jones this morning. She must know he hadn't swallowed her tale of a chance meeting, but he didn't want to challenge her openly. This mustn't become a fight. He had to know what she was up to.

She concentrated on Sam as she said, 'Not sure. And by the way, I'm afraid I mentioned to Ayaan that it was me who told you about Edith Stevenson. I hope that won't cause any bother.'

The words in his head were that he wouldn't let her duck out of Will Jones, but he kept his tone mild as he said, 'It'll be fine. Did you tell him how you knew about her?'

'I said I happened to know someone who'd known them all years ago. I didn't mention Joyce's name. He didn't ask.'

'And where did you say you'd got Will Jones?'

'Oh yeah, from Joyce. I just need some more detail …'

'Mel, you haven't spoken to Joyce today.'

She glared at him. 'OK, OK. It was Ayaan. I didn't want to get him into trouble.'

Webber was amazed. 'Ayaan gave you his name? But ...' He stopped. Of course Ahmed hadn't divulged the name.

Her stance radiated defensiveness. 'I saw an email on his phone. I knew it was about the case because of the subject line. It just said Will Jones and an address.'

'Mel, you didn't go ...?'

'Of course not,' she snapped. 'Anyway, I had to get back across town.'

'OK, I'll check tomorrow. I'll find out for you. I don't know who he is. This is the first I've heard of him.' He pointed at the board, but wasn't concentrating on Will Jones any more, he was thinking about Mel talking to Ahmed.

'Where exactly did you bump into Ayaan?'

She told him.

'That's not far from the Tippets' ex neighbour,' he said, watching her. 'Ayaan will have been on his way to see her.' She was quite capable of having tracked down the woman herself. Mrs Bell hadn't been hard to find.

'I thought you said you didn't know what they were doing?'

'I was at the early briefing.' He couldn't decide whether Melinda had been there to talk to the woman herself, or if she'd known Ahmed would be there and had hung about to catch a word. He had a memory of letting something slip about intending to put Ahmed on to chasing up the old witnesses.

'I've still not congratulated Ayaan on the wedding thing,' he said at random. 'Not that I've seen much of him.'

'Don't worry, I did. We had quite a talk about all their plans.'

'So is it true it's an arranged marriage?' He'd been curious since he'd heard but didn't know if it was an appropriate question to ask.

'Yes,' she said. 'What of it?' Her tone claimed the moral high ground, which irritated him. She'd been curious too. They'd talked about it before the thing with Harmer erupted.

'I'll go and get changed,' he said, and headed out of the room.

◉ ◉ ◉

It was mid-evening. Sam was in bed. Webber could see something about cookery unfolding on the TV but, half dozing and not interested, wasn't taking it in. He didn't think Melinda was really watching either. Having Suzie Harmer in the middle of the cold case had put a damper on relaxed conversation on that topic. The television was a convenient way to avoid conversation about anything else.

Melinda stood up and left the room. She didn't look at him. Webber watched her go, saw the glow from the kitchen as she turned on the lights, then heard the click of the back door. He wondered what she was doing.

The sudden ring of the phone made him jump. He stretched back to pluck it from its rest.

'Could I speak to Melinda,' said a woman's voice. 'It's Joyce Yeatman.'

Webber eased forward to see through the open doors. The kitchen lay empty, the back door ajar.

'She had to pop out,' he said into the phone. 'But she asked me to take a message if you rang.'

'Oh ... well ... I'm not sure ...'

'Is it about Will Jones?'

'Oh, right, you know about it. You must be Martyn.'

He hovered on the brink of saying no. If this woman wormed her way into the live enquiry, it would be awkward to explain prior contact with her. He settled for an indeterminate grunt that she could take for assent or not.

'She asked me if I'd come across the man, and the answer's yes. I met him once in the summer of 1996.'

Keeping the back door in his line of sight, Webber reached for a pen. 'That's very precise, Joyce. What can you tell me about him?'

'Oh, I couldn't give you an exact date, not after all this time, but it was that summer. I know because my husband died in the November of that year.'

'I heard. I'm sorry. It was a car crash, wasn't it?' As the ghost of Gary Yeatman hovered over the exchange, Webber thought about the official report on Yeatman's death. Suicide ... old-fashioned cruise control set to smash him to pieces ... and Arthur Trent ... jammed cruise control. It wasn't supposed to happen in a modern car. The toxicology results were due back tomorrow. 'You said you met Will Jones only once.'

'He turned up on the doorstep one day. A nice enough young man as I remember. He asked for Gary but Gary was out. I took an address off him.'

'Can you remember what it was?'

She laughed. 'You're as bad as your wife. After all this time, no.'

'But you only saw him once?'

'I told Gary when he got back and he went straight off to see him. When he came back he told me, "You won't see him again, but if he shows up, call the police." I remember that clearly.'

'Why? Who was he to Gary?'

There was a pause. Webber heard Joyce pull in a breath. 'It's a long time ago,' she said.

He knew better than to push. Melinda would have to get the detail out of her. 'Thanks for ringing,' he said. 'I'll let Melinda know.'

'There was something else. Would you tell Melinda that I've remembered the quintets thing, the photograph. Oh, and tell her I know she wasn't serious when she left the message, but bizarre as it sounds, she could be right.'

It was an effort to bite down on a myriad of questions but it would be foolish to press for more. She didn't trust him. He heard the click of the back door, became aware of movement from the kitchen. There was a fraction of a second to make up his mind. Hand over the phone with Joyce still on the line or cut the call and talk to Mel first.

'I'll tell her,' he said into the phone. 'Thanks.'

As Melinda re-entered, he was setting the handset back on its rest. 'There you are. Where have you been?'

'Putting the bins out. Why? Who was on the phone?'

He told her it was Joyce Yeatman, that he'd called out to her – fingers crossed behind his back – but she hadn't replied. 'She knows Will Jones,' he said. 'Or rather her husband did. But she held something back. I think she'd tell you.'

'I'm surprised she told you anything.' She sounded miffed.

'I said you'd asked me to take a message,' he confessed. 'I mentioned Will Jones. But there was more, about the quintets.' He repeated Joyce's message word for word.

Her face puckered to a frown. 'She knows Will Jones and she's remembered the quintets thing? What, like they're connected?'

'No,' said Webber, shaking his head. 'She said it like they *weren't* connected. But what could you be right about? What did she mean?'

'No idea, I just asked if the name Will Jones meant anything to her. Who is he?' She gave a huff of frustration. 'Couldn't you ring Ayaan?'

'Not without him tying it in with talking to you. Did he know you'd seen his phone? How did that happen anyway?'

She looked at her hands. 'I borrowed it to make a call.'

Having extricated him from a sticky situation in Scarborough, Webber wondered if Ahmed was heading for equally deep water here as unwitting intermediary stuck in the crossfire between Mel and Suzie Harmer.

'Oh! Wait a minute …'

He saw her eyebrows shoot up as the memory came to her. 'What?'

'I asked if she knew Will Jones, then I said something like, he's not the one cut off the photo, is he? I really wasn't serious. It just popped into my head while I was leaving the message.'

He lifted the handset from its rest and passed it to her. 'Ring Joyce Yeatman back before it gets too late. Can I ...?'

He indicated that he wanted to stand close enough that he could hear the call. She hesitated. He wondered if she'd tell him to listen on the other line, but she didn't. Wisps of her hair feathered his cheek as he leant over her listening to the ring tone and then to Joyce Yeatman's voice apologising for talking to him.

Melinda reassured her and steered the conversation back to Will Jones. 'I take it Gary didn't like him, whoever he was.'

'Gary went wild. I remember it clearly. He was such an even-tempered man usually. I never did find out why. When Gary was wound up about something, he went into his shell. He'd have told me in the end, but he hadn't got to it when ... well, his accident that November.'

Webber could see that Melinda's expression was troubled as she murmured sympathetic words into the phone, adding, 'But Jones never came back?'

'No, I wondered if he might show for the funeral, but no, nothing.'

'So you don't know anything about him at all.'

'No, but why are you interested in him? I thought it was Pamela Morgan's death you were looking at.'

'I don't know,' Melinda admitted. 'His name cropped up in relation to events back then, but without any detail.'

Webber wondered exactly how much Joyce knew about Melinda's informal enquiries. Too much, he was sure.

'Well, Gary did say that thing about the past,' Joyce said. 'I'd forgotten that.'

He glanced sideways to exchange a questioning glance with Melinda. 'What thing?' she said into the phone.

'I asked who Jones was and Gary said, "He's a real blast from the past, but not *my* past". That was before he went off looking for him. I don't even know for certain that he found him, though I think he must have. Warned him off, I suppose. I'd like to know what it was about. It would close a loop. And you'll tell me what you find, won't you? You promised.'

Webber was aware of some discomfort in Mel as she answered, 'Yes, of course.' He couldn't gauge if it was because he was there to witness that she'd made a promise she shouldn't have or if it was a promise she didn't intend to keep.

'But Joyce,' she went on. 'You said I was right in my message. Did you mean the photograph? Was it Will Jones cut off the end?'

'It's odd. I really don't know. I'm unravelling memories I'd forgotten I had. I'm not sure what's a real memory and what's speculation. It was all such a long time ago.'

'But when I showed you the photo,' said Melinda, her voice animated, 'you remembered about it being cut … well, you said it rang a kind of a bell.'

Webber's mind went over the last few days. She'd *shown* Joyce the photo? But they'd only talked about it themselves on Friday evening and she hadn't seen Joyce today. He began a mental track of the weekend that had just gone.

'It's so long ago,' Joyce repeated. 'It was just a photo of a gang of Gary's old school friends. I barely knew any of them and Gary had lost touch, apart from Pamela. But I've just got this picture in my head now of Gary cutting someone off the end. But maybe I'm making it up out of the things we've been talking about.'

Webber drew back so his voice wouldn't leak into the handset. 'When?' he murmured. 'Ask if it coincided with Will Jones?'

'Was it a reaction to Will Jones turning up? Is that when he did it?'

'Oh no, nothing like that. If it's a real memory and he did cut that photograph, it was way back.'

'But why did he do it? Didn't you ask?'

Joyce sighed. 'If it happened at all, I must have asked why, but it's too long ago. I can't remember. If I ever saw that complete photograph, I only saw it once. And I know I only saw Will Jones once in 1996. But there's something in my head telling me it's the same person.'

Melinda glanced at him. Webber gave her the ghost of a shrug. He couldn't think of anything useful to pursue along this line.

'Was there something about the quintets, Joyce?' Melinda changed track.

'Yes, there was. Tilly Brown.'

Webber crouched to add the new name to the list as Melinda asked for detail. He straightened to hear the voice say, '… wasn't the quintets originally, it was Tilly *and* the quintets. There were six of them. Then Tilly left and they were the quintets on their own.'

Melinda looked at him wanting guidance. That the group had been six strong in their earlier years at school seemed an irrelevance. He mouthed, 'So what?' as he mimed a pair of scissors with one hand.

'Are you saying it might have been Tilly Brown cut off the picture, not Will Jones?' Melinda asked. 'Or was she the one taking the photograph?'

'I don't know. I think Tilly would have left before that photo was taken. They were the quintets in the sixth form.'

By the time Melinda ended the call, Webber had added the new information to the board and his mind had been back over Saturday and Sunday. The only time they hadn't been together had been when Melinda had been out somewhere with Sam. But right at the start of all this, when he knew Joyce Yeatman had been in this house, she'd told him Joyce was never in the same space as Sam.

'What do you make of that?' she said, standing beside him looking at the new information he'd written down.

'Mel, when did you see Joyce at the weekend?'

'I nipped round while Sam was at Jess's. Her little boy's one. He had a party. I told you about it. You could have come along.'

She spoke impatiently. He nodded, relieved. He'd forgotten about the party and wondered if he should have gone with her. It hadn't occurred to him. He never went to things like that.

'Tilly Brown,' he repeated. Saying it out loud generated a flicker of unease. The name suddenly had the familiar feel of a long-ago memory. It wasn't unlike the feeling he'd had of Robert Morgan's name reaching out from his past. Tilly Brown.

'I wish you'd found out about Will Jones,' Melinda said.

'If he was the one in the photo,' Webber pointed out, 'then he was next to Edith Stevenson. Ayaan will have had the name from her. She was on his list this morning.'

Melinda shook her head. 'She wouldn't see him. He rang her, but she wasn't playing ball.'

'How do you know?'

'He told me.' Webber thought his jaw must have dropped visibly. Her lips pursed. 'I'm not making this up. He didn't tell me much, but he told me that. I think he thought I knew the woman. Will Jones's name didn't come from Edith Stevenson.'

'Maybe it was the Stevenson woman who sent Ayaan the address. He'll have left his contact details.'

'The email was from Harmer.' Her words were coated in ice.

'But whoever they have and haven't found, Mel ...' He looked at her and saw she was ahead of him. 'They haven't found Joyce Yeatman. And they need to talk to her.'

'I suppose so.' Her expression hardened and he knew the spectre of Suzie Harmer was centre stage once again.

chapter twenty-one

Ahmed surreptitiously rubbed his arms and stamped his feet beneath the table. The hard frost from outside seemed to have seeped into the building, creeping up through the floor. His feet were freezing to the point of numbness. It didn't help that he'd put himself in the draughtiest corner away from the radiator where Suzie Harmer sat leaning her back against the heat. She'd moved there when DI Davis had vacated the spot. Davis and his team had dispersed, though Ahmed could still see the DI in the room across the corridor in a huddle with a group that included Webber. Davis stood facing the door and if Ahmed concentrated hard, he could lip read most of what he said.

He felt a stab of unease about his conversation yesterday with Melinda Webber.

Suzie Harmer flicked through a sheaf of papers. Ahmed glanced across the corridor and saw Davis's lips shape themselves around 'crime scene', and then a moment later, 'toxicology' with a satisfied nod at Webber.

Progress was being made in the search for Jenkinson's killer. He gathered the scraps and squirreled them away.

'Who the fuck's Tilly Brown?' Suzie Harmer's voice jerked him back.

The question hung in the air. She hadn't aimed it at him, but he was the only one who had an answer.

'Um … Tilly Brown,' he said. 'Superintendent Webber gave me the name. Uh …' Hadn't Webber said something else, said he might have another name for them? He tried to pull his mind back to the job in hand. Whatever else Webber had said, he'd only given him the one name. 'He said to see what we could find on Tilly Brown. She was an old school friend of Robert Morgan.'

Suzie rolled her eyes. 'Oh Christ! Not another of his hunches. Saints preserve us from dinosaurs. Someone should pension him off.'

'He gets results,' Ahmed's colleague murmured. It was the usual mantra about Webber – awkward sod to work for but gets results.

Suzie met the comment with a sharp stare. 'And saints preserve us from 20th century crimes. Do we even have a crime scene?'

It was clear she didn't expect a yes, and she didn't get one. They all knew that the scene of Robert Morgan's murder would have told every nuance 30 years ago. Even now, if it had survived, it might have secrets to release, but three decades ago, the investigation had gone down the wrong line and missed what must have been a blazing trail. Now, they'd probably never find out where he'd been killed.

'Except we know it's on their damned patch,' Suzie grumbled referring to their Dorset colleagues who had recently sent on the rest of the case files. Ahmed watched her. She was in a snappy mood this morning. 'It's bad enough doing their job for them, without going off on tangents after old school friends,' she went on, tracing a circle around the name, Tilly Brown.

The colleague beside him leant in to whisper, 'She found the old dinosaur good enough on one count.'

Ahmed coughed long and hard, convinced the words had echoed round the room. Suzie didn't seem to notice.

'Why are we taking the lead on this?' he asked, with a hard glare at the man beside him. Because Suzie was right. The crime scene was hundreds of miles away. It had to be. Robert Morgan hadn't been long dead when the tigers found him, not long enough to have been carted down the length of the country.

'They don't have the resources to spare.' She said it with a sneer, then sighed. 'But also there's the car. It was stolen round here and it found its way back.'

'And took a lead role in a post office raid carried out by three brothers who have no link with any of the rest of it.'

'Yeah well, that's an interesting one because big brother post office, the one who was never caught, gets a mention in that latest batch of case files from down south.'

'Really?' Ahmed stared, surprised. He'd seen the volume of material that had been generated back in 1986; thankfully most of it had been digitised. The publicity surrounding the escaped tigers and the animal rights group had sparked a huge public response.

'Here, Ayaan.' Suzie pushed a piece of paper across the table towards him. 'Check it out. And do it before you go chasing red-herrings for Superintendent Webber. Now, you reckon the neighbour's on the level? Tippet's in the clear?'

'I don't think he drove that car to Dorset.' Ahmed picked his words with care. 'And I'm wondering about Tippet's relationship with Michael Drake, his ex-brother-in-law, if that has a bearing.'

'How so?'

'Tippet can't stand Drake. They worked together for Tippet's father, but Drake was the competent one. Tippet ended up side-lined in his own family firm. I didn't get the impression of any particular animosity the other way, just exasperation. I think Drake tried to stay out of Tippet's way. There's a lot in the original file from way back, from when Tippet accused Drake of killing his sister. It's all in there.'

'Wasn't there a life insurance policy?'

'Yes, but she'd taken it out without telling Drake. That was his version anyway, but it pans out. In fact it was Tippet and his sister who went to a broker together and took out policies that covered both couples. Tippet admitted that his own wife didn't know.'

'But Drake didn't get any money, did he?'

Ahmed shook his head. 'No. She died about six months too soon for it to pay out. The odd thing was that if Drake himself had died at that point, she would have got the money. It was a different sort of policy.'

'Anything in any of this?'

'I did some digging,' said Ahmed. 'Tippet's wife died a couple of years ago. He got a tidy sum out of the policy he took out at the same time.'

Suzie Harmer threw back her head and laughed. 'Christ, Ayaan, don't go finding us another murder.'

Ahmed smiled. 'No, it's not. She was ill for a good while. She died in hospital. Nothing untoward. It's just odd, all the insurance business. Tippet was so antagonistic towards Drake. Not that I've interviewed Tippet or anything but Martyn has and he said he's still holding a grudge. It's in the notes. I just wondered if he knew his sister was dying and got her to take out a policy so he could finger Drake when it happened.'

'That's a bit convoluted. Is there any evidence to support it? Not that we're going to go after Tippet for that after all this time. I just want to know about the car.'

'Ah, well … yes. That's where I'm going with this. When Tippet fingered Drake he claimed his sister had been the one behind the insurance policy business and that Drake must have known all about it. The broker had a different story. He said Tippet's sister was the reluctant one and that it was Tippet in the driving seat.'

'So?'

'Well, it looks like Tippet pushed her into taking out an insurance policy, not the other way round.'

She narrowed her eyes at him. 'OK, I'm thinking tenuous, insignificant and barely circumstantial. Is that the best you have?'

'The car,' he said, with a touch of smugness because he liked the feel of this theory. 'When Quintina Tippet was alive she used to borrow her brother's car. And Tippet didn't seem to mind until she took up with Drake and then he made a real fuss over it, but when he accused Drake, he might have thought …' Ahmed paused. The theory that had felt so good in his head sprouted holes as he tried to articulate it.

'What? Where are you going with this, Ayaan?'

'OK, so maybe … maybe he genuinely thought Drake had taken the car and he didn't say anything because … because he wanted to get him into trouble over it,' he finished in a rush.

After a moment, Suzie said, 'Why would keeping quiet get Drake into trouble?'

'Well … maybe not that, but he was so fixated on Drake. I just think that might be behind why he didn't report the car straight off.'

'Wouldn't he be more likely to report it at once and get Drake picked up for car theft?'

'Yeah, but it doesn't work like that, does it? Family member, used to borrowing the car. It'll get put down to a misunderstanding.' He pulled in a breath. He was sure there was something here to explain away the mini mystery of Tippet's failure to report the theft the night it happened. 'Drinking! He thought Drake was going out drinking … wanted him pulled up and breathalysed.'

'Tippet and Drake weren't working together at that stage, were they? Did they even have much to do with each other?'

'No, Drake stopped working for the Tippets a couple of years after Quintina died. As far as I can work it out, he kept in touch with the parents for a while longer, but not Brad.'

'We're talking a ten year gap,' the man at his side pointed out. 'And it hadn't been Drake who'd been in the habit of taking the car anyway, it was the sister.'

'Yes, that's true, but …' Ahmed found himself wishing he'd rehearsed this theory in private. He might have realised how thin it was.

'Wait a minute,' said Suzie. 'The Ford Tempo was only a couple of years old when it was stolen.'

Ahmed slapped his head. 'Oh yeah. OK, junk that theory.' It was the wrong car. Tippet hadn't bought it until eight years after his sister died. If Drake had had keys, they would have been for Tippet's previous car. 'So big brother post office gets a mention in the files from Dorset, does he?' he said.

'Yes and he's the one who disappeared into thin air after the raid. I want you to chase that. So far there are no known links between the Morgans and the post office raid. We know Morgan was in Dorset in that car boot after he died, so we know the car must have been there, too. Now it looks like big brother post office was there that day. That can't be coincidence.'

◉ ◉ ◉

Webber feigned concentration on the reports that lay open on the desk in front of him while keeping an eye on activity across the corridor. Ahmed was busy with paperwork of some sort, his gaze flicking back and forth between his computer screen and the notepad at his side. Suzie Harmer would leave soon. She'd booked time for a hospital appointment. He wanted to swap information via Ahmed, to find out about Will Jones as he'd promised Melinda, but also to get Joyce Yeatman's name into the cold case enquiry.

The toxicology report focused under his eye. Its subject was Arthur Trent, the driver who'd died in a car with a jammed cruise control. There was satisfaction in being proved right, but mounting anger, too. He could see Trent's sister-in-law … hear her voice as she'd talked about him.

A good family man. Nothing out of the ordinary to most people, but …

A senseless killing that almost felt careless in its execution. The needle mark had been found beneath one of Trent's fingernails. The inescapable conclusion was that Trent had been killed because he knew too much about Jenkinson's death. Webber thought back to the muddy expanse up by the fishing lakes.

'What have you got?' Davis had come into the room, a file in his hand. He looked curiously at Webber as he asked the question, adding, 'You were miles away.'

Webber narrowed his eyes as the thoughts took shape. 'If you were planning a murder and going to dump a body like they dumped Jenkinson, where would you go to get your concrete?'

Davis tipped his head to one side as he considered. 'Canvass the pubs probably. Ask around.'

'But look at the trouble our mystery man got into canvassing for expertise to gridlock the traffic. He might not have wanted to risk that. Maybe he already knew someone.'

'Yeah, but I'd steer clear of someone I knew if I was planning … oh, I see … unless I was going to knock them off, too. You think this is someone that Trent knew.'

Webber pulled a face. 'No, I doubt it. Jenkinson's killing wasn't planned, was it? Not really. He was pulled in and he found out too much. He followed a car up to those fishing lakes.'

'The wrong car, he told Ayaan.'

'Was it, though? He thought it was wrong because there was a woman in it, not just a man, but they'd lost it for long enough that he could have picked up a passenger. OK, so suppose Jenkinson's become a liability. He's done the traffic light thing – I wonder if our mystery man thinks that was kosher – but he's learnt too much, so he's got to go. Dump him in that pit, cover him over, assume he won't be found for decades.'

'And dump his coat in the lake,' murmured Davis.

'Yes, because it's too bright, can't risk it showing through what isn't a very thick layer of concrete.'

'It wasn't properly encased; the body. It was half in the rubble. The concrete hadn't seeped through properly. Wrong sort. It was meant for the wind turbines. The smell would have had it found as soon as they got back to work on that walkway.'

Webber watched as Davis reached out to put down his file,

his gaze losing focus. He wanted to see if Davis's line of thought matched his own or if he was over-thinking it.

'The car thing.' Davis pointed at the toxicology report. 'That's nothing to do with all the traffic bollocks, is it? It's just a rush job to get rid of Trent so he can't finger anyone for the concrete, but what would he know?'

'He might know who paid him the back-hander,' said Webber. 'He might have seen the body in the rubble.'

'And he certainly knew the location,' Davis said. 'But he'd have kept quiet anyway. It was his job on the line.'

'Maybe he wasn't going to keep quiet about murder.'

Davis half nodded, picked up his file again. 'I wonder if he got his pay out,' he said. 'There's no sign of it. No unexplained cash, no bank deposits. Was he done in so he didn't have to be paid?'

Webber shrugged, disappointed. Davis's line of thought had petered out in a cul-de-sac.

Then as he turned away, Davis swung round again. 'No, hang on, that isn't right. Jenkinson's a rush job, you reckon. So the concrete, the lakes, it's all opportunist. And Trent puts himself in the firing line somehow or other, so his killing's even more of a rush job than Jenkinson's.'

Webber allowed himself the ghost of a smile, giving Davis a raised-eyebrows invitation to complete the picture.

'The car … the cruise control thing … That's not opportunistic. That's planned. How do you explain someone doing that if it's a rush job?'

'All I can think of,' said Webber, 'is that it's tried and tested. Our mystery man's done it before.'

chapter twenty-two

Footsteps … the bang of a door. Webber caught a glimpse of Suzie Harmer's profile through the frosted glass before she disappeared.

He didn't like the patterns that swirled in his head. Arthur Trent … Jenkinson … the traffic chaos … the old fishing lakes … their link to the cold case via the car. The car with its link to Robert Morgan; the death that had been a murder all along.

More cars. Jenkinson and his flashlight stunt … Trent in a car with a jammed cruise control. And Joyce Yeatman's husband. Webber had made enough enquiries around Yeatman's death to know the unlikelihood at this distance of distinguishing deliberate sabotage from the disasters and near disasters caused by early manual cruise control systems, but in any case, Gary Yeatman had left a note. Melinda had made a friend of Joyce Yeatman so she could work out what had happened to Pamela Morgan who had also left a note. He'd seen the coroner's report. It was comprehensive. Pamela Morgan had killed herself with an overdose. But he couldn't get that certainty across to Mel. She just said that neither of them had seen the note. Apparently, Joyce Yeatman had never read it all through; didn't know if she still had it. How could anyone not read something like that? He imagined Joyce Yeatman stringing Mel along, keeping her on side, pushing her to reveal details of more recent cases. No, that was paranoia. Mel wouldn't miss anything like that. She knew what she was doing. He wasn't thinking straight, there was too much in his head.

The office walls pressed in, the space made gloomy by the winter weather. He grabbed his coat and made for the door.

'Ayaan,' he called. Ahmed's head jerked up and turned his way. 'With me. Get your coat.'

Webber braced himself against the rain that whipped across him in sheets and, taking advantage of a snarl-up in the traffic, zigzagged between the vehicles and jogged towards the café where he'd sat with Trent's sister-in-law. He didn't look back until under the shelter of an awning, and saw Ahmed, head down, sprinting to catch up.

'Grab that corner table,' Webber said over his shoulder as he pushed through the door and headed for the counter, seeing at once that his concern was unnecessary. The impression of a crowded space had been the condensation misting the windows. There would be no fight for the one table that afforded a degree of privacy.

'Uh ... thanks.' Ahmed radiated both surprise and unease as Webber thumped the coffee down in front of him.

'I needed to get out, clear my head,' Webber told him. 'And I've some intel for you.'

'Yes, you said you'd another name, as well as Tilly Brown. Is it another of his school friends?'

His? Webber frowned. 'Did I say one of Robert Morgan's friends? I meant his wife, Pamela. Tilly Brown left the school a few years before they did. I assume her parents moved away.'

'Oh, then Robert Morgan probably wouldn't have known her at all. He didn't go to school here. He came over from Canada.'

Webber nodded. 'Yes, I remember. So have you found Tilly Brown?'

Ahmed shook his head. 'I ... um ... I haven't looked yet. I've been after the missing brother; the eldest. Big brother post office, the one who was never caught after the raid.'

'He's surfaced, has he?'

'Not as such, but his name cropped up in the Robert Morgan files from Dorset.'

'Really?' Webber, about to switch to Will Jones, pulled back surprised and signalled Ahmed to go on.

Ahmed blew out a sigh. 'It's barely a mention. It was never followed up. You know they went all out to make a cast-iron case. They did house to house, went in all the pubs, big public appeal. They were snowed under. The whole circus thing and the animal rights had split the community even before all of it kicked off. Everyone wanted to have a say. It's something from a guy in a pub. It was taken as drunken rambling, someone with a grudge wanting to put the boot in. The guy was a known petty felon, much like big brother post office. I've an address from 30 years ago and that's about it. It was one scrap of intel out of an avalanche. I can't even find out who recorded it.'

'The address, is it still current?'

'I was just about to make a call when you … uh … when we came out. And I was going to get on to Tilly Brown after that.'

'OK, give me a quick update. I haven't had a chance to catch up today.'

'I … um … thought you were looking busy. I heard a report had come back about Tom; that you've found where he was killed?'

Webber relaxed as he sipped his drink, amused more than irritated to hear Ahmed trying to pump him for information. It was understandable, but he didn't want him distracted from his job which he would be if he were to tell him what they were finding. Jenkinson had kept reams of data online. They'd found no computers in his rooms but he had an account with one of the large cloud storage companies. Davis had had to get heavy with them to prevent the files being junked. Jenkinson had hacked his way to free use of what should have been a premium account. The files, all encrypted, were fighting their corner for scarce analytic resources. There was a part of him that longed to pull Ahmed into the team and set him to work, but he knew he couldn't.

'We're getting there, Ayaan,' he said. 'We'll have the bastard who did it. Now tell me about Will Jones. Who is he?'

'He was ring-leader of the animal rights group gaoled after Morgan's death,' Ahmed told him. 'He's known to have come back to this area when he was released. He rented a room, stayed less than a month then disappeared leaving his stuff and a pile of debts. He's the nearest we have to a suspect at the moment, him and big brother post office.'

Webber buried his face in his cup, hoping the shock didn't show. This man had approached the Yeatmans and been warned off. Joyce claimed not to know why. And the Yeatmans had known the Morgans. And now Mel was mixed up with Joyce.

He struggled to keep his voice level. 'That's interesting. It fits with the other name I have for you. More old friends of the Morgans.' He gave Ahmed the outline.

'Joyce and Gary Yeatman? That's interesting.' Ahmed echoed his words back at him. 'That links Robert Morgan's friends at the time with the animal rights people. But why would he do that?'

'Why would who do what?'

'If you'd been instrumental in killing someone like that, why would you go back to his friends afterwards?'

'Maybe Jones found out that he'd been sent down for a killing that hadn't been to do with the tigers at all. Look into Yeatman. Why did Jones go to him? Did he go to any of the others? Look at them all, especially Edith Stevenson. Joyce Yeatman has an old school photo of her husband's. Someone next to Stevenson has been cut out of it. She thinks it might be Jones.'

Ahmed had put down his coffee and was scribbling furiously. When he looked up, Webber could see the question in his puzzled expression and provided the answer before it could be asked.

'Joyce Yeatman is someone my wife got to know recently.' He wanted to tell Ahmed to keep Melinda's name out of it, but it wasn't something he could ask outright. He'd have to hope that Ahmed's natural instinct to keep on an even keel with Suzie would do the trick.

'Oh, right …' Ahmed's pen hovered but didn't touch down. 'Did they meet at the fishing lakes?'

Webber felt the thump of his heart in his chest. 'Why on earth would they have met at the fishing lakes?'

'Oh, it was just that I remember Mrs Webber's name on the witness list from that weekend … the bystanders up at the site. She told me about you being out together when the call came in.'

Webber thought back to Mel wrapping Sam in his thick jacket and insisting they accompany him. The PCSOs had rounded everyone up. Mel had been caught in the trawl. But he'd skimmed that list, hadn't he? He couldn't think of any credible reason for Mel's new friend to have been out there that drizzly Sunday.

'Are you saying Joyce Yeatman was on that list?' he asked Ahmed.

'No, I don't remember the name.'

Swallowing the urge to snap, *Then why scare the shit out of me by saying it*, Webber looked up at the plate glass where beads of condensation coalesced into tiny reservoirs that swelled until they burst their banks and skittered down the smooth surface. He waited a moment then stood up 'Right then. Back to it. And let me know about Tilly Brown.'

As he strode towards the door, he was aware of Ahmed almost upending his chair as he leapt to follow.

◎ ◎ ◎

Webber was barely back at his desk when a call came through.

'Mr Webber, I'm so sorry to bother you at work.' It was a young woman's voice. 'I'm ringing from play school.'

An icy hand scrunched his insides. 'What's happened? Where's Sam?'

'No, no. He's fine. Sam's here with me. It's just that I'm new and …' Deliberately, Webber drew in a slow breath as he took in the words. Someone had been called away. The woman was on her own … some query she couldn't answer. He glanced at the clock. Surely all the children would have been collected by now.

'When someone who isn't the parent comes to collect a child, when we don't know in advance, we have to check. It's the procedure. I'm sure it's all right. Mrs Webber sent a note with the woman but I don't know her and Mrs Webber's phone's off and yours is the other contact number.'

'Yes, of course. You were right to call. Who is it who's come for Sam?'

'It's …' He heard the rustle of a piece of paper. 'It's Mrs Joyce …'

'No!' Webber cut across her. Shock pricked his skin in a rush of retreating blood. 'Keep Sam there with you,' he barked into the phone. 'Don't let him out of your sight. I'm on my way.'

chapter twenty-three

....

'Grandpa Larry's not here,' the voice said.

Ahmed felt a surge of optimism as he heard the words. It was a young girl's voice but the name was clearly familiar. The Larry who had dropped big brother post office's name into a statement all those years ago was still at the same address.

'Is your mum or dad there?'

A pause, then a sing-song response. 'Well, I'm not on my own.'

It sounded rehearsed. He hoped he wasn't going to have to escalate this and alert a child protection team. 'Who's there with you?'

'Teddy and Tinker but they're asleep.'

'Can you wake them up?'

'No, I won't. They're very tired.'

'OK, if I tell you my name again and my phone number, will you ask one of them to ring me back?'

She giggled. 'Not Tinker.'

He supposed Tinker was a pet of some sort; maybe Teddy was too. Speaking slowly and clearly, he spelt out his name and recited his number. From the grunts and huffs of concentration she was making an attempt to write it down but he wasn't confident the message would get anywhere.

'I'll ring back in a while,' he told her before saying goodbye.

He'd told Webber he would get on to Tilly Brown after he'd made that call. The thought sparked a swell of resentment. He'd been made to look like he'd taken an early break but only managed to choke down half a cup of coffee. Webber himself had raced off out again almost as soon as they were back. Suzie had left for some appointment or other. His remaining colleague had made it abundantly clear that he wasn't best pleased to be landed with a mountain of old case files while he, Ahmed, swanned off with the boss.

In his head he could hear Melinda Webber. Without putting it into words she'd managed to express sympathy that he'd been forced to work with Suzie. The more the conversation came back to him, the more uncomfortable he felt about the things he'd told her. No matter what Suzie's failings might be in other directions, at least she didn't talk in riddles and keep everyone guessing. He'd rather work for her than for either of the Webbers.

He glanced at the phone. His brief exchange with the little girl hardly counted as a call. Tilly Brown could wait. She was just one of Webber's hunches along with the new name, Joyce Yeatman. He'd made the appropriate note but they could both wait until he'd arrived at a satisfactory conclusion on Larry from the old statements. Larry, after all, offered the glimmer of a link between the post office raid and Robert Morgan's death. He could be the key to the whole case. Suzie Harmer had homed in on that scrap of intel from Dorset right away. He would have something solid to report to her when she returned.

◉ ◉ ◉

Webber could see nothing through the kitchen window but the haze of lights from next door through a dank evening drizzle. He swished the knife blades through the hot soapy water in the sink and rinsed them under the tap. The dishwasher thrummed but Mel didn't like these knives in there; the detergent blunted the edges. For years he'd been tactically absent-minded about it, tossing the knives in with everything else, claiming to have forgotten if she noticed. Washing them by hand made for a futile gesture in amongst everything else, but at least it would be one less thing for her to have a go about. He laid them in a row on the draining board and turned his attention to the pan that he hadn't been able to cram into the machine. As he laboured with a wire brush, he heard Melinda's steps down the staircase and, as a backdrop, the high fluting sounds of Sam singing himself to sleep.

Behind it all, the words echoed in his head. *It's Mrs Joyce ...*

Melinda's voice floated through. She was on the phone again, laughing. He paused to listen, a frown creasing his brow. Her father. Visiting the in-laws was an ordeal yet to be faced. He hadn't asked outright but presumed they knew about Harmer. As Melinda had said when he'd tried to touch on keeping things quiet, 'It's not the sort of thing that can be brushed under the carpet. If we're not upfront about it, all it means is that people talk behind our backs.' At least she'd said 'we'.

He balanced the pan upside down on top of the knives as she wound up her call. Drying his hands on a tea-towel, he went through to the living room.

She met him with a hard stare. 'I feel really bad about Jess.'

He said again, 'I thought she said Joyce.' He'd lost count of the number of times he'd said it. If he'd let the woman finish what she was saying, he'd have heard Mrs Jess Eberhart which he surely wouldn't have misheard as Mrs Joyce Yeatman. Mel's good and trusted friend, Jess, had waited at playschool to ask him what the hell he was doing implying she wasn't a fit person to look after his child? He'd apologised at the time, then later by phone with Melinda standing over him. For all her indignation, she'd revelled in his discomfort, going out of her way to call people to tell them what he'd done.

Part of him wanted to feel anger, to tell her to wrap it up, to shout that she should take her share of the blame for her illicit investigation that was at the root of his paranoia. But the fact remained that he'd put himself irretrievably in the wrong and ought to welcome any means that Melinda could find to even the balance. Once she'd deemed him to have repaid the debt, maybe they could resume normal life. Even as the thought formed, he knew he was kidding himself. Life never balanced out as neatly as that.

He tossed the tea-towel on to the back of a chair; watched her gaze track its flight, half expected her to carp at him about returning it to its hook in the kitchen. She tightened her lips but said nothing. He supposed they would work their way through this. There would be no dramatic reconciliation. Everything swung wildly out of kilter, but it would settle in time. All he had to do was avoid tipping the balance while it was still too new, too raw. If she really wanted to leave him, she'd have gone by now. She'd never been one to shilly-shally over decisions. He had to hold on to that.

'I've persuaded Joyce to have a look for that note,' she said.

He tensed as he heard the name, and looked across to see her pulling the boards from behind the TV.

'Good. That's good.' He didn't know what else to say. He'd be reassured if Joyce Yeatman actually produced the note. He was certain it would make everything clear; less certain that the Yeatman woman wasn't hiding something. How could she have left it unread all these years?

'So you thought I'd send Joyce to collect Sam, did you? A woman he's never met? Someone I hardly know?'

He shivered at the coldness in her voice. 'No, of course not. I knew you wouldn't.'

'For someone who's supposed to be good at listening, good at reading people, this has been a real cock-up, hasn't it? Are you losing your touch? What else are you going to mess up? Are you going to be out of a job?'

'No, I'm bloody well not! For fuck's sake, it was Sam. Of course my judgement was out. You've got yourself involved with this woman. You don't know her from Adam. And now her name's cropped up in a murder enquiry. I was fucking terrified for Sam! Can you fucking blame me?'

He couldn't hold back the outburst and found his fists clenched as he stared at her. She looked taken aback but her expression was bright, animated. Was she amused? He couldn't read her.

'Enough with the swearing,' she said, her tone mild. 'Sam might not be asleep yet.'

'Sorry.'

'So you thought Joyce was trying to kidnap Sam. What did you think she'd done with me?'

'With …?' He stopped. He hadn't given her a thought. His head had been full of Sam.

She took three strides across the carpet, stood facing him for a moment before putting her hand on his chest and giving him a sharp push. Off balance he fell back into the chair. He stared up into her face; still couldn't read her. Unexpectedly, she held out her hands, taking hold of his.

'Martyn, I don't think you get it,' she said. Her tone remained mild, her grip on his hands firm. 'I don't think you get how bloody angry I am with you.'

He wanted to say he did, that he understood, that he'd make amends in whatever way she wanted. As he opened his mouth to speak, something in her expression made him shut it again.

'This is not some stupid transgression that'll blow over in a few months.' He could sense her anger, but couldn't hear it in her voice. 'This is going to be with us forever. We can't move past this, Martyn. We have to live with it.'

'But you won't leave me, will you? Please, Mel, I can't lose you.' It felt like the wrong thing to say and the wrong time to say it, but he couldn't stop the words tumbling out.

She drew in a breath, narrowed her eyes. 'If you want the truth, Martyn, I'm too bloody angry to know.'

But he'd started and couldn't stop. He found himself pleading with her. 'We can't throw it all away. It's too precious.'

'The trouble is, Martyn, I'm not the one doing the throwing. That was you. I have to work out whether or not I can live with it. And if I stay it won't be for some sham of a marriage. If we're to get through this, you're going to have to buck your ideas up.'

His mouth felt dry. He didn't know what she was asking. 'I love you, Mel,' he blurted out, semi-shocked by his own words; remembering the easy way that Davis had spoken with affection to his wife on the phone.

Melinda looked surprised. Her expression hardened. He kept a firm grip on her hands. 'I'm not saying it, Martyn,' she snapped. 'You don't deserve to hear it. And never mind what I have or haven't decided. What about you? Have you written off this marriage?'

'What?' He stared, fought to find the words to say what should have been obvious. Of course he hadn't given up on their marriage. He was the one begging her to stay. 'No. No, of course not. Mel, if I could undo things …'

'Don't give me any garbage about changing things that can't be changed. You're going to have to do better than that.'

Sensing that she was about to back away, he held tight to her hands, trying to work out what she wanted, desperate not to hear himself come out with something truly pathetic like telling her he'd washed the knives by hand.

'Mel … What do you want me to do?'

'Let go of my sodding hands for starters,' she snapped, jerking them from his grasp and standing upright. She stretched her head back and muttered that leaning over him was making her back ache. 'And you can bloody well …' She paused, glanced towards the stairs and lowered her voice. 'Bloody well stop treading on eggshells round me. Have you any idea how irritating it is!'

'Sorry.'

'And stop bloody apologising.'

That seemed unfair as she'd spent the afternoon demanding that he apologised to all and sundry for his mistake over Sam. He supposed it was part of the penance that he be battered with inconsistent and contradictory demands. Opening his hands in a gesture of helplessness, he asked again, 'What do you want me to do?'

'How about you stop treating me like some favourite little sister who's a bit simple and has to be humoured at every turn?'

'I'm not, Mel … I …'

'That little bitch gets pregnant …' She spoke over him, her voice rising again, 'and I have to live like a nun. What's that about?'

'What!' His mouth dried. Was she saying …? If he hadn't been sitting already, his legs would have given way. A seam of resentment came close to the surface. He saw himself creeping back into the house the evening after Harmer's visit – only about ten days ago, though it felt like months – not knowing what to expect, finding her encased in an impenetrable shell, presenting a normal face to the world but cold as ice to him. Sam's cot had been through in their bedroom, the spare bed made up. He'd said nothing, just waited until the small hours, until she was sound asleep then crept into bed. She'd been annoyed to wake beside him, but Sam had been right there standing up in his cot jabbering at them, so she hadn't been able to make anything of it. He'd employed the same tactic the next night, and the following day Sam's cot was back in its own room. But every time he touched her, contriving to hug her and Sam together, she'd tensed and turned away. He wasn't the one keeping his distance.

But this wasn't the time to overthink things. He hadn't misheard her, nor misunderstood the look on her face. He was on his feet, reaching to pull her close. She pushed him off and shook her head. He caught a gleam of triumph in her eye. Was this just a ruse to wind him up? What was she playing at?

'Come on, Martyn,' she said. 'Let's have a bit of thought here.

You reckon we're going to rip all our clothes off and shag like rabbits, do you?'

With emotion boiling inside him, he fought to hold back the desire that would drive him mad if she was just toying with him. He didn't know whether to shout or plead; hadn't a clue where she was coming from. Years of training kicked in. Remove the passion, keep it practical. He heard himself say, 'I was going to close the curtains first.'

She laughed. A real laugh. He stared at her, thought he must look like some kind of doleful puppy, but couldn't do anything about it.

'This is going to be on my terms,' she said, 'not yours. Sit down and cool off. We'll give Sam time to settle.'

He swallowed against a dry throat as he let his legs give way and thumped down into the chair.

'While we're waiting …' Her voice was cool, but the gleam still sparkled in her eye. He had to dig his fingernails into his palms to stop himself reaching out for her. He was under no illusions that she knew exactly what she was doing to him.

Her gaze ran over the lists on the board as though her whole attention was there and not on him at all. He sensed again the reckless streak in her that had kept him so on edge. She wasn't just looking for the truth about Pamela Morgan anymore; she was after Robert Morgan's killer. She was determined to beat Suzie Harmer to it. He wanted to tell her it didn't matter; tell her to stop now before things became any more entangled. Because she couldn't outpace Harmer's team and their access to official records. The minute Mel found anything of value, he would have to feed it back into the enquiry, just like he had with what she'd found so far.

She turned to him, gave him a speculative stare as she ran her tongue around her lips. He felt frozen to the chair, unable to move. Her glance flicked towards the stairs. The gentle crooning had stopped a while ago. Webber had consciously to tell himself not to hold his breath.

Her gaze returned to him, a steady stare, then she looked at the clock. 'We'll give him a few more minutes,' she said, not meeting his eye as she spoke. They both knew that Sam was fast asleep. 'And while we're waiting ...' She picked up a marker pen and twisted one of the boards towards her. 'So Joyce's name has cropped up in a murder enquiry, has it? Robert Morgan, I assume. Tell me all about it?'

chapter twenty-four

Webber sat at his desk, a set of aerial photographs spread out in front of him. He slid them one way then the other, completing the jigsaw of overlapping images. Nothing leapt out at him. He supposed he shouldn't have expected it to, but he would get the shots pinned up in plain sight; let the collective subconscious loose on them.

Publicity surrounding Jenkinson's death had been muted; both Jenkinson and his mother had records that auto-labelled them as dregs not worthy of real outrage. The news that Trent's death had been reclassified as suspicious hadn't made much of a dent either. Trent was too old and too ordinary to create a splash, although a note had arrived from a psychic offering his services to scan what he'd called the 'vortex of evil that surrounds the death site'. Caught by the phraseology, Webber had checked the letter and seen it referred to the road where Trent died. He would have been more impressed if it had been the fishing lakes the guy had homed in on. 'Vortex of evil' would have been an apt tag. The grass and shrubs blurred as his eyes lost focus.

John Farrar had been on the phone earlier, harassed over myriad issues, but beneath a grumpy veneer had wanted to talk. Webber had been able to report a slow but inexorable chipping away at the edges of both Jenkinson's and Trent's last hours, and a gradual composing of a picture of Jenkinson himself and his activities since he'd come to York.

'No suspect we can put a name to so far, but I'm confident he's in the net. We just have to find him.'

'Him?' Farrar had queried. 'You're confident it's a man?'

'It's still open,' Webber told him, remembering the exchange with Ahmed in the interview room almost two weeks ago. ... *when we get near enough to see, there's two of them, and it's a woman driving* .... 'You know we've found a stack of data online. It's not straightforward. We're not shouting about it but it's clear now that Jenkinson was involved in far bigger things than petty car crime.'

'You mean all the time he was being mentored through the "Kids with Potential" scheme.'

'Yes, every step of the way. And I don't want the wrong angle on that getting out into the press. It'll just be more ammunition to have what funding's left pulled.'

'Not a great advertisement for the scheme,' Farrar had said dryly.

'That's where you're wrong.' Webber's teeth had clenched as he'd heard the words emerge. Farrar didn't like being baldly contradicted. But he'd started so he ploughed on. 'All the signs were that Ayaan Ahmed was turning him. No doubt he started on the scheme with very different ambitions, but by the end of that first year he had real respect for Ayaan. If we'd only known what size of fish we might have been reeling in.'

'So you think his Mr Big found him out?'

'We've found nothing either way on that yet. And nothing links the Mr Big, if he exists, to the mystery man of the traffic lights scam. Might be the same person, might be unrelated. But one of them was responsible for Jenkinson's death. If this is an organised crime hit, we could be talking hired assassin.'

'Do you think that's likely?'

'On balance, no. It was all too hurried, too panicked.'

He ended the call and let his mind drift over the angles, the fishing lakes, the gravel pits ... he thought he might talk it over with Mel later. The thought suffused him with a warm glow.

'What are you looking so content about?'

The voice made Webber jump and pulled him back to the present. Suzie Harmer leant in the doorway. He gave her a half smile. He knew he was a long way from being out of the woods, but was more relaxed than he had been since all this had blown up. She was right. Content was exactly what he felt.

'No law against contentment as far as I know.'

'I hear you have a possible crime scene for Jenkinson's murder,' she said.

'It's pretty clear he was killed where he was found up at the fishing lakes.'

Both Suzie and Ahmed were deliberately being kept out of the loop on the extent of Jenkinson's underground network. He didn't trust Ahmed not to do some unsanctioned digging if he discovered the extent of Jenkinson's betrayal.

'Ayaan's pretty cut up about the whole thing. He's forever hassling people for the latest on Jenkinson.'

'You can't blame him. He put a lot of work in with that family and it seemed to be leading somewhere. I mean Jenkinson wasn't heading towards model citizenship, but without that scheme he might have dropped out of school and spent his life a typical brick-through-window merchant.'

'Better educated criminals? That's not going to persuade anyone to retain the grants.' She pulled in a breath as though to say something more, but her gaze dropped.

Webber waited, curious to see what was to come. She shot a glance around as though checking the corridor, looked at him again. 'So … uh … you're OK, are you?' Her tone made it sound almost like an apology.

'Yes, I'm fine.' Webber sat back in his chair, fingers laced. This woman carried his child, but there had been too much stress and hassle to confront the reality of it. Now it felt weird in a way it hadn't before, but he wasn't lying. He felt fine, relaxed even. After a moment it occurred to him he should return the query. 'How are you?'

She pulled a face. 'I've felt ropey this week.' She pushed herself away from the door frame and came inside, sitting down to face him. He hadn't meant his enquiry to be an invitation to come in.

'Should you be here at all?'

'It's only hormones.' She waved her hand in a dismissive gesture. 'It'll pass. There are plenty worse off. At least I'm not with a fleeing convoy of refugees trying to cross a border under fire or anything.'

She looked across at him, giving him a flash of the sunny smile that was her trademark. Stray memories of overheard comments replayed in his head ... *Sunny Suzie ...everyone's friend ... just as long as she has things her own way ...*

Up to very recently he'd liked Suzie. Everyone did. She was hard not to like. And despite everything this was the same Suzie, efficient, bright and mostly straightforward, not trying to hide the discomforts of her pregnancy but not asking for sympathy. He smiled back at her. 'How's Ayaan doing?'

'OK. He's good at his job. Can I send him to Dorset?'

'What? Why?' The abrupt change of tack disconcerted him.

She told him how Ahmed had tracked down a man called Larry who had given a statement to the escaped tigers enquiry almost thirty years ago. 'Tried to give a statement,' she amended. 'As far as we can unravel it, the guy was drunk. Can't blame anyone. Whatever he was saying must have seemed way off-beam and the name wouldn't have meant anything.'

'Big brother post office,' Webber murmured. 'But the post office would have been hit by the time they were doing door to door down there.'

'Sure, yeah, but it was hundreds of miles away and nothing to link it.'

'The records have been digitized, haven't they?'

She curled her lip. 'Kind of. Crappy scanning for the most part. It'll be a slog but this name cropping up ... that's promising. And we're lucky the guy's still around. Ahmed found the family. His daughter and grandkids still live in the same house, but the guy himself is in a home. Compos mentis but deaf. We can't do anything over the phone.'

'You could ask someone local to go and get a statement.'

She gave him a pleading setter look. 'They're busy. They won't want to take it on. They'll skimp it. It'll need some work to get anything out of an ancient ex-drunk. Ayaan'll get everything there is to get. This could be the key to whole thing. And ... uh ... we'll get after that name you gave Ayaan. Tilly Brown. I'll get them on to it today.'

He read the whole story into the slight pause. They'd pushed Brown aside as irrelevant, only kept her on the list at all because he'd fed them the name, and now Suzie was kicking herself that she had nothing positive on Brown to offer him. He might have used it against her yesterday, but he and Melinda between them had moved things on beyond that sort of pettiness. And if he was honest, old school friends did look like an irrelevance in amongst everything else. He wouldn't have deployed his resources differently.

'No, don't stress over it,' he told her. 'The line you're on looks more promising.'

She looked relieved, must have expected the reprimand. He felt a moment's disappointment that she hadn't thought better of him. He remembered Melinda comment as she'd run her gaze over the name.

They don't think Tilly Brown's important, do they?

He hadn't contradicted her, hadn't really been paying attention to anything except answering her questions, telling her way more than he should have about the case. But of course she was right. Tilly Brown wasn't important to the official enquiry, not with a possible link between Robert Morgan and the eldest brother from the post office raid.

While he was on duty, his priority had to be Tom Jenkinson, but off duty, he could help Mel to tie all the loose ends around

Pamela Morgan. They'd find Tilly Brown on their own without Harmer's shadow sitting between them, and maybe this old school friend, number six of the group of five, would be the catalyst that persuaded the Yeatman woman to hand over Pamela's suicide note.

Looking down at his desk, the aerial photographs focussed in front of him. The fishing lakes, the old gravel pits, the surrounding terrain unusable for being too boggy and unstable. The deep ruts of the vehicle were still visible despite the incessant rain. The tracks showed where Trent must have driven his lorry to tip concrete over a body that had still been breathing. They already had a record of all that. He wasn't sure what he'd expected to see from this angle, but the traffic helicopter had been over-flying the site anyway and he'd asked them to photograph it.

'OK,' he said to Suzie Harmer, 'send Ayaan to Dorset, but don't let him be all week over it.'

chapter twenty-five

Friday morning Ahmed arrived at work on the cusp of being late, lead running in his veins. He'd spent the whole of Thursday on a trip to Dorset to interview an old man called Larry Scott. The motorways had been busy, visibility poor. It had been close to midnight before he was back in York where he'd fallen into bed too tired to write up his notes. He tucked himself away at the edge of the room hoping to escape notice.

Larry Scott had not been an easy witness. Apart from having to conduct the interview at full volume to counter Larry's bad hearing, he found the man had embroidered his memories of the tiger incident over the years, embellishing it into a tall tale with which to entertain strangers.

As he'd taken in the ravaged features, the outward signs of long dependency on alcohol, it had seemed wildly optimistic to ask Larry to recall detail from 30 years ago. 'In 1986,' he'd said, 'you gave some information to a police enquiry.'

The old man's face had lit up. 'That's right. The business with the tigers. I remember it like it was yesterday.'

It had been an encouraging start. Larry had been caught up in the extensive trawl for witnesses and information to bury the animal rights group. 'I saw it all,' Larry had told him. 'I'd seen all the faces in the photos and more besides. I'd not only seen them, I'd heard them plotting. If they'd listened to me the whole tragedy might not have happened. The whole gang of them it was, round a table, voices low. I could hear in those days. Heard the lot.'

That had been the point Ahmed knew he was in for the long haul. Larry's contemporary statement had been skeletal, no hint he'd seen or heard any of the people the police had actively been looking for. It was the mention of big brother post office by name that shone out like a beacon 30 years later, but all he'd said about it at the time was that he'd overheard the man on the phone talking about a car.

It had been when Ahmed had pushed on both the name and the car that he'd had a reaction. Larry's face had paled. Suddenly he'd been remembering the real events not his later embellishments.

Larry's scrap of a statement at the time had been ascribed to one petty criminal trying to put the boot in another, which implied that the name had been run through whatever systems existed in the mid-80s and unearthed the eldest brother and his record, though not at that point his role in the post office raid.

The topics Ahmed had battled through with Larry were those passing mentions of an overheard phone call and a car.

He had Larry on tape declaiming, 'That's what I said!'

There had been a measure of triumph as the real memory had surfaced.

'His exact words. "That's what I said!" There was a crowd, see, lots of noise, but he raised his voice when he said that … excited by spotting this car, he was. That's what made me take notice. Then he said "pulling it" and I thought he meant the car, but then he says, "a week". I think it was a week; might have been a month. It was time. It made me see he wasn't talking about pulling a car. Different sort of pulling.'

Larry had been in full flow, delighted to have someone show interest in his old tales. 'I can see his face now,' he'd said. 'Smile as wide as the Frome. That's why I had a good dekko, the way he jumped when he saw it. I thought I was going to see something special.'

When Ahmed asked him to look at photographs of cars the vibe had changed. As he'd put a photograph of a Ford Tempo in front of him, Larry had tensed and shivered, saying, 'After all this time? How can I remember anything about how it looked on a dark road?'

'Dark road?' Ahmed had said. 'Surely it was in a well-lit pub car park.'

Larry Scott had nursed a key piece of information, but he had no credibility as a witness after all these years.

Ahmed pulled his thoughts back to the briefing that was happening around him. All eyes were focussed on Davis and Webber at the far end of the room. He allowed himself to stretch and surrender to an extravagant yawn, familiar patterns running past him as he tipped his head – the busy office walls with their notices thumbtacked haphazardly, the flaking paint of the ceiling, down again as the yawn subsided, catching sight of a whole new set of pictures on the big board, the gravel pits from the air – what was that about?

Through the crowd, he met the narrowed eyes of Suzie Harmer giving him a hard stare. He pulled himself upright with a mouthed, 'Sorry.'

He'd returned to find Suzie on her own with the heap of old files. That was fine because it meant the other enquiry, the real enquiry, was soaking up resources as it closed on Tom's killer.

He tried to concentrate on what they were saying. No solid suspects, but useful work on reconstructing Tom's last days … last weeks … his whole time in York. Computer files had a brief mention but someone said something about analysis and changed tack. It depressed him to listen. Tom hadn't turned a corner. He'd used his opportunity to open the wrong doors. His gaze tracked up and down those aerial shots, the scrubland, the trees, the muddy expanse by the walkway foundation. He waited for Davis or Webber to refer to them, to explain what they were doing there.

'What do you think, Ayaan?'

Davis's voice jerked his attention back to the briefing. Suzie was standing now, in the cramped corner that was all they'd been able to carve out for the cold case. They'd moved on from Tom's murder, the new photographs ignored. Someone had asked Suzie about Morgan. She was going through their suspects list.

'Uh … yes … no …' He struggled upright.

Suzie had him pinned with that hard stare but she was helping him out. Her index finger lay across Pamela Morgan's name.

'Pamela Morgan's obviously in the frame.' He played for time as his brain caught up. 'But we don't fancy her for it. No one was looking for alibis at the time, but hers looks pretty solid. She wasn't in Dorset.'

'Doesn't mean she didn't get someone else to do it,' Davis said.

'There's the suicide,' Ahmed added. 'That was odd. Fifteen years later. Could have been bad conscience. But she's still an outsider.'

'Will Jones is a better bet,' Suzie put in. She gave Ahmed a brief glare, then drew attention back to her list 'And we've added big brother post office now we know he was in Dorset at the time.'

Ahmed thought back to Larry's face when he'd shown him the image on the small screen. It hadn't been easy to find a picture of a Ford Tempo at all, never mind one that showed up well enough on his phone, but Larry had reacted.

Suzie was outlining it. He made himself concentrate. 'What we're thinking,' she said, 'is that the overheard phone call was big brother post office pulling the date of the raid forward by a week. It's a bit of a leap but it fits with what we have.' Ahmed contemplated their sparse information base. They had so little, it wasn't hard to fit any theory to it.

'It's the timing,' Suzie went on. 'The big money in that post office was on a fortnightly cycle. To make sense of hitting it, they should have gone for the week before or the week after. It's clear from the investigation that the brothers had watched the place. So why hit it when they did? Why go for the wrong week unless something else cropped up, say like the chance of grabbing the perfect getaway car? I know it's a stretch but now we have this guy in Dorset saying that the brother spotted a car and got excited over it, and it sounds like it was Tippet's car. That's right, isn't it, Ayaan?'

'He's hopeless as a witness,' Ahmed said. 'He can't tell what really happened from stories he's made up over the years, but the car thing was new, something that came back to him when I got him down to the hard facts of what he'd said at the time.'

'It puts the car in Dorset,' said Suzie. 'All we had to start with was the car stolen from Tippet's drive, then at the post office, then 30 years later in the gravel pit. All within a fairly small radius. This puts it several hundred miles south at the time Morgan was killed. On paper, that car had the best part of three decades to have stuff shoved in its boot. Well … obviously it didn't. It was dumped soon after the robbery, but without Larry Scott's story, the brothers could have killed Morgan in Dorset, come back in their own car, nicked Tippet's to do the raid and shoved the evidence from the murder in the boot.'

As he listened, Ahmed's eye was drawn again to the aerial photographs of the fishing lakes and surrounding scrubland. The gravel pit where they'd found the car looked smaller from the high angle, picture-postcard pretty, the reflective surface taking away the cold feeling of depth, of darkness. It was a vile place. He shuddered, repelled at the thought of anyone choosing to relax by that stretch of water.

'… be in later to pick it up. You and Ayaan need to catch her for a word …'

Ahmed's gaze snapped back to the briefing. Catch who? It wasn't Suzie who had him under close scrutiny this time. It was Webber. He swallowed against a dry throat. Concentrate.

The briefing was all but over. The real enquiry was revving up to get to work. He and Suzie would be on their own again soon. Someone had asked about Gary Yeatman, the newest name on their list.

'Turns out he knew Will Jones.' Webber answered the speaker, but his glance flicked to Ahmed. 'And he was at school with Pamela Morgan. It gives us a link between Morgan and the animal rights group.'

People stood up to leave. General conversation broke out. Ahmed, staying put, didn't realise at first that Webber had remained behind. He looked up to meet an unsmiling stare. Webber signalled him across with a jerk of his head.

'What did you see there, Ayaan?' Webber pointed at the aerial photographs.

'Uh … nothing. I was just having a look. I hadn't seen them before.'

'You were engrossed in them. Why?'

Ahmed could only shrug. 'They give me the creeps. There's something not right about them.'

'What? What's not right?' Webber's stare bored into him.

Ahmed cleared his throat and struggled to articulate the unease with which the pictures filled him. 'They look so … so peaceful, so quiet. But some bastard buried Tom alive in the middle of that lot. I was wondering how anyone could think of fishing where something like that had happened.'

'Hmm.' Webber fixed him with a look as though checking that he was hiding nothing, then he seemed to lose interest, his stare turning to the photographs.

Ahmed watched the movement of Webber's eyes as they tracked up and down, back and forth. He glanced again himself. He'd heard about the letter from the psychic. *Vortex of evil.* It would make a good label for this collection.

chapter twenty-six

It was mid-afternoon. The monochrome gloom from outside let in a premature dusk on which the overhead lights could make no dent. Ahmed screwed up his eyes and fought a series of yawns. Trying to pull sense from a set of documents had never felt such an uphill struggle. He'd given up trying to skim the text for general meaning. His brain simply wasn't taking anything in. But he was determined to get another piece of the Morgan jigsaw in place. There were pearls buried in this avalanche; there had to be. But not only had he to find them, he had to avoid missing them. Swimming into focus in front of his eyes, he saw yet another account from someone who had been caught in the 30-year-old net following the release of the tigers.

Before he could fix his concentration on it, the sound of footsteps caught his attention. Voices approached from down the corridor. He sat upright. Any interruption was welcome.

It was DI Davis and Suzie with a tall blonde woman he'd never seen before. Her tailored suit marked her as an outsider, but she had an air of someone in familiar surroundings. Davis peeled off, and it was just Suzie and the woman who entered.

'Since you're here anyway,' Suzie was saying, 'we thought we'd grab a word.' She led the woman to a table stacked with photographs; 30-year-old crime scene shots and the newer ones of the Dorset warehouse taken by the woman from forensics who'd gone down there without Webber's permission. This must be her. Ahmed stood up and offered his hand. 'Ayaan Ahmed. I was in Dorset myself yesterday.'

She returned the handshake but all her attention was on the pictures as Suzie spread them out. 'I doubt there's anything I can tell you that wasn't in my report,' she said.

There will be, thought Ahmed, there always is, and sure enough it popped out almost at once. In response to Suzie saying, 'Contemporary photos don't go that far towards the rear of the space, presumably because they thought everyone had come in through the front, but we're now assuming they backed the car through that entrance and dumped the body.'

'Well, no, they couldn't have,' the woman said. 'It wasn't there. There'd have been no access back then.'

'Are you sure? It doesn't look new.'

'No, it's not new, but it wasn't there 30 years ago.'

Ahmed flicked through the paperwork and pulled out the floor plan of the warehouse. 'This is what we have.' He pointed to the boundary lines. 'That's the original and the blue lines are where it's had extra walls put in over the years.'

The woman looked at the plan, then reached for one of the photographs. 'That's the wall there. You can see where it was knocked through. Look at that RSJ. That's no more than 25 years old, tops.'

Ahmed exchanged a glance with Suzie. Her fixity of expression matched his own annoyance. He hated wasting time over other people's carelessness. Why couldn't the woman have said this in her report? Why wasn't it obvious from the floor plan? Why hadn't the case notes been explicit? Were they all supposed to be specialists in building materials now?

'Let's run through it again,' Suzie said. 'We want to be clear. They found tracks from the lorry with the tiger cage round the front. The tigers were released into that small annexe. And they reckoned everyone bar Robert Morgan had arrived in the lorry.'

'How was he supposed to have got there?' the woman asked.

Suzie rolled her eyes. 'If only someone had really thought that through at the time. It seems certain he was in Wetherby earlier in the day. He could have caught a train down there. He didn't take his car. Who knows? The assumption was that he'd climbed in through the other side, but couldn't get back that way because the tigers trapped him.'

'But of course we now know he didn't get in there under his own steam,' Ahmed put in. 'There were car tracks round the back.' He pointed to the plan. 'That was the off road parking for the place when it was in use.'

Suzie tapped her finger on the floor plan where the woman had identified the likely starting point for the gruesome feeding frenzy. 'Now we know he didn't walk in, we're working on the theory that he was dumped right there, but if they didn't back a car in and tip him out of it, how did they get his body to that spot?'

Ahmed looked at the drawing, trying to see it in 3-D. 'If there was no vehicle access, then either he came on the lorry with the rest of them or he was taken round the back.' He paused as he thought of the reams of statements and reports. 'Simplest scenario seems to be that he was with the gang on the lorry. Did they kill him? Was there some kind of accident and they left him to the tigers? It was a very basic tractor unit. They were all crammed in the cab. There wasn't anywhere else.'

'What are you getting at?' asked Suzie.

'If he was on the lorry, alive or dead, then they all knew about it.'

Suzie frowned. 'But they didn't. I'm sure they didn't know about him, not all of them. Does that mean they weren't all on the lorry? Did some of them get to the warehouse some other way? In a car that parked round the back maybe.'

'So was Morgan in the car or on the lorry?'

'If you wanted to dump a body in that place, where would you go?'

'Round the back, for sure,' said Ahmed. 'Much more discreet. And you know what else, I'd have dumped him right there in that

219

car park. It's out of the way, deserted, no one's going to find him for ages.'

'Or you might carry him inside the offices at the back,' put in Suzie. 'Then it'll be even longer before he's found.'

'They checked the office space,' the woman said. 'There was no forensic trace. He hadn't been in there.'

'No, but there were tracks,' Ahmed said. 'And marks across the floor inside. The place was criss-crossed with tracks. It had been a warehouse not so long before. Stuff carted back and forth. They thought Morgan had been alive so they weren't looking for signs of a body being carried in.'

'But how can you know?' the woman said.

'Balance of probabilities,' said Suzie. 'We have to look at what fits and what doesn't. There are several reasons to think he wasn't brought in on the lorry, so that leaves a car, and of course a car could get round the back. What do you think? They've got him wrapped up in the boot. They get a wheelbarrow or something and take him through the offices at the back and to the point where the tigers found him soon after.'

'How about he's alive in the car,' said Ahmed. 'They kill him in the car park and wrap him in the sheet to avoid leaving traces while they wheel him inside.' The woman looked from one to the other of them. Ahmed could see she thought the debate pointless. They would never find hard evidence for any of this, but they'd known from the start there would be no smoking guns to find or confessions to hear at this distance in time. 'The point is,' he told her. 'They didn't leave him in the office, they carted him all the way through. If that vehicle access wasn't there, that's a really odd place to leave the body.'

'So why would they do it?'

'Because there were three doors between those offices and the warehouse,' Suzie told her. 'If they'd left him in the back, the tigers couldn't get at him. They knew.'

'Knew about the tigers?' the woman queried. 'Wasn't that clear anyway?'

'It was always a possibility, but it's good to see it supported by a scenario that stands up.'

'Does that mean it was deliberate on the part of the group who released the animals?'

'It's starting to look that way. Whoever dumped the body knew the detail of the scheme. Morgan was killed down there or very nearby. Someone went into the heart of that warehouse to dump the body and they did it just before the tigers arrived. You wouldn't want to get that timing wrong and find yourself face to face with a big cat.'

'Best way to be sure,' Ahmed said, 'is to have your mates hold off with the tiger cage until you're safely out again. The car boot was protected by that sheet. They drag him out and into some kind of barrow, wheel him through leaving no forensic trace in the office space. They'll have tipped him out, and run for it.'

'If they'd dumped him still wrapped in the sheet,' the woman said, 'we'd have had no evidence at all.'

Ahmed exchanged the ghost of a raised-eyebrows glance with Suzie. Take these techie types outside their comfort zone and they hadn't a clue. 'I'm no zoologist,' he said, 'but I don't think tigers eat thick plastic sheeting.'

The exchange invigorated Ahmed. Pieces were falling into place. The lab woman wandered away to look at the aerial photographs of the gravel pits as he and Suzie batted scenarios back and forth; scenarios that had begun to lean towards Will Jones and Gary Yeatman.

It was Suzie's glance that alerted Ahmed. He turned to follow the line of her gaze and saw Webber in the doorway. Webber's face wore the same intent stare he'd turned on Ahmed following the morning's briefing. The focus of his attention this time was the lab woman who was leaning forward to peer at the same pictures.

They watched as her finger reached out to trace a line across two interlocking images.

'What is it?' Webber had stepped behind her.

She didn't answer at once, but kept her contact with the surface of the print. When she spoke, her tone was hesitant. 'It's odd. Isn't that …? I'm not sure. Do you have this in close-up?'

'Get your coat,' said Webber. 'We can do better than snapshots.'

Ahmed watched as Webber spun on his heel, his stare landing first on Suzie, then on him before casting further afield to the opposite office. Ahmed held his breath. Were he and Suzie the only ones not currently out and about? He didn't want to be taken away from these new ideas on the Morgan case.

'Suzie. With me. Get your coat.'

Webber marched out. Ahmed lip-read the expletive as Suzie rose to follow.

It wasn't until he felt soft mud under his feet that Webber wondered about the advisability of bringing Suzie. She'd been a silent presence in the car, radiating resentment. He hadn't wanted Ahmed. Ahmed had seen nothing in those aerial shots; he'd have been asking questions the whole time, crowding out any embryo ideas that anyone else might be brewing. The woman from the lab had felt some anomaly even if she hadn't been able to articulate it. She wasn't one to explore unevidenced theories; she was only comfortable with facts. He'd learnt that much about her in their short acquaintance. But she would work out whatever it was that bugged her and she would explain it to him if he had to keep her here all night.

He held aside the tape to let them through. Suzie shot him a glare. The mist closed in like a sodden blanket. Moisture leached from it to settle on his hair and clothes. Suzie had had the foresight to bring a hat. The lab woman's coat sported a massive fur-fringed hood. Webber hoped it wouldn't restrict her vision. She'd seen whatever she'd seen from a wide angle, not that any of them would be able to see much in the failing light.

'Straight across that way.' He leant close to the lab woman and pointed out into the gloom. 'Those trees are the ones that ran along the middle two photos. OK?' He waited for her nod before going on. 'Pictures at the top of the board show the other side. I was going to suggest we take a direct line, but it's not much of a path. We could have done with better light.'

'Like tomorrow morning?' A grumpy comment from behind. He ignored it.

'We'll follow the perimeter round. It's a better path, but it'll take us out of sight of that stretch, and we'll be coming at it from the side.'

'OK, let's go.' The woman sounded impatient now, not understanding his worry that the unfamiliar angle would fail to spark her subconscious about whatever she'd seen.

They trudged in silence up the track to the highest point, where the woman stopped and peered out across the vegetation. The water in the gravel pit shimmered through the trees. Webber watched her as she held out her hand framing sections of the landscape. Then, as though happy she knew the way, she gave a nod and set off again, striding ahead of them.

'What do you think she's going to find?' Suzie's voice was low, her tone resigned rather than resentful. 'And why now? Why not tomorrow?'

Webber glanced at the woman in front, too far away to hear the exchange. He would look silly if it all turned out to be nothing, but he gave her a truthful response. 'Something's been bugging me about this site, but don't ask. I've no idea what.'

'You never said anything.'

'Didn't have anything to say and you know how it is when you start putting ideas in people's heads. Their imaginations go into overdrive, but she saw something.' He pointed to the woman ahead whose form was vanishing into the gloom. He quickened his step, not wanting to miss her reaction when they arrived at the stretch she'd studied on the photographs.

They caught up with her at a tangle of wire that had once been a fence. The mist and failing light made the wire hard to see. Webber pulled out his torch to illuminate the tangled obstruction.

'Why isn't this side taped off?' the woman asked as they forced a way through.

'No vehicle access. No sign anyone came this far. The walkway foundation's back that way.' Her gaze followed the line of his pointing finger. 'Concrete lorry would have come in from the road up there. No one uses this bit. It's too boggy. Watch your step.'

She climbed clear of the trailing wire and peered ahead. 'Torch,' she said, reaching back.

He passed it to her. She played the beam ahead into the scrub as she moved forward. 'Now, that's unusual,' she said, walking up to a tangle of misshapen branches. Her tone was light. She might have been commenting on a piece of jewellery.

Webber tried to read her expression, but her features were losing clarity in the fading light. Suzie had a point. He should have left this till morning.

'That's unusual, too,' the woman said, waving the torch towards a lush stand of waving grasses.

'Talk to us,' he said, trying not to snap. 'What are you seeing?'

She shrugged. 'I just wouldn't have expected to see that … oh, look, there's more.' She strode forward. He and Suzie, without the torch beam to guide their feet, followed as best they could. 'It must be something about the land,' she said. 'What was here before?'

'Nothing,' said Webber. 'There's never been anything here. It's …'

He stopped as the woman jerked to a standstill, her face frozen as though she'd seen a poisonous snake curled in the grass. He and

Suzie exchanged a glance, then moved together to the woman's side.

Her gaze seemed fixed on the twisted woody stems of some kind of bush tangled in a stand of tall grass that shimmered in the dusk.

'What is it?' he asked, fighting an urge to grab her well-tailored lapels and shake the answer out of her.

'I don't know.' Her voice was high, unsteady. 'I can't see properly in this light, but look … There and there. Maybe there, too. It might be animals. I can't tell. It's substantial. It's …'

He could see her hand trembling and strained his eyes to try to draw something … anything … out of the bland scrubland in which they stood. Animals? The association of ideas sent a tremor through him. He imagined tigers springing out of the mist.

The damp air hung heavy. The only sounds were the swish of the grasses and the distant rumble of traffic. The path behind them had dissolved into the twilight. All around were the stands of woody stems … tall grasses … Out of place in this barren stretch. The torch beam was no match for the incoming dusk. An invisible hand carved a hollow inside him. His mind took the scene ahead and overlaid it on to the distant memory of a long-ago case. He knew what it was that didn't look right. She'd said, maybe animals. Yes, it might be some kind of illegal disposal. He could only hope.

'Back off,' he said. 'We're in a graveyard.'

chapter twenty-seven

The light in the kitchen gave Webber hope that Mel had waited up for him, but the house was silent, the living room dark. He hoped someone had been in touch; that was how it was supposed to work, but he hadn't checked. He supposed he should feel relief. If she was asleep he didn't have to worry about what to tell her, what to hold back. He would gloss over going out there with Suzie but whoever rang to say he'd be late might have let it slip.

He sank into a chair, too tired to think about foraging for something to eat though hunger gnawed at him, but with too much in his head to think about sleeping. He'd wanted Melinda up and about so he could share the details that spun around in his mind. She could have had the satisfaction of being in the know before it broke in the press. It wouldn't be long. It might be unfolding on the late news right now. It wasn't something they could keep quiet; a whole new stretch had been cordoned off and this time properly. The initial team had been quick to unearth small animal bones. He recalled the relieved sigh with which Suzie had greeted the find. He supposed she'd been tired too, ready to clutch at straws, wanting to get home. 'Too shallow,' he'd told her, and could have added too recent, way too recent to account for the abnormal growth. She would work it out in her own time. This whatever-it-was had no bearing on the Jenkinson case, nor on Robert Morgan. It might even pre-date the latter's demise.

Footsteps sounded on the stairs. Relief suffused him. Mel was still up. Her tread was soft. Maybe Sam had woken during the evening.

'Hi,' he greeted her. 'Sam OK?'

She nodded and eyed him curiously. 'I thought I heard you come in.'

Pre Suzie, she'd have been concerned at his tiredness, she'd have asked if he'd eaten, what had happened, why was he late?

'Someone called you, didn't they?' he asked. 'It was all a bit chaotic.'

She reached down for the switch on the standard lamp, then walked across to the television, but held back from flicking on the plug. He was pleased. The last thing he wanted was to see that the late night news had picked up the story. 'You're not as late as they said you might be.'

His eyelids grew heavy. Simply having her here had calmed the turmoil in his head. Straight to bed was his best plan but he couldn't immediately summon the energy to stand up.

Melinda gave a small sigh. 'Have you eaten?'

He looked at her surprised. They had a script for this. Were they still allowed to use it? He would say that he was OK, that he'd sort himself out in a moment. She'd say either that she'd saved him something or that she'd cook him a snack. He would give her a grateful smile and then doze in the chair until she put a plate in front of him. And just occasionally if they'd had a row, she would say, fine, sort yourself out. Since Suzie, all bets were off. She was still standing by the TV looking down at him.

'No, I haven't. I'm starving.'

She hesitated, then said, 'Cheese sandwiches? Cheese on toast?'

He let out a sigh of contentment. 'Thanks, Mel. Anything. Whatever's easiest.' He attempted a laugh. 'I'm getting too old to be out following hunches. If I'd known where this one would lead, I'd have left it for next week.'

She marched through to the kitchen without a word. He heard the clatter of plates. It struck him she'd looked irritated.

'I've been out to the gravel pits again,' he called through.

No reply.

'That's why I'm late.'

An uninterested, 'Yeah.'

The plate landing in his lap jerked him awake from a doze. He smiled his gratitude and fell on the warm toast biting off a huge mouthful savouring the tang of the cheese. 'You had a good day?' The boost of calories reminded him to ask, though the words were muffled.

'Yeah, pretty good. This gravel pit thing, whatever it is, it's not going to pull you into work tomorrow is it?'

'I'm not sure. No, probably not.' He reflected that whatever they'd found up there could probably wait another year or two without spoiling. He was about to expand on the idea when she spoke again.

'Good, because I need you to have Sam while I'm out tomorrow.'

'Why? Out where?'

A smile of satisfaction spread across her face. 'Because I don't trust Joyce enough to have her and Sam in the same space, and because I've arranged to go out with her tomorrow to see someone.'

He realised belatedly that her initial move towards the TV had been nothing to do with late night news. She'd been heading for her evidence boards, but probably changed her mind when she saw how tired he was. He felt impatient that she didn't want to interrogate him on why he'd been out at the gravel pits. He needed her to ask; couldn't make the effort to explain it from cold. And his find had to trump whatever small progress she'd made on her case. He looked up and met her eye, seeing his impatience reflected back at him. She too thought she had momentous news to impart and was waiting for questions.

'Who are you going to see?' The line of least resistance was the only one he had the energy to follow, and if he wasn't the one speaking, at least he could focus all his attention on his food.

The blackboard clacked against the television casing as she pulled it free.

She said something about a teacher; a filler to bridge the gap while she gathered her thoughts. Sam rarely came home from playschool without a new achievement to be announced. Whatever it was, it would be told again. He didn't need to listen.

'I thought you didn't believe in hunches.' Her tone was sharp; it penetrated his drowsiness. Hunches?

'Oh, you mean the gravel pit. I don't. It was my subconscious seeing that abnormal growth. In summer it must be obvious, but no one's really looked.' It seemed a good moment to expand on the story, but tiredness was settling over him like a heavy blanket. It was easier to let her words roll on unheeded.

As he climbed into bed later he flinched at the touch of the cold sheets. He wasn't sure if the bed was empty when he climbed in, but she was there beside him at some point. He turned, gathering her into his arms pressing her head to his chest, a comforting presence to drive out the demons and soothe him to sleep. She said something but he didn't catch it.

The next morning with Sam chirruping happily over his cereal and Melinda humming to herself as she clattered about in the kitchen, he eyed the boards behind the TV. She'd told him all about it last night ... fragments came back to him ... she and Joyce had pushed forward another step ... a trip out ... he was to look after Sam. He struggled to recall whether or not he'd told her what they'd found up at the gravel pits, but only remembered gathering her to him as he slipped into sleep and wondered if she'd tried to pull away.

He felt refreshed, happy that she seemed happy, yet the previous evening's lassitude still wrapped him in a haze, giving a sensation of disconnection from the world around him. Once the chaos of Sam at breakfast was over, he would sneak a surreptitious look at those boards, see if he could jog his brain into completing the pattern without having to ask.

'Get that lot out to dry when the washer finishes.' Melinda was at his elbow, smiling at Sam, reaching out to smooth the boy's hair and wipe a stray cereal flake from his chin. 'Plenty of stuff in for lunch if I'm not back, but I will be. Probably.'

She had her coat on; her bag swung from her arm. She leant down to kiss the top of Sam's head, then turned to Webber to give him a brief goodbye, her lips brushing his cheek. A few days ago it would have been unmistakeably an act put on for Sam. Now it might be real again, but maybe that was wishful thinking. The thought stalled him until the slam of the door snapped him to alertness.

'Mel, where are you …?' As he set off after her, Sam wailed panicked disapproval as he saw his second parent set to disappear, and Webber was distracted until it was too late.

He watched her car drive off, saw her face briefly in profile; she didn't look back. All the demons crowded in; the anomalies of senseless traffic chaos, bodies buried in concrete, an ancient site spitting out a decades-old secret. He stared after her. It was mundane scenes like this that came back to haunt people. If something terrible happened, this might be the last he ever saw of her. He wanted to etch every detail on his mind.

chapter twenty-eight

Ahmed stifled a yawn. This was turning into a waste of a Sunday evening. He'd come round to be with Cari not to make small talk with her family. They should revive their plans to sneak off to the registry office with a couple of friends in tow. It was as though her mother had picked up on his thoughts because the nearer the day approached, the more subterfuge it took for him and Cari to get any time alone together. There was her mother now, wrecking what little was left of his time here tonight by determinedly taking her away to talk wedding details in which he, as a man, was deemed to have no interest. Her brothers were on shift work so he'd be left with the three young cousins, a trio whose heads he would happily knock together. As Cari trailed after her mother, she peeped back and caught his eye. They exchanged the ghost of a raised-eyebrows glance. The door closed behind them and Ahmed slumped into his chair blowing out a sigh.

One of the cousins said something in the sing-song tone they used to goad him. He ignored it; he'd learnt to ignore them months ago; couldn't even be bothered to make sense of the words, though the sly looks that shot between them told him they were making something of the call he'd taken just after he arrived.

It had been from Suzie. He'd been careless enough to use her name. Much adolescent hilarity that he should be talking to her in the presence of his wife-to-be. Muted hilarity, though, because he'd blown up at them last time he was here. There had been one too many snide remarks about his boss being a woman. For all their youth this trio were fresh out of the ark.

He felt his mouth curve to a smile as he imagined their reaction should they know about Suzie and Webber. Then a bolt of frustration shot through him. He could curse Martyn Webber for unearthing another ancient crime. Webber should have been concentrating on the job in hand not mulling on botanical anomalies. What Ahmed really wanted was to have another go at Tom's mother. Davis and his team thought she had nothing more to tell, but Ahmed was convinced that Tom had been back to see her in that gap before he disappeared. He'd get it out of her if he had her face to face. He'd tried putting it to DI Davis but been rebuffed.

'... hey, Ayaan?'

One of the cousins held the coffee pot, ostensibly offering a refill.

Ahmed gave him a hard look but no other response and returned to his dilemma over Tom's mother. He'd thought about engineering an accidental meeting and having a go at her himself, but he'd have to be very creative to find a credible reason to be in any of the woman's haunts. Or he might approach Webber about it, but then he'd end up in bad odour with Davis and Suzie. And the carrot of a permanent move to York was in front of him. When he thought about starting his married life 50 miles from Cari's parents and her antediluvian cousins, as opposed to in Scarborough practically on their doorstep, he couldn't jeopardise it. His only option was to do nothing, keep his eyes and ears open and look for his chance.

Monday eased its way into late afternoon, the light long gone, rain battering the windows. Webber stood with John Farrar in the otherwise empty office. Farrar's presence wasn't to do with any of Webber's cases, but he asked about the makeshift graveyard up beyond the fishing lakes.

'Looks like illegal disposal of cattle carcases from the 1960's,'

Webber said. 'Coincides with a foot and mouth outbreak. We're checking but there's nothing recent turning up.'

'And Tom Jenkinson?'

Webber outlined the strands of the net they had closing around Jenkinson's killer.

'But no one in the frame.'

'No names yet,' Webber admitted, 'but we've shone a spotlight into every corner of Tom Jenkinson's life, we have to have him … or her in the net somewhere.'

'Links?' Farrar asked. 'Jenkinson's behind-the-scenes contacts and the traffic chaos business. Are you still seeing them as unrelated?'

Webber nodded. 'Jenkinson's mystery man was offering a sizeable sum for the traffic lights scam. Jenkinson kept his ear to the ground. He'd go for something like that. He was after the money. His other contacts were more arms' length. He was playing the long game. From one side it's clear he was keeping that area of his life very low key while he had Ayaan actively on his case. This was no stranger killing. It wasn't random and it was a rush job. It fits with Jenkinson trying to do a double cross on the traffic scam. The story he gave Ayaan won't have been far off. He was a clever lad. He'd have dressed up a few angles to keep things from us, but he knew how to spin a convincing line close to the truth. If we could have had him back a second time when we knew a bit more, we'd have been home and dry on that side of things, but maybe someone else figured that out.'

'You said from one side. What about from the other?'

'Not good,' Webber said. 'The theory there, is that someone got wind that he was moving into Ayaan's camp and decided to get rid before he could do any damage.'

'Did he know enough to do damage?'

Webber wobbled his hand in a yes-no gesture. 'Doesn't look like it. We've copies of everything off his cloud storage, and we'll get notice if anyone else tries to access it, but no one has to date, which says to me no one's worried about it. His computer disappeared but that might be just to make it look like a robbery, though it's possible they destroyed the hardware without realising he'd kept copies.'

'OK, so you're going with the mystery man for now. Did you have CCTV or have I got that wrong?'

'Yes, we have someone from the street round the back at about the right time. It's indistinct. Shows an odd gait.' His gaze searched the space, running down the myriad lists plastered about the place. 'There.' He pointed, showing Farrar the *Mystery Man* heading with its scant data attached.

'Funny walk,' Farrar read from the board. 'Is that the best you can do by way of distinguishing features?'

'I'm afraid so. It shows on the CCTV. We've tried enhancing it but it just becomes less distinct. It's nothing much, just a bit odd. Like this.' He pulled back his shoulders and minced across the floor trying to emulate his memory of the grainy footage.

Behind him Farrar laughed. 'You look like you're trying to walk in stilettos, Martyn.'

Webber smiled. 'Such witnesses as we have, Jenkinson included of course, say a man, but it could be a woman. And I'm sure I didn't do justice to the walk. It's odd whichever sex the mystery person is.'

Farrar's gaze swept the empty space. 'Where is everyone?'

'They're out talking to a group of students who lived in the same block practically on top of Jenkinson. They're just back from a three-week exchange trip abroad but they'd have been on the spot when Jenkinson was claiming to have had his visits from the mystery man. Students keep odd hours. We're hoping to flesh out the bits of sightings we've already had. We'll be catching up in the morning,' he added, in case Farrar had been expecting a briefing tonight.

Farrar moved forward to study the photographs of Jenkinson's room. 'No forensics,' he murmured.

'Not a trace,' Webber said. 'Cleanest student flat in history.'

The long second-hand on the wall clock ticked its way towards the hour. He didn't expect Davis's team back tonight, but Suzie and Ahmed would probably return to dump whatever they'd gone to collect from the gravel pits. The old cases weren't high on his radar now he'd solved the mystery of the anomalous growth on that deserted stretch, but he wanted to have things wrapped up before Suzie got back because Melinda was dropping off her car to be serviced and would call in any time now for a lift home.

They'd spent an uncommunicative weekend together. He'd scrutinized her boards while she was out but the new entries were crammed in, written in shorthand that he couldn't decipher. She wasn't keeping it from him, just using contractions to fit everything into the inadequate space.

Looking back, it seemed they'd both got stubborn. When she'd arrived home on Saturday he'd been irrationally annoyed that he'd been so worried about her. She'd clearly been bursting with something to tell, but she'd been sniffy about talking in front of Sam. Then the local news had shown the gravel pits; his name had been mentioned. He'd waited for her to ask but she'd feigned indifference.

Once Sam was in bed he'd assumed they'd have it all out but wasn't going to invite another snub so hadn't asked any questions. Maybe she too had decided she wouldn't be the one to initiate discussion, so they'd watched a DVD in fairly frosty silence that had leaked over into Sunday.

Tonight he would make the effort, unthaw relations between them again, but he didn't want her arriving at the front desk at the same time Suzie returned with Ahmed. Time was getting on.

'Do you think we're done with the traffic shenanigans?' Farrar's question popped out of nowhere. It took Webber a moment to realise that the Chief Super had intercepted his glance at the clock. This was the time of night the strange events had kicked off.

235

'Nothing for almost three weeks now, nothing since Jenkinson.'

'Do you think he told his mother anything?'

Webber thought over the briefings he'd had from Davis. 'Yes,' he said. 'It's pretty clear he went to see her and he wasn't one for family visits for the sake of it. But we need to get an unembellished version out of her. Davis is going carefully with it.' He smiled. 'Ayaan Ahmed's itching to have a go at her himself.'

'Any mileage in that?'

Webber shook his head. 'Ayaan's influence was with Tom, not his mother. It's a shame. Ayaan would have won the war. Jenkinson was tipping towards mentoring some of the youngsters the way Ayaan had mentored him, getting a taste for the straight and narrow.'

'Until some bastard cut him down.' Farrar's gaze turned to the shots of the walkway; the foundations where Jenkinson had died. 'Where's Ahmed, anyway?'

'Out at the gravel pits with Suzie. They had a call.'

'Why the interest? I thought they'd found animal remains.'

'Yes, they've excavated three pits. So far cattle and small animal bones – dogs and cats. All very degraded. Someone called in about something in the third pit. I don't know what.'

Farrar heaved a sigh. 'Well, don't turn the place into a cold case unit, Martyn, and certainly not a veterinary one. But tell me about Davis. Are you happy with him? Is he pulling his weight?'

'Yes.' Webber was surprised at the sincerity he could put into the affirmative. Davis had an oddly quiet way of working but he made steady progress; kept his team up to scratch. He was about to comment on the transformation from bored DI sitting it out to retirement to safe pair of hands when the clatter of footsteps and voices stopped him.

Ahmed and Suzie, dripping wet, boots caked with thick mud marched into the big office, their chat and laughter cut off abruptly at the sight of Webber and Farrar standing there.

Webber took in the evidence bag that swung from Suzie's hand. 'What have you got?'

'I'm sending it for analysis,' she said with a touch of defensiveness, 'but we want some better photographs before we let it go.

'What is it?'

'If I knew that I wouldn't need the photos,' she muttered.

Ahmed shot her an alarmed glance and leapt in with, 'We don't know. We've got pictures of it in situ but with the weather, we thought we'd just take a couple here in a proper light.'

'OK.' Webber nodded. He took the point. The site had swallowed more resources than he'd wanted, but he'd kept it to a minimum for old animal carcasses. And an artefact older than the car they'd pulled out a scant few weeks ago wasn't going to climb anyone's priority list. He was surprised they were even thinking of sending it for testing. It might never reach the top of the list with everything else that was queuing for attention.

Farrar voiced the thought. 'Why do think it's worth testing at all? What's so special about it?'

Suzie shrugged. 'We don't know, but it was at the same depth as what they think are more remains. It's plastic so it's not rotted down. Possibly a large box that's been crushed over the years. This could be part of a handle. It's conceivable there's forensic trace caught in the twisty bit.'

She held up the bag for inspection. Orange plastic, an unusual shade. It wasn't a shape Webber could make sense of. It could almost have been a section ripped from a plastic football except for the small protuberance and that the curve was more egg-shaped than spherical.

'Suppose it's the handle off a box,' Ahmed put in. 'It might have had a body in it. A plastic coffin.'

'What makes you say that and if it hasn't rotted where's the rest of it?'

Suzie pulled a face. 'They might find more … it might have been crushed. It's just that they found a tooth, a human tooth. That's why they called it in.'

One tooth doesn't make a crime, thought Webber, no matter how deep it's buried. 'Any bones?' he asked.

Suzie shook her head. 'It's the terrain, and after this length of time, they say we're lucky to have an odd tooth in recognisable shape. They think they'll be sifting soil for bone fragments.'

Farrar gave an irritable gesture. 'They unearth Roman remains all over the place in pretty good shape. Why should modern bodies crumble to dust? And what's to say we don't have Romans here?'

'The archaeologists have had a look,' said Ahmed, 'but they're pretty certain it's not. They'll know for sure when they get some soil analysis done.'

'And they didn't bury Romans with plastic artefacts,' muttered Suzie.

Farrar glared at her. No longer the blue-eyed favourite, thought Webber. She should watch her step.

She turned to him with a bright smile. 'What do you think, Martyn?' He was taken aback by her coquettish tone. Was she deliberately winding Farrar up? She could be a real idiot at times.

No. The train of thought froze. Not an idiot, a vicious little cow, stirring things just because she could. Reflected in the glass partition barely even in his peripheral vision he caught a familiar shape, familiar colours. She shouldn't have been allowed through. Suzie would have a clear view from where she was standing, but with just enough angle to pretend she hadn't noticed Melinda in the corridor outside.

'Get the thing photographed and sent off,' he snapped. 'Then do something with that lot.' He pointed at the suspects list that Ahmed and Suzie had compiled for Robert Morgan. 'Just because it happened 30 years ago doesn't mean you can swan about for another 30 years. Focus on the job in hand.'

Suzie flushed and pursed her lips. Ahmed shuffled his feet, a picture of guilt; clearly he had been focusing on the wrong things, but that wasn't news.

'Come through,' he said to Farrar, turning his back on the two of them. 'Interesting development on Jenkinson.'

Racking his brain for some new detail to tell Farrar that might come under the heading of interesting development, he strode towards his office and was able to put on a credible start of surprise to see Melinda standing waiting for him.

Farrar greeted her warmly which was a relief. He might have bawled someone out for letting her in unchaperoned. 'A sight for sore eyes, Melinda. It'll be good to have you back on the team. Not long now, is it?'

Webber watched his wife drag her attention away from Suzie and Ahmed, scurrying about their tasks, and return Farrar's smile. 'Yes,' she said. 'Yes … I'm talking dates with HR.'

Was she? He didn't know that. She hadn't talked dates with him. He watched Farrar gallantly wave her ahead of them into the office and saw her peep sideways over Farrar's shoulder with such a piercing glance that he looked back himself. It seemed to be Ahmed in her line of sight, not Suzie. Ahmed holding an evidence bag up to the light, the gaudy orange of the plastic fragment undimmed by age.

chapter twenty-nine

Ahmed stared at the suspects list. After all these years wasn't it pretty good to have found five names and unfair of Webber to have a go just because they hadn't yet cut it down? Robert Morgan's death hadn't even been classified as a murder until the other week. But maybe there was some trimming to be done. Pamela Morgan could surely be crossed off. She hadn't been anywhere near the scene; she hadn't gained from her husband's death.

He opened his mouth to suggest they put a line through her, but Suzie was rubbing at her hair with a towel, her stare targeted across the corridor at Webber's office. Seeing the look on her face, he closed his mouth and turned back to the list. There was the suicide of course. They should dig deeper into that before discounting Pamela, but not yet because she was a long-shot and they should concentrate on the more promising leads. Mentally he bracketed Brad Tippet with Pamela Morgan as another outsider. Enough time had been spent on them. He thought about the neighbour, Mrs Bell. He'd been coming from her house when he'd bumped into Melinda Webber that time, or rather when she'd bumped into him. Instinctively he shot a narrowed-eyed look towards the closed door where she'd disappeared with Webber and Farrar.

'What're you thinking, Ayaan?' Suzie watched him from across the office space.

He looked again at the list before he answered. 'Mrs Bell … Tippet's neighbour. No one's ever asked her about the car, beyond did she see it that night?'

'And?'

He shrugged. 'Don't know. It just struck me, that's all.'

'D'you want to go back to her?'

He shook his head. 'No. Tippet and Pamela Morgan are way down the bottom of the list. We need to focus on the top end.'

'Who are you putting up there, big brother post office?'

Again he shook his head. 'He's in the mix somewhere but I think Will Jones is the front runner. He was the ring leader of the animal rights lot.' Ahmed plucked a marker pen from the table and drew a circle around the name. 'And Gary Yeatman,' – another circle – 'Jones went to see him when he got out of prison but Yeatman wouldn't have anything to do with him. We need that first hand. Can we have a word with Yeatman's wife? She's still around.'

'She's the one who knows the Webbers, isn't she? I wonder how.'

'Melinda Webber,' corrected Ahmed, as they both turned to look at the closed door. 'I think she met her somewhere recently. I don't think they know her well. I don't think Martyn knows her at all.'

'Yes, well, if we need to talk to her, we'll do it. We don't need their say-so. Her husband's death was a suicide wasn't it, like Pamela Morgan?'

'Suicide, yes, but not like Pamela Morgan. She took an overdose; he drove his car off the road.'

'Yeah, that cruise control thing,' Suzie said, her gaze unfocussed. 'Like Arthur Trent in the Jenkinson enquiry.'

'Coincidence,' said Suzie. 'Don't look for complications. God, is that the time already? Come on, let's get that thing photographed and packed up.'

Ahmed arranged a desk lamp to show the plastic fragment to best effect and held a ruler next to it leaving Suzie to click the camera. After Webber's outburst he was no longer sure why they were bothering and said so.

'Because they think they've got human remains,' Suzie reminded him, 'and this was at the same depth.'

He nodded, depressed at the implications. Yet another ancient case to be untangled that would leach resources from the here and now of Tom's death. Suzie looked tired. He offered to stay and tie loose ends and she accepted with alacrity, shaking out her still sodden coat before putting it on. He raised his hand in acknowledgement of her, 'See you tomorrow,' and bent over the orange plastic, carefully repacking it to avoid any disturbance to the twisty bit that might yield secrets to a forensic probe.

The fading of her footsteps down the corridor coincided with the click of a door opening. He read the situation immediately and felt no surprise to hear Melinda Webber's voice greeting him. It was an effort to look her in the eye with any semblance of a pleasant smile. *It's just as though you were waiting for her to leave.* He'd have liked to say it aloud.

She murmured something about leaving them to discuss things, which was all very well but she shouldn't be here at all. Webber should have escorted her back to the reception area, not just let her loose like this.

'What on earth's that orange thing, Ayaan?'

'Oh ... well ... we don't really know. Probably nothing.'

'I heard about the work you did with the lad who was killed.' He watched her gaze stray to the evidence boards. She shouldn't see any of this. 'Martyn said you were winning; said you'd have turned him right round in another few months.'

'Did he?' He looked at her surprised. The things that had come to light about Tom since his murder suggested almost the reverse; that Tom had been after recruiting him, Ahmed, to a life of crime and given the duplicity of his dealings it looked on paper like he might have been succeeding.

'Oh yes,' Melinda said. 'Martyn was quite clear about it.'

She picked up the evidence bag and held it to the light, turning it slowly as she inspected it. Ahmed felt a sudden certainty that she wanted to touch the object, that she would pluck it free of its protective polythene. He found himself hovering at her elbow ready to grab it back.

She turned to face him, giving him a half smile from close quarters. 'I know how to handle evidence, Ayaan.'

He relaxed a little but didn't move away. 'Are you planning to make the move to CID?'

'Hell no. It's too slow for me. I'd get bored to tears doing it all the time. I like the front line stuff.'

What did she mean by *all the time*? She'd always been in uniform.

'Anyway, I really need to get going.' He eased the bag out of her hands and laid it on the desk. She relinquished it without a struggle.

'Will Jones and Gary Yeatman?' She seemed to ask the question under her breath, her attention now on the list with their circled names. He thought she sounded shocked.

'Well … um …' He tried for a breezy tone as he grasped her arm and drew her away. 'I need to be on my way. Are you waiting for Martyn?'

He felt relief that she let him lead her towards the door. 'My car's in dock,' she said absently.

'Right, well …' He glanced across towards the frosted partition the other side of the corridor. It showed Webber and Farrar still deep in conversation. *Wrap it up, guys!* He aimed the thought crossly, certain he'd be the one to catch the flack if Melinda's meddling became an issue. 'I'll walk you through to reception. Can I get you a coffee while you're waiting?'

She seemed to snap back from wherever her thoughts had wandered and gave him a grin. 'It's all right, officer, I'll go quietly.'

He dropped her arm and followed her out of the office, clicking off the light plunging the space behind them into darkness. She paused at Webber's door and pushed her face close to the glass, waving her hand in an extravagant gesture to attract his attention. Ahmed saw Webber glance up. Farrar had his back to them. Melinda flicked her hand in an unmistakeable get-a-move-on gesture and then headed for the exit.

Ahmed blew out a sigh of relief to have her back in the public space. His intention to usher her to a chair stalled as he looked at the stained and broken furniture. Someone really should do something about that.

As though reading his dilemma, she said, 'I'll be fine, Ayaan. I'll wait here for Martyn. You get on. Sorry to have kept you.'

As he scurried away he thought about her holding the evidence bag to the light, turning it this way and that. There was a temptation to go back and ask if she knew what it was. But no, she'd have said. Far better to get clear of the firing line.

Sam spluttered and squealed as a sheet of rain cut under Webber's protective arm and hit him full in the face. He kicked and wriggled against the strap that held him in the chair. Webber had the carry-handle awkwardly over his arm as he wrestled with the key in the front door. He could hear the rustle of carrier bags as Melinda hauled the shopping from the boot and hurried up the path.

'Come on, Martyn, get Sam under cover. He'll get soaked.'

Webber forced the key home and gave the door an irritable kick to open it. Replaying the trip home he could hear Melinda's inconsequential chatter as she'd gone on about what he could now see were irrelevant details about the shopping she wanted to stop for. She'd filled the time until they arrived at Jess's house and once Sam was in the car, she'd twisted in her seat to talk to him and side-tracked all Webber's attempts to ask questions.

He needed to know about her return to work. It affected him as well. And where did that leave their plans for a sibling for Sam? Did he have to assume now that they were going to wait a few years?

Didn't he have a say any more? But he couldn't concentrate on the traffic as well as Melinda or his bad temper would have shown, so he had bitten his tongue.

Now they were indoors. Melinda was clattering about in the kitchen putting things away. He carried Sam to the doorway as he eased the boy out of his damp coat. Maybe she'd already agreed a date to start again. Where would she be stationed? Would she go back full time? How would it work with play school?

'Come on, Mel, tell me what's going on.'

Fleetingly her eyes met his then she looked at Sam. 'When he's in bed,' she said turning back to stack tins of beans in the cupboard.

'Why?' he said. He wasn't letting her off the hook on this one. 'Why shouldn't Sam hear about your plans … our plans?' Sam strained in his arms, reaching for a high shelf. Webber plucked a packet of spaghetti down and gave it to him, leaning his head away to avoid a smack in the face as Sam rattled the packet vigorously. 'It'll affect him too, certainly if you end up on shifts.'

He saw surprise in her expression, mingled with disapproval as she looked at Sam scrunching the crackly cellophane in his fists. 'Uh … yeah. Yes, of course, but I don't have a date yet. I've been on to HR but we haven't talked dates. I just said that to John for something to say.'

Webber realised that she'd been expecting an interrogation about something else, not her return to work. 'So you're definitely going back. I mean now rather than in a couple of years, say?'

'Yes, Martyn, I am. I want to keep my career on track. And Sam's great but I don't want two children under three. I want to wait a couple of years.'

He couldn't hold back a smile. This was long-term planning. And in a couple of years he might be able to take some leave; there'd be no Suzie Harmer hovering in the background. Except that there would. There would be her child; he couldn't think of it as his. Maybe it would have become nothing more than a standing order on his bank account. Fiona would be fine with that. He wasn't sure about Suzie, and oddly he wasn't sure about Mel either. Dangerous territory. He shook the thoughts out of his head.

'Have you considered CID?' He was pleased with the question. It flowed neatly, avoided dangerous ground and segued into the territory that she was trying to avoid.

She gave a short laugh. 'Ayaan Ahmed asked me that.'

'Ayaan? When?'

With a delighted shriek, Sam ripped apart the spaghetti packet tipping pasta needles down Webber's shirt front and on to the floor where they bounced and skittered across the lino.

Melinda let out a sigh. 'I'll get his tea on while you clear that lot up.'

Webber reached for the dustpan and brush as he lowered himself and his son to the floor and began to gather up the brittle rods. She must have spoken to Ahmed after she'd left his office. Had Suzie been there too? He remembered Melinda's backward glance. It hadn't been Suzie she'd focussed on.

'Mel?' He looked up at her. 'When Sam's in bed, I want to know about it.'

'Yeah, OK. But I want to make a call first. I want to be sure.'

He nodded and returned to his task, surprised at how far the pasta pieces had spread. He didn't know what it was or what she wanted to be sure about, but she assumed he'd guessed. Hearing the clicking of the keyboard, he stretched across to look through into the living room as the computer screen burst into a palette of colour then flicked to a single orange rectangle.

'What's that?' He spoke more sharply than he'd meant to.

'Dulux colour chart,' she replied reaching for the phone.

A chuckle from behind alerted him. Sam's eyes were bright with mischief; his fist descending. Webber dived but wasn't quick enough. The dustpan flipped, sending a shower of fractured spaghetti high in the air. Through Sam's shrieks of laughter and the crackle of breaking pasta, he heard Melinda say that she'd emailed a link ... she was asking someone to check something.

He assumed she was calling Joyce Yeatman, but later while she was upstairs putting Sam to bed, he looked at the last number dialled. It wasn't one he recognised.

'Who did you phone, Mel?' he asked as soon as she came back down.

She sat down before she answered him. 'A guy called Johan Meyer. He's the one we went to see at the weekend, me and Joyce. I needed to check something with him. I wasn't sure if I was making too much of it.'

'Too much of what? Who is this Johan Meyer?'

'Retired teacher. He knew the quintets, taught them ... I've got it all written down for you. And no, I don't think I was making too much of it.' She had a look on her face that was almost sulky. Like a child who's found a wonderful treasure but knows they have to give it back. Webber waited for her to go on. 'There's something you need to know. It's about that plastic thing that Ayaan Ahmed had in the evidence bag.' He noted in passing that she'd airbrushed Suzie out of the way. 'He claimed not to know much about it,' she went on. 'But then he wouldn't tell me, would he?'

'No, of course not. You shouldn't have asked.' As he spoke he knew he should shoulder the blame; shouldn't have given her the opportunity.

'OK, Martyn, then you tell me. They know what it is, don't they?'

'No,' he said, taken aback. 'No, I don't think so. I don't think they know anything about it.' He thought of her excursion on Saturday to the mystery Johan Meyer. He still didn't know where she'd been. 'Why?' he asked. 'Do you know what it is?'

'Yeah. I think I do.' She turned to the computer and knocked the mouse so the screen sprang to life. Leaning across she typed in a URL and the screen was filled with photographs of rocking horses.

He stared but saw nothing that looked in the least like his memory of the gaudy orange plastic.

'It was the colour,' she said. 'That's what I wanted to check. I mean orange comes in all sorts of shades, doesn't it?'

Webber nodded. There was no trace of orange in the pictures on the monitor. 'Where do the toy horses come in?'

'Something like that one, I'm guessing.' She homed in on an elaborate old-fashioned model and enlarged the image. 'The saddles are plastic. Imagine ripping it so you get part of the pommel thing and a bit down the sides there and there.'

He stepped across to scrutinise the picture rolling the mouse wheel to enlarge it further. 'I suppose it could be.' He could just about make a match, but he was sure he could find another dozen plastic toys where he could argue an equally good fit with the ragged artefact Ahmed and Suzie had collected. He voiced his doubts.

'Like what?' she said. 'Where are you going to match the twist of that pommel? And you know whose it is, don't you?' Her eyes narrowed as she looked at him.

Webber shook his head. 'No, Mel. All we know is that it was dug up from a pit that might contain human remains, but there's little trace of anything left down there.'

'The land behind the fishing place!' She looked startled. 'I didn't realise. I thought they'd dug up cattle bones.'

'They did in two of the pits.'

'Definitely human remains?' she asked.

'No, there's nothing definite yet. Mel, why do you think that that thing was part of a bright orange plastic rocking horse saddle? And whose was it?'

She looked troubled as though fighting to work something out, then stood, turning away from the computer screen and went to sit in an armchair.

'The rocking horse was her big thing,' she said. 'She used to cart its bridle and stuff about with her. The saddle got broken in a fight. But it can't be her. Not there. If she's anywhere, she's in Dorset.'

'Dorset? Who are you talking about Mel?' He strode across the room, crouching in front of her chair and taking both her hands in his. Her skin felt cold; he felt the ghost of a tremor. This had suddenly become real to her.

'Shit, Martyn, what's wrong with me? I've been treating this like a game, pleased I'd found her before you did. It's Tilly Brown. Remember? Tilly Brown and the quintets.'

chapter thirty

Webber studied the screen that showed the soft interview room. The man sitting there craned his neck to survey his surroundings. It was the retired teacher, Johan Meyer. His face wore a half smile; he held himself upright but relaxed. On appearance alone, Webber would have judged him early to mid-60s, but he had to be ten years older. He'd been a teacher until his retirement a decade or so earlier. Meyer had claimed never to have visited a police station in his life before and no one had unearthed anything to contradict that. Webber had rarely seen anyone quite so at ease in an interview room. The man's gaze darted about, taking in his surroundings; his head gave small nods of satisfaction as though approving what he saw. It had been his own choice to be here. He could have been interviewed at home.

'Practically begged to be allowed to come in, Guv, said it would make a nice change.' The PC who'd made the call had given a helpless shrug, adding, 'And he asked if it was about "young Tilly Brown".'

'I suppose we shouldn't rule out that he wants to keep us away from his house,' Webber had murmured, but hadn't seen it as a real possibility. Meyer would provide useful background, nothing more.

The real problem was that they'd hit the wall he'd been dreading since this started. Melinda's investigation had crashed into the middle of the real one. It should be Suzie or Ahmed here watching Meyer cast his gaze around the room whilst sipping pale tea. With no idea how or if to keep Melinda's meddling out of the frame, Webber had muscled in on the cold cases, saying he would conduct Mr Meyer's interview himself.

He'd seen surprise and annoyance on both Ahmed and Suzie's faces. She'd snapped that they'd been planning an interview strategy for Mrs Joyce Yeatman.

'All in good time,' he'd told her through gritted teeth. If Suzie had got her finger out and talked to Joyce Yeatman earlier, she might have got to Meyer before Joyce had given the name to Mel. 'Go and find Edith Stevenson,' he told them. 'See what she can tell you about Tilly Brown.'

That got rid of them from the premises and left him with Johan Meyer, the teacher Joyce Yeatman had dredged up from her husband's old school papers and taken Melinda to see. Meyer had taught them all, Pamela Morgan, the diminutive China Kowalski, Brad Tippet, all three brothers from the post office raid, including the eldest who had been in Dorset the night Robert Morgan died.

Webber remembered the emails he'd exchanged with Kowalski. He wanted someone to talk to her to find out just why she'd approached Farrar's father last May, but she was thousands of miles beyond his jurisdiction, beyond even the reach of the internet. All he had was Johan Meyer. And Meyer, of course, had known Tilly Brown.

Once the old Tilly Brown paperwork had been found, he knew where the sense of familiarity had come from. He'd been barely Sam's age when Tilly Brown was all over the newspapers, but the case had kept popping up over the years as such cases did when unsolved. Peripheral memories floated around his head; his parents discussing the mystery, speculating on what might have happened. It must have been one of the things, along with Robert Morgan a decade and a half later that had lodged in his subconscious and influenced his career path.

Mathilda, always known as Tilly, had left the area with her

family when her father retired in 1971. They'd moved to the south coast. Tilly was 15. She'd stayed behind to complete the school year, lodging with her friend Edith Stevenson before heading for Dorset to join her family. A new school awaited her that autumn, but unbeknownst to anyone at the time, Tilly's studies were over. One day in August, she went out for a walk and never came home. Police enquiries had been extensive. There were unconfirmed sightings; Tilly getting on a train … on a ferry … walking a path high on the cliffs. But she was never seen again. She'd taken nothing much with her, no passport, no money; the only oddity had been the disappearance of the bits and pieces from her rocking horse, its bridle, saddlebags, the broken section of its saddle and a multi-coloured shaffron, whatever that was.

Webber gave the screen a final glance before pulling in a deep breath and marching to the door. He put on his friendly face as he entered and introduced himself, noting that unlike Brad Tippet a week and a half ago, his rank made no impression on Meyer who stood up with a beaming smile to return his handshake.

'Good of you to come in, Mr Meyer … Johan.'

Meyer laughed. 'Jack, please. No one ever called me Johan. I've been Jack forever, after the cricketer, you know.'

Webber didn't know but nodded anyway.

'And you're Martyn,' Meyer went on. 'I met your wife. A very determined young lady.'

Webber acknowledged the point with a smile. 'Back in the late 1960s, early 1970s …' He sat down opposite Meyer and drew him into the past, to his days as a teacher. 'You taught a group who called themselves Tilly and the quintets.'

'Ah yes, Tilly. The little girl with the rocking horse.'

'Yes, the rocking horse. Tell me about them, all of them, not just Tilly Brown.'

Ahmed steered the car through the morning traffic. The rain was a steady drizzle draping a grey blanket over the city. He glanced at Suzie. Her monologue of complaints against the Webbers had run down when he'd stopped responding, bored with it. Grievances notwithstanding, she looked more cheerful this week, brighter.

'God, there's another one,' she snapped suddenly. Ahmed followed the line of her pointing finger to see a driver openly chatting into a phone. 'Is there a dash-cam on this? Can you get her on it? I'll report her.'

'It doesn't do sideways,' said Ahmed. 'If we get close enough, flash your warrant card. That'll give her a nasty jolt. We're not far off now. Edith Stevenson lives in one of the crescents down there.'

'If she wouldn't talk to you, why should she talk to both of us? I'll try on my own. She might be funny about strange men on her doorstep.'

'Martyn said to ask her about Tilly Brown. Maybe that'll spark something.'

'Why should it?'

Ahmed shrugged. 'I don't know. Maybe he knows something we don't.'

'Then he should have told us. Who does he think he is, barging in on our interview like that ... you know why, don't you? That sodding wife of his.'

The traffic was moving properly now, a glimpse of sunlight lighting the sky ahead. Ahmed looked at Suzie as he asked, 'Why are you so mad at Melinda Webber?'

'Who's mad?' Her tone was defensive. 'She's always had it easy because she has some hotshot barrister for a father, plays golf with all the bigwigs. And look at the way she's been talking to our witnesses all over the place.'

'Only Joyce Yeatman,' Ahmed said. 'She knows the woman. That's not a crime.' He flicked on the indicator, aware that Suzie had tossed her head in a petulant gesture. 'Anyway,' he went on,

253

borrowing a little of the goading tactics he suffered at the hands of Cari's cousins, 'I can see why she'd be mad at you, but why should you have it in for her?'

When silence met his remark, he gave her a quick look, worried he might have stepped across a line. Then she laughed. He saw genuine amusement on her face as she looked back at him. 'Welcome to real life, Ayaan. That's how it works.'

He swung the car into Edith Stevenson's road. 'It's just along here.'

'Pull up short, don't forewarn her.'

They both got out of the car but he held back as Suzie marched up to Edith Stevenson's front door and knocked sharply on the wooden panel. He cast a glance up and over the front of the house. Its tall stone façade looked somehow greyer than its neighbours, no splash of colour to relieve the rain-soaked masonry. His concentration focused on the windows, especially those that overlooked the door; he stared unblinking determined not to miss anything. After a while, Suzie knocked again, harder. She lifted the flap of the letterbox and shouted through.

Her voice generated a response but not from Stevenson's house. Ahmed caught the flash of movement from next-door. A woman emerged on to the step and peered round at Suzie who smiled across at her. 'I'm looking for Edith Stevenson.'

Ahmed watched the woman's gaze rake Suzie from head to toe. Curiosity, he judged, not suspicion. 'You've missed her. She went out a while ago.'

'Do you know where or how long she'll be?'

The woman shook her head. Ahmed saw Suzie hesitate weighing up whether or not to divulge her identity. Sometimes it loosened tongues; sometimes it caused unnecessary friction.

'OK, thanks.' Suzie raised her hand in acknowledgement and turned towards the road. She didn't stop or look at Ahmed, just hissed 'Back off,' as she strode past him.

He climbed behind the wheel as she slid into the passenger side. 'Reverse out,' she said.

'It's a crescent. We can go right round.'

'Reverse out,' she repeated. 'Don't go past the house.'

'You think she's in there?'

'Yes. Didn't see anyone though. Did you?'

He shook his head as he twisted in the seat to drive the car backwards around the curve of the road. Once confident he was out of sight of both houses, he stopped then drove forwards a short way deliberately spinning the wheels on the gravel and dead leaves in the gutter. It left them at a slight angle to the pavement where he knocked the lever into neutral and played with the accelerator, mimicking a car going up through the gears as it drove away. He thought it would sound convincing enough to anyone struggling to listen through the rain and gusts of winter wind. As he let the revs die to nothing, he clicked the key to turn off the engine and they both climbed out strolling towards the curve in the road.

'There,' hissed Suzie, her tone triumphant. 'That's her, isn't it?'

Instinctively they drew back and watched, Ahmed straining to catch the detail from the figure up ahead. Certainly she'd come out of Stevenson's house. 'I don't know,' he said. They had no recent pictures of Edith Stevenson.

They watched the woman who might be Edith Stevenson rummage in her handbag and then hold out a set of keys. A small silver car responded with a flash of its lights.

'D'you want to stop her?' Ahmed said.

'No, let's see where she's off to.'

They ran back to the car. Ahmed listened to be sure the other car had set off before he keyed the engine to life. 'She's going round the crescent,' he told Suzie as he wrestled the steering wheel to execute an efficient three-point turn. 'We'll catch her at the other end.'

He nudged the car out into the main road, eyes straining ahead to watch for a vehicle leaving the far exit of the crescent.

'Shit, she's coming this way,' snapped Suzie. 'Don't want to be too obvious about this. No, it's OK … she's going the other way.'

Ahmed watched Edith Stevenson make a meal of detouring around a parked car before she joined the main road in an unnecessarily wide arc. It looked like her mind wasn't on her driving. Traffic on the main road was perfect; enough to keep them out of her line of sight but not enough to swallow her up. In this weather they were invisible behind her.

'She's turning right up ahead,' Suzie warned him.

The traffic queue slowed giving them an unimpeded view of her car as it snaked around the entrance lanes to a supermarket car park. By the time they reached the junction, she was out of sight and a dozen or more cars had gone in behind her. 'See if you can spot where she went,' he said. 'Towards the main entrance by the look of it.'

'She'll not get a place near the door in this weather,' Suzie commented, then, 'Oh yes, she will. She's going in the disabled bays. Is she disabled? Right then. Park up and let's grab a word while there are people around. She hates being the centre of attention. I'm sure I've read that in one of the old reports. We might bounce her into something.'

'OK, I …' Ahmed stared across the car roofs towards the reserved parking bays. Her figure was indistinct in the haze and milling crowds, but …

The blare of a car horn jerked him from his reverie. They were blocking the lane. He turned the car towards the supermarket's wide entrance, nudging it along behind rows of parked cars then swinging it to a standstill across one of the yellow grids that denoted special parking.

'What are you doing, Ayaan?'

'I want her on camera when she comes back out,' he said. 'Did you see her when she got out of the car?'

'No,' said Suzie. 'I'm surprised you could. Why, what was she doing?'

He felt building excitement in the prickle across his skin. 'The way she walked,' he told her.

Suzie looked blank. 'You mean she's putting on a limp to justify the parking? I saw her walk to her car in the crescent. She looked normal enough there.'

Ahmed thought back. Had she looked normal enough? 'We might not have noticed,' he said. 'She was digging in her bag for her keys and whatnot.'

'Noticed what? Why? What's ...? Oh ... there she is. She wasn't in there long. One bottle of Bells whisky and a newspaper.'

'Look how she walks.' Ahmed heard the low almost reverent tone in which the words emerged from his mouth. He hadn't been sure. It had been no more than a glimpse through a crowd. Suzie looked puzzled. He'd tell her on the way back. She wouldn't see the significance. She hadn't spent the hours he had poring over fuzzy CCTV images from a case he wasn't supposed to touch.

chapter thirty-one

Ahmed stretched his legs under the desk, easing closer to the heat of the radiator. His right foot felt damp. He wasn't sure if he'd trodden in too deep a puddle or if his boot was leaking. It was an unwanted distraction as he stared at DI Davis leaning his elbow on the top of a filing cabinet as their footage played out in front of him. Suzie had disappointed him with her reaction, saying that Edith Stevenson was putting on a limp to justify a brief spell in a disabled parking bay; that it was his imagination to make more of it. But she'd agreed to put it to Davis. And she must be able to see it now. Davis was playing both sequences together. Ahmed peered across at the grainy image of the mystery man … person … they'd clocked near Tom's flat.

'It is, isn't it?' He couldn't hold back the question.

Suzie shot him a shut-up look. Davis said nothing as he watched the sequence to its end. When he turned, Ahmed tensed, on edge to hear what he would say. His gaze met Ahmed's; nothing to read in his expression. Instead of speaking he reached for the machine and set both sequences to replay. Ahmed watched intently. The grainy image with its weird off-kilter walk. The bulk was different but that could be down to clothes. The walk was Edith Stevenson's. He'd known it the moment he'd glimpsed her entering the supermarket, and was thankful he'd had the means to film her coming out.

'She didn't walk like that in the crescent,' Suzie had said, but as he'd pointed out, they'd been holding back, peering through vegetation, and she'd been digging about in her bag as she took the few steps across the road.

'We didn't notice. She wasn't walking upright. We weren't looking out for it.'

All three of them focussed on the moving figures, one fuzzy, one sharp as they played out. Davis clicked the mouse, leaving two frozen images on the screen. 'I wish that original had enhanced better.' He turned to Ahmed. 'What do you think now you've seen both tapes side by side?'

'It's her, isn't it?' He didn't even try to suppress the excitement in his tone.

Suzie still didn't look convinced, but that must be for show. She had to be convinced now she'd seen this.

'Heard the voices on tape?' Davis said.

'Voices?' Ahmed struggled for context. 'Uh … no. What voices?'

He didn't know they'd found any recordings of anything. Must be something from Tom's flat. Davis was still watching him, that bland expression on his face, as though he wasn't really paying attention. It was an expression Ahmed had learnt to mistrust. He braced himself; some sort of reprimand was on its way. So far he'd been the subject of no more than a couple of hard stares when he'd admitted the extent of his familiarity with the Jenkinson CCTV footage.

Leaving the images frozen, Davis moved to another machine and tapped at the keyboard. Ahmed began to move to get a view of what he was doing, but retreated under a narrow-eyed glare. Suzie leant forward to look over Davis's shoulder. 'Oh, those,' she said and turned away.

Ahmed shot her a glance. She'd known about this. Why hadn't she told him?

'Listen to this, Ayaan,' said Davis. 'Can you make out the words?'

The crackle from the speakers was over before he'd properly set himself to listen.

'I'll play it again. It's barely a couple of seconds.'

This time he heard something behind the buzz of static. He shook his head. Davis replayed it. Concentrating hard he could almost feel the shape of a brief burst of speech, but couldn't begin to guess at the words.

'Sound analysts can do a lot these days,' Davis commented, 'separating sounds, getting rid of background stuff, all that. Listen to this version. Listen for "post office raid".'

Ahmed leant in as Davis clicked the mouse.

... post office raid ...

'Yes, got it.' The audio still crackled but whatever Davis or his analysts had done had stripped the disguise from it. The words were plain. *Post office raid.* He thought back to Larry Scott in Dorset and the conversation the old man had overheard all those years ago. Had there been a recording? Where was this from? What was it to do with Tom's mystery man? 'What ... who is it?'

Suzie swung round and flounced to the far side of the room, pulling something from a desk and slamming the drawer with unnecessary force. He gave her a quick glance. This wasn't like her, but he thought he understood. Whatever he'd found, she thought it would end in him being taken away from her enquiry and set to work on Tom's murder. That would be fine by him.

'Now listen to this one,' Davis leant in to the keyboard again. He ignored Suzie's sulking. 'Put it back, Ron. Or is it Dan? What do you think?'

Put it back, Ron ...

'Ron, for sure.' Ahmed frowned. The short burst of speech was overlain with the same hard crackle of static but there was no ambiguity.

'And now here's the facer.' Again Davis leant over the keyboard. Suzie wandered over, treating the DI to a glare. 'This is supposed to be the same voice, but is it?' Davis said. 'It says "It's John Bingham". Listen carefully.'

It's John Bingham ...

Ahmed tipped his head, unsure. 'I can hear the words, but ... who's John Bingham?'

Davis reached forward and logged out the machine. He gave Suzie a smug smile to which she responded by putting out her tongue. Ahmed stared from one to the other of them. 'Tell him,' Davis said to Suzie

'Richard John Bingham.' She sighed. 'Seventh Earl of Lucan, murdered a young woman in 1974 then disappeared off the face of the earth. Probably dead by now.'

'But what's it all about?' said Ahmed. 'Where has it all come from? Voices from beyond the grave?'

Davis laughed. 'Spot on. That's exactly where it came from. Some psychic con merchant, couple of years ago.'

Suzie shot an annoyed look at Davis and said, 'It's all the same audio, Ayaan. He was playing the same recording over and over. When no one tells you what to hear, you hear nothing. When you're told it says post office, that's what you hear. Lord Lucan ... aliens from Mars ... whatever.'

Davis walked back to tap the screen where Edith Stevenson's frozen form stood upright by her car in a strangely unrealistic pose. 'There are good reasons for keeping people off cases where they have an emotional involvement. You're seeing what you want to see ... making links that aren't there. You're snatching at straws because you want Jenkinson's killer found and nicked. It's understandable but it's unfortunate that the cases have run so close together geographically. Just remember they're 30 years apart. And keep your head straight.'

Ahmed realised his mouth had dropped open as he stared from one to the other of them. 'Then you didn't think ...?'

Davis's gaze followed his to the screen. 'No, I didn't. If I worked at it, I could convince myself of a resemblance, but it's not the same person ... Ayaan.' There was an unaccustomed sharpness in Davis's tone as he spoke his name. Ahmed's gaze snapped up to meet the DI's. 'Don't meddle. You saw what you wanted to see.' With that he left the room.

But I didn't, Ahmed wanted to say to Davis's retreating back. I wasn't even thinking about Tom. 'You saw the similarity, didn't you?' he appealed to Suzie.

She shook her head. 'You heard the words, didn't you? Lord Lucan … post office raids? He didn't have to make such a meal of it but he's right.'

'If I hadn't known Tom, he'd have taken me seriously.'

Suzie gave him a despairing look. 'Ayaan, he did take you seriously. He ran that footage several times through. If it helps, I can see where you're coming from with the walk, but it's not the same person. Look at it again if you must, really look this time. But then leave it alone. We have work to do.'

So she *had* seen it. And they couldn't possibly say it wasn't the same person. The figure scurrying down the road by Tom's flat had obviously taken the trouble to disguise herself. For a while he and Suzie stared at each other, then he allowed his gaze to drop. Hanging over his head was the unspoken threat to his proposed move to York if he should step out of line. Next to that was a debt he owed not just to Tom Jenkinson but to all the young kids who might be mentored out of a life of crime. He must pretend to have accepted Davis's verdict, but he wasn't going to leave it there.

chapter thirty-two

Jack Meyer's interview that morning had taken shape in Webber's memory as an oasis of ordered calm in an irritating mish-mash of a day. He should have debriefed Ahmed and Suzie hours ago, but told himself he didn't know they were in. It wasn't an easy pretence to uphold, even in his own head, as Ahmed's excited tones drifted down the corridor. He ducked into his office, went to close the door then thought better of it. It was less of an annoyance having a stream of people knocking at an open door than a closed one.

Slumping into his chair he clicked on his email letting out a sigh of exasperation as the new mails began to download. 64! Who in hell had time to write 64 emails since he'd last checked? He skimmed the headers.

Nothing from Farrar or anyone else who warranted immediate attention. One from Melinda, subject 'DON'T FORGET!!' One from a coroner's office, subject 'Yeatman'. That would be the report on Gary Yeatman's death. There might be information here that he could use to divert Mel. He had to find something. The conversation with Jack Meyer played in his head. Another quick look at the list half expecting to see the name Kowalski, but it wasn't there. He'd toyed with setting Melinda on to China Kowalski as a way of keeping her out of the path of the live enquiry, but that had been his intention with Tilly Brown.

He clicked on Melinda's email. No detail, just an admonition not to forget the shopping task she'd given him.

'You're over that way anyway,' she'd told him this morning. 'Pick it up on your way home.'

He no idea what it was ... something to do with Christmas. But she hadn't relied on the detail staying in his head. She'd written it all down and shoved a note in his jacket pocket. He would make the effort because he wanted to be in her good books this evening; wanted her receptive to backing off from both Tilly Brown and Joyce Yeatman. There was a well of relief inside him that he'd conducted the interview with Meyer. Suzie would have made a meal of Mel's contribution. Her name couldn't stay out of it altogether but he could minimise her involvement now, gloss over it as the enquiry moved on until it no longer had a bearing.

Melinda was out this afternoon at some toddler-related do with Sam. If he could slip away early, he could be back before her, scrutinize those boards of hers. He needed to know if she'd been holding out on him and now he had Jack Meyer's insights he'd be able to decipher her shorthand. Joyce had lied to Mel about her husband's death, hadn't told her it was suicide, and as far as Webber knew Mel hadn't challenged the woman about it. There would be something in that to drive a wedge between them. He glanced at the time then towards the corridor. Things had quietened, the day was running down.

As he stood up, there was a flurry of sound from the window. Rain battered down as though someone had opened a sluice gate. As quickly as it had crashed down, it eased off, the wind gusted taking the brunt of the storm in a new direction. Ready with a hard glare should anyone appear, he pulled the door closed and returned to his desk where he opened the coroner's report and began to read.

It was familiar in style, a dry formal account of events that had turned lives upside down, but with an odd feel to it. It was 20 years old. He kept tripping on phrasing and structure that jarred. It would have been done differently had it happened last week.

Yeatman had left a note for his wife. Unlike the Pamela Morgan file this one gave the full text. It wasn't long and was oddly impersonal for a husband to his wife in these circumstances.

It's one of those risks where you know just what's at stake, the house, the car, everything you've worked for in hock for years to come, but there's no big reward without high risk and the potential reward on this one is big. Just no way out bar a bottle of pills.

Yeatman hadn't taken pills; he'd crashed his car. His impression, from what Melinda had said, was that Joyce Yeatman was comfortably set up. Had her husband really left her in a financial black hole two decades ago?

Looking up, Webber found his gaze locked with Davis's the other side of the glass. Davis peered in, respecting the closed door but making sure he was seen. Webber signalled him inside. It struck him he could give Davis the detail of his interview with Meyer, let him pass it on.

'How's it going?' he said.

'Yeah, good. Forensics and door-to-door coming together nicely to give us a second-by-second account of Trent … well, more or less. But you know all that.'

Webber nodded. They'd been on to the anomalies in Trent's death soon enough to throw resources at tracking his final minutes.

'And we're building a useful picture around Jenkinson's last days,' Davis added. 'Plus a possible lead on the bigger crime syndicate. There's a Scandinavian link, a Norwegian connection. We're wading through treacle with it but we've two names who look like possibles. One goes by Boots Boy and the other's Streetwise. I say names but I don't know if anyone has more than those handles. We're waiting on Europol. What we're seeing is the contacts being built, possibly rebuilt, as the mentoring scheme came to an end. Maybe our mystery man's one of them, maybe not. The images just won't enhance to anything very clear. But anyway, the Chief Super's talking to some of his contacts.'

Boots Boy and Streetwise? Webber nodded. 'One of those handles sounds familiar … had a mention in a briefing.'

Davis shook his head. 'Doesn't ring a bell with me.'

Webber screwed up his eyes, but the memory hovered tantalisingly out of reach. 'I'll get on to the Chief Super,' he said. 'I was probably with him.' There was nowhere else he could have heard the names where Davis hadn't also been present, yet all his recent dealings with Farrar had been fraught enough that they lay sharp in his mind. 'And the mystery man?' he asked. 'Killer or not, we've some scores to settle with this guy on the traffic chaos front.'

'Too right.' Davis nodded. 'But that's not what I wanted to see you about. I thought you'd better have a heads-up on Ayaan Ahmed. He's been doing a bit of freelancing on Jenkinson.'

Webber gave a tut of annoyance as he listened to Davis's account of the film footage Ahmed had shown him, and smiled at Davis's creative use of the audio files. He recalled the shock with which he'd first realised how easily his brain could be persuaded it had heard voices. 'And have you convinced him?'

'Maybe.' Davis tipped his head in a yes-and-no gesture. 'Suzie'll keep him in line. I just thought you ought to know.'

'And you're sure he's wrong?'

'If I'm honest, I could see where he was coming from. It's an odd walk. But it's not the same person. Have a look, it's been uploaded.' He indicated Webber's computer.

Davis came round the desk to stand beside Webber as they watched the images. Webber felt a bolt of surprise. He too could see where Ahmed was coming from, it was the weird walk he'd tried to imitate for Farrar. Why would she walk like that? Had she felt the whisky bottle slipping from her grasp? Would she have continued that way if she'd had to walk the length of the car park? He turned his attention to the original footage, the fuzzy image of the mystery man. There were pointers other than the walk, things that could be measured, proportions that couldn't be disguised.

He'd seen a lot of these things over the years and his gut told him that these were two different people. It was just the coincidence of the oddball gait that jarred. Of course it wasn't possible to be sure on a visual check. He looked up at Davis who seemed to read his thoughts.

'Call me paranoid,' he said, 'but I've asked an analyst to have a look, only let's not tell Ayaan.'

Webber smiled. 'Speaking of which, let me tell you about Mr Meyer. His info will fill a few gaps. Background stuff but it might keep them out of trouble.' He waved Davis to a chair as he spoke. 'Useful to put the various players into context. I didn't put him on tape but I had detailed notes taken. They can have a dig through those as they want but these are the headlines ...'

Headlines that happened not to mention Melinda. Webber took in a breath. Melinda was in the notes; he hadn't tried to hide anything. As he went to speak, a burst of laughter sounded from the corridor. Davis turned in his seat. A bustle of activity went by trailing a line of glittery tinsel.

'God, only ten days to Christmas,' Davis muttered. 'We're due at the in-laws this year. Any overtime going?'

Webber gave him a raised-eyebrows look. 'Get in the queue.' He paused on a mental image of Melinda's parents where he, Mel and Sam would be staying for the festive season. Her father, tall, imposing, able to shrink anyone with a glance. To date he'd approved of his daughter's choice of spouse, never felt the need to belittle him though Webber always felt that he had the power if he chose to use it. He would find himself in the crosshairs this year for sure.

'Meyer.' He returned to the matter in hand. 'He taught Robert Morgan's wife, the whole group of them. He remembers them well.'

It had begun to dawn on Webber before he'd talked to Meyer, that everyone who had encountered this group remembered them well, partly for their remarkable academic potential, in the end realised only by China Kowalski, and mainly for the magnetic personality of Pamela Morgan – Quinliven as she was then. Everyone loved Pamela. Even after all these years they could take the limelight at alumni events or open days if one of them turned up. Webber had come away with the impression they'd been the highlight of Meyer's career, perhaps of his life.

'Tilly Brown and the quintets,' he told Davis. 'Meyer doesn't know who gave them the handle but he said it was a volatile group that ruled the roost. The girls were the bright sparks, Tilly Brown, China Kowalski and Pamela Morgan spent their whole school career vying for the academic top spots, way out ahead of anyone else. Brown was top dog. Her gimmick was a rocking horse. She used to bring bits and pieces of it to school, saddlebags, bridle and such. Meyer said one of the biggest rows he ever witnessed was when someone broke Tilly Brown's rocking horse saddle. Edith Stevenson was the quiet one. Happy to be anonymous in a crowd but hated the spotlight. He said the group wouldn't have stuck together if Tilly Brown hadn't left. There was too much animosity between her and the others. Oh, and it was Pamela Morgan, Quinliven back then, who was nicknamed Quinny, not Quintina Tippet, but only the quintets were allowed to use the name.'

Davis frowned. 'Why?'

'He didn't know. According to Meyer it was Michael Drake and Pamela who held the group together after Tilly left.'

Meyer had laughed as he'd talked about them. 'Michael wasn't as pushy as Tilly,' he had told Webber. 'Didn't stand a chance while she was around, none of them did. I don't know what it was about Michael, but he made them a more cohesive unit.'

Davis asked, 'Did they keep in touch as a group when they left school?'

'Not really.' Webber shook his head. It was the same question he'd asked Meyer.

Meyer had said, 'They started out with big ambitions. They

were going to Oxbridge, all six of them together. They didn't much mind if it was Oxford or Cambridge. Gary and China made it to Cambridge, did very well. Pamela had a place too but she went off travelling instead. Edith went to York I think.'

This much had been on record. It had been the detail of the relationships Webber had wanted.

Meyer had needed no prompting. 'Me and a colleague had a bit of a side bet on,' he'd said to Webber. 'We used to try to spot the forthcoming nuptials. Would it be Michael or Gary for Pamela? They were both devoted to her of course … well, everyone was devoted to Pamela. She was special, and she might have landed with either of them. We didn't think Edith would marry at all unless someone popped up out of the blue and swept her off her feet, she liked her own company too much, hated the limelight, but happy to direct from behind the scenes. Except that then Tina Tippet of all people came out of left field and married Michael. No one saw that coming. Do you know, all I remember about Brad and Tina Tippet from schooldays comes from her marrying Michael Drake. If she hadn't, they'd have been just another brother and sister in the rump of nonentities that went through the mill.'

'There was bad feeling between Brad Tippet and Michael Drake,' Webber had prompted.

'Oh yes, he saw Michael as taking his place in the family firm. I knew their father. He despaired of Brad. He was glad to have Michael on board. But Brad never stopped needling Michael.'

'Brad Tippet once accused Drake of stealing his car.' Webber had dropped the comment in, curious to see if it would chime with Meyer's memories.

The man in front of him had laughed. 'More than once, I'm sure. It was Tina. She used to borrow it. I suspect Michael did take it a time or two, with Tina's keys, but I told Brad not to show he minded, then they'd stop doing it. They always brought it back before he needed it. But then Tina died of course.' Meyer's face had clouded. 'Far too young. She'd been ill a good while. I don't think they ever got to the bottom of it. And that certainly showed the naysayers. Young Michael was devastated, had to be sedated at one point I remember before he did himself harm.'

'Did you keep up with the rest of them? How about Gary Yeatman?'

'Gary married someone he met at University. I think he was pleased to get away from the group. I remember him in trouble once, trying to blame Michael. He told me he didn't like Michael always being in charge.' Meyer had laughed. 'I can't remember what it was about now, but I remember saying to him, "It was your idea Gary, not Michael's," and he had to take his medicine, but I'm glad he settled down. He was a steady lad, Gary Yeatman. China and Tilly were the real high-flyers. I don't believe China ever married.'

'And Pamela's marriage to Robert Morgan,' Webber had asked, watching for Meyer's reaction, 'was that on the rebound?'

Meyer had given him a speculative look. 'I wondered that at the time. She could have done better than the Canadian, I always thought so. I was at their wedding, you know. All the quintets were there, and Tina Tippet … Drake by then. Not all, of course. They sent Tilly an invitation … the family thought it was in very poor taste, but the quintets were resolute, it was what she would have wanted wherever she was. When that group stood together, they were an immovable wall.'

Webber related the bones of the conversation to Davis, adding, 'That photograph of the group of five, Meyer was adamant it was taken earlier than it was dated. He was convincing, recognised the school hall in the background, said it was at an end of year prize giving and it would have been Tilly Brown on the end of the line.'

'Did he know Will Jones?' Davis asked.

'No,' said Webber, getting to his feet. 'He didn't rule out having known a boy of that name but said if he'd been attached to the quintets he'd have remembered him. Right, I need to be elsewhere. We'll catch this up in the morning if need be.'

As he stood up, Davis said, 'So not Will Jones cut off the photo then?'

'Apparently not. Meyer said he might have a copy, said he has a box full of old school photos. He's going to see what he can find.'

Davis's brow creased to a frown. 'Yeatman's wife got it wrong then. Which begs the question why did Gary Yeatman cut Tilly Brown out of the photo?'

Webber pulled on his coat. 'Got it wrong or lied about it,' he murmured before turning and heading for the exit.

chapter thirty-three

'We have a timeline for Arthur Trent.'

Harsh morning sunlight leached colour from the room. The windows nearest the trees displayed a criss-cross of streaks where the night's storm had made cat-o'-nine-tails of the branches, leaving the glass frosted. Every reflective surface flashed a blinding spotlight. People huddled into jackets, rubbed their arms, clutched polystyrene cups for warmth more than caffeine. A buzz of conversation died as DI Davis dropped the words into the general bustle of preparation for the morning briefing.

Webber stayed at the edge of the space, leaning on an empty desk, watching. Everyone knew some of the detail, they'd been working at it for days, but only he and Davis had the full picture.

'Parts of it we can pin down for definite,' Davis continued. 'Other bits we can back up with strong circumstantial. And some of it's speculation based on lack of viable alternatives, so pick holes in it.' He turned to an enlarged map showing the stretch of road where Trent's mangled car had been recovered.

Webber raised his head to look across at Suzie and Ahmed, sitting together at the periphery. Ahmed's mouth hung slightly open as his unblinking stare locked on to Davis's briefing. It was OK for him to hear about this side of the Jenkinson enquiry. Suzie's attention was maybe 20 percent on Davis and the rest on a case file that she flicked through, occasionally reaching forward to scribble a note. She was probably putting the final polish on their strategy for Joyce Yeatman. Things had worked out well. She'd been waiting for Webber first thing, saying she didn't want to do the interview, didn't want any contact with the woman. She'd got it in her head that Joyce and Melinda were close friends; she'd been defensive expecting him to fight against her. He hadn't. He'd listened to get the gist and then faked reluctance in letting her hand it on to Ahmed, inwardly heaving a sigh of relief. The last thing he wanted was for Suzie to get her teeth into Mel's involvement with the case.

He glanced out of the window. Bare branches waved languidly in the cold air. The atmosphere was crisp as though everything had been swept clean in the night. It felt like a new beginning. He was free from Suzie's dagger-sharp glare for the time being. Mel too was pleased with him, both for picking up the shopping she'd ordered and for arriving home with the contents of Gary Yeatman's suicide note. They'd talked late into the evening reconstructing the lives and loves of a gang of 1960s school friends.

'The car stopped here.' Davis tapped the map at a junction two streets away from the crash site. 'Trent was in the front passenger seat unconscious but not dead. He was pulled across behind the wheel, finished off with a needle under his thumbnail. The car was driven from the passenger seat at least as far as this point here ...' – tap – 'Then it drove along from here ... ' – tap – '... down to the crash site, here ... ' – tap – '... where he was in the vehicle on his own.'

Davis looked around inviting comment. Webber knew exactly which parts of the scenario were backed up by evidence and which by speculation, and listened with interest to hear who homed in where.

Questions and comments focused initially on where and when the car had held two passengers or one.

'Forensics and toxicology can't be 100 percent,' said Davis, 'but they've done some pretty clever stuff with the injuries, modelling when death occurred in relation to them.'

'From what you said, we're talking minutes ... seconds even. How sure can they be?'

'We'd have difficulty standing some of these timings up in court,' Davis admitted, 'but I want to leave this room confident we all know what happened, where to focus to find what we need.'

'Does this mean re-analysing some of the stuff where we came up blank?' That from the officer sitting beside Ahmed. Webber assumed he'd fed him the question and supposed he was thinking about Jenkinson's flat.

'It's the boffins who've put this lot together. It's up to us to get the real evidence. We have no lab result to say that Trent didn't inject himself and then wrap himself round that tree. No trace of anyone else in the front of that car.'

'So how do we know there was?'

'Scraps of witnesses. It was the small hours. We've a gang of girls doing the midnight feast thing on a sleepover; a young couple up with a sick child; a shift worker going home, half asleep but he was first on the scene. The kids' stories are all over the place, but they saw something. The couple with the sick baby only took note because they thought it was the doctor's car, but it gives us a time. The shift worker was pretty much on autopilot; better on what he didn't see than what he did. Their statements would all be shredded in a courtroom but they give us a location and a time where the car stopped.'

Webber smiled to himself. The more they shone their spotlight on the crime scene, the more it told them.

'Did the lab come up with anything at all about who else had been in the car?' someone asked.

'Signs of Trent's family and a couple of mates he routinely gave lifts to. We've checked them all and eliminated them. There was someone else there that night taking pains to leave no trace. One of the kids described a ... what was it ... space zombie or something. Man in forensic overalls basically.'

'Or woman.' The words were barely audible. Webber's stare snapped across to Ahmed in time to see him flinch as he took Suzie's elbow in his midriff. She pulled Ahmed's attention to the file in her hand. Webber could see it was a lab report. Something back from that graveyard up at the gravel pits probably.

'How do we know it was driven from the passenger seat after Trent was killed? Why didn't the killer do the business once he'd got it lined up with the tree? Far easier that way.'

Davis tapped the map again. 'The shift worker,' he said. 'Doesn't remember seeing it but heard it stop then start up again. He clocked it as odd to pause at that junction at that hour. Road's clear ... you can see both ways as you approach. The killer stopped the car to get out. He had that cruise control gizmo in place.'

Someone went to pin up a diagram of the workings of the car the way the lab had reconstructed how the trick had been pulled. The complex diagram of wires was met with a chorus of disbelief. 'Yeah, yeah,' said Davis, 'Nothing like this in the car, but remember those odd bits of stuff ...' He pointed to a photograph showing the vehicle's interior after the crash. Short lengths of string and wire hung from one of the seatbelt anchors and the door handles. 'Suppose he had it fixed so he could set it off then yank the whole mechanism out, just leaving those odd scraps behind. Who's going to look twice at a bit of string?'

Webber's attention wandered as they argued for a crude but effective mechanism against something more sophisticated. Again he glanced at Ahmed whose whole bearing radiated irritation with Suzie who was taking his attention away from the discussion on Trent.

A couple of dissenters spoke up, arguing that Trent might have been killed at the junction where the car had been heard to stop. '... makes more sense than trying to drive from beside him ...' but Davis shook his head. 'Doesn't fit with what we know,' he told them, 'and anyway, that junction's too exposed. The car stopping caught someone's attention. If he'd hung about long enough to pull bodies about, our half-asleep witness would have woken up and seen him.'

'Did the witness see the crash?'

'He heard it. And he remembered running footsteps too once he was pressed for a second-by-second account. Running footsteps *before* the impact. Only no one else was there when he got to the wreckage. Our phantom driver trusted to luck the car would hit hard enough to be taken as cause of death, because Trent was a dead man by then.'

'If Trent was definitely killed back there, do we know for certain the killer stayed in the car with him at all?'

'If he got out earlier,' Davis said, 'he'd have needed some kind of remote control on the car and there's no trace of anything that clever.'

Webber thought about the traffic light scam. There had been nothing clever about that either. It was clear now that Jenkinson had told Ahmed the truth. Handheld lasers operated by children at his signal. They'd never fully unravelled what it was all about and wouldn't until they ran Jenkinson's mystery man to earth.

The set up with Trent was uncomfortably reminiscent of what had happened to Gary Yeatman. Back in 1996 no one had thought about looking for anomalies of timing, nor conducted house-to-house enquiries in the area. Like Trent, Yeatman had died in the small hours when no one was about. His car might have been seen but no one had asked the right questions. This time, they'd got themselves out into the surrounding streets quickly enough that memories were fresh and intact.

Davis moved to the wider aspects of the case, talking about the reams of footage from various security cameras that might hold a missing piece of the jigsaw. Wading through that lot would be a tedious job for someone. Ahmed would be good at it but Webber daren't let him that close to the case. A shame because a finicky arduous task would be just the thing to distract him from any freelance enquiries on his own account. Webber didn't like the gleam in his eye as he listened to Davis's team bouncing ideas around; didn't like it that he occasionally leant in to say something to the officers nearest to him, and he wasn't impressed that Suzie hadn't pulled him up far more sharply. She needed to keep a closer rein on him.

His phone sounded from across the corridor, the tone signalling an external call. He pushed himself up from the desk, briefly meeting Davis's eye as he left the room and went to pick up the handset.

'It's a Mr Meyer, you spoke to him yesterday.'

'Put him through.'

'Martyn Webber? Jack Meyer here. I've been looking out photographs for you.'

Webber watched through the glass. Suzie was talking to Davis now, presumably briefing him on the latest on the cold cases, that lab report maybe. Ahmed's attention was all on Davis's team as they bustled about preparing to head off to get started on their allotted tasks. The look in Ahmed's eye showed how badly he wanted to be setting off with them. He wasn't paying any attention to Davis and Suzie.

'Ah, the group of five,' Webber said absently into the phone. 'Did you find it?'

'Not yet, but I'm sure it's here somewhere. It's that other name, Will Jones. Blow me down if that didn't crop up as I was going through the albums.'

'Will Jones?' Webber made himself turn away from the scene across the corridor and concentrate on the call. 'Have you remembered him?'

'Vaguely. At any rate, I remember the fight. And when I saw the photo, it came back to me. The names were on the back and there was Will Jones in amongst the quintets. He wasn't a pupil … wasn't at school then. He'd been through the secondary modern system, left at 15 or 16, I imagine.'

'He was into the animal rights movement apparently,' Webber prompted.

'If you say so. It wouldn't surprise me. He certainly caused trouble at school that year.'

'You said there was a fight.'

'Yes, in the quintets' final year. Gary and China hammer and tongs with Edie as I remember it. Nothing physical. There never was. Pamela and Michael the peacemakers. It was all tensions and fights by then. Michael was set to marry Tina Tippet. Pamela had taken up with her Canadian and planned to go off travelling the world with him. And Brad Tippet a coiled spring of resentment against Michael for nabbing his big sister.'

The early 1970s. Webber tried to imagine the mores of the time. He knew that Pamela Morgan hadn't had children, but wondered about the other unexpected marriage. 'Was Tina Tippet pregnant when she married Michael Drake?' As he asked the question he knew that they wouldn't have confided that snippet to Meyer even if it had been true.

Meyer gave a forced laugh as though embarrassed at the question. 'No, no. They never had children. I expect they would have if Tina had lived. It must have been 1976 she died. Yes, because it was the year Gary and Edie graduated. Michael couldn't go because Tina was ill, but the quintets were there at Tina's funeral to support Michael. They rallied round when one of them was in trouble. In fact, I'm not sure that Will Jones wasn't there too. I couldn't swear to it, not after all this time, but now I've remembered him ...'

'But where did Will Jones fit in? Why did he become one of the group?'

'Ah, now that was a reaction to Michael's marriage, I'm sure. Edie trying to make him jealous. I think she had her eye on him. Leastways if he wasn't going to marry Pamela I think she wanted him for herself. Young Edie Stevenson, I mean. Will Jones was her boyfriend.'

So the woman with the weird walk on Ahmed's film had been

the adolescent girlfriend of Will Jones of the tiger stunt. After ending the call, Webber stood as he was, handset to his ear listening to the buzz of the dialling tone as he looked through the glass panels watching the activity across the corridor.

His first thought had been satisfaction at having such a chunky nugget to take home to Melinda; it boded well for another comfortable evening. His second thought was to be horrified at his first. What had become of his professionalism? Of course he shouldn't tell Mel. He didn't need to. Things were not exactly fine, but getting there. The next stage of his penance would be a painfully uncomfortable stay with Melinda's parents over Christmas. His job would be to contain things, act the model husband and father, and resist the temptation to explode.

He could see the whole excruciating week as though it were scripted. Cold shoulder to start with from all of them; then Melinda's mother would soften towards him for Sam's sake. This would infuriate both her husband and daughter who would join ranks to raise poison levels to unbearable. Then his father-in-law would succumb to the habits of a lifetime and start telling his daughter what to do. At this point the Bryants would turn their fire on each other and leave him alone. On the last day of the visit they would take their leave with everyone exclaiming over Sam and being cold and wooden with each other. Mel would thaw on the journey back because otherwise she would have no audience on whom to vent her frustrations about her father, and normal life would resume.

He thought of Davis's comment about overtime and let out a sigh. There would be no bolthole for him. If he let Mel go on her own, the dynamic would be disastrous. They might persuade her not to come home.

His task following Meyer's call was to keep a close enough eye on things that Melinda's name didn't get entangled in any way that might damage her future prospects – or his, come to that. The buzz in his ear turned to a low-level siren as the handset protested its separation from its base unit. He replaced it and strode to the door, signalling to Davis to join him in his office.

'Where are we with these cold cases?' He jerked his thumb towards Suzie and Ahmed. 'They're costing us an arm and a leg. I don't want to go throwing good money after bad if we're not going to get any further.'

Davis tipped his head. 'The post office job is wrapped up as far as it'll go. We can place the eldest brother in Dorset at the same time as the car. The teacher Meyer didn't remember him, did he?'

'Not really,' Webber said. 'He was aware of three brothers gone bad but they weren't a part of the quintets clique. It was a hierarchical set-up. The quintets were the cream, the post office brothers would have been the scum. They'd have known of each other's existence but little more than that.'

'Circumstantial says that big brother post office didn't drive the car to Dorset, but we're betting he drove it back. If he blackmailed someone about Robert Morgan then maybe he got enough money to disappear abroad. That was always the working hypothesis. The sticking point was that the money should have run out and he ought to have resurfaced, but maybe he had enough to make a clean break. Probably drank himself to death on a beach somewhere years ago ... assumed name ... who'd know?'

Webber nodded. He'd never given the post office brothers high priority. 'What about Robert Morgan? How far have Suzie and Ayaan got with that?'

'To be fair, they were taken off course by that note in the missing girl's file, Tilly Brown and her orange plastic rocking horse stuff. The Morgan case went on the back burner while they looked at that.'

'Just coincidence then. The plastic's from something else, is it?'

Davis's face betrayed the frustration he felt. 'We can't be sure. It's proving a negative ... and after all these years ... but it was in the file. The only things she took with her were the bits and pieces from the rocking horse, the broken bit of the saddle, distinctive shade of orange, the bridle and something called a shaffron. Both her parents are dead now. Her mother died early this year. Of course no one thought the rocking horse was important enough to photograph at the time, or if they did the pictures are lost. There's no analysis we can do even if we wanted to spend the money. Nothing to compare against.'

'And after all,' Webber completed the thought, 'what are the chances? Was there anything from the original paperwork that suggested she could have come back here?'

Davis shook his head. 'The school friends were interviewed in case she'd been in touch. The one she'd always been at daggers drawn with, Michael Drake, they had a bit of a go at him but it was a long shot, and anyway some stray footage of him turned up on a security camera showing he'd been … I can't remember where it was, but anyway, he was out of the frame before even being in it. They were clutching at straws once they were asking questions back up here. The search was extensive.'

Webber felt uncomfortable that he'd been the one to divert energies into this dead end by passing on Melinda's theory about the orange plastic. He pulled in a breath preparatory to changing topic and knew that something fundamental had changed. He didn't regret putting his marriage ahead of the job; he was thankful he'd realised how much he valued his family before he'd lost them, but it was time to regain balance.

'If we can wrap things up,' he said to Davis, 'I want you to get Ayaan working on the Jenkinson case. Background obviously,' he added, forestalling Davis's objection. 'He's meticulous. He'll be useful and we need every hand we can muster. So exactly where are they on Robert Morgan?'

Davis gave a quick glance to where Suzie and Ahmed sat heads down over a heap of old files. 'Our big problem with Morgan is that all energies at the time were aimed the wrong way. It was about a watertight case against the animal rights group, no one touched on premeditated murder.'

Webber nodded. Morgan's death had been taken as unintended collateral damage. The original team had milked it, but they hadn't investigated it. Extensive paperwork had arrived from Dorset all slanted just the wrong way, like pictures of a crowd that showed no faces.

'Suzie's done what she can to profile Morgan,' Davis went on, 'but he's a difficult one. He didn't keep up any links with his Canadian family. His whole network in this country was tied in with his wife's friends. I don't think he knew anyone other than through her. They're talking to people still around from back then, trying to build a picture … well, everyone other than Edith Stevenson who won't talk to us, but I'm not reading anything into that. Not yet. She's probably just a bad-tempered old bat. That teacher you talked to said she was reclusive even back then.'

'Jack Meyer,' Webber said. 'I've just had a call from him. And let's keep an open mind on Stevenson. It turns out she was Will Jones's girlfriend.'

Davis's eyebrows rose. 'The animal rights guy? The one who turned up briefly round here. That's interesting. Oh, and I'm saying they haven't found much on Morgan, but there is one thing. He and his wife won an enormous amount of money on the football pools in the mid-1970s. They opted for anonymity but I imagine the close circle of friends would have known. Suzie's been chasing Pamela's will.'

'Come on, let's see what she's found and we'll get them both up to speed on what Meyer had to say.'

chapter thirty-four

Suzie tapped the page in front of her. 'And that's another angle for you,' she said.

Ahmed leant across to take a look. Once everyone else had left, he and Suzie had gravitated to the wall with the radiator and returned to Robert Morgan, the topic they'd been pulled away from after those remains turned up at the gravel pits. He was pleased the body hadn't been Tilly Brown; pleased too that it was all going to unravel into some scam-gone-wrong to do with an outbreak of foot-and-mouth disease half a century ago. He didn't want anything else cropping up, no more cases to hop on to. He wanted Robert Morgan in the bag and then they'd have to let him help out on the hunt for Tom's killer.

'If Joyce Yeatman was that close to Pamela Morgan,' Suzie continued, 'she must have known Robert too. With luck she'll have a few insights and fill some gaps.'

Ahmed drew in breath to speak but it was Davis's voice that answered her. 'You mean they must have been close because Morgan's suicide note was addressed to Yeatman?'

She nodded. Ahmed said, 'Pamela Morgan and Gary Yeatman had known each other for years, but we've no evidence they kept in touch after school. Gary's death might have been the thing that brought Pamela into Joyce Yeatman's life, but we don't know that they were close when Robert Morgan was alive.'

'You're going to get that out of her when you interview her,' said Suzie, 'and anyway, it's not just the note, it's the will.' She looked up at Davis. 'Pamela Morgan left most of her money to good causes, but those apart, Joyce Yeatman was her chief beneficiary.'

Ahmed saw Webber run his hand through his hair as he stared at Suzie. Finding money entangled in a murder case wasn't unusual but Ahmed thought Webber looked more worried than the revelation demanded.

'When you were working with Tom Jenkinson, did you ever worry about him being recruited into something bigger than the petty theft stuff he'd been involved in?' Ahmed saw Suzie's surprise as Webber posed the question out of nowhere. Davis looked taken aback too.

'Yes, of course, but I think he'd have told me if he'd had an approach.' He spoke the words confidently but as soon as they were out, he felt foolish. Tom had been up to all manner of junk behind the scenes; garbage he'd known nothing about. 'Why?' he asked Webber. 'Has anything come up like that?'

Webber just gave a shrug that could have been a yes or a no. Ahmed looked at Davis who was clearly as surprised as any of them. it was almost as if Webber had asked the question out of the blue to divert the discussion away from Pamela Morgan's money. He wondered how well Melinda Webber knew Joyce Yeatman.

There was a moment's pause, then Suzie said, 'Yes, that note. You're going to have to get it off Mrs Yeatman if you can … if she's kept it. We know it said something about Robert Morgan's death. We need to know what exactly.'

She glanced towards the grey vista outside the window. Ahmed's thoughts stalled. Tom involved in something big? He *had* been making headway no matter what had been uncovered since Tom's death. He looked Webber in the eye. 'Tom would have said something … or at least hinted … if he'd been threatened or anything.'

'Suzie's right,' Webber said. 'You need to get that note.' Webber's words ignored what he'd said but the tone and slight inclination of his head told Ahmed he'd accepted the point. 'We need to dig into the money side,' he said, 'now we know how much the Morgans had.'

Pamela Morgan ... all that business with the other old school friend, Kowalski, telling Farrar's dad that it wasn't a suicide at all. Of course she was wrong. He'd seen the coroner's report and the coroner had seen the note. It was just another frayed edge because the case was so old.

'Will Jones, the animal rights man,' Webber said. 'He was Edith Stevenson's boyfriend in school. I've just had that from Jack Meyer. He has photos should we need them. Jones wasn't at the same school, in fact he'd left before sixth form. The others in the group didn't approve.'

Edith Stevenson. Ahmed felt the prickle of anticipation over his skin. She was the one who'd walked the same way as Tom's mystery man. Tom must have known who he was dealing with. It was Tom all over to pretend a woman was a man, to hold his secrets close until he decided what to disclose. And it was Edith Stevenson who'd refused to talk to him, then hidden from Suzie. A link with Will Jones connected her to the events surrounding Robert Morgan's death rather than Tom's, but she was the key to something, somehow.

Suzie pushed herself to her feet and reached for a marker pen to add the link. 'Could Will Jones and Edith Stevenson have worked together? Why would she have wanted Robert Morgan out of the way?'

'Why would any of them?' Ahmed said. 'We haven't had a sniff of a good motive. If it's not a psychopath it's more like a fight gone wrong or that someone targeted the wrong man.'

'Don't underestimate petty jealousies,' Webber said. 'Meyer talked about tensions in the group, and that would be about the time that Stevenson became involved with Jones. Maybe we need him in again, get a bit more about the whole dynamic.'

Ahmed cast his mind back to his own schooldays, the jostling for position within his peer group. The staff were on the outside. 'He was their teacher,' he said. 'I think we need to hear it from their classmates if we want the real story.'

Suzie gave him a quizzical look but was prevented from replying by an insistent beep. She glanced at the computer screen. 'The lab,' she said. 'I'll take it.' She moved to sit the other side of the desk. They heard the video call open.

'Go on,' Webber said to Ahmed.

'Michael Drake,' Ahmed said. 'The only way we're going to get a real picture of Robert Morgan is through his wife's friends. And it's the old school network that keeps cropping up. Edith Stevenson won't talk to us. China Kowalski's out of reach. God knows where Tilly Brown is. Pamela Morgan and Gary Yeatman are dead. I want to call round on Michael Drake again. He was one of the inner circle and he was happy to talk.'

'OK.' Webber glanced at Davis as he nodded. 'Then Meyer again if need be. He'll come in like a shot if you ask him.'

'Well …' Ahmed hesitated. He didn't think Webber and Davis had got the point. 'I was thinking Brad Tippet ought to be the next port of call. He was sort of one of them. He was a pupil I mean, not a teacher. He'd know the dynamics.'

'Yes, but we haven't entirely unravelled the business with his car,' Davis pointed out, 'and I'm not sure we'll get him in again voluntarily.'

'He's a real outsider for the murder,' Ahmed said.

Webber looked at their list of suspects. He didn't like the way it resonated with Melinda's lists scrawled on boards stacked behind the TV at home. Ahmed was right; Tippet was pretty much in the clear for the Dorset murder, but Davis had a point too. Tippet wouldn't be falling over himself to cooperate.

A voice said his name. He looked up to see Suzie swing the computer screen around to face them as she said, 'Yes, it is. He's here with DI Davis.'

Webber saw a familiar overalled figure framed on the screen; the woman from the lab, fully kitted out, the tools of her trade around her. He took in the hint of a self-satisfied smile playing at the edge of her mouth. The last time she'd looked at him like that had been to tell him she'd confirmed the presence of Robert Morgan's DNA in that plastic sheeting. He pulled in a sigh and braced himself for whatever grenade she was about to toss out to them.

'Do you want the bad news or the bad news?' she said.

His gaze met Suzie's in a glance of complete understanding. 'Just get on with it,' Suzie snapped.

The woman's eyebrows rose briefly as though surprised at the bad temper aimed her way. These lab types saw some nasty stuff, Webber knew. When feeling charitable he excused their inappropriate levity on those grounds. Just now though he didn't feel charitable.

'The remains are not Tilly Brown ...' she began.

'That's good news,' Suzie growled at her, 'and we already know that. It's a man.'

'One of them's a man,' the woman continued smoothly. 'And I can give you a name.'

'One of them?' from Ahmed.

'Who is it?' Webber could see Suzie's hand resting on the desk next to the screen. He saw her index and middle fingers slide to cross each other and became aware his own fingers were making a similar move. His silent wish was for this to be someone clearly tied into the illegal disposal of animal carcasses, a tight-knit closed loop, no complications.

The woman's mouth curved again to that hint of a smile. 'It's a Mr William Jones.'

Webber watched Suzie's hand ball into a fist as Ahmed smothered an expletive. He clutched for the straw. 'Is this the same William Jones who was gaoled in 1986 after the release of tigers in Dorset?'

'It was '87 before he was gaoled.' She looked pleased to have caught him out. 'But yes, that's the one.'

Webber's mind grappled with the fragments trying to sort fact from speculation. The information about Jones going to see Gary Yeatman had come from Joyce Yeatman via Melinda. It seemed partly corroborated by the landlady who had suffered Jones's presence in her house for a few weeks around the same time. He wondered what would come back to bite them out of all this. Ahmed would be interviewing Joyce Yeatman in a couple of hours. If she talked about Melinda there was nothing he could do about it. Mel hadn't done anything wrong, not really.

Davis spoke into the pause. 'What did you mean, *one* of them?'

'There's a second body underneath Jones.'

'What the … hell's been going on up there?' Webber had to hold back an urge to kick something.

'It's not Tilly Brown, is it?' Ahmed's tone held a plea.

'It's looking like this one's a man too. I'll have more in a while. They're both badly decomposed.' She looked slightly disappointed to have given Ahmed the negative he'd wanted.

When Suzie ended the call, Webber pulled out a chair and sat down. 'The summer of 1996,' he said. '10 years after the tiger thing, Jones supposedly turned up at the Yeatmans' house looking for Gary. Joyce passed on the message. Gary went out to see him and later he told his wife that Jones wouldn't be back.'

Suzie's stare remained on the now blank screen as she said, 'So did he take him up behind the gravel pits, knock him on the head and bury him?'

'That would take some doing on his own,' Ahmed said, scribbling a note. 'I'll quiz her on timings. See if she can remember how long he was gone.'

'Maybe she was in on it.' Davis voiced the thought that Webber was trying to suppress. Melinda was too close to this woman.

'Do we have a date for Jones calling on Yeatman?' asked Ahmed, reaching for the file. 'His landlady reported him when he did a moonlight. I looked it up. It was 1996. July … no, was it August …? It must have been about the same time.'

Suzie pulled a face. 'After all this time if she's innocent she won't remember, and if she was in on it, she'll say she's forgotten.'

'Give it a try,' said Webber. 'Get Joyce Yeatman to pin it to something we can date. Is she into sports? Was she watching TV when Jones called round? The Olympics were held in Atlanta that July. Charles and Diana got divorced in the August. And–' Ahmed's surprised stare pulled him up. He cut short the litany. He'd looked it up with Melinda when he was coaching her to quiz Joyce on exactly this. Thankfully, she'd held back. He changed tack. 'It's going to be interesting if that was the last time anyone ever saw Jones.'

'But if he was an item with Edith Stevenson maybe he went to her,' Suzie said.

'Maybe, but that was when they were eighteen. This is 22 years later.'

'Gary Yeatman died a few months later. It's down as a suicide.'

'Crashed his car, didn't he?'

'Jammed cruise control.' Ahmed said the words with studied casualness, his gaze fixed on the paperwork in front of him.

Webber narrowed his eyes. Ahmed was snatching at anything to veer towards more recent happenings. But of course he was right; it had been a jammed cruise control, but the two incidents were decades apart. Coincidence, he told himself, recognising a tinge of desperation in the thought.

'It doesn't look good for Gary Yeatman,' he said. 'And it's not looking great for Edith Stevenson either, but we've nowhere near enough to drag her in.' He thought back to Meyer's comment about Pamela and Michael being the peacemakers. 'Ayaan, when you talk to Michael Drake, find out if he kept in touch with Edith Stevenson. He might be our way in there.'

chapter thirty-five

Ahmed closed his eyes for a moment in silent exasperation. The lights had finally shown green just in time for everything to come to a standstill to wait for an ambulance to pick its way through the traffic, taking long enough that the signal was back at red before he could make any headway. It was always like this when time was tight.

He'd scrabbled about for ages looking for Michael Drake's mobile number, having had no luck on his landline. Drake had answered from the chaos of a pre-Christmas supermarket queue and done his best to put Ahmed off until the following day, but Ahmed hadn't allowed him to end the call. Drake was a compliant sort. Ahmed imagined he'd been doing other people's bidding his whole life; not the type to say no to a police officer. It hadn't been too difficult to hustle him into agreeing to hurry home where Ahmed promised to meet him.

'You can be a real bully,' Suzie had said as he'd ended the call. 'The poor guy didn't deserve that. Where was he off to?'

'He'd been shopping. He was calling in on a friend on his way back. Said his wife wanted a couple of hours peace and quiet to have a lie down.'

'She's not well, is she?'

He'd sniffed. 'That's what they told me, but my impression was that he's the sick one. She's only 30, half his age.'

Suzie had given him a look. 'So how come she didn't answer the phone when you rang the house?'

'Good question. Maybe she had other plans for her couple of hours peace. Maybe she's gone out somewhere she doesn't want him to know about.'

'Yeah, well, it's not your job to incite marital disharmony.'

Ahmed had turned away, his eyes narrowing at the hypocrisy of her rebuke.

At last the signal showed green again and he set off following the route of the ambulance that had impeded him, its flashing blue disappearing into the distance. He needed to get across to the Drakes, talk to Michael and then get back in time for Joyce Yeatman. She'd agreed to come in, but instinct told him he wouldn't find her as accommodating as Michael Drake. It wouldn't enhance the interview if she arrived on time and found she had to wait for him. He'd tried to push Suzie into fielding her if he was late back, but had had only a vehement, 'No way. I have a hospital appointment, and anyway I told you I'm not going anywhere near that woman.'

Drake had been one of the inner circle. He was key to finding Robert Morgan's secrets. Did he know Gary Yeatman's wife? Had the rest of the quintets known her? Drake would be able to tell him and he wanted this stuff in his head when he talked to Joyce Yeatman. If she was a liar hanging on to her own secrets she'd had decades to hone her stories.

He wished he'd asked the questions the first time he'd met the Drakes. Voicing the thought to Suzie, he'd added, 'But we didn't know the half of it then.'

She'd looked up and said, 'I doubt we know the half of it now.'

Unspoken between them was the phrase; and we never will. Webber had talked to him about cold cases, told him to manage his expectations; witnesses die, evidence degrades, people forget. Webber had gone as far as to say this one had yielded more hard forensics than they could reasonably have expected given it had never had the trappings of a murder enquiry attached to it until recently. And now their best prospect, the animal rights protester

Will Jones, had been found buried by the gravel pits, and left them with the question of whether or not he and Gary Yeatman had worked together, and the further question of whether Edith Stevenson or Joyce Yeatman had been in the know.

Nearly at the Drakes now. The flashing blue of the ambulance was still visible as a pale reflection that bounced around the rain-washed vista ahead. It must be wading through Christmas traffic not to have broken free of the city's grip.

The Drakes' road was just ahead. Michael would be back by now and it occurred to Ahmed that if he had returned to find his wife missing, he would be in no mood for a chat about his old school friends. Well, as Suzie said, he could be a bully when he wanted. He didn't intend leaving empty handed.

He swung the car round the turn and let out a huff of frustration. There was the explanation for the continued presence of the pulsing blue light. The ambulance sat foursquare in the middle of the road, parked cars solid either side. He was near enough to get out and walk but he couldn't just abandon the car …

His line of thought crashed to a halt as he took in the scene; the open front door, the bustle of reflective jackets. The chaos of an emergency in full swing was all focused on Michael Drake's house.

Ahmed slammed the car into reverse, slapping on his own set of blue lights as he did so. He slewed the vehicle across the end of the street blocking it to traffic, keeping the ambulance's escape route clear. He leapt out and sprinted back towards the action, pausing only to be sure he heard the clunk of the lock as he clicked the keys behind him.

Michael Drake stood just outside the open front door, a man in green coveralls at his side grasping his arm. A woman by the ambulance called across. Ahmed heard an exchange of medical terminology between the two of them. As he came closer he took in Drake's ashen face, the beads of sweat at odds with the hard cold of the December air. The paramedic's voice was robust and reassuring. 'She's in good hands, Michael,' he said. 'Now come back inside. We need to keep you safe as well.'

Briefly Michael's stare moved from the ambulance in the middle of the road to the face of the man holding his arm, then to Ahmed rushing up beside them. Ahmed forestalled objections by flashing his warrant card. 'Come on, Michael.' He took Drake's other arm to help ease him into the house. Michael's stare had returned to the ambulance, held as though by a magnetic force that wasn't broken until the two men at his side had eased his body far enough round that his head had to follow.

'I need him lying down,' said the paramedic. 'He's going into shock.'

'Oh my God!' The words strangled themselves as they emerged. Drake suddenly locked on to Ahmed as though seeing him for the first time. 'Thank God, thank God, thank God,' he babbled, trying to raise his arm to grasp Ahmed's. 'If you hadn't called me ... oh my God!'

The shivering beneath Ahmed's hand intensified, Drake's voice lost coherence in the chattering of his teeth.

Between them, they lowered Drake to the floor lying him on the rug by the fire. The paramedic barked orders, 'Cushion ... blanket ... pull that coffee table closer ... get his legs up...' which Ahmed leapt to obey.

Calm began to settle. Ahmed stood looking down at the back of the paramedic's head as he bent over Michael Drake whose shaking had subsided into ragged breathing that threatened to become sobs.

The paramedic twisted his neck to look up at Ahmed, tipping his head to summon him closer. 'Check if the responder car's still out there, will you?' He kept his voice low. 'I'll stabilise him and get him in that. I don't want him in the ambulance with his wife.'

'It will be,' said Ahmed. 'The road's blocked. No way out.' He paused, then mouthed, 'What happened?'

The man rolled his eyes towards the fireplace, mouthing back, 'Mantelpiece.'

Making sure to keep out of Michael Drake's line of sight, Ahmed stepped towards the fireplace. The hand-written note was prominent, propped against a clock whose second hand ticked past the hour as Ahmed looked at it.

To Michael, he read.

He reached in his pocket pulling on a pair of latex gloves before lifting the page and opening it out. The writing was even and neat.

Make no mistake, if you'd come right back after the supermarket you'd have found me in time, but you won't, you'll do like you always do. What's the betting it's 2 hours on the dot. Are you reading this and panicking or have you already found me. I'm upstairs by the way.

Footsteps. More people came in. He kept his back to the room to hide that he was reading the note but was aware of the paramedics talking to each other arranging to get the Drakes to hospital. A woman's voice said, 'She did what? Selfish little bitch.' He felt sympathy with the sentiment but was shocked she'd spoken the words aloud and within earshot of Michael Drake who was now being eased on to a stretcher.

'DC Ahmed.'

He turned. Michael was staring at him, pale, shaky, struggling to get out the words. 'Thank you … so much … If you hadn't…' His voice cracked.

'Just you try to relax, Michael,' the paramedic said, his tone both reassuring and authoritative. 'You're in safe hands now, both of you.'

Ahmed gave Drake what he hoped was a confident smile as the stretcher was manhandled away. He turned back to the note.

I don't care what the doctors say, I know I'm finished. I'm not carrying on like this. Why should I? You wouldn't if you had to live with this pain. You're selfish wanting me to. Why should I do anything for you? What have you ever done for me? You want to know my only regret? I can't stomach doing it with a knife and leaving you with a real mess to clear up.

A scrawled signature and today's date.

More footsteps. More uniforms. Police this time. The paramedics must have called them. Despite the evidence of Tiffany's note, he was not taking any chances with anything connected with this set of people. He would ask them to treat this house as a crime scene. The mantelpiece clock told him he had plenty of time to put them in the picture.

It was as he positioned his phone and clicked the camera to take a record of the suicide note that the words he'd heard replayed in his head. *She did what? Selfish little bitch.* He'd heard that voice before – on the phone. It hadn't been the woman paramedic. Of course it hadn't. She'd stayed in the ambulance with Tiffany. And no professional would have come out with a comment like that in front of Michael Drake.

He strained his memory for the sight of her. Someone had left the room when he turned to respond to Michael saying his name. Maybe hearing his name had hastened her exit. He marched outside. They couldn't get out until he'd moved his car and there was time enough for a quick word with Michael if the paramedics would let him. Maybe there would be a simple answer to her appearance just here, just now, but he was pretty certain the voice had been Edith Stevenson's.

chapter thirty-six

By lunchtime the day had brightened. Webber strode briskly as he hurried back from a brief foray to the sandwich shop. It wasn't just the weather or the determined beat of Christmas carols behind the thrum of the traffic that lightened his mood. There was Tom Jenkinson too. The case was moving, new intelligence coming in almost by the minute. If Jenkinson had trodden on the toes of organised crime, he might have put himself in the firing line, but the killing had had an air of rushed incompetence, not a seasoned assassin, and yet it had been followed by the calculated murder of Arthur Trent, an act that had needed some nerve.

Whoever was responsible would be uncovered soon. They had left too wide a trail. Their only hope had been that no one would look, or anyway that no one would look while the footprints were fresh. If they'd done it before, and Webber suspected they had, then their luck had deserted them this time. It was frustrating to be without a named suspect but the net drew tighter with every interview, every new witness.

No one would slip through. He began to think they would wrap it up before Suzie and Ahmed had a lid on their cold case.

As he'd left for the shop, Ahmed had sprinted in past him. Cutting it fine for his interview with Joyce Yeatman, Webber thought, though he'd already checked that she hadn't arrived. It was hunger that drove him out and he had quickened his step, determined to be back in time to observe, to get to know if Joyce would drop any mini bombshells about Melinda's involvement.

He ripped the cellophane from his sandwich as he took the steps, grabbing a bite as he entered.

'Ayaan's woman's here,' the desk sergeant greeted him. 'He only just made it ahead of her.'

Webber's mind replayed the fleeting glimpse he'd had of Ahmed's face as he'd rushed inside. Ahmed had been distracted by more than just worry about being late.

'What's happened?'

The sergeant shrugged. 'Something's up. He flew in like a whirlwind. Suzie'll know.'

Webber strode through to his office. He thought Suzie had left. Her official excuse for keeping clear of Joyce Yeatman was a hospital appointment. He didn't want to watch the interview with Suzie at his shoulder; he wanted time to absorb what Joyce said and work on any damage limitation that might be necessary. At any rate, he didn't want her seeing it live while he skulked in his office. Ahmed's agitated entrance was excuse enough to go and talk to her.

'What's going on, Suzie?' She jumped round as he walked in behind her. 'I gather Ayaan came tearing back like a hurricane.'

'Since when is that news? He does everything at a million miles an hour. But yeah, there was a bit of an incident. He went out to talk to Michael Drake; wanted to have a word before he tackled Mrs Yeatman.' She nodded towards the screen.

Webber glanced at the image showing three people milling about the interview room where he'd talked to the teacher, Meyer. Someone had brought hot drinks. Joyce was being settled in with tea and small talk.

'What sort of an incident?' he asked moving round so that she had to turn away from the screen to face him as she drew in breath to answer.

'Both the Drakes are in hospital,' she began.

He listened amazed as Suzie took him through the account she'd had from Ahmed.

'Another suicide?' He wondered if there was something about this group of friends that predisposed them to self-harm. It might be interesting to try that thought on Meyer. Yet Tiffany Drake wasn't one of them. She was way younger than her husband, probably hadn't known the other quintets.

'Attempted suicide,' Suzie corrected. 'She's fine. They might keep her in overnight but no damage done. They were more worried about the husband. He was in shock. Ayaan told them to be careful with the scene just in case, but there doesn't seem to be much doubt.' She reached across for an A4 sheet which she passed to Webber. 'He took a photograph of the note she left.'

Webber read through it, commenting, 'There's some malice in that. What's the matter with her, health-wise, the *living with pain* bit?'

Suzie shrugged. 'They told Ayaan she was ill the first time he met them. The husband retired early to look after her. Ayaan was sceptical from the off, thought it was the husband who looked more decrepit. Mind you, he's 30 years her senior. She wasn't even born when his first wife died.'

'Brad Tippet's sister,' Webber murmured thinking of the complaint against Farrar all those years ago.

'One thing that's odd, though. Ayaan's pretty sure that Edith Stevenson turned up at the Drakes' house just after he did.' Webber listened as Suzie outlined the summary that was all Ahmed had had time to pass on. 'Ayaan knows her voice,' she said. 'He's spoken to her on the phone, and it sounds like she cleared off sharpish as soon as she realised who he was.'

'So Michael Drake has kept up with at least one of the old gang. That could be useful once he's back on his feet.'

'First time Ayaan met them Tiffany mentioned Pamela Morgan too; called her Saint bloody Pamela; said she'd never met her which sounds credible. She and Michael have only been married a couple of years. She'd have been 15 when Pamela died.' A pause.

'Martyn, what was that stuff about Tom Jenkinson being involved in something big? What have you found?'

'I don't want Ayaan doing any digging behind the scenes,' he said.

She gave him a look of exasperation. 'I'm doing my best to keep him hemmed in, but you don't help dropping things like that in.'

Webber took a quick glance at the screen. Just Ahmed and Joyce Yeatman now. They'd be getting down to business soon. 'Just trying to cover all the bases,' he said. 'Weren't you off somewhere this afternoon?'

'Hospital appointment. I'm going at half past.' Her tone slipped into defensiveness. 'I've cleared it with DI Davis.'

Annoyance rose inside him that she expected him to object; just the sort of attitude that might have pushed him into finding her some time consuming last minute task. OK, he would surprise her. He allowed his gaze to stray briefly to her midriff. Was it his imagination that the material across her stomach looked tight? Wasn't it too early to show?

'Are you OK?'

The enquiry took her aback as he'd intended it to. 'Yes, fine,' she said. 'A lot better this week.'

'You may as well get off now. You've to get through the Christmas traffic.'

She stared and then roused herself. 'Uh ... right. Yes, that'd be great. Thanks.'

As she scurried out, he strolled after her as if heading for his office, but once the door had slammed behind her, he turned on his heel and was at the observation screen playing with the volume and straining to hear what was being said.

The ring of his phone sounded from across the corridor, muffled by the closed doors. He ignored it. After half a dozen rings it stopped and was immediately replaced by the phone behind him. He leant over to check the display. Front desk. They could wait. But as soon as that phone quietened, his mobile buzzed. With a sigh of resignation, he answered it.

'Sorry, boss, I couldn't raise you in the office. We've just had a call from across town. A woman walked in off the street and asked to speak to you about the cold case.'

His first thought was Tiffany Drake. Had she discharged herself from hospital? Why would she ask for him? Someone else could deal with this. He wasn't traipsing across town.

'She'll have to come over here and no guarantees I can talk to her today.' Out of the corner of his eye he could see Ahmed lean forward as he showed something to Joyce.

'They tried that. She won't; says she doesn't have time, it must be face to face and she won't talk to anyone else.'

His frustration rose as he watched the on-screen interview playing out beyond his reach. 'Who is it and why are they bothering us with this? I'm busy. I can't be racing across the city.'

The voice in his ear held a touch of uncertainty. 'I know, I said all that, but when I heard the name I thought you should know. It's Dr China Kowalski.'

chapter thirty-seven

Ahmed struggled to retain focus. Joyce Yeatman sat in front of him. He was word perfect on the strategy he and Suzie had devised, but his mind kept flashing up pictures of the chaos back at the Drakes'. An image of Tiffany Drake's pallid face superimposed itself on Joyce Yeatman's features smoothing out the lines, blending Joyce's open countenance with a demeanour that was troubled even in unconsciousness, the mouth a petulant downward curve. He shook his head and blinked. This was absurd. He hadn't seen Tiffany this visit. She'd already been in the ambulance. He hadn't seen Edith Stevenson either, though his mind kept rerunning that moment when Michael Drake had said his name. He had caught up with them outside.

'I think your friend was here.' He'd peered over the shoulder of one of the paramedics so he could see Drake's face. 'Edith Stevenson.'

Michael had been encased in crinkly silver by then as they'd tried to warm him. His face had shown mild surprise at Ahmed's words. 'Edie? What's she doing here?' Then his expression had crumpled to something like despair. Ahmed had heard him murmur, 'Tiffany,' as he'd had to back off to go and clear the road.

'Do you keep up with any of Gary's school friends?' he asked Joyce Yeatman.

'Not really,' Joyce replied. 'Not now. There was Pamela of course. Gary took her under his wing a bit after Robert died. She was a lovely woman, too sunny to be sad for long but she was really devastated by what happened to him. She got back on her feet but Gary always said she'd lost something fundamental when she lost Robert.'

'Do you know what he meant by that?'

'There was something about her, something indestructible. Everyone loved Pamela, that's what they always said. I remember when I first met her, I expected a smug, self-centred bitch who had all the boys round her little finger. Well, the little finger bit was accurate enough.' Joyce laughed. 'But there was nothing smug or self-centred about Pamela. She really was a lovely woman but she lost something of her spark when Robert died. It was as though she blamed herself.'

'Why would she have blamed herself?'

'They'd been talking about splitting up only a year before. It might not have been the world's best marriage but they were working things out.'

'How did Pamela and Robert meet?'

Joyce spread open her hands and shook her head. 'I've no idea. I didn't know them then. I met Gary at university. He never talked much about his schooldays, not that sort of stuff anyway. And Pamela would never talk about Robert, not after I'd got to know her.'

'Pamela and Robert ...'

China Kowalski's tone softened as she said the names. She smiled for the first time, her eyes focused somewhere far from a cold cramped corner of an office that was the only space Webber had been able to find for them both. He watched her expression as her mind roamed back across the decades.

He'd arrived to find her fast asleep, curled cat-like in a chair in amongst the noise and bustle of a busy public entranceway.

Unconscious, she'd looked far younger than her 60 years, skin smooth, hair without a tinge of grey pulled into a high ponytail.

'Jet lag,' they told him. 'She flew into Leeds–Bradford this morning, but she's got a plane booked tonight. She reckons she has an hour to spare, tops.'

'She's travelled in from Malaysia?'

'No, she's come from Easter Island. I don't know where she's going on to. Quite a journey, though. She said to wake her when you arrived but I don't know how. We had a gang of Christmas revellers kick off just after I rang you. She never stirred.'

But when he'd touched her shoulder, saying, 'Dr Kowalski? I'm Detective Superintendent Webber,' her eyes had opened. She'd looked blank for a second and then swung her legs down to the floor and stood up. She was tiny and had to tip her head right back to look into his face.

'I'm China Kowalski. How do you do?'

Her hand was proffered without a smile. She maintained a serious air through the initial verbal to-and-fro as he led her to the closest he'd been able to find to a private corner. It might have been the jet lag but she seemed unable to take the lead and articulate exactly why she'd come all this way to see him, so he'd plied her with bits of questions touching on all the angles he could think of.

It was when he'd prompted with, 'Tell me about the Morgans, Pamela and Robert,' that she'd repeated the names, her expression softening. The smile broke the perfection of her skin, creasing it to myriad tiny lines, giving a clue to her real age.

She drew in a sigh. 'Poor Quinny.'

'That's what you said to Don Farrar. What do you mean?'

'Oh, it was just the nickname we had for her. I never really thought of her as Pamela Morgan. She was always Pamela Quinliven to me.'

'Why *poor* Quinny?' he pushed.

'She had the world ahead of her. She could have done anything, but Robert Morgan came along and that was the end of it.'

'How so? I hadn't heard it was an unhappy marriage.'

'Oh, they weren't unhappy with each other, I didn't mean that. It was all the other stuff. Winning all that money, Robert dying the way he did. It left her with nowhere to go. But it wasn't suicide. It couldn't have been.'

'What makes you so sure?'

'I knew Quinny. She'd never have done that.'

Webber shot her a hard stare. Had this woman made a detour of a few thousand miles on such a flimsy basis? 'How ... uh ... how frequently were you and Pamela in contact after her marriage?'

'Oh, hardly at all. We got together a couple of times. And I saw her at Robert's funeral of course, and then at Gary's. Gary Yeatman. He was one of our set.'

'Yes, I know who Gary Yeatman was. Pamela would have changed a lot since you knew her at school. She was 45 when she died. Do you have any specific reason to say it wasn't a suicide? She left a detailed note.'

'Not Quinny.' China Kowalski shook her head decisively and Webber knew she had nothing, just the memory of an old school friend. She needed a psychologist not a policeman. It was something inside her that had caused this preoccupation with Pamela Morgan's death. He was reminded of Brad Tippet's fixation on Farrar's supposed negligence.

'Did you know,' she said, 'that Quinny deferred her place at university to go travelling with Robert Morgan? Of course, she lost out. It stifled her future choices. Our set wasn't a good advertisement for marriage. I suppose Gary did OK but looking back I think part of the reason Edie and I never married was that we had Quinny and Michael's examples in front of us.'

'Edith Stevenson? Are you still in touch with her?'

She shook her head. 'I haven't spoken to her in years.'

'How about Michael Drake?'

'We spoke briefly at Gary's funeral. That's the last time I saw him.'

Webber thought of Michael's brief marriage to Brad Tippet's sister. Her death had made an untimely end to it but this was the first he'd heard, other than from Brad, that it hadn't been a happy marriage. 'He married Quintina Tippet, didn't he?'

'That's right, Tina Tippet. I was struggling for the name.'

'Why was it such a bad example?'

She looked at him as though to say it should be obvious. 'He had to give up any chance of university and go to work for her father. He must have hated her for that. What sort of marriage can it have been?'

Webber considered the woman in front of him. She'd smiled only when she'd talked about Pamela Morgan. *Saint bloody Pamela.* He found himself with an inkling of sympathy for the second Mrs Drake, and wondered about the first. 'Not everyone sees university as the be-all and end all,' he said. 'I understand Michael landed a very good job with the Tippet's firm.'

'I'm sure he did, but he had a place at Oxford. You've no idea what that meant, how hard he must have worked for it. We'd talked about the six of us going up together, but it didn't happen. In the end it was just me and Gary at Cambridge. Quinny should have come with us but she chose to go globetrotting with her Canadian ...'

As she paused Webber bit back on a verbal prompt, wanting to see where she would go with this. He wondered how often she'd taken out these memories and if she'd ever inspected them closely. Could she see the way she'd imposed her own values on to the rest of them? By her reckoning avoiding university was Pamela's downfall and a reason for Michael Drake to hate his first wife.

'And Edie went off the rails,' she went on. 'She missed out entirely, ended up with some sort of degree, but such a waste.'

Webber was aware from Ahmed's background enquiries that Edith Stevenson held a first class honours degree from York University. He made a small adjustment to his view of China

Kowalski. It wasn't a university degree that was her key to life, it was Oxbridge or nothing.

'You said six of you talked about it. Who was the sixth?'

Tilly Brown, Ahmed thought suddenly, giving himself a mental kick. He was sleepwalking through this interview the way others had sleepwalked through interviews in Dorset three decades ago. They'd let a murder slip past. He mustn't let himself miss the perpetrator.

He looked down at his notes. They gave an outline, a summary of Joyce Yeatman's knowledge about the quintets. She'd known Pamela Morgan but had only a passing acquaintance with Michael Drake and Edith Stevenson. When he'd mentioned China Kowalski she'd closed her eyes in thought, saying eventually that yes, she remembered her from her husband's funeral. 'A tiny woman,' she'd said. 'Very neat.'

It was Edith Stevenson he really wanted to know about, but he and Suzie had talked this through. Joyce had claimed barely to know her. Ahmed would let her think he'd accepted what she said for now, but he would be back pecking away at the topic from different directions. If she wasn't being straight with him, he would find out.

'What can you tell me about Tilly Brown?' he said.

'Tilly Brown?' She looked surprised. 'To be honest I wouldn't even have remembered the name if I hadn't heard it again recently.' She smiled as she reached forward for her drink. 'One of Gary's old teachers, a Mr Meyer, he talked about Gary and his friends to Melinda Webber. Tilly Brown was one of the ones he mentioned, and yes the name rang a bell from years ago; someone Gary had mentioned but I'm sure I never met her.'

Ahmed briefly closed his eyes. In the middle of this speech,

Joyce had raised her cup to her lips and sipped at her tea. It had had the effect of muffling her words. She might have said Melinda Webber or Martyn Webber. Inwardly he sighed. What he really meant was that he had an excuse to think she'd said the latter and not the former. These were complications he could do without.

'What did your husband tell you about Tilly Brown?'

◉ ◉ ◉

'Tilly Brown!' China Kowalski repeated the name and treated Webber to a second smile, this one wider and more open than the first. Then her expression clouded. 'Have you found her? Did anyone find out what happened to her?'

'Sorry, no.' He shook his head. The image shimmered in his mind of that night at the gravel pits, the realisation they were standing on old graves. He was glad the two bodies had been male. It would have been terrible to have to tell her they had an unidentified body that might be her old friend. 'What do you think happened to her?' he asked.

'We had all sorts of theories,' she told him. 'I think we spent that summer talking about nothing else. Gary made up a tale about her running off with an Indian prince, going across the ocean in a jewelled boat to rule a faraway kingdom. That was the version I wanted to believe.' She laughed without warmth. 'Michael was the realist, said she was dead. He was like a broken record. If she was alive, she'd let us know. She'd run out on her family, but she wouldn't desert us. I thought he was being overdramatic at the time, but looking back now, I know he was right. She came to York to die.'

'Came to York to die?'

'I don't mean she meant to die, but she must have. They didn't find her in Dorset, did they?'

'No one found anything anywhere,' Webber pointed out.

She is dead though, isn't she?' She turned her gaze on Webber.

'We can't know that for sure,' he said.

'No word for all these years? I think we can. Gary said she went off on a boat with someone, probably not a jewelled one, and fell overboard or was she pushed? If she'd fallen in the sea close to shore, her body would have washed up. Though, Edie–'

She stopped abruptly. Webber tensed, waiting. Her eyes were unfocussed looking back on a past she didn't like to remember. 'Edie?' he prompted gently. 'What did Edie do?'

'Uh … well, we were all full of bizarre theories. The police came and talked to us all, wanting to know what contact we'd had with her after they moved away. I'd forgotten … never thought about it before, but …' She gave him a poor attempt at a carefree smile. 'Unfortunate coincidence. It's odd what comes back to you when you start to think about it. There can't be anything to it.' She stared down at her hands. Webber knew that if she'd been less tired, given more thought to what she was saying before she said it, she would probably have filtered out whatever she'd remembered about Edith Stevenson, but it was clear she would tell him now so he waited.

When she spoke, she made an effort to inject a casual tone, but behind it Webber detected something close to fear.

'Edie said that Tilly had probably been eaten by tigers.'

chapter thirty-eight

Ahmed pushed his way through the doors. The acknowledgements he received and returned were muted, a nod to a new day that was too dark and too cold to deserve either a 'good' or a 'morning'. He was deliberately early. His gaze raked the corridors and offices to see who had arrived before him. No sign of Davis or Webber. He let out a sigh of relief that was tempered by there being no sign of Suzie either.

She had rung him the previous afternoon just as he'd emerged from his interview with Joyce Yeatman. She'd been in a hurry, asking, 'Anything new? Anything that won't keep?'

He'd said, 'Bits. Nothing much.'

'Cover for me,' she'd said, 'if I'm late back.'

Davis had asked after her ten minutes later. Ahmed had given him a half-formed sentence around the words 'delay' and 'Christmas traffic' which Davis, his attention elsewhere, had accepted. Ahmed had then buried himself in writing up his notes and following the few new lines that Joyce Yeatman had provided, while dreading the order for an update that was bound to come at some point. The more that time moved on, the more likely it became that it would be Webber bursting in to hear the latest. He wouldn't be fobbed off with half a story.

But the afternoon grew chaotic. People were in and out. No sign of Suzie and she wasn't answering her phone. Webber himself had disappeared at zero notice disrupting several people's schedules. Ahmed found that he, Suzie, and their cold case fell so far down the list that Davis never came back to him, and by the time Webber returned, Davis was gone and Ahmed was finishing up. Webber put his head round the door but clearly assumed whoever he was looking for had gone home. Ahmed felt relief but was also annoyed with Suzie. Keeping his head down meant he'd had to keep well off Davis's radar and hadn't been able to catch up with what had been happening in the hunt for Tom's killer.

Given that her 'if I'm late back' had become a complete non-appearance, Suzie would surely have the sense to arrive early this morning. He glanced at the clock. People would be piling in soon. Where was she? He clicked her number into his phone.

'Ayaan, what's up?'

'Where are you? Where *were* you? I thought you'd be in early.'

'I'm on my way. Was there any bother yesterday?'

'No one noticed. It was chaos what with one thing and another. I fobbed them off with a traffic delay.'

'Good man. Sit tight and keep shtum. You won't believe what I've got. I'll be with you in five.' Her voice sounded animated with an underlying excitement, but before he could frame a question the line went dead.

He paused long enough for a couple of deep breaths and then called the hospital. Both the Drakes had been discharged. Michael yesterday afternoon, his wife in the evening. Cradling his phone in the still quiet office, he punched in the Drakes' home number. Like yesterday it rang for a long time, but eventually a voice answered him. It was snappy and heavy with tiredness.

'Hello Michael. It's DC Ahmed. How are you?'

'Oh … uh … Yeah, sorry. Not been up long.'

It sounded to Ahmed as though Michael Drake had just woken from a deep sleep; he didn't think he'd been up at all, never mind not for long. 'And how's your wife?' He put on a deliberately breezy tone.

'Yes, fine. She left the hospital last night. She's not here. She's with a friend.'

Ahmed remembered the venom of Tiffany's suicide note. 'But she's OK now, is she?'

'How should I know?' snapped Michael. 'Uh … sorry, I mean yes, as far as I know. They didn't allow her any visitors; they didn't even let your lot in to talk to her. I haven't seen her since … since … But you're the last person I should get annoyed with. If you hadn't … well, anyway. I won't say I'm happy about it. She's gone to the friend she was with the first time.'

'What first time?'

'The first time she got ill. I know, I know, you'll tell me it's coincidence and I shouldn't say these things just because I don't like the woman.'

Ahmed hadn't been going to say anything close to that. 'What exactly is the matter with Tiffany?' he asked.

'They don't know. They've never pinned it down. We've had batteries of tests done.' Michael sounded exhausted now.

'Who's the friend she's gone to stay with?'

'Oh, I'm sorry, I can't tell you that. She'd kill me for sure.' Ahmed heard genuine worry in the man's voice.

'It's not Edith Stevenson, is it?'

Michael's tone relaxed as he laughed. 'Why on earth would it be Edie? She and Tiff don't get on.'

Ahmed noted that he hadn't actually said no, but wasn't sure there was anything to read into it. 'But Miss Stevenson was there yesterday. Wasn't it Tiffany she'd called in to see?'

'Are you sure it was Edie?' Michael sounded puzzled.

'Pretty sure, yes.' Ahmed crossed his fingers to neutralise the lie. The fleeting visitor hadn't been one of the paramedics but he'd been coming round to the idea it might have been a neighbour.

'Well, I've no idea, unless she'd heard that Tiff had … um … had heard what had happened. We'd spoken on the phone in the morning; she knew I'd be out.'

Footsteps reverberated from the corridor with a swell of voices.

People were crowding in out of the cold. Ahmed looked up and saw Suzie. She caught his eye and winked, putting her finger to her lips telling him to keep the secret she hadn't yet relinquished.

As he ended his call and gathered both thoughts and paperwork together, Michael Drake's voice echoed. *We'd spoken on the phone in the morning; she knew I'd be out.*

The pace quickened during the morning. There was none of the usual jockeying between Davis's team for position at the radiator, no lazy huddling into overcoats and yawning over files. And it wasn't Davis's presence that animated them. He hadn't yet crossed their threshold. He and several others had been closeted in Webber's office since they'd arrived. Ahmed glanced over heads towards the corridor. He could see people milling about. Things were moving. There was an energy about the place that he hadn't seen before. Yesterday afternoon's activity must have borne fruit and now they were about to discuss it, to debrief everyone.

He found himself holding his breath as Davis entered, an unmistakable spring in his step. Ahmed wasn't sure he'd ever seen Davis move faster than a relaxed stroll, but he was striding as he cut a path to the warm end of the room.

'Something's happened,' Suzie murmured in his ear, looking the question at him.

He gave a brief shrug. 'It's from yesterday,' he told her. 'No idea what.'

They both turned to listen as Davis began to speak.

'You two,' he began. 'Suzie and Ayaan. Martyn wants a word.' He tipped his thumb in the direction of Webber's office. 'Go on. Look sharp!'

Ahmed felt his jaw drop. This wasn't fair. Suzie had been caught out, whatever she'd been up to, and they were about to get bollocked for it. He wanted to plead with Davis to let him stay and listen to the briefing. This wasn't his fault. He hadn't known anything about it. Suzie would back him up, but by the time they'd sat through Webber ranting on about it, it would be too late. He closed his mouth and pulled himself to his feet. There was no succinct way to say anything that would do any good. He hung behind Suzie as they left the room dragging his feet with rapidly diminishing hope that Davis would say something significant while he was still in earshot.

Webber was on the phone and scribbling figures on to a notepad as they reached his open doorway. He waved them inside, pointing Suzie towards a chair. Ahmed saw irritation and impatience in every line of his body. He supposed Suzie was invited to sit because she was pregnant. She would be ordered to her feet when Webber was ready to deliver his reprimand. He tried to catch her eye but she stared stonily ahead of her.

'Sit down, Ayaan,' Webber barked suddenly taking Ahmed by surprise. The handset was back on its rest. He pulled out a chair and perched at its edge.

'China Kowalski.' Webber looked from one to the other of them.

Ahmed glanced at Suzie. She looked as mystified as he felt. 'Um … yes … she's one of the ones … one of the school friends … Robert Morgan. She's somewhere on a research trip … works in Malaysia.'

'She's been on Easter Island,' Webber said. 'And on her way back home yesterday she called in here.'

'Here?' Ahmed's stare met Suzie's. The conversation had taken a surreal turn.

'Not here,' Webber amended. 'The other side of town. I went over to see her. She didn't have long before her flight out.'

Ahmed digested this. Remembering the annoyance of the people disrupted by Webber's sudden disappearance he wanted to say, Why you? But as he formed the question he realised there hadn't been anyone else, no one who knew anything about the case, anyway. He'd been with Joyce Yeatman, Suzie had gone for her hospital appointment and everyone else was out. 'Did she have anything?'

'I don't know if she came with the intention of passing on something specific. I'm inclined to think she must have done. It's one hell of a journey. She flew via Santiago, Lima and Amsterdam to get here, the best part of two days travelling, and another 24 hours journey ahead of her when she left. She was tired beyond exhaustion, completely on autopilot. I just kept her talking. She knows a lot about the key players from back then. Hopefully there's something useful in all of it.'

'Why couldn't she just have rung you?' from Suzie.

Webber shrugged. 'She's a very intense woman. I think she wanted to see someone face to face to make sure she was taken seriously. You know that she spoke to Don Farrar, the Chief Super's father, back in May. She got Brad Tippet's son to engineer a meeting. She knew Brad from school. They were both supposed to stay under the radar but Don Farrar recognised the family likeness in the young Tippet.'

'Brad Tippet claimed not to know about this meeting, didn't he?' Ahmed asked. It was one of the loose ends that flapped around Tippet for all his watertight 30-year-old alibi.

'I'm inclined to believe that,' said Webber. 'He looked genuinely shocked when I told him. What do you think? You've been through all the notes.'

Ahmed did a mental recap of the files. It was two weeks since Webber had interviewed Tippet. 'I haven't spoken to Brad Tippet myself,' he said, 'and this is speculation but I wonder if it was a bit of a wake-up call for him. He's conducted a kind of low-level stalking of the Chief Super for the past three decades. It's how his son knew Farrar senior's movements. Maybe he realised just how much he'd pulled in his family over the years. Why did China Kowalski go to the son, not to Brad?'

'Chance. She rang and got the son. He agreed to help her.'

'And Pamela Morgan?' Ahmed said. 'Does she have anything? I mean why the insistence it wasn't suicide?'

Webber shook his head. 'She and Pamela were obviously close at school. China disapproved of the match with Robert Morgan. I think she's just held on to some idealised version of Pamela as someone who would never kill herself. In her own way she's become as obsessed as Tippet is with John Farrar. She knew the woman as a school friend but beyond adolescence they didn't really keep in touch. She doesn't seem to appreciate that the Pamela Morgan who killed herself was a completely different person from the Pamela Quinliven she used to know.'

'But she still insists it wasn't suicide?'

Webber nodded. 'Nothing I could say made a dent. She was adamant there must have been foul play.'

'And yet she waited 15 years to speak up,' said Suzie.

Webber leant back in his chair and rested his hands behind his head. 'And yet she waited 15 years,' he repeated. 'Something got to her earlier this year but I couldn't get it out of her. She told me she'd been … unsettled was the word she used, she'd been unsettled for years, right back from when Robert Morgan died.'

Ahmed gave Suzie a quick glance which she returned. She'd got away with yesterday's escapade whatever it was.

'Do you mean she had her doubts about that being accidental?'

'That's not what she said. It wasn't as concrete a concern as that. At Morgan's funeral someone told her that Pamela was pleased he'd died. That it saved her the hassle of an expensive divorce.'

'Was she saying Pamela had engineered his death?'

'Kowalski's a very clever woman,' Webber said, 'but she doesn't have much emotional intelligence … no empathy. Everything's judged rigidly by her own standards. She said Pamela's grief had looked genuine to her but could have been remorse or guilt for wishing him dead. She certainly wasn't saying Pamela was involved. She still has Pamela on a pedestal like they all seem to. She was critical of Michael Drake, thought he wasn't as sympathetic towards Pamela as he should have been, Edith Stevenson too.'

'If Pamela knew more than she let on about her husband's death,' Ahmed said, 'maybe Drake and Stevenson knew about it. I had no hint of anything untoward from Michael Drake. Pamela was just a good friend who's sadly no longer with us.'

'What did Kowalski think of Robert Morgan?' Suzie asked.

'She didn't like him; thought Pamela had thrown away a university place because of him, Cambridge at that, and believe me, in China Kowalski's world that's a biggie.'

'Big enough to be a motive to kill him?' Suzie spoke the words as though trying them for size.

Webber pulled a face. 'I don't think so. I mean I've seen worse done for flimsier motives ...' *Worse?* Ahmed felt his eyebrows rise ... 'but no, I don't much like it as a theory. The teacher Meyer said the group fought a lot but never anything physical.'

'I guess we should get back to him.' Ahmed made a note as he spoke. 'Check out her story against his recollections. Michael Drake too.'

'I've spoken to Meyer. I rang him on my way back yesterday.' Ahmed was aware that Suzie tensed in annoyance. He felt the same. Webber might have been the only one on hand to tackle Kowalski but he needn't have butted in on Meyer again. It was as though he didn't want anyone else talking directly to the man. 'The university thing,' Webber went on. 'Kowalski, Gary Yeatman and Pamela Morgan all had places at Cambridge. Edith Stevenson tried but didn't get in. Kowalski told me that Drake had a place at Oxford. Meyer says not. He was pretty sure Drake was advised against applying to Oxbridge. He can't remember if he did but said he wouldn't have got in. And in the end he didn't go on to university at all.'

'Because he married Tina Tippet.'

'Well, that's another thing I got from Kowalski. According to her Tina Tippet was pregnant when they married. An old-fashioned shotgun wedding. She was convinced Michael Drake must have resented his wife for stopping his career in its tracks.'

'That's not how it comes across,' said Ahmed.

'No, I don't think it's how it was. Drake landed on his feet in the Tippet's firm. Tippet senior was glad to have him. He was a better prospect for the firm than Brad.'

'And I didn't think Drake had any children.'

'Kowalski said Tina miscarried. I wonder if it was a face-saving thing for Drake. Once he knew he wouldn't be going to any university, he told the quintets he'd given up a place at Oxford.'

'Could he have got away with that?' Suzie said.

Webber nodded. 'I ran the idea past Meyer. He said Pamela would have seen through it but she might have backed him up all the same. And if Pamela said she believed something, the rest of them followed suit. Kowalski mentioned the Yeatmans too. She was at Gary's funeral. She told me Pamela had sung their praises about the way they'd helped her after Robert's death. You were right, Ayaan, Pamela Morgan didn't know Joyce Yeatman well before Gary died. Kowalski thought they'd become closer afterwards for mutual support, both husbands dying suddenly.'

'Did Kowalski know that Yeatman's death was classified as suicide?' Ahmed asked.

Webber narrowed his eyes. 'I got the impression she'd known but had forgotten. I also thought she might have contradicted me if she'd had the energy, tried to argue foul play for him too. But it was Pamela's death that was the important thing for her. So what about Joyce Yeatman? We know she doesn't talk about her husband's death as suicide but there might be all sorts of reasons for that. What did you get on that, Ayaan?'

'Uh ... well ...' Ahmed tried to gather his thoughts. He wanted to be back across the corridor listening to Davis, not discussing ancient history with Webber. 'Frankly the suicide verdict looks dodgy to me. It's all based on his note which isn't exactly clear. I haven't found anything to back up the financial problems. Oh, and you know Mrs Yeatman seems to have had a big insurance pay out. I asked about it and she was cagey.'

'Cagey? How do you mean?'

He'd tried to read Joyce Yeatman. In some ways she'd come across as transparent, in others he hadn't been so sure. 'It was as though I was touching indelicate ground; her profiting from her husband's death. She said he didn't kill himself, said the verdict was a nonsense. She'd have challenged it but there was no point. It wouldn't bring him back. That's when I asked about the insurance. Accidental death … suicide … it can make a difference.'

Webber nodded. 'Oh, and I got an interesting snippet about Tilly Brown,' he said. 'If Kowalski had Pamela on a pedestal, Tilly Brown was on a higher one.' Webber outlined what he'd heard.

'Edith Stevenson said Tilly Brown had been eaten by tigers?' Suzie said. 'What would have made her say that?'

'Will Jones,' replied Webber. 'Turns out Edith Stevenson knew Will Jones even back then and he was already involved in campaigns against circus animals.'

Ahmed whistled through his teeth. 'That's a turn up. So Jones was around the quintets longer than we thought.'

'And he was the result of quite a bit of in-fighting. It went under Meyer's radar because it happened outside school. Michael Drake fell out with Edith Stevenson, he thought Jones was an idiot. Kowalski clearly thought much the same. She told me she recalled advising Stevenson to steer clear of trouble.'

'How about Yeatman?' Ahmed asked.

'Seems Gary Yeatman was the peacemaker in this one, but Kowalski told me he didn't like Will Jones either. None of them did.'

'Except Edith Stevenson,' murmured Suzie.

Webber looked at her. 'Kowalski said she didn't think Stevenson thought much of him either, just let him hang around. The last time she remembers seeing him was at a reunion in 1985, the year before Morgan died. She told me Stevenson had told them she was fed up with Jones and his campaigning. He shouldn't have been at the do, it wasn't his school. As far as Kowalski remembered, Jones had tagged along as Edith's plus one. She and Yeatman were ready to throw him out and it was Michael Drake and Pamela Morgan who stopped them. Anyway …' Ahmed saw Webber glance at the clock. Maybe they'd be allowed back in time to get the nub of Davis's briefing after all. 'There's some kind of mess of motives in all that lot that need unravelling. Jones and Morgan. It's all on tape, my chat with Kowalski. They'll have uploaded it by now. I think those were the headlines.'

'Why would Michael Drake and Pamela Morgan pitch in on Will Jones's side?'

Ahmed shot Suzie a furious glare. It was all on the tape. Why was she keeping Webber talking?

Webber nodded. 'Didn't like him but didn't want to see him publically humiliated is the way she remembers it.'

'And the rocking horse?'

Ahmed felt his jaw tighten. They'd never get away if she kept on with the irrelevant questions.

'Yes, I mentioned it. It certainly got a reaction. She was … how can I put it … as though I was accusing her of something. It made me wonder if she'd been responsible for the broken saddle all those years ago. She said "That's got nothing to do with Pamela." She was cagey, didn't want to talk about it. It was odd.'

When they were finally let go, it was to return to a rapidly emptying office. Ahmed's gaze raced across the boards and desks, looking for new names, new ideas, anything to give a clue about what had been happening.

He sidestepped the crowd, losing Suzie and cornering the colleague most likely to leak details. 'What's the latest?' he hissed.

In answer, he found himself on the receiving end of a friendly punch on the arm and a whispered, 'Still no name, but we're not far off now.'

He turned to see Suzie beckoning. She had claimed the corner by the radiator as everyone else bustled away. 'Ayaan, quick before we're disturbed. I need to get you up to speed. You know where I was yesterday.'

'No, I don't.' He spoke with a level of indignation thinking of the briefing he'd had to keep away from so as not to betray her absence.

'Yes, you do. I was at the hospital. And you know who else was there?'

'Who?'

She gave a tut of impatience. 'Come on, Ayaan. Wake up! We want the inside story. Who's going to be in just the right frame of mind to dish the dirt? And what better way to get it than to catch her when she's at her most vulnerable? Tiffany Drake, of course.'

chapter thirty-nine

Ahmed tensed. Suzie was flirting with professional suicide. He wondered if he would be able to steer clear of the fall-out when it came. Behind her head, beyond glass panels that cut out all sound, the group that contained both Davis and Webber shifted around as it focused on something Ahmed couldn't see. Webber pulled a face. Davis looked up, said something. Ahmed saw his lips shape themselves around the words Boots Boy. He could be imagining it, but his lip-reading was good and Boots Boy was a term he'd heard tossed about. Boots Boy ... something ... streetwise... He grasped at the straws knowing he had barely got his finger ends on to anything solid.

'Uh ... yeah ... OK.' He murmured a response to a half heard comment from Suzie. She was going to have him sitting with earphones on all day making sense of Webber's talk with Dr China. He mustn't feel annoyed with her. Webber was right about all that stuff the year before Robert Morgan died; Will Jones had been involved for way longer than they'd realised. It had a bearing.

Will Jones had become their prime suspect for Robert Morgan's murder. Gary Yeatman might also have been involved. The problem was that it left them chasing dead guys. And nothing he'd heard filled the gaping hole labelled 'motive'; mild dislike of Robert Morgan didn't fit with such a brutal killing.

Of course Edith Stevenson was still alive and well. According to what Webber had said, she had wanted to be rid of Jones. The tiger stunt had certainly done that for her, but it hadn't needed Robert

Morgan's death. He had no idea what her role might have been 30 years ago, but hadn't lost his certainty that she had a role to play in something right now and nearer to home.

'How did Michael Drake react to what Tiffany did?' Suzie asked him. He pulled his gaze back to her. The conclave across the corridor was breaking up. 'I mean was he angry, upset, indifferent ... what?'

Ahmed shook his head. 'Angry upset I suppose best describes it. By the time I got there, he was in shock, physically. His body was shutting down. They were seriously worried about him. If he hadn't grabbed the phone he might have collapsed and that would have been the last of them both.'

'That's a point,' said Suzie. 'Find his emergency call, listen to that. I'd like to know. Tiffany told me he'd been really angry with her for what she'd done.'

'Can you blame him?'

'Have you any impression of how he feels about her? It was clearly never a love match, I've had the story from her, but she's a player. Tiffany Drake is very much out for number one.'

Takes one to know one, Ahmed thought as he went over his brief interactions with the Drakes. 'I think he cares about her more than she cares for him. She seemed to resent having to rely on him. I've only met her the once. Do you know where she went when she left hospital?'

Suzie shot him a warning look. He became aware of Davis approaching. Suzie pointed towards the headset lying on the desk. 'We need to concentrate on that reunion a year before Robert Morgan's death ...' She stopped as though just aware of Davis and looked up at him.

'OK?' he said. 'How's it going?' but even as he turned his attention to the screen and paperwork in front of them, Ahmed could see that his mind was elsewhere.

Suzie pointed at the headset, outlining their plans to go through Webber's encounter, ferret out the nuances of what China

Kowalski had said. She settled into her seat as she began to expand the detail. Ahmed ducked his head to hide a smile as Davis held up his hand to stem the flow. 'Yes, yes, good. You carry on. I'll catch up later.'

Suzie's stare tracked his departure. 'Right, that's got shot of him. If he comes sniffing round, tie him up in the psychology of it all. He won't stick around for that. How old would they have been at that reunion?'

'Uh … 29. Yes, it was the year before the tiger stunt.'

'Why 29? Wouldn't you normally wait for a round number, like 30?'

'China Kowalski was going to Malaysia. It was the last time they'd all be together in England.' As he spoke Ahmed realised he'd paid better attention to Webber's account than he'd thought. It had been Suzie's attention that had wandered. 'But as it went they were all together the next year; solidarity with Saint Pamela at Robert's funeral.' He nodded his head towards the door where Davis had disappeared. 'Why the diversion? What aren't we telling him?'

'I'm going to have a dig around the records on the first Mrs Michael Drake. I didn't like what I was hearing yesterday. I'm not seeing a link yet but we have Pamela Morgan's husband targeted for no good reason. What if someone has it in for Michael Drake's wives?'

'If that's a possibility, then shouldn't we be alerting someone, not keeping quiet?'

Suzie blew out a breath and shook her head. 'Not after the way I got to know stuff yesterday. I might have been sailing close to the wind lately …' She patted her stomach, 'but I'm not ready to throw myself under the disciplinary express just yet.'

'So where's she gone, Tiffany Drake?' Ahmed returned to the topic Davis had interrupted.

'I don't know. It was one of the first things I asked but she skirted round it. The best part of an hour and some strong coffees later I'd got her talking. I'd listened to her sodding life story, then we were getting on to the nitty gritty when the nurse came in.'

'Hang on a minute. Michael said she hadn't been allowed visitors. How did you get to see her?'

'I know some of the medics. I used to work the rape crisis centre. They let me slip in. As far as Tiffany's concerned I was just another patient in a hospital gown. I think she thought I was an attempted suicide too. She didn't ask much, just wanted to talk ... well, complain. The thing is, when I first went in she was asleep. Her records were there. I wanted to know about this mystery illness she's supposed to have.'

Ahmed felt his eyes widen as he swallowed involuntarily.

'I know, I know,' said Suzie, watching him. 'If it comes out, I'm dead meat, but can you imagine trying to get at her medical records through official channels? I wasn't letting that chance go by. Not that I was expecting to find anything. And I didn't. Not really. But she's not been making it up. She's had a whole swathe of things wrong with her. Blurred vision, dizziness, nausea, sensitivity to sunlight, bone pain. None of it explained. She was hospitalised once with what should have been a minor infection. Turned out she hadn't fought it off because she was immunosuppressed, but they never found out why. Sort of effect you might see in HIV patients or people on chemo.'

'Are you saying it was something she'd taken ... or been given?'

She shrugged. 'They didn't find anything. Apparently it can happen, but it's rare. It's usually attached to some kind of chronic condition. They just haven't pinned down what hers is. Or, like you say, it's something she's taking but if she's self-medicating she's got to have cottoned on by now that it's not a great idea. I know she's dabbled with herbal stuff. She told me. But she stopped when it wasn't doing any good. She's a real whiner but apparently she wasn't exaggerating about the pain.

'What if someone's been feeding her stuff,' said Ahmed. 'Like the mystery friend she's gone to? Michael told me she'd first got ill after staying with her.' He found himself forming the syllables to say Edith Stevenson, but swallowed the words; mustn't get obsessed with the woman.

'Yeah, well, that's why I want to dig a bit more into the first Mrs Drake … just check out what was wrong with her. And at least she's been dead long enough that I can get at her records without causing a riot.'

Ahmed looked at her doubtfully. 'It's a long shot. What's put you on this track?'

'It was something she said. The thing about dabbling in herbal remedies. They hadn't been married long. She said it was the first time she'd seen him angry. She suggested something or got something from somewhere. He went apeshit, said his first wife had lost a child through messing about with her own medicines.'

'It's a long time ago, Suzie. And it's a bit tenuous.'

'I know, I know. I can't quite put my finger on it but get this; she wasn't into herbal stuff before she married him. Someone talked her into it, advised her to give it a try. When I asked who, she said she wasn't sure, but soon after that she went quiet – this is the woman who hadn't stopped complaining since she woke up. It was like something had clicked. I have a feeling she remembered exactly who was involved in the herbal stuff. She changed tack, and started repeating what she'd said at the start, that she wasn't going back to her husband; she was going to stay with a friend, only now she wasn't sounding so sure. The way she said it, I think she was linking homespun remedies with who knows what in her head. She was having second thoughts, and if I'd had just a few minutes longer with her I think she'd have told me just what was bothering her and where she was planning to go.'

'Why did she marry him? You said you'd had the full story.'

'She went all round the houses about it, but what it boils down to is that she thought he was older and sicker than he is. He wanted someone to look after him. He has no family. She was working as a carer, badly paid, thought why not take on a longer-term job and get some real money out of it. She didn't dislike him. They both went into it with their eyes open.'

'So it was a bit of blow when she got ill and he had to look after her.'

'Exactly. Sounds like he was on his own and lonely. Having a wife around perked him up. Didn't do much for her though. D'you think Michael would come clean with you about the friend?' Suzie looked across at him as she asked.

Ahmed shook his head. 'I doubt it. I could push him on most things but that seemed to be a matter of trust between them.'

'Hmm, OK then. Probably best if you go after Edith Stevenson.'

'Why? What do you mean?'

'Depending on what I find on the first Mrs Drake, we're going to have another go at this. I'll take Michael Drake this time, and you go for Stevenson. She was one of the quintets. She must have known Tina Tippet, the first Mrs Drake. Wouldn't it be interesting if she turns out to be the mystery friend that the second Mrs Drake is staying with? And I can't risk turning up on her doorstep in an official capacity if Tiffany might be there, not after the stunt at the hospital.'

'But what is it that you're chasing here?'

'Remember Brad Tippet and his grudge against the Chief Super? What if there was something in his accusations all those years ago?'

'That his sister was murdered? But she wasn't. Tippet's delusional.'

'What if he isn't? What if Tina Tippet was bumped off just for being Michael Drake's wife? And what if whoever targeted Drake's first wife now wants a go at his second? Who's still on the scene from the old quintets days?'

'Edith Stevenson.'

'Yes, and Michael Drake himself. Never discount the nearest and dearest.'

After a pause, Ahmed added, 'There's Brad Tippet too.'

'Brad Tippet? Do you think he could have killed his sister? Why?'

'No, I was thinking that maybe she died of natural causes just like her death certificate says, but we know he's never believed it. He's nursed one hell of an obsession for a long time. He thinks Drake killed her. Maybe this is payback time.'

◉ ◉ ◉

Ahmed huddled into his jacket as he tucked himself close to the radiator. He slipped the headphones over his ears and picked up a notebook. Aware of Suzie's scrutiny, he clicked the play button and settled back to listen. While she was watching, he would take the recording step by step, documenting, cataloguing. He read her motives. She would wait for him to become engrossed; wait until confident he was well embedded in the task, and then she'd be off.

She had covert plans just as he had. He could see her now, her focus shifting from keeping an eye on him to the online databases she was trawling, probably for Michael Drake's first wife … Brad Tippet's sister … part of the tangle of old friends, old jealousies, disappearances, suicides and at least one murder. He wondered what she would find, his attention shifting for a moment to her agenda and away from his own. Was she right? Were the elusive motives tied in with who the victims were married to and not who they were?

Was Tiffany Drake at risk? She could have died yesterday but suicide wasn't murder. An image of Pamela Morgan floated in his mind … a straightforward suicide … but China Kowalski hadn't travelled thousands of miles on a whim, whatever Webber thought. Somewhere she'd nursed a solid certainty.

Suzie's surveillance lost its intensity, but it was too soon to fast-forward the recording. His plan was to listen in detail to Kowalski talking about the 1985 reunion. What had Webber called it? A

327

mess of motives in there somewhere. Once he had that part of the recording analysed the key job was done and he would be free to root about for Boots Boy, clearly the handle of someone they'd identified as close to Tom, maybe even his killer.

He became aware that Suzie was standing over him. He paused the recording and removed the headphones.

'Robert Morgan died a long time ago,' she said. 'Thirty years … a lifetime.'

He murmured agreement.

'Tom Jenkinson's the here and now.' Her stare remained hard.

He nodded again, wary. This sounded like it was leading to tacit approval to get digging on the wrong case, but that wasn't what he read in her expression.

'Suppose they don't find anyone,' she said. 'Despite everything, just suppose they don't get a viable suspect. What if the case goes cold?'

A chill ran through him. 'That's not going to happen.'

'It could,' she said. 'Then there'll be some future version of you sitting in a space-age incident room looking back and wondering why no one did better at the time. Tom Jenkinson's death will seem as irrelevant to them as Robert Morgan's seems to you now.'

Ah, so she'd seen through him. 'It'd be different,' he said. 'At least we'd be leaving a proper enquiry behind us. Robert Morgan was treated as accidental death.'

'Doesn't he deserve justice then, because we got it wrong?'

'Of course he does,' he snapped, clamping the earphones back over his ears and turning away. She had no right to imply he wasn't giving everything to the case. OK, so he'd been following the other enquiry as closely as he could, but no one would get short-changed. He risked a sideways glance. She'd turned away. He un-paused the recording.

Webber's voice asked Kowalski why she'd insisted on speaking to him personally. Ahmed listened to her precise tones as she outlined her reasoning. He was surprised to learn that Webber had interviewed the Chief Super's father at some point and Kowalski seemed to know about it. And there'd been some kind of contact between her and Webber,

'... I thought about your email and what you'd said about the quintets ...'

Ahmed wondered why none of this was clear in the file. Maybe Melinda Webber had had a hand in it somewhere.

'... decided that I needed to talk to you and it may as well be on my way home so I took a bit of a detour.'

'A bit of a detour?' Ahmed heard his own incredulity echoed in Webber's response.

It wasn't an easy recording to follow. Webber had warned them there hadn't been an interview room free. The background buzz of conversation and bustle was a constant irritant. He had to concentrate so hard that he wasn't aware Suzie had crossed to the far side of the room until a movement caught his eye. He paused the recording again as he watched her. She was absorbed in something and paying him no attention. Time to act.

It took a while ... stop-start ... fast forward ... check on Suzie ... He found it late in the recording, four fifths through he judged. A quick glance round at Suzie then he adjusted the window on the screen so the slider didn't show. If she looked over his shoulder she wouldn't see that he'd jumped almost to the end.

Webber sounded calm enough and Kowalski probably didn't notice anything but Ahmed could hear the underlying irritation as Webber cast about trying to keep the woman focussed, fishing for how well she'd stayed in touch and with whom. Her replies were heavy, Ahmed could hear the sleepiness behind her words until Webber said, 'You all met up in 1985, didn't you?'

At once her tone lifted as she leapt on the question. 'That was it. Yes, that was the start of it. The 1985 reunion. We were all there.'

Webber murmured prompts, but Kowalski didn't need pushing

now. She scrabbled to articulate what might be the specifics that Webber had been sure had brought her all this way. She should have written it down, Ahmed thought, should have anticipated the effects of jet lag.

'Are you saying that's the first time you thought something was wrong?' Webber's voice.

'I thought something wasn't right … first time? I'm not sure … let me think. It was a bit like meeting strangers. I cut ties with them after Quinny's Canadian died.'

'But you're talking about the reunion that happened the year before he died, aren't you?'

'Yes … yes, I suppose so. It's all run together over the years. I hated the way they treated Quinny, like they were trying to jolly her out of it. I mean we all knew it was a big mistake for her to marry him, but she was pretty cut up about his death, especially the way it happened … those animals hunting him down. And there were Edie and Michael trying to take her out of herself. At the funeral for heaven's sake! I met Gary's wife there. She was OK, a nice woman. Not Gary's calibre of course but she was kind to Quinny, diverted the others, smoothed things over.'

Ahmed nodded to himself as he made a note. This matched what Joyce Yeatman had told him about Robert Morgan's funeral. She too had taken against Michael Drake and Edith Stevenson; said they'd been callous.

'Robert Morgan wasn't chased,' Webber's voice told China Kowalski. 'We now know it didn't happen like that. He … uh … wouldn't have known anything about the tigers.'

'He wasn't …? But everyone said … Quinny needs to know that … needed to know … it's too late now. Do you know how much it must have haunted her? Why didn't anyone know at the time? Are you sure?'

'You say you cut all ties, but you were at Gary Yeatman's funeral ten years later?'

'Of course I was!' Ahmed heard indignation in her tone. 'We went to all the big events, the graduations, the marriages … the funerals. Except that Tilly never had a funeral … and Michael couldn't be at Gary's graduation because his wife was dying.'

A buzz that didn't belong to the incessant background noise from the recording pierced Ahmed's shell. The phone behind him was ringing an incoming call. A glance at Suzie. She stared at a piece of paper, one of her fingers tracing something along the screen as her gaze bounced back and forth, screen to paper. He wondered what she'd found.

Blowing out a sigh, he pulled off the headphones and reached back to pluck the handset from its rest.

'DI Davis?' a voice rapped out before he could speak. He recognized the clipped tones of the woman from the lab. In his head he toyed with a comment about not realising she knew how to use a standard phone.

'Out.' He matched her economy with words. 'DC Ahmed here. Can I help?'

'Yep. Second body … gravel pit. The one underneath William Jones. It's your post office guy. The big brother.'

'OK.' He grabbed a pen. 'Any timings for us?'

She grumbled something in an undertone before replying. 'Hard to say. Might get more when we've run tests. Best guess? Jones has been down there 20 years; the other one longer by ten years. At least.'

'Can't be any more than ten years longer,' Ahmed pointed out, 'assuming he was alive when they did the post office job. Sounds like he was killed on the spot when the car was dumped, and someone's been stacking bodies. Anything to say it's the same person coming back to the grave?'

A huff of exasperation. 'You guys seem to think we dig up a log book with each artefact. We'll find what's there to find but it'll take time. One thing we have that you should have found for us;

there were some excavations done. There would have been diggers on site, the means to dig large holes. It wouldn't take long in that terrain to get really deep.'

Ahmed pursed his lips in annoyance. He'd checked the history of that site himself. It hadn't been touched in the right time window. 'Do you mean the animal remains? We've dated those more or less. There were no records of anything official.'

'Only just found this one myself and no, not the animal remains. That's a different pit.'

'What then? Does it coincide with the time of the robbery or of Jones's burial?'

'Test pit to see if they could reroute the bypass. Land wasn't stable enough.'

Ahmed drew in a breath as he struck a line through the note he'd just written. 'Yes,' he said coldly. 'I know what you mean. I found that. It predated the post office job by 15 years if I remember right. That makes it 45 years ago. How the …?' He paused and forced his voice to remain even. 'How does that help? The guy was alive at the time of the robbery so he clearly wasn't buried 45 years ago.'

'No,' she said and he could tell from her tone that a half-smile tinged with smugness had curved her lips, 'but the third body, the one they've just found underneath him probably was.'

chapter forty

Suzie was getting ready to go now. She'd pulled a face when he told her about the latest find up at the gravel pits. 'Too long ago to be relevant,' had been her comment, 'but what's the betting whoever buried the second body knew who'd buried the first. Father … uncle … that sort of thing. Otherwise why go back to just the same place? Can't be coincidence.' Their eyes had met briefly. They both wanted to shove this latest development on to the back burner as they chased their own priorities. Her parting shot had been a nod towards Webber's office. 'Tell one of them before you go out after Stevenson.'

As soon as her footsteps receded, he was across the room grabbing a heap of new paperwork, returning with it to his desk, switching his computer away from the Kowalski recording and firing up the databases that were going to give him the answers he needed. He riffled through the papers, jotting down new areas, wanting to have skim-read everything and returned it to its place before he was disturbed.

Everyone was out chasing down witnesses, tightening the noose around Tom's killer. They had someone called Boots Boy in the crosshairs. They'd linked Tom to him … or her … the paperwork he'd read so far didn't specify. Having gleaned as much as he could from the documents, he replaced them and went back to his online search. He couldn't hide his electronic tracks but he'd worry about that when someone challenged him. For now, he needed to know.

It didn't take long. The groundwork had already been done.

Solid links had been unearthed between Tom and Boots Boy, solid links that went back months. As the story unfolded a heavy weight pressed on his shoulders. Boots Boy was the handle of the wingman to a big player referred to as Streetwise. For all the progress that had been made, neither handle was attached to a real name. Tom had been in deep. This hadn't happened overnight. Tom had deceived him so comprehensively it was like reading about a different person. He felt the crease at his brow as he sat back to pull in a couple of deep breaths. How could he have been so wrong?

Something inside rebelled at the idea. He had been turning Tom's life around, he knew he had. OK, so Tom had been a bigger player than he'd realised and he'd hidden it well, but that didn't mean he hadn't wanted to get out from under the yoke. He remembered Melinda Webber's words, *Martyn said you were winning; said you'd have turned him right round in another few months.* He didn't know if he liked Martyn Webber's wife but there was a side to her that he found appealing. She'd seemed genuinely interested in his forthcoming marriage, that made a nice change. On the other hand she'd taken shameful advantage at times of being Webber's wife.

The story got no better the deeper he dug. It seemed to be a Scandinavian connection they were following, a major drugs cartel.

Why hadn't Tom confided in him?

A sudden thought. He looked round. No one to challenge him. Pulling the keyboard on to his lap he typed furiously, linking in to different systems, gritting his teeth at slow connections. *Kids with Potential,* the familiar logo filled the screen. He logged in and typed Tom's name. He'd spent hours with Tom, written reams of notes. He knew that the current enquiry would have been all over his records, but they hadn't known Tom the way he had. It had taken a long time to build trust, to learn to decipher Tom's defensively coded pronouncements. Maybe Tom had already told him and he'd missed it.

He searched for every term he could conjure up that might be relevant; he read the notes, scoured the plans they'd hatched together. There was nothing. He'd been so certain, but there was nothing. He banged his fist on the desk as the frustration bubbled up. Tom would have told him all about Boots Boy and this Streetwise character, of course he would. If he'd only done it sooner they might have been able to protect him.

He logged out. He'd been searching the system for a long time. No ground gained. He had to get past this and get on with what he was supposed to be doing. His line of thought paused. Edith Stevenson. Despite Davis he'd not lost his certainty that she was the so-called man on CCTV heading to see Tom. But the cold case … Robert Morgan, the quintets, animal rights groups releasing tigers years ago … it was a million miles from Scandinavian drugs rings.

Or was it? Who had ever checked up on those sorts of contacts? China Kowalski thought nothing of circumnavigating the globe on a whim … Edith Stevenson was keeping out of their way for a reason. And … his thoughts went back to something that had bugged him all along … no one had ever questioned Brad Tippet's old neighbour, Mrs Bell, on anything other than the car.

His theories were as nebulous as Suzie's, but he was determined to follow them up. She wanted him out after Edith Stevenson anyway. It wasn't so much of a detour to go via Mrs Bell's.

Voices … Davis and Webber … a door swinging open. Good timing. He had one task to complete before he could set off.

They were standing in the corridor outside Webber's office. Davis had a sheaf of papers in his hand. They were looking at them, talking. Their faces were turned away, no lips to read. Ahmed moved quickly but quietly, picking up his coat. He slipped through the far door, the bend in the corridor would partly obscure his approach.

As he drew nearer the low rumble of conversation became audible as words. He paused.

'... if that's right, that corroborates the positive ID on Boots Boy.' Satisfaction underlay Davis's words.

They both paused and glanced up as footsteps approached. Ahmed pressed himself to the wall and slid backwards a couple of steps, bending over his phone simulating interest in the blank screen as people pushed past. No one challenged him. Neither Davis nor Webber noticed him.

'... can rule him out then.' Webber's voice didn't sound as upbeat as Davis. Ahmed felt bleak with him; he wanted to hear optimism. He wanted suspects caught and charged.

'Exactly' – Davis again – 'which cuts the suspect list down to one.'

'Hmm.' Webber's tone was noncommittal. Ahmed clenched his fist, a silent tribute to the triumph in Davis's tone. They'd homed in on a prime suspect. It was just a matter of time.

'Ayaan? What are you doing?'

'Oh ... uh ...' With a guilty start, Ahmed juggled his phone. 'I was just coming to see you. Um ... just checking a message from Suzie. I'm going out to see Edith Stevenson.'

'Agreed to see you, has she?' Davis gave him a hard look. He felt a slight flush warm his face. It must be crystal clear that he'd been eavesdropping.

'Well ... not yet, but Suzie's going to see Michael Drake and I'm going to call in on Mrs Bell before I go to Stevenson's. We're confident we'll get something to loosen her tongue.'

'Which one of us were you coming to see?' Webber asked. He looked distracted, mildly irritated at the interruption.

'Er ... either of you really. It's that body underneath Jones behind the gravel pits, it's big brother post office ... uh ... I mean the eldest brother from the post office raid.'

Webber nodded. 'Predictable,' he said. 'I wonder if that makes it a family feud after all. Dumped about the same time as the car, right?'

Ahmed murmured assent. 'Only that's not all …'

'Oh God, what now?'

He told them about the third body deep in the makeshift grave.

'45 years ago?' Webber sounded incredulous.

Ahmed outlined what he'd learnt from the woman at the lab. 'Probably dumped at the time they were testing for rerouting the bypass.' He explained about the digging equipment. 'Next one in the same pit was the post office brother about 15 years later, and Jones is the most recent about 20 years ago which matches the time he was known to have come back to the area.'

'Who is it, the third one?'

'We don't know. They haven't estimated age or sex or anything yet. She's optimistic they'll get something. The remains are better preserved than the one above it. Something to do with the depth and the soil and so on. But she hasn't anything so far. She was just … um …'

'Getting in quick with the bad news,' completed Webber dryly. 'What's the link between these bodies, any ideas?'

Ahmed shook his head. 'As yet nothing …' He swallowed the word *concrete*. 'Nothing solid, but circumstantially it has to be the same person coming back, doesn't it?'

'Or someone who knew about the earlier grave,' put in Davis. 'OK, get on to missing persons, all that, you know what to do.'

Webber let out a sigh. 'We've no extra resources for a 45-year-old body, not just now anyway. Have the press got it?'

Ahmed shook his head. 'We talked about it. We think it should stay under wraps. We have 24 hour surveillance on that site. It's possible someone might get twitchy about how far down we've dug, if they've heard about the first two and know there's another one down there. We've had our share of ghouls out sightseeing. We're logging them all. No one of any interest to date.'

Webber nodded his approval. 'OK, let's see what happens. You get on with wherever it was you were going.' He turned to Davis, drew in a breath to speak and then stopped, looking round at Ahmed again. 'What? Is there something else?'

'Well, no … yes … um … I couldn't help overhearing. Tom. You've found a link to a big drugs cartel.'

Webber shot a sideways glance at Davis who answered with the ghost of a shrug. 'You can't be involved, Ayaan, you know that. But we're close. This case won't go cold.'

'He'd have told me,' Ahmed burst out. 'Maybe not two years ago but he'd changed. He was turning his life round. I know he was. Whatever he was in, he was in too deep, but he'd have told me.'

Webber's stare bored into him. 'Did he tell you anything, Ayaan? Anything at all?'

With a feeling of defeat, Ahmed shook his head. 'I've been over and over the past two years. I've even had his "Kids with Potential" records out. I can't find anything that matches something as big as this.'

'For what it's worth, Ayaan, I think you're right. He would have told you. I just wish he'd made up his mind to it sooner.'

As Ahmed hurried away pulling on his coat he reran the overheard fragments. Boots Boy was wingman to someone called Streetwise, and now Boots Boy had been eliminated from the suspects list for Tom's murder. That left Streetwise. As far as he could work it out, they still struggled for a name but their positive ID of Boots Boy had been the bridge they needed. They'd have this Streetwise character soon and could only hope he'd be within their jurisdiction when they found him … or her.

Suzie wanted him to go straight to Edith Stevenson, but Suzie wasn't here. His first call would be to Mrs Bell, the interview he'd done just before Melinda Webber had collared him in that coffee shop. This time he would ask all the questions about the Tippets that should have been asked 30 years ago.

He was on his way through the door when his phone buzzed. It was Suzie. Her voice was low, her tone urgent. 'Ayaan, where are you?'

'Just setting off now. I had to update–'

'Never mind that.' She cut across him. 'Find some excuse to ring Michael Drake. I'm with him now. He's out of the room. He won't be long. Ring him. Push him to trust me with intel about his wife … where she's gone … anything. He's on the verge of telling me. I need you to push him over the edge.'

'But … Why am I ringing him? What …?'

'Just do it!' The line went dead.

He paused, didn't want to go back to the office and risk being quizzed by Davis. On the other hand it was freezing outside. The foyer was quiet. He pushed his mind over what he and Michael had talked about the times they'd met. He supposed he could be calling just to check on how they both were after the trauma of Tiffany's suicide attempt. The ring tone sounded in his ear. Three … four … five … then it was answered.

'Hello Michael, it's Ayaan Ahmed. How are you?'

'DC Ahmed? One of your colleagues is here.' Michael sounded surprised. As well he might, thought Ahmed rerunning Webber's perennial comments about lack of resources. Here was Michael Drake getting personal service from two officers.

'Oh yes, that'll be Sergeant Harmer,' he said. 'Is your wife there too?'

'No, she's still away. She …'

'Talk to Sergeant Harmer, Michael. She's just the person to help you and Tiffany. She used to work with …' He tripped mentally on the phrase *rape crisis centre*, not at all appropriate, and gabbled out a jumble of words '… special training … relevance … problems … You should talk to her about Tiffany.'

Michael must know he was spouting rubbish; he could only hope the man's instinct for compliance remained strong.

'Sergeant Harmer,' Michael's voice was low, hesitant, 'she's quite a … forceful sort of person.' It was almost as though he was asking for help.

Ahmed smiled. Now who's the bully, he thought.

Webber watched Ahmed stride away from the station. He had a vague idea he should know where he was off to, hadn't he said when he'd been telling him and Davis about the third body in the old grave? His mind wasn't on Ahmed. It was on Tom Jenkinson. It troubled him that Boots Boy had been so easily eliminated. Davis was cock-a-hoop to have shrunk his suspects list after the frustrations of the past week but Webber wasn't ready to celebrate. They had a strong front runner but he wasn't comfortable with the idea that this Streetwise man had killed Jenkinson.

'If Streetwise is as big a player as he's painted, then what's he doing getting his hands dirty with Tom Jenkinson? I mean who is Jenkinson to an outfit like that? A possible new recruit; small fry? He steps out of line and they get rid of him, but how is he more than a minor irritant? Guy like that, he'd send in one of his wingmen, not do the job himself ... or herself,' he added after a pause. He'd be surprised to learn that Streetwise was a woman but it didn't do to close off any avenues.

'From what we know he's an out-and-out psychopath,' Davis said. 'Enjoys the hands-on. It's how people like that climb the tree, no one wants to get in their way.'

Webber conceded the point with a shrug. 'I'm not saying he isn't a strong frontrunner, but without hard evidence to put him in the frame, we can't eliminate the rest of the list.'

Davis let out a sigh. Webber understood his frustration. They *did* have a good frontrunner but this wasn't ancient history like Ahmed and Suzie were chasing. He wanted solid evidence. The crime was recent, evidence was there for the taking if they could find it. They had to uncover it before it began to dissolve into the landscape. He didn't want to think about Streetwise evaporating from the enquiry the way Boots Boy had, because that would open up the possibility he'd told Ahmed wouldn't happen. The leads petering out one by one, resources having to be pulled, the case gradually going cold.

'You were chasing some CCTV,' he remembered suddenly. 'Where did that go?'

Davis pulled a face. 'Useless. For whatever reason they can't enhance it, not the stretch with the guy we want. Or did you mean that footage of Edith Stevenson?' he added. 'The analysis is back but I haven't looked yet.'

'Come on.' Webber turned to head for the office. 'Let's see if we can at least cut her out.' He didn't have any real doubts but it would be a relief to strike a line through Edith Stevenson's name. She didn't belong in Tom Jenkinson's realm; she belonged with the cold case. Edith Stevenson ... wasn't that who Ahmed had said he was on his way to see?

Davis was at the keyboard, searching emails for the report. 'Here we are. The odd walk. The style ... hang on ... more or less identical. No, wait a minute ...' Webber had to hold back from barging Davis out of the way to see for himself. 'They remark on the similarity,' Davis continued. 'I was unfair on Ayaan. He wasn't making it up.'

'They're not saying it could be her?' Webber's mind began to spin with the implications.

'No, no ... They say ... chances of it being the same person ...' Davis reeled off the percentages, skipping over the statistical jargon, clearly as impatient as Webber to get to the final verdict. 'It's not her. Definitely not. Chance in a million ... thank God for that.'

Webber nodded taking in a breath to slow his heartrate which had begun to race. There was no link between Tom Jenkinson and the cold case. It was a link that had never made sense and now it was severed.

He became aware that Davis's attention had shifted. There was a notepad propped against a telephone handset. Webber looked at the rough sketch, recognised Ahmed's writing in the captions. This must be where he'd taken the call from the lab. It was a cross section of a grave, three stick figures on their sides, the topmost labelled 'Jones 20 yrs,' the middle 'PO guy 30 yrs,' and the deepest simply labelled with a question mark and the number 45.

More links, he thought. Robert Morgan's murder ... the stolen Ford Tempo ... the ring-leader of the gang that released the tigers. But what relevance could attach to this latest find from so long ago?

Davis gave him a quizzical look. '45 years ago,' he said. 'That's when that schoolgirl went missing. The one from Dorset. Tilly Brown.'

chapter forty-one

Ahmed felt impervious to the cold as he walked away from Mrs Bell's neat bungalow. She'd fed him hot mince pies and a steaming cup of strong tea. He hadn't tried to hurry her reminiscences but wondered just how relevant they were after all this time. Someone should have talked to her like this 30 years ago. She'd not only known the Tippets but several of the quintets. She was of their parents' generation, not theirs but if Robert Morgan's death had been correctly categorised at the time, Mrs Bell could have been a goldmine. Now her memories were fragmented, skipping from weddings to the car theft to thoughts of schooldays. Some of her observations predated the time of the killing by years.

'Young Tilly Brown, it was heart-breaking,' she'd said. 'They shouldn't have taken her away. She didn't want to go. She could have finished her schooling here. Any of her friends would have taken her in. One of them offered, I know … got her parents to agree and everything. Tilly was a lovely girl and every bit as clever as that little one; so much nicer too.'

'That little one …?'

'Oh I don't remember all the names. A little madam, miserable as sin, I remember that much. Very sniffy about young Michael Drake getting married. He wed Tina Tippet, you know. Such a tragedy when she died. It tore the family apart, all those accusations Brad made. I told Michael off once for ribbing young Brad, but who could blame him really? It used to infuriate Brad when Michael took his car. Tina had keys, you see. I said to Brad once, stop minding so much and it'll not be sport for them. But then it was properly stolen, wasn't it? Turned out not to have been Michael that time. But yes, that small one who never smiled, she minded more than Brad about Tina and Michael getting married so quick.'

'Edith Stevenson …? China Kowalski …?'

'China, that's right. Silly name.' She'd paused in thought and then laughed. 'And that's right, Edith … Edie. I liked Edie. She was the one who offered young Tilly a place to stay. Oh, and she tore a real strip off young China, told her it was up to Michael who he married.'

The names Gary Yeatman, Pamela Quinliven and Will Jones had sparked no recognition. Robert Morgan's gruesome death didn't seem to have registered either though she couldn't have missed the news reports at the time. Ahmed assumed she'd never matched it to the children she'd known and, as she didn't know any of the players, he hadn't enlightened her.

'No one asked me any of this at the time,' she'd said at one point. 'Nothing about the family, just where was Brad that evening. And he was right there the whole time.'

Ahmed's phone buzzed a call from Suzie as he reached his car. He was pleased to see her name on the screen. He wasn't sure what he'd got from Mrs Bell. Talking it through with someone was the way to unravel it. But when he clicked open the call, her voice was low.

'Are you with Stevenson?'

'No, not yet. I've just –'

'Don't go. Not yet. I've a couple of names for you to try first.'

'Are you still with Michael Drake?'

'Yup. He's upstairs looking for the notebook where Tiffany keeps her passwords. He's going to let me look at her email. She emails her friends a lot and he thinks she's been emailing Stevenson. He's convinced himself that it'll be OK as long as he doesn't read them himself. Only he's taking forever going through her stuff. Won't let me help in case I don't leave it just so.'

Ahmed climbed into the car and started the engine. The warming effects of Mrs Bell's mince pies were wearing off. 'She'll have taken it with her, won't she?'

'No, she hasn't been back since the hospital. I had to offer to make tea. I'd have exploded if I watched him much longer lifting old magazines practically page by page.'

Ahmed laughed. 'Michael Drake has hidden talents if he can persuade you to make tea. Anyway, you can probably get into her emails without a password, can't you?'

He heard a huff of frustration. 'Don't tempt me. The computer's right here. But I can hardly say, can I? I'm chipping bits out of him. There's the two friends she might be with, but get this, you were right ... half right ... about Edith Stevenson. Sounds like her and Tiffany have been swapping emails. That stuff about them not getting on; he says they didn't when he and Tiffany first got together, but just lately they've become quite close. He's not best pleased about it either. I think he's a bit jealous, like his old friend Edith has betrayed him by making friends with his wife.'

'But are you saying he doesn't know where she's gone? I got the impression he knew but wasn't going to tell me.'

'Give me a sec, Ayaan.' Ahmed kept quiet as he listened to silence at the end of the line. After a few seconds Suzie's voice was back in his ear. 'It's OK, I thought he was coming down to see where I'd got to. I'd better get this kettle on.' Her voice became slightly distant and he heard sounds of running water. He guessed she had the handset balanced between her head and shoulder. 'No, he doesn't know for sure. He said he was ashamed to admit it to you, that he didn't know where his own wife had run off to. Edith Stevenson's still a possibility but I've two other names.'

He clicked the phone to speaker and rested it in its cradle so he could make a note as Suzie recited names and addresses. Behind her words he could hear cups clinking.

'Oh yuk!'

'What?'

'There's a bowl of raw meat on the top shelf of the fridge, not covered or anything. Honestly, some people haven't a clue. Anyway, where are you? How are you getting on?'

'OK, but shouldn't you be getting back to Michael? He'll be wondering where you are.'

'Pah! Not him. I don't think I could get any sense of urgency into him if the house was on fire. And I can't bear to go back up there and find he's only half way through the first heap of stuff.'

Ahmed told her about Mrs Bell. 'Nothing new really,' he ended, 'but it was interesting to hear it from someone who was there. It'd have been a lot more interesting at the time when she could have remembered it better. The feud was quite something, Brad and Michael. She said in hindsight she can feel sorry for Brad but face to face he's so obnoxious that it was no wonder everyone took Michael's side.'

'You know what I think. I think Michael Drake was the dummy of the group.' Suzie said. 'At school I mean … the quintets. They were all academic high flyers bar him and Edith Stevenson and even she wasn't behind the door. Those lies about a place at university. Who does that? I know everyone says how well he did at Tippets' firm, but that wasn't the currency that counted to that lot.'

'He didn't stick with it, though. He broke ties two years after Tina died.'

'I've had that conversation with him,' Suzie said. 'It was interesting. You've been right through the paperwork, haven't you? Give me an overview and then I'll tell you what I think.'

'The way it seemed to me – and Mrs Bell said the same – for a couple of years he was the rock the family clung to after Tina died. Not Brad of course. Michael did everything he could to keep things going but Brad never stopped trying to unseat him from his place in the firm … his place in the family by then. It's a puzzle to me that Brad succeeded. Michael could have stayed on and had the lot.

Tippet senior was ready to disown Brad. If there'd been a child, if Tina hadn't miscarried, there'd have been no perhaps about it. Then a year after Tina died, Tippet senior got ill. He changed his will. He didn't disinherit Brad but he put the firm in Michael's hands. God knows how that would have worked. Michael had started fighting back a bit by then.'

'Fighting back? How do you mean?'

'This is what I got from Mrs Bell. Nothing much, just like he'd had enough of the constant bad-mouthing from Brad. You know the thing about Tina having keys to Brad's car and borrowing it when she wanted ... Michael never gave the keys back and he took Brad's car a time or two without asking. Just to wind him up. And if you remember, Brad always claimed he thought it was Michael Drake when it disappeared that final time. Mrs Bell said that's what they all thought.'

'Well, it couldn't have been,' said Suzie. 'That car was new. Michael wouldn't have had keys to the Ford Tempo.'

'I know. I said that to Mrs Bell. She'd obviously never thought it through, said maybe Brad had given him a set for Tina. Only Tina had been dead eight years before he bought that car. Clearly Brad Tippet was paranoid enough to overlook an inconvenience like lack of keys. Thing is that if Mrs Bell swallowed it as possible it means that Michael Drake was poking a stick through the bars at Brad Tippet for longer than we realised.'

'Hang on ...' Again the line went quiet, then Ahmed heard Suzie's voice, muffled. 'Sorry, Michael. I got a call.' He heard her footsteps echo. 'Here you are,' she said. 'How are you getting on?'

'Aren't you having one?' Michael Drake's voice. 'Yes, I'll have it for you any minute.'

'Lovely, yes I can see you're almost down that first pile ... uh ... if ...'

'No, please, Sergeant Harmer, please don't disturb anything. Tiffany mustn't know.'

'OK, well if you don't mind I'll pop down and get my tea and I'll just make a call.'

'Do you want to use the phone?'

'No, no, that's fine, thanks. I have my own.'

From the muffled thuds that came from the speaker, Ahmed surmised she'd patted the pocket where she'd slipped the phone. More footsteps ... the echo of a staircase ... a grunt of exasperation and her voice was back. 'Ack, he's barely down a single heap of stuff. He's clearly started in the wrong place. He'll be all bloody week. I'll give him a few more minutes then I'm off. But go on, this feud, Tippet and Drake, what were you saying?'

'That it went on longer than we thought ...'

'Oh yes, that's what I was going to say. That fits with the conversation I had earlier. He could have had that firm, couldn't he, the whole caboodle even after his first wife died. The father liked him, they all liked him bar Brad. But he kind of bowed out. Now he didn't tell me a coherent story. I got the impression he doesn't know why he did what he did, but here's what I think. He carried on after Tina died. He tried to work with Brad, tried to make it work, but he couldn't. He was heading for taking control of the firm and I don't think he could square it ethically. Brad was the son who should inherit, not him. Different if Tina had lived. She was the eldest. I don't think he liked the idea of taking it all off Brad, not with Tina gone. And I wonder if he tried to talk any of this through with the quintets, the ones he was still in contact with. Can you imagine how those conversations might have gone? China Kowalski ... Gary Yeatman ... trample over Brad and take the lot, that's what they'd have said. Maybe Pamela Morgan and Edith Stevenson said different, maybe that's why he kept up with them and not the other two.'

'Money,' said Ahmed as a memory sparked. He'd been listening to Suzie without thinking much of her theory, but maybe she was right. 'I'd need to check the timings but according to Joyce Yeatman,

Pamela Morgan lent him money. If she's right it would have been round about the time he cut ties with the Tippets.'

'Yes, that's interesting. Think about it, he didn't have anything else, only that job. Did Pamela Morgan give him the means to break free? Didn't she lend money to Stevenson as well round about the same time? What was that about? Remind me, who gained from Tina Drake's death?'

'Michael, nothing. He lost his wife, and eventually his job. There was that insurance policy but it didn't pay out. She died six months too soon.'

'And she took the policy out on him, yes? At Tippet's prompting. In a way, I suppose Tippet got something out of it. He got Michael Drake out of his life.'

'He didn't though, did he?' said Ahmed. 'Or not at once. And if Tippet cared enough about his sister not to want Drake to marry her, is he really going to kill her? But how about he's still convinced that Drake did her in, so he's going to pay him out by killing his second wife?'

'After all this time, and anyway how? They don't have anything to do with each other these days.'

'I know, it doesn't make much sense.' He sighed. The car windows were misting over. He couldn't see anything outside with any clarity. Bit like this case, he thought, looking back in time there were just too many gaps to be able to see a clear picture. 'But still, Tippet's held on to that grudge against the Chief Super all these years. Why not Drake too?'

'Or how about Stevenson?' said Suzie. 'Maybe she wanted Drake to herself all those years ago and bumped off Tina Tippet. Now he's gone and married again.'

He pulled a face and reached forward to rub his cuff over the windscreen opening a small window of visibility. 'She's had a lot of years to get together with him or come to terms with not. Do you really think there's anything there?'

'You're the one trying to persuade us that Stevenson's involved, remember?'

'With Tom Jenkinson, not with some plot to kill Michael Drake's wives. And where's Robert Morgan in all this? We're building on quicksand, Suzie.'

'I know I know, but there's something in here somewhere.'

'What did you get on the first Mrs Drake? Did you find her medical records?'

'Nothing explicitly untoward, though no definitive cause of death. Batteries of tests, months of ups and downs. Symptoms: blurred vision, dizziness, nausea, sensitivity to sunlight, and bone pain. Sound familiar? If there's something going on with Michael Drake's wives, the links are the Tippets and the quintets; three of the quintets anyway; Stevenson, Drake himself and Kowalski.'

'Kowalski's been at the other side of the world,' objected Ahmed.

'Has she? We've only her word for that.'

'Well, it's easily checked.'

'Yeah, right. It's so easily checked we haven't bothered. Who was it raked all this up with John Farrar's father in the first place? And who turned up in York yesterday supposedly jet-lagged so she didn't have to appear too coherent?'

Ahmed paused. She was right. 'Suzie, if someone's targeting Tiffany Drake, we ought to take this higher.'

'We don't have enough.' Suzie sounded troubled. 'Hell, Ayaan, I don't have enough to convince myself let alone anyone else, and I don't want to have to come clean about how I found Tiffany Drake's medical data until I have to. Hang on …'

Ahmed heard a voice in the background, then Suzie's shout, 'That's great, Michael, thanks.' Her voice lowered again. 'Wonders will never cease, he's found it. I'd have put money on this being a waste of time.'

'I told you, don't underestimate him. This is the guy who got Suzie Harmer to make the tea.'

'Ha ha. Right, I'm going to go through these emails. Hold off Stevenson until I get back to you, but have a go at those other two names, only don't bounce them into trying to chase her if she isn't there.'

'OK.' He closed the call and set the blower to maximum to clear the windows, sitting back while it did its work, disjointed thoughts floating at random.

Names ... Tom ... Edith Stevenson ... major drugs cartel ... *Tom, why didn't you tell me?*

Webber's voice: *Did he tell you anything ... anything at all?*

He remembered the guilty flush on Tom's face when he'd walked into the interview room in York. That had been about the kids and the traffic lights scam. As far as he knew no one had unravelled what that had been about but it had been somehow tied up in Tom's death.

Something wasn't right. He closed his eyes. Tom facing him across the desk ... sitting there in his battered jacket. 'Oh, Tom.' He spoke the words aloud, slapping his forehead in exasperation. Pulling out his phone he opened a new text message and began to type. Of course, he'd found nothing in the mentoring notes. It was that interview in York. Tom had been digging, wanting to know how much they'd found about his drugs contacts; and in doing so he might have passed on a key scrap of information.

chapter forty-two

Webber strode through the crowded reception area, Davis at his heels. They clattered up the stairs. Webber felt good. Things were moving now. An identity had been unearthed for the man called Streetwise and with the identification had come the intel that they weren't the only ones interested in him. A Europol operation had him flagged for drugs trafficking. They had been close to stepping on the toes of a long-running, highly resourced operation that was building to a climax. Information had been swapped and Webber had asked John Farrar to add his weight to a forthcoming teleconference.

They would run into a level of resentment, he knew. Streetwise had had a team after him for a long time. They'd worked meticulously and wouldn't want Webber stepping in to pluck the prize at the last minute, but that's just what he intended to do. He wanted Streetwise arrested by his team for killing Tom Jenkinson, not under another country's warrant for drugs running; didn't want the Jenkinson case left in official limbo because the perpetrator was behind bars for another crime.

Farrar had organised the teleconference in his own office. Just the three of them from this side of the enquiry.

As he arrived at Farrar's door, his phone buzzed a text. Farrar signalled him inside. The space was awkward for three of them to sit the same side of the screen. Webber manoeuvred his chair to allow room for Davis. A glance at his phone showed Ahmed's name on the screen. Ahmed could wait.

Farrar's hard stare alerted him that Davis too had pulled out his phone. Webber glanced across to see Ahmed's name on Davis's screen. Whatever Ahmed had found, he'd sent it to both of them. Davis slipped the phone into his pocket.

'We've sent them everything we have, yes?' Farrar looked from one to the other of them as he spoke.

Webber nodded. 'Everything. They couldn't wait to get their hands on it. He's killed before but not like this; they've never had enough to make charges stick. We seem to have come in from left field, picked up things we didn't know we had, things their surveillance team missed.'

'What's the point of these fancy analysis systems,' grumbled Davis, 'if we don't even get to know they've had a surveillance team in York?'

Farrar's pursed lips told Webber that the question had been asked at a higher level. 'We know now,' Farrar rapped out. 'Though strictly speaking it wasn't York where they linked him to Jenkinson, it was Hull where he and his sidekick first went to recruit the boy. They said nothing because it didn't come to anything.'

'Streetwise came to York to kill him,' Webber growled, 'and he has to be brought back here to be charged.'

'They'll fight you, Martyn,' Farrar said. 'This is a trophy scalp. They'll want it.'

'They can't get him for murder. We can.'

Farrar tipped his head. 'Only if their surveillance gives us the missing pieces. OK, let's see, shall we?'

Farrar leant forward to tweak the controls. The monitor flashed into life. After a moment, a face came into focus, filling the screen. Webber took in the florid complexion, the lined forehead, the hint of jowls. The face drew back as Farrar identified himself and introduced the two of them. Their Scandinavian counterparts sat around a table, three women and two men.

The florid-faced man took the lead, aiming his comments at Farrar. 'Let me first give you a frank appraisal of our planned strategy,' he said. 'And then I should like to talk about the data we have from your Inspector Davis.'

Webber saw Farrar's glance flick briefly to Davis who shuffled in his chair. The message was plain – any cock-up in the data provided would not go well. Webber hoped Davis hadn't cut any corners.

The planned strategy unfolded. Webber fought to keep his breathing even. It was worse than he'd thought. They were open about wanting to use Jenkinson's killing as a bargaining chip.

'Make no mistake,' said the man, 'this man is a killer, but if he killed this Jenkinson boy we reason that it was a rush job, heat of the moment. If your data fits with ours, the case is strong. But a man like this, to be pulled down for the murder of someone so insignificant, he would hate that above all.'

'He killed Arthur Trent too.' Webber struggled to keep his tone neutral. Two weeks ago Trent's sister-in-law had sat across from him, cradling a hot cup of tea, telling him about *good family man* Arthur Trent.

'An added irritant.' The face on the screen acknowledged his comment with a smile and a nod.

Webber's fists clenched. He listened to the silky tone glide past Trent and talk about Jenkinson's death as leverage, a means to loosen tongues; there was even a side-swipe at Davis about potential anomalies in the data that would have to be straightened out. He thought of the text they'd received and was thankful Ahmed would never get to listen to this.

'It's a case of clearing up some details of timing and then deciding what is needed so we can be the best help possible to each other's enquiries. We should get what we need from the final section of your data, which we have yet to look at.'

'I've sent that across.' It was Davis's first intervention. He sounded worried.

'Yes,' the voice said smoothly, 'but it has only just arrived. We haven't had time to study it.'

Webber looked into the smiling face on the screen and couldn't hold back. As he drew in breath to speak a movement from Farrar stopped him. Farrar's hand, below the line of the camera was upraised in a clear signal to him to keep quiet. Briefly he met Farrar's eye and clamped down on his anger.

Smiling into the camera, his voice as smooth as his Scandinavian counterpart, Farrar said, 'A brief recess I think. Ten minutes? Will that be enough for you to analyse the data from Inspector Davis?'

'Ten minutes will be ample.'

As soon as the screen blanked Webber burst out, 'Trent was no rush job. They could have kept him quiet with money. He didn't have to die. And Streetwise knocked out that boy and buried him in concrete before he was dead. We can't do deals. This is murder.'

Farrar turned to face him. 'I'm not happy about it either, but we have to think big picture. Which is not to say I'm going to agree, but I'm not ruling it out.'

'The "Kids with Potential" initiative struggles for funding as it is,' Webber said. 'If we start labelling its participants as insignificant pawns in some bigger game, what message does that send to the next generation? What message does it send to our own officers?' As he spoke, his phone buzzed a call. He looked down to see Melinda's name on the screen and red-buttoned her to voicemail.

'Those last details you sent across,' Farrar turned to Davis. 'It's all there, is it? All checked?'

'Yes, dates and times, chapter and verse.' Davis didn't sound confident. 'I don't know why they're making a song and dance. It's nothing new.'

'Then what is it?'

'It's a summary they asked for after they'd seen the rest of the file. They wanted the timeline in a different format, needed it spelling out apparently. It's only a page.'

Webber looked at Farrar. Farrar had the contacts to make sure Jenkinson's killer wasn't allowed to dodge responsibility for his death. He tried to imagine the effect on Ahmed if the killer was never brought to book for the crime. Again he felt his phone buzz. His glance showed two new text messages, one signalling receipt of voicemail and the other from Melinda.

'Do you have everything there for when we reconvene?' Farrar barked the question at Davis.

'Everything.' Davis nodded and patted the fat files that he'd carried in and placed on the desk.

Farrar narrowed his eyes, then said, 'I'll be back in a few minutes.'

Webber watched him go. He left the door swinging open which seemed to say no discussion while he was away. Davis flicked through the case files. Webber thought he looked like a schoolboy doing last-minute cramming for an exam.

'Let me see the chronology.' Webber held out his hand. Davis passed across the single sheet of paper. Webber ran his gaze down the list, checking, looking for mistakes … Jenkinson ID'd on the footage by the traffic lights … the interview with Ahmed … the death of Arthur Trent … Jenkinson's jacket pulled from the gravel pit … his body from the concrete foundation of the walkway tower. He couldn't find any anomalies and handed the page back.

No sign of Farrar yet, so he pulled out his phone. The text from Ahmed said,

Tom did tell me something. Interview in York. Can't recall exact words but he said traffic lights were nothing to do with the drugs Mr Big. If it had been he wouldn't have touched it.

Webber turned to Davis. 'You had a text from Ayaan just as we got here. He sent me one too. Are they the same? Do you know what he means?'

Davis pulled out his phone and clicked through it. He shook his head. 'I'd have to get the recording out. If he's right, then …'

'Check it later,' Webber said. If Ahmed was right then it suggested that the traffic chaos had not been down to Boots Boy. It would leave the mystery man of the traffic lights business in limbo but made no difference to the case against Streetwise for murder.

He opened Melinda's text. It said simply, *I've left voicemail. Listen to it. You've 5 mins to let me know if there's a problem.*

He clicked to voicemail and put the phone to his ear. 'I've had a message,' said Melinda's voice. 'Joyce Yeatman. I need to follow it up while she's still worried enough to come clean with me. Jess'll pick Sam up from playschool but if I'm not back I need you to go and get him on your way home. I'll probably be there, but just in case ...'

Webber cursed under his breath; he didn't want to be tied down just at the moment, not with news due to land about Jenkinson's killer. He shoved the phone back in his pocket, couldn't risk getting into a heated discussion with her for Farrar to walk in on. He'd play it by ear and like she said, she'd probably be back.

They sat in silence for a short while until Farrar strode in. Webber had expected to see a cup of coffee in the Chief Super's hand but there was nothing.

'All set?' Farrar aimed the question at Davis.

Davis nodded.

Farrar reached forward to reconnect the call. It was the same group but this time the florid-faced man sat back and one of the women from the other side of the table spoke first.

'Inspector Davis.' Her voice was heavily accented. 'These informations ... these dates ... they are accurate, yes?'

Farrar's eyes narrowed. His glance speared into Davis who looked steadily at the screen, one of his hands resting on the case file in front of him. 'Absolutely accurate, yes,' he said with what Webber prayed wasn't misplaced confidence.

'Are you sure?' The voice was smooth, the tone reminded Webber of a barrister leading a witness.

Davis hesitated, shot a puzzled glance at Webber and opened the file in front of him. 'Yes, I'm sure,' he said and recited the key dates again, holding the page up to the camera. Webber watched intently. What was the issue here? It occurred to him to wonder why on earth the florid-faced man had been upfront about their intention to use Jenkinson as a pawn to make sure of Streetwise's scalp. Had positions been reversed he'd have played it differently.

The woman on the screen paused. Looks were exchanged around their table. 'Well in that case,' she said, 'I'm afraid that you have been more help for us, than we for you about your Mr ... uh ... Streetwise ... and Mr ... Boots Boy ...'

Webber saw Farrar's lips purse in annoyance at this deference to their supposed inability to pronounce Scandinavian surnames. He let his gaze slip to the papers on the desk. This would be a good time to interject with the men's real names but this was his first sight of them and as his eyes took in the unfamiliar character combinations he kept his mouth shut.

The woman sat back. Florid-face took the floor. 'Indeed, you have provided us valuable corroboration,' he said. 'They were under very close surveillance throughout that time.' He paused to shuffle through some papers. 'I will provide a summary of our surveillance for the relevant period.'

Webber sat up aware of the heightened tension. For whatever reason they were going to hand over what they had. They would give up the killer. They weren't going to fight for their bargaining chip. Had Farrar's brief trip out of the room been to make a strategic call to someone? He clenched one of his fists as a prickle of anticipation touched his skin. The man was reciting their own chronology now. Boots Boy nowhere near; they knew that already ... knew exactly when he and Tom had been seen together.

'... and Streetwise ...' Webber found his stare locked on to a paper in the man's hand. It gave a tantalising glimpse of a neat list. 'We have him in York briefly on two occasions. The first was a wasted trip. The person he wished to see took some trouble to avoid him ...'

That would please Ahmed, Webber thought, Jenkinson trying to keep a distance. A date was mentioned. Webber was aware of Davis scribbling it down. The chronology was clear in his head; that Thursday in late November was the day before Ahmed had interviewed Jenkinson in York. If only Jenkinson had gone straight to Ahmed or at least come clean in the interview. He glanced down at his phone on the desk remembering the text.

'... it was an attempted contact from which we could make nothing ...' the voice went on, 'but Streetwise returned some days later and this time he had his meeting. No one refuses him ...'

He couldn't read florid-face's expression and wondered suddenly how close the surveillance team had been when Jenkinson had been killed. He thought of a concrete lorry backing down that rutted path, its reversing signal blaring out its presence to anyone within earshot. He was alive when the concrete went in. Had they watched without knowing what they were seeing? Had they been down to look after Streetwise left the site? Had they missed the opportunity to save Tom Jenkinson?

Another date was mentioned; a Tuesday at the beginning of December. Webber did the calculation in his head. Two days after Jenkinson's body had been found. His thoughts stalled. That couldn't be right. Had he miscalculated? He looked at Davis who was staring at the sheet of paper, his brow furrowed. What had the man said? ... *contact from which we could make nothing* ... What was that supposed to mean?

The voice went on, 'Now as to the times on Inspector Davis's summary when the unfortunate boy met his end ...' The man tapped his finger on a page, a copy of the one Davis had in his hand. 'Streetwise was where he went immediately after his first trip to York. You will find him on the inventory of your Leeds and Bradford airport. He was in Germany doing deals.'

'In Germany?' Webber queried, exchanging a glance with Farrar.

'Yes, his first trip to York made him late for his business dealings in Munich. He was in a bad temper. He went back to York as soon as he could. A brief visit. But no, at the time your young boy died, he was nowhere near. Whoever killed Tom Jenkinson, it wasn't Streetwise. And we can be clear it wasn't done at his order, not even for a nobody like Jenkinson. We know them well enough to be sure of that. It is one of the reasons we cannot snare them through third parties. They do their own dirty work.'

Webber stared. This couldn't be true. They'd had it tied in tight. It had to be Streetwise. He thought about the suspects list, the single name, evaporating to nothing. What had the man said about a meeting two days after Jenkinson's body was found?

'The contact,' he said. 'The one you made nothing of ... what was it about? Who was it?'

Florid-face turned to his colleague who glanced down at a file and shrugged. 'As to what it was about, we assume drugs.' She gave them a wintry smile. 'We always assume drugs ... but we found no link. She didn't want to see him but no one refuses Streetwise. They met briefly that second occasion. He has not returned and she suffered no consequences for her earlier stubbornness. That in itself is something to be remarked, but we found nothing of interest on record about her. Her name is Stevenson. Edith Stevenson.'

chapter forty-three

The call had ended. Webber saw the distorted reflections of their three faces in the now blank screen. They could have been sitting there for minutes or hours. After the volley of questions they'd fired at their Scandinavian colleagues, teasing out every last nuance, the silence felt somehow too loud to breach. When Davis spoke, it seemed wrong, as though he'd stolen a march on them. Webber listened to the DI tell Farrar about Ahmed's text. And as soon as Farrar caught the sense of Davis's words, he had him pull up the recording right there in front of them.

The screen gave a window on to the past, showing Jenkinson alive, weaving more of a story than anyone there at the time had realised. Webber looked at the garish orange of the torn jacket.

Davis fast-forwarded it through the 20 minutes before Ahmed entered the room. Jenkinson looked as relaxed as Webber remembered, his form barely moving until the moment his head shot up as he recognised Ahmed. Webber strained to see every gesture, catch every trace but there was nothing to suggest the specific message Ahmed thought he'd heard. Maybe he should call him to get more detail. Whatever he thought he'd remembered, he might be able to point them to a particular stretch, to narrow the search. And it might be no more than wishful thinking on Ahmed's part. He fingered his phone but said nothing, let it run further.

When it came, with hindsight to colour his interpretation, it was crystal clear.

Ahmed said, 'Who is he, Tom?'

Jenkinson shrugged and said, 'I don't know, Mr Ahmed. Honest. I never met him, never saw him. I tried once ... we had a go. Wouldn't have gone that far if we'd thought he were Streetwise ...' the ghost of a pause as Jenkinson looked Ahmed in the eye, 'but ...'

The agenda behind his words was plain – now.

'He was fishing!' Farrar's tone bordered indignation.

Webber nodded. 'I guess if Ahmed already knew about Streetwise and Boots Boy, then Jenkinson had lost his route to big money. I think he was wavering anyway. If he'd seen any sign of recognition he'd have earned the brownie points and confessed to the contact.'

'But we didn't know,' Davis said. 'The name hadn't cropped up at that point.'

Webber felt his jaw clench. The name *had* cropped up. An outside surveillance team had already clocked Jenkinson as a potential recruit for Streetwise, but they were chasing a bigger prize and hadn't passed on what they knew. Jenkinson had seen that Ahmed knew nothing, none of them had known anything at that stage.

'Edith Stevenson,' he burst out. 'How does she fit into this?'

'Ayaan always had it that ...' Davis let the comment fade into an expression of puzzlement.

'Who had it that what?' Farrar's hard stare bounced from one to the other of them. He wanted every detail.

Webber explained about the fuzzy image of the man/woman with the odd walk, the one who'd been with Jenkinson, and Ahmed's dogged fixation on Stevenson as somehow involved. Davis, displaying a surprisingly deft touch with the networked systems, found and opened the analyst's report on Farrar's screen.

'We went through it.' Davis's tone was uncertain as he looked from Webber to Farrar and back again. 'It wasn't her.'

Webber nodded. That was how he remembered it too. Definitely not her. But the report hadn't said that. It had given numbers and stats. *Definitely not* was the interpretation they'd put on it.

While he and Davis struggled to pull a clear conclusion out of the morass of detail, Farrar was on the phone having the report's author chased down. The voice that eventually came from Farrar's speakerphone was relaxed. 'Yes, of course I remember it, sir. Two recordings from DI Davis. What's the problem?'

A few minutes into to a fierce grilling from Farrar, her relaxed tone had vanished, but Farrar couldn't make her waver. And as she talked through the measurements she'd made, the analyses she'd done, Webber found himself convinced and saw that Farrar and Davis were too. The mystery person who had met Tom Jenkinson might have been either sex, the odd manner of the walk was close to identical in both samples, but the original CCTV was not Edith Stevenson.

'Have we spoken to this Stevenson woman yet?' Farrar asked.

Davis shook his head. 'Ayaan Ahmed spoke to her on the phone briefly ten or eleven days ago. She wouldn't see him. And when Suzie tried a week later, she pretended to be out. We haven't had a reason to haul her in.'

'We have now,' said Webber, looking briefly to Farrar for endorsement which came in a curt nod. 'I'm pretty sure they were planning another go at her this afternoon,' he added as he pulled out his phone and clicked through for Ahmed's number. The last thing he needed was Ahmed getting a hint that he'd been right about Stevenson's involvement while he was alone with the woman.

From the echo of the speaker and buzz of engine noise, it was clear Ahmed was on the road. 'Where are you?' Webber asked. 'What are you doing?'

'Trying to track down Tiffany Drake,' Ahmed told them. 'Suzie got me two possible addresses. She wasn't at the first. I'm on my way to the second.'

'Is Edith Stevenson one of them?'

'No, but she'll be next on my list only Suzie said to hold off until she'd got back to me. Turns out Stevenson and Tiffany have been in contact, exchanging emails. Suzie's going to look through them.'

'How's she accessing these emails?' The question came as a bark from Farrar.

'Uh … her husband … he's given her access.' Webber heard Ahmed's voice snap to attention as Farrar revealed his presence in the conversation.

'Do you think she's with Edith Stevenson?' As Webber asked the question he exchanged a perplexed glance with Davis and before Ahmed could answer, he added, 'Where's Suzie and why the rush?'

'Well … uh … no, Tiffany's probably with the woman I'm going to see now. Suzie's with Michael Drake … well, she was when I last spoke to her. We've nothing solid but … one or two things … we thought …'

'Spit it out, Ayaan.'

'We think it's possible someone wants to harm Tiffany; that it could be tied up with the first Mrs Drake.'

Webber's puzzlement deepened. He saw his concern reflected in Davis's face. Farrar had narrowed his eyes. 'And you think it could be Stevenson who wants to harm her?'

'Possibly yes. If there's a link with both wives then it has to be one of the surviving quintets or Brad Tippet. But we don't think Tiffany's with any of them now. That's why I'm trying to find her. She's not answering her phone and the friend isn't either, but we think she'll be there.'

Webber was aware of a reaction from Farrar as Brad Tippet's name dropped out. 'When you say remaining quintets, you mean Stevenson and Drake?'

'And Kowalski.'

'She's been thousands of miles away.'

'Well … um … has she? We've only her word for that.'

Webber opened his mouth to contradict Ahmed, then paused. He was sure they had more than Kowalski's word, but without stopping to think it through he couldn't be clear what they'd found themselves and what had come from Melinda. 'Are you anywhere· near Stevenson's address now?' he asked.

'No, I'm heading for Melton on the outskirts of Hull.'

'Ayaan,' Davis broke into the conversation, 'I want to know what's happening. Call me when you get there, when you find her. And don't go near Stevenson without my say-so, ok?'

As he ended the call, Webber turned to Farrar who fixed them both with a hard stare. 'This is becoming a bit of a mess. Get it sorted. Keep me in the loop.'

As they hurried away from Farrar's office, Webber said, 'I don't want Suzie Harmer anywhere near Stevenson either.'

Davis nodded. 'I'll send a couple of uniforms for Stevenson. Given her track record I don't know that we'll get her in voluntarily.'

Webber paused. He didn't want the clock running on Edith Stevenson of all people. On the other hand, her name had cropped up in a context that couldn't be ignored. And if Ahmed and Suzie were on to something it lent an air of urgency even if he couldn't quite pin it down. 'I want her in,' he said, 'even if we can't keep her. Tell them to bring her in under caution if they can but if they have to arrest her, so be it. Only keep it low key. For now.'

He flicked through his phone for Suzie's number. The ring tone sounded in his ear as they went down the stairs. As they reached the ground floor, Suzie's voicemail cut in.

'Call in for an update before you do anything else or go anywhere. Neither you nor Ayaan are to tackle Stevenson,' Webber said into the phone. 'That's on Suzie's voicemail,' he said to Davis, 'but keep trying. I don't want her or Ayaan anywhere near Stevenson now we have a link with Jenkinson.'

Davis nodded and was pulling out his phone as he peeled off to organise Edith Stevenson's detention.

Webber pushed through the main door, the icy cold air making him shiver. He pulled his jacket tight around him, catching a glimpse of the wall clock as he did so. His gut told him this would be a long day. With a muffled curse he snatched out his phone again. It was over an hour since that text from Melinda but maybe he could catch her. The phone rang twice then went to voicemail. She'd red-buttoned him. He didn't leave a message. Instead he flicked through for the number of her friend Jess.

'Hello, Martyn Webber here.' He could hear childish shrieks in the background – surely that was Sam shouting 'Digger!' and felt awkward. The last time he'd spoken to Jess had been with Melinda at his elbow making him apologise for his mistake when he hadn't allowed her to collect Sam from playschool.

'Yes … Hi.' There was a hint of frost to her tone. 'Mel said you might be coming for Sam. Any idea what time?'

'That's the thing. I've only just got Mel's message. I don't know that I'll be able to. I might have to work late.'

A pause. 'Well, will Mel be back? I can't keep him beyond six. We're going out and I can't leave him with our baby-sitter. They don't know each other.'

'No, no of course not. I'm sure Mel will be back. Or I'll be able to get away. I just wanted to warn you.'

'As long as someone picks him up … uh …'

'What is it?'

Another pause, then, 'You know where she's gone, don't you? That woman left her a message, the one you mistook for me that time.'

'Joyce Yeatman. Yes, that's all I know. Mel left me voicemail. Why?'

'I'm … it's probably nothing … I was a bit worried. She doesn't know her well, does she? Do you trust her, Joyce Yeatman, I mean? I'm not sure I do.'

'Have you met her?'

'No, have you?'

'No … I've spoken to her … I don't know much about her. Why don't you trust her, Jess?'

He didn't like the turn the conversation had taken. Mel's friend Jess didn't like him. For her to say these things she must be worried.

'It's nothing I can pin down, it's just some of the things she's told Mel, like not reading that suicide note. How can that possibly be true?'

There was a ripple of shock through him at the revelation of how much Melinda had confided in Jess, but he pushed it aside as unimportant for now. As soon as he ended the call he rang Melinda's number again. This time it went straight to voicemail. Either she was on another call or she'd turned it off. He left a short message asking her to ring him. He'd slowed to make the calls and the cold had begun to make him shiver. As he upped his pace and strode towards his car Jess's words replayed in his head. *That woman had left her a message …* As far as he knew Joyce had never used Melinda's mobile. She'd always called the house.

He speed-dialled his own home number and started to jog, pausing to punch in the access code as the answerphone cut in.

He could barely hear anything over the rising whistle of the wind. An empty doorway was the best shelter the street had to offer. He ducked his head away from the brunt of the winter weather and hunched over the phone trying to fashion a makeshift cocoon in which to hear what was being said. No new messages; six saved. He prayed Melinda hadn't deleted anything recent from Joyce. The first two were quickly skipped as his own voice spoke out to him. The next was Melinda to herself, a reminder about something for Sam. Then Jess, a non-message asking Melinda to ring if she was going to some event or other. Then with the penultimate message he tensed and pressed the phone hard to his ear. Joyce Yeatman's voice, calm enough but with an element of tension.

Melinda hello, it's Joyce. Uh … could you call me back? Um … if you have the time.

The final message had come in less than 20 minutes later. It was Joyce Yeatman's voice again, the tension more marked.

Hello, Melinda. I'm sorry to be on to you again, but if you're free there's something I'd like to talk through with you. It's ... well, it's one of Gary's friends from the old days. I ... uh ... we ... have some of her stuff. I should have told you sooner probably, but ... anyway. She's been in touch again, wants to see me. To be absolutely frank I'm not keen on meeting her on my own and I wondered if you might come along. She knew Pamela. In fact it's Pamela she wants to talk about.

The chill that ran through Webber as he stared at the phone was nothing to do with the icy blast of the wind. *One of Gary's friends from the old days ... she ... in touch again ...*

It could only be Edith Stevenson or China Kowalski. As he turned to sprint back the way he'd come, his phone again at his ear, he couldn't find a shred of comfort in either name.

chapter forty-four

It was clear that Farrar was pulled in too many directions to fully take in what Webber was saying so he kept the summary short and sharp, sticking with the key points. He wanted to operate with Farrar's explicit backing. He'd do what he had to do without it ... had already set someone on to tracking Melinda's phone ... but the panic hadn't yet risen high enough to override caution. He'd been wrong not so long ago when he'd flown from behind his desk to rescue Sam from, so he thought, the malevolent clutches of Joyce Yeatman.

'But where's Melinda in all this?' Farrar's tone reflected the bewilderment of his expression as his embattled PA, glaring at Webber, harassed him about people waiting, deadlines slipping.

Webber responded briefly, reassuringly ... dropping out the phrases that might yet keep Melinda out of trouble and his own rank intact once the dust had settled. Melinda knew someone ... didn't know her well ... a coincidence ... the Pamela Morgan saga ... public domain ... And now she'd been asked to go and meet a friend of a friend ...

'Edith Stevenson!' Farrar looked shocked as the realisation hit him. 'But she's the one ...'

'Nobody knew,' Webber told him. He swallowed the thought, *it might not be Stevenson, it might be Kowalski*, because there wasn't time to muddy the waters with the implications of that.

'Yes, do it!' Farrar said as his glowering PA hurried him away. 'Find Melinda. Get on to Suzie ... tell her ...'

'I'm on it.' Webber had been backing off the second the affirmative was out of Farrar's mouth. He turned and ran back to the main office. His phone was at his ear. Melinda's number was going straight to voicemail, but it hadn't the first time he'd rung. She'd red-buttoned him. She was on another call. Who was she talking to? Where was she? Just as long as her mobile remained on, he'd soon know.

He kept his phone in his hand, a talisman, she'd ring him back soon, everything would be fine. Melinda knew how to look after herself.

Trying to keep a lid on any outward show of anxiety, Webber peered over the shoulder of the woman who was setting up to track Melinda's phone. 'How long will it take?'

'As long as the phone's on, it should be quick … minutes…'

He was aware of a nervy edge to her voice, aware it was his looming presence that was causing it. He had to pull back, let her get on with her job. It would be quicker that way. 'How closely can you pinpoint her?' He couldn't hold back the questions.

She stopped, twisted round to look at him, the worry of unrealistic expectations was clear in her expression. 'I can't pinpoint your wife, guv. I can only find her phone. It's a smartphone with GPS. As long as it's on I can get within a few metres.'

'OK, OK. Get on with it. Let me know as soon as …' His voice tailed away. Of course she would let him know. She might have found Melinda by now if he hadn't kept hassling her. He forced himself to turn and walk away.

The far door opened and Davis came in. Webber leapt on this new focus to distract his thoughts. 'Have you spoken to Suzie?'

Davis shook his head. 'Her phone's still going to voicemail. But I've just heard from Ayaan. He's had no joy with Tiffany Drake or the friend. He's had it from a neighbour that the friend went away a couple of days ago. Not due back till after Christmas. The thing is he's heard from Suzie. He wasn't too clear but she'd got something out of some emails and she was on her way to see another witness. He thinks it was Stevenson.'

'Ayaan's on his way back here, is he?' Webber spoke the words mechanically, knowing he should be pissed at Suzie for pretending she hadn't had their messages; had she targeted Stevenson because she knew Mel was on her way there with Joyce Yeatman? Behind him the woman at the desk was chasing Melinda's phone. He had to force himself not to spin round to look at her.

'He wanted to do a bit more digging,' Davis said. 'Speak to a few people. Apparently Stevenson has a neighbour primed to tell callers she's out. He wants to be sure this one is really away.'

Webber nodded. 'Where is he?' His voice sounded far away. He didn't care where Ahmed was and anyway he should already know. Where's Melinda? That was the only question that mattered.

'Outskirts of Hull,' Davis said. 'Melton way, not far from the Humber Bridge.'

'… not far from the Humber Bridge …'

The phrase seemed to echo. It took a second for him to realise the words had come from behind. Then he was at the woman's shoulder staring at the screen, Davis at her other side, no memory of the steps that had brought either of them across the room. It was more a grid than a map … not his thing … didn't make sense. He wanted to see a flashing blip, a cartoon tracker overlying a map. It didn't work like that.

'Where …?' He had to stop to gulp in a breath.

Davis came to his rescue. 'What have you found?'

'I've got it,' she said. 'Outskirts of Hull, not far from the Humber Bridge.'

Davis peered closer. 'Can you get an exact location, show us on something that looks a bit more like a map?'

'It's … she's moving. I can't tell … I'm guessing she's in a car on the A63 heading out of Hull towards the bridge.'

'Is she going to cross the bridge?' Webber raked his memory for anything that linked Pamela Morgan, the quintets or anyone to the south bank of the Humber.

'I don't know.' The woman's voice was close to a despairing wail.

Davis had found a road map. He slapped it down on the desk open at the page showing the network of roads west of Hull. She grabbed it, shot Webber a glare and directed her words to Davis. 'I got a signal in that area,' she said, 'and there ... then there ...'

Davis nodded. 'So it would be a reasonable guess that she's travelling west out of Hull.' He looked up at Webber. 'But she could be on a parallel road. If she's going to go across the bridge she'd turn off on to the A15.' His finger traced the route. 'But it wouldn't show up with that level of accuracy until she's definitely made the move. And until we get in touch with her, all we know is that that's where her phone is. It doesn't mean she's with it.'

The woman shot Davis a grateful glance and turned back to her screen.

Webber pulled in a deep breath and closed his eyes for a second. He was behaving like an idiot, practically asking for an IT trace on Melinda's thoughts and intentions. It put a block on rational thinking. He had to take a mental step back. If it wasn't Melinda what would he do?

Ahmed!

'Get on to Ayaan,' he rapped out. 'He's practically on the spot. Patch him in somehow. Get him there ... wherever it is.'

As Davis reached for the nearest handset, Webber cast about for his own phone. It had been in his hand. He scrabbled through his pockets. Where had he put it? He spotted it gleaming at him from an empty desk and dived across for it. As he reached out it sprang to life, the shock sending a shaft of fire through him. He had to make a double grab to stop it tumbling to the floor. The screen told him it was Melinda's friend Jess.

'Jess? Is Sam OK?'

'He's fine but I'm afraid my baby-sitter's cried off. She isn't well.' A sudden hope that she'd rung to say they wouldn't be going out and would look after Sam for as long as necessary died as she went on. They weren't cancelling their trip. They were taking their child to its grandparents. They would drop Sam off with him. She'd rung to know exactly where he was.

'That's good,' she said when he told her. 'I thought you might be the other side of town. We'll be there in about quarter of an hour.'

There was no option but to agree. She added that she hadn't heard from Melinda, though she'd tried to get in touch. 'It just went to voicemail,' she told him. It did nothing to relieve his anxiety that she'd been worried enough to try.

As the phone disconnected, he was aware of Davis talking to someone on another phone about Edith Stevenson. He wanted to hear that they'd found her, found her with Melinda, that they were nearby. But Melinda's phone was somewhere west of Hull.

He saw Davis pull a face. Edith Stevenson's house was empty; no one there. As he listened to Davis interrogate someone on how closely the house had been checked, his thoughts raced at random. They didn't know enough about Stevenson ... didn't know anything except that a killer and major league drugs dealer had sought her out after Tom Jenkinson's murder. Why?

Webber wanted to be on the road right now heading for Hull. He couldn't. He was tied to this place ... had to wait for Sam ... was there anyone here who might be persuaded to play child-minder? As he drew in breath to speak, his handset pinged a message. He stared at the small screen. Disbelief hollowed out a void deep inside him.

It showed a missed call from Melinda.

'Mel!' If Davis's head hadn't shot up, Webber wouldn't have known he'd spoken her name aloud.

His fingers seemed to lose all sense of touch as he fought to find the right buttons to return the call.

There was no ring tone. Melinda's voice crackled from the speaker telling him she wasn't available to take his call.

He felt stunned. The handset stood out in sharp relief against the activity around him. Davis was talking to Ahmed, telling him where to go, where Melinda had last been tracked. The woman following the signal bent over her task. They sat in his peripheral vision out of focus as though draped in gauze. He didn't know why he had his phone on speaker. Melinda's message morphed into a robotic voice inviting him to speak after the tone.

'Ring me,' he snapped at it, hearing anger in his words. That wasn't right. It wasn't anger he felt. 'Ring me,' he said again, softening his tone. If the whole room hadn't been listening he would have said something else … maybe … but what?

The moment he cut the call the phone beeped again. She'd left voicemail. He stared at the small screen. Then Davis was at his elbow saying something, gesture more than words easing him on to a chair.

'Ring her back, Guv. You were both on the phone at the same time.'

'She's left a message.'

'Yes, you're right.' Davis's calm tones were reassuring. The DI plucked the phone from his hand and clicked through to retrieve the voicemail. 'See what she said. If she rings it'll cut in.' The phone was back in his palm. 'Listen to her message.' The intonation behind Davis's words made it more an order than a suggestion. 'Tell me what I need to know; anything I need to pass on to Ayaan.'

Webber shook the lethargy out of his head. He had to get a grip. This was no time to worry about Melinda leaving anything inappropriate; they had to find her. 'Put it on speaker.' He slapped the phone back into Davis's hand and reached for the nearest landline. He'd call her from that while they listened to her message.

Melinda's tone was a mix of excitement and indignation, the words rattled out.

Martyn, are you ever off your bloody phone? You won't believe what Joyce has done. Stupid cow's been holding out on me. Some damn-fool idea of loyalty to her husband.

Her voice rose and fell. Traffic noise overlay everything she said. A shiver of anticipation ran through him. She was driving fast. The message began to break up. The handset on the desk cut across her words with the ringtone from her mobile. One ... two ... and it cut out. Davis reached across to disconnect the line before her voice could invite them to leave a message. It had been the wrong number calling. She'd cut it off.

... suicide note ... unsigned ... been on to the paymasters ...

Her voice was hurried now. He heard Davis say, 'Paymasters?' The woman at the desk looked up. 'I thought she said papers.'

Stevenson ... I can't go into it all now ... Joyce has gone to pieces but I want you to pick her up before she does any damage ... I'm going to get–

She stopped abruptly but the line remained open. Webber found himself holding his breath.

Stevenson's gone completely off the ...

The words disappeared into background noise. Webber imagined Melinda turning away from the phone which, he hoped, rested in its cradle. The quality of the sound suggested it wasn't held to her head.

... anyway, Jess ... can't get ... Joyce ... tried to call you ... Ring me.

Her final volley of speech was all but inaudible and the line disconnected.

'She's moved.'

Webber was at the desk in a stride looking at the screen that made no sense to him. 'Where? When?'

'It showed up just before you picked up the voicemail. If she was on the A63, she's turned off. She might be heading for the bridge.'

Davis's voice; 'Ayaan, have you got that?' As Webber looked round, he saw yet another telephone handset ... everyone was on the phone ... this one passed from Davis to the woman at the desk,

Davis telling her, 'He's coming in from the other direction. He'll come off at the A15. Keep him on track.'

'What's over the bridge?' Webber floundered, struggling to pull detail out of his head. It was the wrong case. He knew more about it from his discussions with Melinda than from briefings at work.

Then Davis was in his face again. 'I've sent someone to get Joyce Yeatman.'

'But she's with Mel.'

'She's not. She answered her phone at home not ten minutes ago.'

'What did she say? What's she told Mel?'

'Soon as she knew it was the police she burst into tears and slammed down the phone; hasn't answered it since, but like I say, I've sent someone out to get her. Edith Stevenson isn't at home but I've left someone there in case.' Davis pointed to the mobile that Webber clutched in his hand. 'Ring your wife, Guv. She might answer now.'

Webber pressed the buttons and stared at the small screen, resenting every microsecond of the time it took to make its connection. Then it was ringing again. Once … twice …

Connected.

Melinda's voice loud and clear. 'At last! Where have you been?'

His heart thumped hard at the sound of her voice. She was breathless, her words disjointed as though she was running.

'Mel, are you OK? Where are you?'

'Listen Martyn, its Edith Stevenson … Joyce didn't tell me until … The note. She read it, all of it when she first found Pamela. She … coroner didn't see it all … Then China Kowalski … Hang on, is that …?'

'What? Mel, where are you? What's happening? Are you with Stevenson? Are you OK? Stand still, you're breaking up.'

He heard a tut of exasperation. When she spoke, her voice came through clearly. She breathed heavily but he had the impression she'd stopped moving. 'I'm fine.' The words were snapped impatiently. 'And no, she's here somewhere, but I can't find her. If I'd known what I was coming into I'd have ...' A pause. 'I got on to the pay...' She'd turned her face away from the phone. It was that word again, paymasters / papers.

The woman at the desk behind him was speaking to Ahmed. 'Not the bridge. Don't go to the bridge.'

Webber glanced at her but it wasn't what she said that sent a tingle of ice through his core. Paymasters was a word that belonged with people like Streetwise and Boots Boy. And Streetwise had gone out of his way to meet Edith Stevenson.

'Mel, listen to me. Wherever you are, get back to ...'

Her voice cut across him. 'Oh no! That isn't ...' Her clear tones had become a low murmur. He heard shock and an element of fear. 'Edith?' It came over as a question, a whisper. Then suddenly it was a shout. 'Edith! No! Shi–!' The expletive cut off mid syllable.

'Mel?'

The sounds from the phone were chaotic, as though she'd shoved the handset into a pocket full of crackly sweet wrappers and begun to sprint.

'Mel!' He shouted her name.

The crackling noise stopped, replaced by a gentle buzz. The sound of her breathing was gone. He heard the distant bark of a dog. After a volley of yaps it stopped, leaving birdsong the only sound that punctuated a low background hum.

chapter forty-five

Ahmed eased his foot off the accelerator and stared round in perplexity. Don't go to the bridge? Then where? He wasn't even sure who he was looking for or why, just that he was being guided towards a mobile phone signal. Melinda Webber's? Had he got that right? His mind had raced through scenarios. She'd walked out on her marriage – no great surprise there – and was heading to the Humber Bridge to end it all. But no, not Melinda Webber. She might take her husband there to throw him off but she wasn't the self-harm type.

He stopped the car, keeping one eye on the mirror. It was a clearway and this wasn't the moment to have to argue with Hull's traffic division. 'I'm going to give you my coordinates.' He spoke into the phone, taking it from its cradle and clicking through for the app that would give him his exact location. 'And you can tell me what direction I need to go.'

'It's not moved for a while now … uh …' She lowered her voice. 'What's it all about? What's happening?'

Ahmed blew out a sigh. 'Don't ask me. I was out looking for someone else. But it is Melinda Webber's phone you're tracking, isn't it?'

'Yes, and he's going frantic. Pacing up and down like a tiger in a cage. He was called downstairs just a minute ago, thank God. But it's not just her, DI Davis has been hassling people on the phone. I can hear him arguing with someone now. He was on about someone called Joyce Yeatman. That mean anything to you?'

'Yeah, she's our case, not theirs. They're supposed to be tying the noose tight round whoever killed Tom Jenkinson.' Ahmed watched the sweep of the wide road up ahead. It curved to meet a landscaped roundabout on its way to the Humber Bridge, the route he'd thought he was taking.

'There's been a call about that from across town,' the voice in his ear told him. 'Something about someone called Emmett.'

Emmett? That was the kid Tom said he'd recruited for the traffic lights scam. 'Emmett? What's that about?'

'Search me. It's all chaos and raised voices here. I'm not asking questions. No one's where they need to be. They want Webber and Davis back across town. Farrar's gone off late to something he's not allowed to be late for. Take my advice, don't show your face till tomorrow.'

Ahmed smiled. That mirrored Suzie's last message. Whether or not she found Stevenson in, she was going to string it out and go straight home. Had she said Stevenson? Whoever it was, she knew when trouble was brewing.

'OK, so how close am I? Can you give me a compass bearing and a distance?'

'Yes, you're practically on the spot. Let's see ... from those coordinates you want to be ... 142 degrees.'

'OK, just a sec.' Ahmed clicked his phone to compass mode and balanced it on his hand. He climbed out of his car and turned to look. He was in no man's land here, stretches of rough farmland tracking the estuary, out of sight of the big trading parks, the edge-of-town supermarkets and big car dealers. The way she told him was at right angles to the road. A barbed wire fence marked the border between the wide grass verge and the mess of trees, bushes and scrubland beyond. 'Distance?'

'Bear in mind there's a margin of error here, but round about 650 metres.'

That was the best part of half a mile. He looked out across

the empty wasteland, then glanced up and down the road. A roundabout lay at either end of the dual carriageway, the major routes led on into Hull, onwards to the motorway or out across the bridge to Lincolnshire. He fought to orientate himself. He knew this area reasonably well.

'There must be a road nearer than this,' he said into the phone.

'Yes, how about … there's Ferriby Road, runs sort of parallel to where you are.' Behind her words he could hear someone else. Her tone changed. She was no longer alone.

'Got it,' he said. He'd been momentarily confused by this featureless scrubland criss-crossed by roads but now it clicked into place. He had been here with Cari. 650 metres would take him right over that stretch of scrub, across the road at the other side and on into a woodland park. 'It's the Humber Bridge Country Park. He jumped into the car. 'I know where to go but there's no direct road. You'll need to help me out again when I get there.'

The phone was back in its cradle; the line remained open as he sped towards the roundabout that would give him access to the network of smaller roads that embraced the park. 'Um … was that Martyn Webber who came back just now?'

'No,' said Davis's voice, 'it was me. What is it?'

'Who am I searching for? Is it Mrs Webber? And … uh … why? I mean I'm not sure what I'm supposed to be looking out for.'

'It's Mrs Webber's phone we're tracking,' Davis told him. 'Martyn talked to her on it less than 20 minutes ago, but she's not answered it since.' There was a pause. Ahmed could feel the tension. 'There's a possibility that she's with Edith Stevenson.'

Edith Stevenson with Melinda Webber? But that was where Suzie was going. He felt his hands grip the wheel as he slowed to take the turn, then pushed the car forward, too fast for the narrower road.

'Listen to me, Ayaan.' Davis's voice had hardened. 'We found a possible link …'

'Stevenson and Tom!' he broke in.

Davis sighed. 'It's not the link you thought it was, Ayaan, and it's not a definite link between them. It's through a third party. But listen to me, if she's there and you find them ...'

'Don't worry,' Ahmed said. 'I'm not going to do anything stupid.' He felt his mouth curve to a smile and hoped the tone of his voice didn't give away the satisfaction he felt. 'If she had anything to do with it, I'm not going to jeopardise a prosecution.'

'And you might find nothing more than Melinda Webber off on a wild goose chase,' Davis added, 'but she seemed to think she had Stevenson in her sights.'

Ahmed's thoughts stalled for a moment wondering how on earth Melinda Webber had got herself into the frame, but there had been a hard edge to Davis's voice as though he'd been wondering just the same. Now wasn't the time to ask those questions.

'The CCTV footage?' he murmured.

'It wasn't her. I had it analysed. You can consider the cost of that a black mark on your record. It wasn't her. That's not the link. It's doubtful they ever met.'

Ahmed knew he wouldn't get any more out of Davis, not just now. The car was no longer buffeted by the wind, he'd left the exposed scrubland behind and moved into the shelter of the wood at the south end of the park. He slowed and bumped the car up off the tarmac and on to the dirt track that led into the trees. Behind him the Humber sparkled as the breeze whipped the surface to a mass of tiny jewelled peaks. There was a proper car park not far along but he would have to drive round in a loop to get to it.

'OK.' He jumped out of the car, and checked his phone for his current position, reading the figures aloud. 'Where do I go from here?'

'83 degrees. 150 metres near enough.'

He looked at the terrain ahead trying to estimate the distance. It gave him a gentle incline for maybe 100 metres, and then rose sharply. He set off between the trees, his feet sinking into the leaf mould as though he was walking on a giant sponge. He had to reach out to the rough bark of the tree trunks to keep his footing. It was hard to stay on a straight line but he pinpointed a distant tree and tracked towards it.

'Can't be far off now,' he said, hearing a slight breathlessness in his tone. It was hard going.

'Is there anyone nearby?' asked Davis.

'No, not a soul, but who'd be out in this lot? It's freezing. I can hear dogs barking in the distance. There are no proper paths here.'

'Well, watch your back. Melinda Webber cut off mid call almost half an hour ago. Something startled her. Don't know if she was attacked or if she dropped the phone, but if the latter she didn't stop to pick it up. It's on but it's just ringing through to voicemail.'

The slope's gradient increased. Every step was a struggle as the weight of his feet pushed aside the top coating leaving him to flounder on smooth mud. There was more of a breeze than he'd realised. The musty aroma of leaf mould rose as his feet sank into the mushy ground. Glancing behind him it was as though an invisible hand with a broom had swept the leaves back into place, all but obliterating his tracks. He stopped, breathing hard and holding on to a tree branch. 'I can't be far off. Give it another try.'

He heard the woman murmur something about margins. 'I'm ringing her phone now, Ayaan,' said Davis. 'Stop and listen.'

He tried to stand motionless, but although the crunch of his footsteps had stopped, a thousand small beasts continued to forage, making what should have been a tranquil spot bustle with sound. Underlying it all was the continuous rustle of the wind through the trees, the taste of salt on the air from the estuary. No other sound. He pulled himself a few more steps up the hill and stopped again.

A bird in a tree somewhere above him chattered furiously. Up ahead, the breeze scythed through the fallen leaves leaving stragglers to eddy around and settle against the tree trunks. The terrain steepened. He moved forward, felt his calf muscles strain against the gradient. In a few more steps he'd be up against a miniature cliff face that reared out of the treeline.

The long mournful wail of an air horn from a tug boat on the Humber cut across the noises of the woodland. And as it died away a tiny sound crept into the mix, so fleeting he wasn't sure he'd heard it.

'Gone to voicemail,' said Davis.

'Ring it again,' urged Ahmed. 'I think I heard something.'

It was muffled, might have been distant traffic. He took two more steps up the incline, the crunch of his shoes on the soft ground smothered the noise, but no, it was there … louder … he scrambled further. It was unmistakeably a phone ringing. But where?

'Mrs Webber?' he called out feeling foolish. There was no one in sight. He had the wood to himself.

Any second now it was going to cut out again. His hand reached for the rough bark of a tall tree, and as he pulled himself up to move out from its shadow, the phone sang out clearly. He stared. It must be buried in the detritus of the woodland floor. Then he caught the gleam. An eerie light glowed from the leaf mould packed at the base of the trunk.

'Got it!' he screeched, diving to his knees, pulling on latex gloves and carefully easing it free.

'Any sign of Melinda Webber?' Davis was in his ear.

'I'm halfway up a slope under the trees,' he said. 'The path's way down below me. I've not seen anyone.' He pulled in a breath, didn't want Webber to be listening, wondered where he was. On his way here maybe? 'I can't see any disturbance on the ground, but it's fairly easy to cover tracks on this terrain. It was in the curve of the roots at the bottom of a tree, tucked round the back. Looks like it was deliberately hidden.'

chapter forty-six

Webber carried Sam across to the window feeling the boy's fist clutch the back of his collar, a sure sign of insecurity in strange surroundings. There was no shortage of people ready to look after him, to allow Webber to get back upstairs to find out what had happened over in Hull, but Sam had clung tight, his face threatening to crumple. He wouldn't be palmed off on to strangers in a place he didn't know. Webber concentrated on breathing evenly as he pointed out to Sam the comings and goings outside the station. It was clear that his son had already picked up his worry. The child's face was sombre, eyes big as he stared out from the security of his father's hip. No smiles, no chatter. He'd only spoken once, saying 'Mummy?' as his gaze searched the crowd when Jess had handed him over. Now his head snapped round each time the door opened.

Webber was desperate to know what was happening upstairs but daren't go up there. If Sam heard Melinda's voice from the phone it might be enough to set him off.

He paced up and down by the window, murmuring to Sam, struggling to keep a lid on his frustration. This wasn't what he'd envisaged. Sam had been into work before. He'd even stayed one time for half an hour while Melinda went off somewhere. He'd been no trouble at all, hadn't clung to Webber or threatened screams if he tried to pass him on to someone else.

Now there was an added worry. There'd been a call and he needed to send Davis back across town, but was loathe to remove him from direct contact with Ahmed.

Emmett, the young girl who had been Tom Jenkinson's contact, had turned up out of the blue offering information about the traffic scam. Feeling Sam's grip tighten at the back of his collar it struck him that two children were obstructing a team of professional investigators. It shouldn't happen.

Sam's face turned to him, his brow creased to a frown. 'Mummy?'

'Mummy's back soon,' Webber reassured him. 'You've been with Daddy at work before. It was fun.' The way he remembered it he'd spent the entire 30 minutes on the phone while Sam played happily across the corridor surrounded by a willing crowd of volunteers. Of course it hadn't been here. Different station, different set of people not all of whom were complete strangers, that was the difference.

The grip on his collar loosened. Sam's attention was taken by someone flicking through a heap of files. They could go upstairs, stay at the edge of things. His arm began to ache. He reached behind his head to prise the tiny fingers free and shifted Sam to his other hip. Sam stared unsmiling into his face, then returned his attention to the bustle of the office around them. The small hand clamped into position again at the back of his neck. Who was he kidding? Sam already knew something was wrong. He couldn't risk going back into the thick of it, but there had to be something he could do. He turned to a nearby terminal.

Ahmed and Suzie had been chasing a theory about Michael Drake's wives, both wives. Webber sat down and logged into the system. Sam struggled to stand up on his knee so he could look over his father's shoulder.

'You keep an eye on things for me, Sam,' Webber said.

'Doy … oy …' Sam murmured. His grip on Webber's collar relaxed and he began to jig about.

Webber sighed. If Sam was going to settle enough to get boisterous but not enough to leave his father's arms then he had the worst of all worlds. He pushed his chair back to keep the small flailing feet clear of the equipment. At least something or someone was holding Sam's attention.

Was it going to turn out that Tippet's accusations from all those years ago had foundation? Had Drake killed his wife? But why? Not for the insurance. It wasn't clear he'd even known about the policy. Tippet had though, and Tippet must have collected a tidy sum himself when his own wife died years later. How closely had that been followed up?

Suzie had been looking out medical records for the first Mrs Drake, but he couldn't see anything of note. He found himself checking the routes she'd used, making sure she hadn't cut corners, but it was a mechanical move. He thought about how Tom Jenkinson's interview had looked from the viewpoint of what he now knew. There were other recordings he wanted to revisit, Kowalski ... Joyce Yeatman ... Tippet ... but he couldn't work out how to get at them from here. Where was Davis when he needed him? Stevenson and Drake weren't on record at all, but he wanted to listen to them too.

When he caught the reflection of Davis's face in the monitor he found himself framing a request to dig out the recordings. Then his thoughts tumbled to a halt. Davis hadn't appeared behind him by chance. He stared at the image, irrationally wanting to know the best or the worst before he turned to look. The DI's expression was impassive. Sam's fist tightened its grip.

Webber made himself breathe evenly. 'I want Drake and Stevenson on record,' he said without looking up. 'We have Kowalski, Tippet and Yeatman.'

He saw Davis nod. 'Stevenson might take a while, but we can get Drake in anytime.' There was a pause. From the corner of his eye Webber could see that Sam had turned his head to gaze up at Davis. 'We've found her phone,' Davis said. 'I think ... it looks like she dropped it.'

Webber's gaze snapped round to stare into the man's eyes. He'd caught the ghost of a pause. Davis wasn't convinced by *dropped it.*

'Found the phone but not … her?' He glanced at Sam not wanting to say Melinda's name.

'No, but there's something kicking off at the bridge. Ayaan's hot-footing it up there.'

'How d'you mean, kicking off?'

'We haven't got a straight story yet, but you know when you were on the phone, she said that thing … I couldn't make sense of it. Did she say papers or paymasters?'

'I thought it was paymasters. I don't know what she meant. Why?'

'If she said she'd been on to the papers, then … I know it makes no sense but that's what seems to be kicking off, some kind of media circus. They were only just picking it up in Hull when I talked to them. They'll get right back to me.' Davis spread his hands in a helpless shrug of apology for half a story.

Suddenly the decision was made. Webber didn't try to analyse the thought processes that had brought him to it but he reached for the keyboard to shut down the systems he'd opened, then stood up.

'We're going back across town,' he said. 'Sam'll settle better over there. I want you to go via Michael Drake's; bring him back with you.'

Davis looked taken aback but nodded. 'OK. Why?'

'I want him on record. I want to listen to him. I've got Tippet, Yeatman and Kowalski, but I don't have Drake and Stevenson.'

'Well, we haven't been concentrating on them,' Davis said. 'Oh and I've said not to bring Yeatman in just yet. They were reluctant because she's so drunk. I told them to see she was safe and leave her be. We'd only be bunging her in a cell to sleep it off.'

Webber shrugged. Part of him wanted to be sure of Joyce Yeatman, but he supposed they'd checked that her inebriation was for real, and he had her on record. Sam had let go of his collar and fixed Davis with an unblinking stare. Davis seemed mesmerised and addressed his next words to the boy.

'That thing Ayaan said about Kowalski. Could she have been in the thick of things all along?'

'No, no.' Webber shook his head impatiently.

Sam too shook his head and said, 'Nooo ...' making Davis smile.

'That's just Ayaan running away with things,' Webber went on. 'He goes off on tangents.'

'What is it you want Drake on record about?'

'All of it. I want to hear him talking like the others. There are limits to what I can get on with.' He nodded his head towards Sam. 'But I can listen to interview tapes. One of them's lying. I want to work out which one and why.'

'It's probably Stevenson and we don't have her.'

'No.' Webber shifted Sam to his other hip. He pulled in a deep breath. Not knowing Edith Stevenson's whereabouts was tied in with not knowing Melinda's.

'This Streetwise thing,' Davis said. 'Her and Tom ...'

'Thomas,' announced Sam.

Davis looked startled.

'Tank Engine not Jenkinson,' Webber translated. 'They approached Jenkinson in Hull months ago. This abortive meeting with Stevenson happened here in York. I don't think they're linked. It's like John said, it's a mess.'

Davis nodded and let out a sigh. 'At least I won't have any trouble with Drake. Ayaan says he does as he's told. I'll see you over there.'

Ahmed jammed Melinda's phone in his pocket and slithered down the slope. Even grabbing at the tree trunks he could barely keep his footing and had to concentrate not to twist his ankle on the slick mud that underlay the surface detritus.

So now he *was* going to the bridge ... should have gone there in the first place. Where had Melinda Webber's phone come from? He wasn't as convinced as he'd been at first that it had been deliberately hidden. The way the breeze eddied and shifted the leaves, it could easily have got covered over. Maybe it had simply landed where he'd found it. But if Melinda had dropped it, then where from, why hadn't she picked it up and how had it sunk so deep? As he reached gentler ground he paused to look back. Up beyond the tree where he'd found it, that mini cliff edge pushed through the vegetation, and above it the land disappeared into thick bushes. Was there a path up there or was it the railway?

His sliding boot prints had cut deep incisions into the terrain. He hadn't been trying to hide his tracks, but it wouldn't be as easy as he'd first thought.

Suppose she'd been up at the top and dropped the phone from there? He didn't like the feel of it. How could the handset have fallen so far unless it had been thrown? And what was up there? Davis didn't want him to take any detours. Straight to the bridge and find out what in hell was going on, that had been the order. Edith Stevenson's name had cropped up. He hadn't had any detail from Davis, wasn't sure the DI knew the story himself.

He should know what was up there. He knew this place. He and Cari had walked here on an outing in the summer with her mother and the obnoxious cousins. They'd managed to lose themselves in the trees for the best part of an hour while her mother fretted over the cousins playing too close to the lake. The memory brought a smile to his lips. But he was a long way from the lake here, somewhere at the periphery, couldn't orientate his memory with the treescape around him. He was thankful, not for the first time, that Cari had no ambition to follow in his footsteps career-wise. What must it be like for Webber having his wife in the same business, getting entangled with people like Edith Stevenson?

But what if Melinda Webber was lying up there injured or worse? It wouldn't matter whose orders he was under, Webber would never forgive him. But Davis had been adamant. Something was happening on the bridge, get up there pronto.

He tried to kick the worst of the mud off his shoes before he climbed back into the car, but could feel his feet slick on the pedals. It took longer to drive there than it should. He could see the giant struts. They kept looming large up ahead or off to one side, but the road twisted round, the whole structure ducked out of sight, giving tantalising glimpses as he closed in on it.

Something going on became clear as soon as he was on the final straight where the road sprouted multiple lanes towards the toll booths. He looked at the crowded trucks trying to make sense of it, but it wasn't until a swelling siren and flashing blue light filled his rear view mirror that he realised what was missing. The vehicles crowding the north end of the structure were all in civilian livery. Some sprouted communications discs and television logos but there was no official presence until the patrol car sped past him.

His phone lit up and buzzed in its cradle. Davis. He clicked it to speaker. 'Just arriving now,' he said. 'TV vans all over the show. Do we know what it's about?'

'I haven't heard yet. What can you see?'

'I've only just got here.' He pulled up clear of the huddle of lorries and watched the patrol car execute a U-turn. 'I think they're closing the road.' He reached into his pocket ready to flash his warrant card, but the local officers ignored him as they left their car askew across the carriageway and began to throw cones out to bar the way.

'Get through there,' urged Davis. 'Find out what's going on.'

'OK, I'm on my way.' He plucked the phone from its cradle, pushing open the door, his stare raking the vista in front trying to home in on the focus of the activity. The wail of sirens swelled from behind him. 'Cavalry's here in force,' he murmured, 'but I can't see anything yet.'

A movement up ahead … one figure in a milling crowd. He paused, half-in half-out of the car. 'Hang on, I think that's …'

'What?' Davis's voice leaked tension. 'What's happening?'

Ahmed stared. Someone had ambled from round the side of one of the big vans, looking neither right nor left, as if oblivious to the pandemonium behind, for all the world a woman without a worry on her shoulders out for an afternoon stroll. He leapt from the car and raced towards her. It was Melinda Webber.

chapter forty-seven

Webber smiled as he listened to Davis's words from the handset. What had he said before he left? *I won't have any trouble with Drake.* Talk about tempting fate. Drake might have been compliant throughout his dealings with Ahmed but he'd chosen now to dig in his heels. No real surprise. It had been a traumatic last day and a half for the man.

'What's his beef exactly?' he asked into the phone.

Across the corridor Sam sat happily, his sack of toys at his side, drinking in the attention from everyone around him. It had been like flicking a switch. One moment Sam had been sombre-faced clinging limpet like, the grip of his fist on Webber's collar tight enough to be uncomfortable, then the news had come that Mel was safe. Webber hadn't immediately known where she was or how she was, but they'd found her and she was safe. And before he'd had time to draw in breath to ask questions Sam was squirming in his arms, shouting 'Digger!' and pointing at the rucksack he'd had from Jess, a toy car peeking out of the top. Someone had stepped forward offering to take him and he'd leapt from Webber's grasp without a backward glance.

'Says he's tired,' Davis's voice told him. 'Doesn't fancy a bus trip back in the dark this weather.'

'He can come in his car, for heaven's sake. Plenty of parking at this time of day.'

'I already suggested that. He doesn't have it. It's in for repairs. I've just stepped outside to ring you but I can see where he's coming from. His wife tried to top herself yesterday morning and now he doesn't know where she is.' Davis wanted to leave things to tomorrow. It made sense. Webber knew that he was in no position to be hassling a man whose wife had gone missing. 'He was going to spend a quiet evening in his garden,' Davis went on.

'His garden!' Webber's glance shot to the window. It looked benign enough from here but the temperature hovered around freezing.

'Conservatory,' Davis amended. 'Gloomy bit of a lean-to at the back of the house. He showed me. Full of plant pots and such, probably got some hard liquor stashed in the corners. I didn't ask but I imagine it's his bolthole when she's here. And before you ask I've had as much of a rummage as I could get away with. He's not hiding any bodies.'

'We're not looking for bodies,' Webber snapped. 'Has he been drinking? Is that why he doesn't want to drive?'

'No, I don't think so. I think he was about to settle down when I got here. And I've had a look in the garage. It's empty. It's not just an excuse.'

'What's he doing now?'

'He's waiting for me to come back and say that we'll leave him in peace until tomorrow. If he comes with me, he'll want to get changed. He's in his potting shed clothes.'

A rising irritation began to counter the calm within Webber. 'It's no big deal. I just want to talk to the guy.'

'He's knackered, Martyn, and he's worried about his wife.'

Webber narrowed his eyes. *You of all people should have some sympathy,* was that the subtext? He breathed out a sigh. Davis had a point. He had Tippet and Yeatman on record already. Kowalski, too. If he got Drake in, what would he do? Have Davis talk to him probably. He might listen in but he had Sam to consider. Realistically he wasn't going to get anything done with Drake before tomorrow.

When Webber didn't respond immediately, Davis added, 'Edith

Stevenson's on his mind too. He knows something's gone down. He tried to contact her. Is there anything I can tell him?'

'Last I heard she was on her way to hospital in Hull. I've no idea what's wrong with her or how she is. Don't tell him enough that he wants to go and find her. Why was he contacting her?'

'To let her know that Suzie was on her way. Apparently she found something in the emails.'

'Found what? Did she think Tiffany Drake was with her?'

'I don't know. Drake says he kept clear while she was at the emails, didn't want to know.'

Webber gave a huff of irritation. 'Suzie should have had my message by then ... and yours.' He checked the time. 'Did she contact you before she went off duty?'

'I've not heard a thing.'

'Hmm, so did Stevenson do a runner because Drake warned her?'

'I don't think so. He says he couldn't raise her.'

Melinda was on her way back with Ahmed. They had skirted round the nub of it which was that Melinda should be back in Hull giving her statement there, but she'd slipped away in the confusion around Edith Stevenson who had been the real focus, and Ahmed had spirited her away from the action. The clock told him they would be here soon. She would want to take Sam straight home. He hoped that she was telling Ahmed everything, because he couldn't imagine trying to keep her here against her will. He felt uncomfortable. It was Melinda he needed to be listening to, Melinda who should be pressured to stay here and talk. But that wasn't going to happen.

'We should go easy on Drake,' Davis went on. 'Can't help feeling sorry for the guy after what he's been through.'

'Feel sorry for him?' Webber heard a level of incredulity in his tone, and knew he was being unfair even as the words emerged. He wanted the loose ends tied before Melinda arrived. 'You know better than to go around feeling sorry for people,' he snapped. 'That's a sure-fire way to misread a witness. Bring him in. Right now. And sod any dressing up lark. He's not in his pyjamas, is he?'

'No but ...'

'This isn't a fashion parade. We're not judging him on the quality of his suit. I've had enough pissing about. I want this sorted.'

As he clicked the phone on to its rest, his gaze rose to meet Sam's unsmiling stare from across the corridor. From within the bustle of the game he was playing, the boy had heard his father's raised voice, picked up his frustration, and highlighted his hypocrisy in that single look. Webber glanced at the now silent handset, feeling ashamed for his outburst, knowing he should ring back, tell Davis to use his judgement. He wouldn't even be here to talk to Drake when he arrived. As soon as Melinda showed up, he intended taking both her and Sam home.

He stood up and marched through to the big office half expecting Sam to call out and want to come to him, but he'd gone back to whatever game he was playing with the group clustered round him. Far more minders than were needed for one small boy, Webber noted with disapproval, but being in no position to object he simply said, 'Someone give me the detail on Jenkinson's sidekick,' and walked to the far end of the space. Jenkinson's contact, Emmett, was one of the loose ends he must tie so as to be ready to leave with Melinda when she arrived.

Mimicking him, Sam had a try at 'sidekick,' making it sound like 'psychic,' which morphed into laughter and shouts of 'Digger ... do it 'gain.'

As he listened to an account of Emmett's unexpected visit, Webber had to struggle to keep his thoughts on track. His mind kept veering towards Hull and the incomplete story there. The flash point had seemed to be Edith Stevenson, but he didn't know how or why. All he knew was that she was effectively in custody with someone at her hospital bed. He had to concentrate, had to be done when Mel arrived or she'd take Sam and go. Apart from anything else she didn't have her car so she'd take his, leaving him a wet trek home by bus. As far as he could gather she'd been in Edith Stevenson's car and Stevenson had driven Joyce Yeatman's. How had that come about?

'Wait a minute,' he said to the officer who was going through the account with him. 'You're saying some man approached this girl Emmett and she says it was the same man who approached Tom Jenkinson? How did she know? I'm sure Jenkinson said he'd met the man on his own; brought the others in later.'

'Yes, that's right,' she amended. 'Emmett didn't know the man. He told them he'd met Jenkinson.'

'And it was definitely a man?'

There was a pause. 'She said it was a man, but when I pushed for a description, she'd seen very little. Or she wasn't giving me anything, anyway. My impression was that she was trying to be helpful, but he'd approached her on her way back from school yesterday. It's a lonely stretch. She was scared.'

'And he wanted the traffic lights stunt doing again?'

'That's what she said. Offered her money. He was in a hurry. Gave her cash with the promise of the same amount again for each junction they disrupted. It's supposed to be this evening.'

They turned to the street map that was spread out across one of the desks. Webber closed his eyes and tried to feel round the edges of the odd tale. 'This Emmett girl, she was on the level, was she?'

'I'd say so. She and the gang of friends spent all day talking about it, then they went together to her mother. It was her mother who brought her in. It was the money that did it.'

Tom Jenkinson's mystery man had overplayed his hand. He'd given Emmett a wad of cash the size of which had both tied her tongue and loosened it. The amount had scared her into confiding in her mother, but she hadn't dared to tell the man that the trick had been sleight of hand, that she couldn't do it without Tom

Jenkinson because it needed practice and precision timing. The best she'd managed had been to tell him she couldn't do more than one location simultaneously.

He learnt that the girl and her mother had asked for Ahmed. They'd come here not so much as good citizens but because they'd talked it through and decided it would be what Tom Jenkinson would have done. If only Jenkinson had made a similar judgement. He'd clearly been close to it.

Webber looked again at the map. 'We haven't had any reports of anything, have we?'

'No, but he wasn't wanting it to kick off yet. He's going for nine o'clock. We've got someone out keeping an eye on things, but they'll miss the rush hour? Wasn't the whole point to cause major snarl-ups?'

'Maybe it's a practice run,' Webber said.

'What for?'

He shrugged and listened to the theories fly back and forth as he studied the map. The targets were smaller junctions than the previous ones; in each case a busy main road intersected by a smaller quieter one. Two were T-junctions where the lights were programmed to let out the traffic from the side street on an as-needed basis. He felt a frown crease his brow. The kid had been asked to switch the traffic light green on the minor road at nine o'clock tonight. When she'd told him they could only work one junction at a time, he'd allowed five minutes leeway either way, but he'd wanted all three junctions sabotaged.

'What does he gain from it?' someone asked.

'One hell of a smash at this one,' said Webber, tracing the path of one of the intersections with his finger. 'Bad visibility. Freezing weather. You don't get a good view of the major road at the best of times with that high wall. If the main lights aren't red and there's something coming down that hill ... classic T-bone RTA. There won't be anyone walking away from it.'

'But why?'

Webber said nothing. None of it made sense.

A voice at his shoulder. 'Call from the Chief Super's office, Guv.'

He turned to head for his own office, hearing a shout of laughter from Sam. It was lucky he'd decided to return here; hadn't realised Farrar would be back this afternoon. He wouldn't approve of Sam's presence.

'Ah, Superintendent Webber. I'm glad I chased one of you down.'

The call had been bounced on from Farrar's office but it wasn't Farrar. It took a second to click into place. It was the voice that had spelled out a plan to use Tom Jenkinson's death as collateral to snare a drugs dealer. He pictured the florid features. His first thought; they'd made a mistake, it would turn out that Streetwise had given them the slip, that he was responsible for Jenkinson's death after all.

'Hello, what can I do for you?' *What can you do for me?*

'I have not rung to hand you Streetwise, I'm afraid. No last minute gap in our surveillance to report.'

Webber pursed his lips; didn't like having his mind read like this. 'But I assume it's on a related matter,' he said tartly.

A gentle laugh. 'Yes, indeed. We like to keep an eye on the people he recruits to his little organisation. As to the ones he lets go … Jenkinson, Stevenson, there have been others … they're of no interest to us, but I thought it might prove useful to you if one of my colleagues were to push Streetwise for information on his trip to York, and if I were to let you know what he said. It was an interesting exchange.'

'Are you saying you've arrested him?' Webber hadn't realised they were that close to a decisive move.

Again that laugh as though he'd said something naïve. 'No, no. It's all part of the game. We have him under *very* close surveillance.'

Webber felt his eyebrows rise. They had someone under cover – deep cover by the sound of it – not a job for which he would want to hold responsibility. He said as much, adding, 'Streetwise and Boots Boy, they're out-and-out psychopaths.'

This time the laugh sounded like genuine amusement. 'Exactly so. They dropped Mr Jenkinson because they didn't deem him reliable, but they didn't follow up with Miss Stevenson for quite another reason. The exact quotation is a colloquialism, but roughly translates that the post of psychopathic killer within their group is taken; they would not risk recruiting another. So yes, you can say we have a tiger by the tail, but it seems that you have one on your patch from whom ours prefers to keep a distance. I cannot offer you anything tangible, no statements, no evidence, but I don't think you need look further for the killer of Tom Jenkinson and I advise you to tread with care.'

Webber looked across the corridor to the crowd around Sam. He could barely see him, just a small fist waving something, hilarity all round that became suddenly muted as though they sensed his scrutiny. 'We have Edith Stevenson in custody.' He listened to his own words as though hearing them from far away. Mel had met the woman.

'Then be sure that you keep her.'

'We will,' said Webber, hearing a hollow note to his voice. He'd yet to hear of a single piece of concrete evidence against Edith Stevenson for anything.

When he ended the call, he stood up determined to go and extract Sam, to get the station back to work. Then he hesitated. If he had Sam on his knee he couldn't be chasing up anyone for details of what had happened down by the Humber. He got as far as the doorway. Sam sat on the floor between two officers, fists at his mouth as he gnawed on a bread roll. Webber wondered whose it was, what was in it.

'DI Davis's car has just arrived, Guv. You said to let you know.'

He veered off his intended path and headed for the window, reaching it in time to see Davis hurry round the corner, collar turned up against the weather. As he watched, Davis stopped and looked back, said something. Another man, tall but bent, came into view. Was that Drake? He'd only ever seen a photograph from decades ago. He took in the slow hobbling gait, the walking stick. Ahmed had said the man wasn't well … at his last gasp more like. Clearly Davis had done as told and not allowed a change of clothes. Drake's topcoat was smart enough but his trouser legs were tattered and frayed. If he'd realised it was that bad, he would have relented. Their progress was painfully slow.

After a few minutes, Davis came in shaking rainwater off his jacket. He glanced at Webber. 'I've put him in the interview room.'

'I didn't realise he was that bad on his feet.'

'He was fine till we came round the corner. Apparently it comes on suddenly, whatever it is. The weather doesn't help.'

An hour later, with no sign of Melinda, Webber's fingers itched to pick up the phone and call her, but he didn't want to have the conversation with Ahmed or anyone else listening. They'd be stuck in rush hour traffic now. Webber didn't want Melinda out on York's streets, not with Jenkinson's mystery man bent on sabotaging traffic lights, but he'd had someone contact Ahmed. They'd be on their guard.

He'd talked to Davis before sending him back to Drake, wanting the DI up to speed on the phone call he'd had about Streetwise's views on Edith Stevenson. It had been planned as a brief update. He hadn't expected Davis to retaliate with his own mini bombshell.

'Hard to know what to make of it,' he'd told Davis. 'Why would we take note of hearsay from someone like Streetwise? On the other hand, we know we've had a killer on the loose. That bloody gravel pit. I just hope they've plumbed the depths of that site now and it's not going to spring any more …' He'd stopped, seeing Davis's gaze drop. 'What?'

'Yeah … um … you were busy … I meant to tell you. I've asked for the DNA profiles on that third body, the deepest one … I've asked for them to be fast-tracked. They came through with some more stuff … artefacts they'd found with the corpse, all that, I got someone to do a comparison with the old missing person files. It's looking like it's going to be the schoolgirl from Dorset. Everything else matches. We just need the DNA.'

Webber blew out a sigh. 'Christ! What in hell does that mean?'

He ran his hand through his hair. Links they weren't close to seeing; it was all tied in together, somehow. It had to be. Tilly Brown 45 years ago, someone else here and now.

'Edith Stevenson,' he said. 'We've nothing on her. Some of the school friends were interviewed at the time to see if they'd heard from Tilly Brown, but that was it. I've gone back to the Morgan files too. They were all interviewed. They looked at them briefly for possible conspiracy but found nothing. Their alibis held up. There was even some CCTV from outside a pub to corroborate their stories. The teacher Meyer told me they always stood out in a group, the way they dressed, the way they walked. They were lucky, that footage took the heat off them. and the real focus of the investigation was to get all the ammo they could find to throw at the animal rights group. Yeatman, Stevenson and Pamela Morgan had arranged to see Michael Drake because it was the tenth anniversary of his first wife's death. More to the point, they alibied each other up here in York. Morgan was killed in Dorset.'

'And Dorset's where Tilly Brown went missing.'

Webber reran the conversation in his head as he struggled to pull some meaning out of it all.

Davis was in the interview room now talking to Drake, recording him for Webber to listen to later. From what he could gather, Davis was walking a thin line close to holding the man against his will, but Ahmed had been right. Drake was susceptible to bullying. And Webber would let them both off the hook soon.

He looked at the screen in front of him. Four recordings were open; Kowalski, Tippet, Yeatman and Jenkinson. He'd been hopping from one to the other, listening to short stretches from different places, closing his eyes as he absorbed them, voice only, no body language to distract him. Deceit and fabrication had a way of shining through raw words in a way that was often smothered by the distractions of facial expression and movement.

The headphones hung round his neck as he sat back and took a break. He'd homed in on Kowalski first, remembering her many hesitations, wanting to discover the root of her dishonesty, but he'd heard nothing untoward. Exhaustion, confusion, pain at old wounds reopened but nothing to suggest she wasn't being straight with him, except maybe when he'd mentioned Tilly Brown's rocking horse.

That's got nothing to do with Pamela ... Why are you wasting time ...

Of course, she was sleep-deprived. It might have been down to tiredness.

Tippet's voice dripped deceit and alarm all around the theft. He'd known the car had gone hours before he reported it. Was it really as simple as him having thought it was Drake and wanting to get him into trouble? How paranoid was Tippet that even after all these years he'd overlooked the fact that it wasn't the car to which Drake had keys? If he'd known all this when Tippet had been sitting in front of him he could have explored it further. It hardly seemed worth the bother of chasing now. And if revenge on Drake was the aim, how did failure to report the theft achieve it? Unless ... Webber sat back resting his hands behind his head ... unless Tippet knew what it had been stolen for. And that raised another question; had it been stolen to do the post office raid or to dump Morgan's body?

He'd told Davis to quiz Drake on the whole Tippet feud. They might be talking about it right now. It was a frustration that he couldn't go and listen as they talked, but for all that Sam was happy playing, he'd already made clear with an indignant wail that his father wasn't to move out of sight. Webber looked across the corridor and felt his lips tighten in annoyance. The game with the toy cars had grown into an elaborate affair involving file boxes and makeshift track. Sam had become a spectator chewing on an apple whilst what looked like the entire staff threw themselves into fierce competition with the tiny vehicles.

He made himself look away. Sam shouldn't be here at all so either he put up with this impromptu tournament or he would have Sam to himself. He was glad Suzie hadn't come back before the end of her shift, didn't want her thinking in terms of precedents.

He pulled on the headphones and switched to the recording marked Yeatman. After what he'd had from Melinda, he homed in on the stretch where Ahmed quizzed her on Pamela Morgan's suicide note. He'd skimmed through it yesterday, curious about how the woman reacted to Ahmed's questions, but beyond a few hesitations he hadn't seen much of note. Now the contrast was stark. Once he cut out her face, there was no air of middle-aged, middle-class respectability to colour his interpretation. Every mention of Pamela Morgan's suicide was spoken through a layer of ground glass especially the anomaly of the unsigned note. He caught hints of anger, confusion, fear … then pulled himself up in case he was manufacturing anomalies in his head. She hadn't had to cooperate with Melinda, so why had she done it? He felt that her account to Ahmed was intended to give a simple gloss to something she didn't understand. Was it something she wanted to understand or not? Why hadn't she been open about it? Was she scared of uncovering something nasty?

Again he stopped the recording and took off the headphones … felt he was marking time … waiting … and not just for Melinda.

It was a relief to see Davis framed in his doorway. The DI allowed his glance to slip briefly to the mayhem in the big office, before meeting Webber's eye. 'Mr Drake badly wants to go home. I'm sure I could keep making up excuses to keep him here all night, but I really don't want to. I've the best part of an hour's chat with him on record now. I've squeezed him dry of everything I can think of.'

'Anything new?'

'Not really. If he's guilty of anything it's loyalty to a friend somewhere along the line, maybe Stevenson but maybe it goes back to Pamela Morgan. Whatever it is, I can't get a handle to prise it out of him. There were a couple of bits ... The finance ... You know Ayaan and Suzie were speculating that he'd had money from Pamela Morgan and that's when he'd broken ties with the Tippets. They were right.'

Webber nodded. 'Anything odd in it?'

'Not that I can see. He was open about it when I asked him. The Morgans had had that big pools win. They were loaded. He told me he asked her for a loan, but she wouldn't entertain it. It had to be a gift. She didn't want him with the debt on his shoulders.'

'I wouldn't mind some friends like that,' Webber commented.

Davis gave half a smile. 'She did similar for Stevenson according to Drake. Stevenson's loan was earlier than his. He hadn't known about it at the time but said he wasn't surprised, or rather wasn't surprised that Pamela had helped her out, but quite surprised to know Stevenson had been in trouble. He says he doesn't know what it was about. I'm not sure if I believe him and I'm not sure if it's important after all this time.'

'You said a couple of things.'

'Yes, I asked him what Suzie had read in his wife's emails. He shilly-shallied, said he hadn't wanted to know, but clearly she'd questioned him about something she'd found. Anyway, apparently she asked him about someone who signed their emails JB, which was J Brown according to the email address. He said he didn't know, but he got the idea she'd found something that made her think his wife was with this J Brown.'

'I thought he said she was going to find Stevenson.'

'Stevenson first, was what he thought.'

'And this J Brown isn't one of the friends she sent Ayaan after?'

'No, she gave Ayaan the two addresses before she looked at

the emails. I'm sure it's nothing but while he was telling me, he remembered a J Brown from years ago, a John Brown who always signed his name JB. Tilly Brown's brother. The missing schoolgirl, the one who's probably ...' Davis nodded his head in the general direction of the evidence boards that held the photographs from up behind the gravel pits. Then he shrugged. 'I mean, chances are it's not even J for John and if it is, then it won't be the same one. Tiffany Drake never knew the Browns. She wasn't born when Tilly disappeared. It was just odd, the name cropping up like that. It's all on record. Do you want me to load it?' He indicated Webber's screen.

Webber nodded.

'Any sign or Ayaan or Suzie?' Davis said as he pulled Webber's keyboard towards him.

'No. Ayaan'll be stuck in traffic and Suzie went off duty an hour ago.' Webber wondered if Suzie had been in the equation that had led Melinda to chase Edith Stevenson to Hull. 'She and Ayaan talked before he picked up Melinda,' he added, 'so she's no excuse for trying to collar Stevenson if that's what she did. But maybe she was after the mystery JB. Anyway ...' He waved the issue aside.

'I need to let Drake go home,' said Davis.

'OK, but I'm going to have a look at the CCTV of him arriving. Call me paranoid but aren't we looking for someone with a funny walk?'

'You're paranoid.' Davis gave him a withering look. 'I'll go and call the guy a cab.'

Webber walked through into the big office. No one spared him a glance. Tension was palpable as all eyes focussed on the makeshift racing track. Sam's attention was on his apple, juice dribbling down his chin. The woman beside Sam leant over to mop his face with a tissue.

The screen in front of Webber flickered to life. He studied the images of the scene he'd watched live an hour ago. Davis stopping to see where Drake had got to ... Drake emerging from round the side of the building, hobbling, leaning heavily on his stick. He clicked over to the car-park's camera, pushing time backwards to watch them drive in. They marched smartly across the tarmac, shoulders hunched against the cold drizzle, the breeze flapping Drake's ragged trousers to invisibility against the grey tarmac, making him look like a man with no legs in the failing light. Webber wanted to see the transition – Drake's upright stride to his bent hobble. It was nothing dramatic. Drake simply stopped as they reached the corner, his head and neck curved forward, and then he set off again slowly, face screwed up against the wind or the pain as he inched the last few paces to the doorway. It was nothing like the indistinct image on the footage with Jenkinson. He hadn't expected it to be. Paranoia, just like he'd said.

Somewhere behind him a buzz of encouragement grew for one of the car racers. Sam's voice rose shrill above the crowd. Webber could interpret the babble as Sam's attempt at 'Faster, damn it!' and kept his face turned away to hide a smile as he returned to his office, picking up the headphones and clicking on the new window that Davis had opened. He used the mouse to pull the slider about halfway along the 48-minute extract.

It was a near perfect guess. He landed in the middle of Davis's interrogation about the emails.

'I didn't want Sergeant Harmer to tell me,' Drake's voice said. 'It's a matter of trust, but like she said I had to balance things against Tiff's safety, but I'm afraid the name meant nothing.'

He listened to the story of JB unfold just as Davis had told him. Drake's voice remained even and bland. He sounded relaxed if a little tired. Davis moved on to the money and Drake cutting all ties with the Tippets.

'You must have needed money to move on,' Davis said. 'Did you get it from Pamela Morgan?'

When the question was met with silence Webber glanced up at the picture on the screen. Drake had nodded.

'Quite a lot of money ...' Davis prompted.

Webber looked away again and concentrated on the sound track.

'Pammy was one in a million.' Michael Drake's words were wrapped in velvet, a sudden warmth animating the bland tones.

Pammy not Quinny, Webber thought. Then Sam's voice cut across everything. Even muted by the earpieces it was a clear, delighted cry. 'Mummy!'

And there was Melinda bustling in to scoop Sam from the chaos of the game that was hastily dismantled as people dispersed, entertainment over, back to their tasks for the remainder of the shift. Ahmed was there too, shaking the rain from his coat, talking to Davis who would be filling him in on Michael Drake.

Webber walked over, caught Melinda's eye and gave her a smile that she returned with a hint of wariness. What on earth had she been up to? The question was secondary. He had no intention of wavering from his plan to get her and Sam back home. Right now.

When the office fell quiet, he thought at first it was his presence that had done it. All eyes had turned his way. What were they expecting him to do? But he wasn't the target. They were looking over his shoulder. He spun round.

The desk sergeant stood in the doorway with a woman at his side. A familiar face out of context. Suzie's partner, Fiona. He'd only ever seen her smiling or glowering. Now she looked scared. Her stare bounced from one to the other of them, homing in on Ahmed who stepped forward. 'Fiona. What is it? What's wrong?'

'I can't find Suzie,' she said. 'She's not answering her phone.'

chapter forty-eight

Ahmed stared at Fiona. He hadn't known her long; wanted to think her outburst meant nothing, the result of some domestic spat. But the spike in tension from everyone around him was unmistakable and these were the people who knew her and Suzie well. Fiona had homed in on him as the one most likely to know something. It was true, he must be the last person here to have been in contact with her. They were all turning to him. He struggled to grab the detail from his head.

'Two hours ago ... two and a half ...' he said. 'She was on her way to see someone and then she was going home. It was ...' He couldn't stop a layer of rising panic obscuring the memories that should be crystal clear. He'd forgotten something vital, he knew he had. 'On her way home ... I'm sure she said it was on her way home, wherever she was going. I thought it was Stevenson but ...'

He tried to imagine a map of York, but someone was ahead of him and had a road map on the desk. 'Ayaan!' Webber snapped. 'Come on, you've been to both. Where's Drake's house? Where's Stevenson's?'

He leapt across, his stare scanning the grid, homing in. 'There ... Drake ... Stevenson ...'

Fiona reached forward to put her finger on the street where she and Suzie lived. There was a moment's silence as they looked at it. It wasn't a difficult route from Drake's to Stevenson's then home, but it hardly merited the comment, 'it's on my way'.

Ahmed thought he heard Webber murmur, 'JB' and looked up into his face, seeing his expression puzzled, his eyes unfocussed.

Before he could frame a question, Webber had spun round shouting for Davis and made for the window. Ahmed took a few steps in his wake trying to peer out to see what he was looking for. Davis wasn't in the office, wasn't in earshot.

'You! With me.' Webber's finger was in his face, the words coming at him like bullets. 'And you!' Webber had swung round on someone else. 'That schoolgirl from Dorset, Tilly Brown. Find out if any of her family moved back up here. Her brother in particular.' And he was out of the office vanishing down the corridor.

Ahmed stumbled as he leapt to follow, his foot landing painfully on something hard. He kicked it aside aware of it skittering away across the floor. The toddler in Melinda Webber's arms shouted 'Digger,' as its gaze tracked the small object.

He caught up with Webber at the door to the street. The cold air hit him as he stepped through. Webber stared up the road. 'He's only just left. I saw him.'

'Who?'

'Michael Drake. He was going at a snail's pace. Can you see him?'

'There.' Ahmed pointed to the familiar figure of Drake striding towards the bus stop.

'Ah, good. I thought we might have missed him.' Webber relaxed visibly. 'Come on, I might need you to persuade Mr Drake to answer yet more questions. I thought we were calling him a cab.'

'What is it that …?'

But Webber had set off after Drake, stopping him with a shout. Ahmed followed. He watched Drake turn as he heard his name, then Drake saw him and his face fell.

'Mr Ahmed, surely there's nothing else I can tell you. I've spent most of the day talking to Sergeant Harmer and Inspector Davis. I really want to get home.'

'Hello again, Michael. Um … this is Detective Superintendent Martyn Webber.'

Drake let out a resigned sigh and nodded to Webber.

'I'm sorry, Mr Drake,' said Webber. 'Just one more thing. It's about the emails that you showed Sergeant Harmer. I understand she told you she was going to go and find one of the people who'd been in touch with your wife.'

Drake opened his hands in a helpless gesture. 'She didn't exactly say that, but I think that's what she meant. I told Inspector Davis. I … look I know she's worried about Tiff, and I'm grateful for all the trouble you've gone to but … really, I think I should be home. What if Tiff comes back and there's no one there?'

'There was an email from a J Brown, I understand?'

Drake pulled his coat tight around him. 'Yes, but I don't know who it is. It's one of Tiff's friends I suppose. I told Inspector Davis, I used to know a John Brown but that was years ago. The family moved away.'

'But this J Brown was the name that Sergeant Harmer mentioned?'

'No … no she didn't. I asked her not to tell me what she'd read. She didn't say Brown, she said did I know who JB was, but I didn't.'

'I understand J Brown came from the email address. How did you get to see that?'

'She left it behind.'

'Left what behind?'

'The email on the printer. She asked me if she could print some of them. Then after she'd gone I found that one in the tray. She'd forgotten to pick it up. I … I shouldn't have looked at it but it I'd read it before I realised what it was.'

'You don't have it with you, I suppose?'

Ahmed saw Drake's glance shoot up to meet Webber's; saw a sudden hope spark in his face. 'If someone drove me back I could get it for you. It's cold to be trailing back by bus, and I'm not too good on my legs at the moment.'

'Yes, I noticed you were very bad just outside the station,' Webber said. 'But you seem to be OK now.'

Ahmed was slightly shocked at the unsympathetic tone. Michael Drake just looked dejected. 'It comes and goes,' he murmured.

'Didn't DI Davis call you a cab?'

'He offered but to be honest I just wanted to get away.' He gave them a wintry smile. 'I thought if I hung about waiting, you might come after me with more questions.'

'OK,' said Webber. 'DC Ahmed will take you home and pick up the email.'

Michael Drake shifted his stance so he could prop his stick against the wall as he rubbed at his arms. Ahmed cupped his hands and blew into them to warm them. It was going to be a long shift. Drake picked up his stick again. The three of them turned to walk back towards the station.

'I think ... well I know she printed more than just that one,' Michael Drake said. 'She must have missed picking up the one at the bottom of the pile. I'm sorry, just a moment ...' They slowed. Drake paused and leant forward breathing hard.

'Are you OK?' from Webber.

'I'll just sit on the wall here and wait for you if I may.'

Ahmed saw Webber give Drake a speculative look. 'Would you let us have a look at your wife's computer? DC Ahmed here could bring it away with him, that way we can leave you in peace.'

'Well ...' Drake looked up at them, lines of worry etched on his face. 'I suppose ... do you really think something's happened to her?'

Ahmed tensed. They both knew that Drake meant Tiffany, not Suzie. 'We'd like to find her,' Webber said, 'to be sure she's safe.'

'Well all right then, but we will get everything back, won't we? Uh ...'

'What is it, Mr Drake?'

'It's ... it's Edie. Edie Stevenson. I know something's happened to her. She's an old friend. I should at least try to get in touch, find out how she is, only I don't know where ... what with Tiff and everything. I ... uh ... I was a bit sharp with her last time we spoke. It's not that I don't want her to be friends with Tiff, but Tiff's easily led and with what happened ...'

Ahmed felt pleased that Drake had asked the question with Webber on hand to answer it, saving him the trouble of working out what he could safely say.

'Miss Stevenson's in hospital,' Webber told him. 'She's injured her leg, not sure if it's broken, but don't worry, she'll be fine.'

Ahmed saw relief in the way Drake's shoulders slumped. 'I'll try and get in to see her tomorrow ... maybe I'll ring when I get home. I can't go tonight. I'm all in. She'll understand.'

'She's not in York,' Webber said, 'so I'm afraid you won't be able to see her just yet. Let's just concentrate on finding your wife.'

Suspicion flared in Drake's eyes as he stared at Webber. 'What aren't you telling me? How bad is she? Please don't keep things from me, it won't help.'

Ahmed watched as Webber hesitated a moment before he spoke. 'She'll be fine, but the fact is that she's currently in police custody. Now let's get you home.'

'I'll nip in and get the keys,' Ahmed said.

Webber walked with him, but glanced over his shoulder as they neared the door. 'I'm not expecting him to do a runner,' Webber said, 'but I'll keep an eye on him all the same. Don't tell him anything else about Stevenson.' He pointed through the glass of the entranceway to where Davis was in conversation at the desk. 'Grab a quick word, see if there's anything he wants you to know from his talk with Drake. Did Suzie definitely tell you she was heading for Stevenson's?'

'No ... no, I don't think so. I thought that's where she was going but I can't remember why I thought that.' Ahmed gritted his teeth knowing he'd forgotten something obvious. Everything had happened too fast, it had knocked something vital out of his head.

'You know what, Ayaan,' said Webber giving a brief glance

towards the hunched figure of Michael Drake sitting on the low wall. 'I can't imagine Suzie being careless enough to leave a printout. Do you think she left it deliberately as something she thought he should see?'

A minute later as he jogged back up the road, Ahmed saw Drake pull himself to his feet and give him a smile. 'I'm grateful for the lift, Mr Ahmed. I hadn't realised how cold it's become.'

'No problem. We're grateful for your cooperation. I'll pick up the printout and the computer and be out of your way quick as I can. Let's hope it isn't long before we find Tiffany safe and well.'

And Suzie.

chapter forty-nine

It wasn't without misgivings that Webber watched Melinda and Sam walk towards the cab that had pulled up outside. It would take her to where she'd left her own car so she could pick it up. He'd talked her through a circuitous route home that would bypass each of the three targeted junctions. She'd pursed her lips but had promised to follow it. Webber was thankful enough to think they'd soon be safe at home that he didn't care he had no more than an outline of what had happened.

The headline was that Edith Stevenson had tried to act out some kind of doomsday scenario in which she disposed of a stack of incriminating evidence and then herself. But Melinda had called on her old press contacts. Working on a hunch from things Joyce had told her, she'd tried to set up some kind of stunt to stop Stevenson in her tracks. Stevenson had summoned Joyce Yeatman to pull her into the plan – maybe Joyce had always been a part of it – but Joyce had been wary, had taken Melinda with her. And once Stevenson had found Mel in the equation she'd taken off. He wasn't clear why Stevenson had been in Yeatman's car and Melinda in Stevenson's; or why Mel couldn't have rung it all in earlier and saved a lot of angst, but she was safe now, that was the main thing.

He wished he could go with her now, but he had to stay behind because Suzie might be missing.

On the face of it Melinda was understanding, one of their own under attack, all personal agendas squashed. She'd offered to draft out her own preliminary statement while things were fresh in her mind, said she'd come back in a day or two for an official chat. She'd even taken semi-charge of Fiona, organising someone to look after her. He could see everyone applauding her professionalism, they all knew the score. She would hold a team together well once she was back in the job, her promotion secured. He let out a sigh. It was the perfect act to give her the moral high ground but he might yet have to pay for it behind closed doors.

He'd wanted to hear that Joyce Yeatman had shown her the suicide note, but she hadn't. Melinda now thought Joyce had destroyed it years ago. Joyce had confessed that instead of rushing to her friend's aid the moment she realised what the note implied, she'd sat and read it through. Her next action had been to remove the final page because of whatever it had said – presumably about Gary, but she was still being cagey about its exact contents. Whatever it had said, it had shocked her into building the story she'd stuck to for years, the story of rushing to find her friend, no thought for the contents of the note.

'Clears up the mystery of why it was unsigned,' Melinda had told him as she'd packed up Sam's toys, 'but she wouldn't tell me what that last page said. Anyway you've got the gist and Ayaan Ahmed has the detail.'

But he couldn't get the story from Ahmed yet because Ahmed was with Drake getting the information that would find Suzie.

With Sam and his miniature cars gone, the station was back at work, doing what they had to do. There was nothing left for Webber that wasn't already being done, nothing he could settle to. He'd wanted to go out and get Mel, not wait here for her to come to him. He felt the same restless urge for Suzie. He wanted to be out there looking for her, not sitting at a desk directing operations. This team barely needed direction. It was nothing to do with it being Suzie. He'd have felt the same whichever of them it had been.

He dipped back into the recordings. At least the headphones

were a physical shackle to his desk that stopped him hassling people who didn't need him at their shoulders.

He listened to Michael Drake tell Davis all about the old school network, noting a marked difference between Drake talking about Pamela Morgan and Tilly Brown. The man clearly idolised Pamela and hated Tilly. Webber knew from the record that both women, girls they'd have been then, were academically so far ahead of Drake as to be out of sight, but Webber's impression, putting together all the scraps they'd learnt about the quintets, was that Michael and Tilly had always butted heads, and Pamela had always supported him. Jack Meyer, the retired teacher, had commented about them being a more cohesive group once Tilly had gone.

Pamela had shelled out serious money to both Michael Drake and Edith Stevenson. He wondered what Robert Morgan had thought about it. Ahmed had noted bits and pieces about the Drakes; that they were Charlie Sheen fans, that the first Mrs Drake had been older than her husband and the second considerably younger. There was no record of the first Mrs Drake's feelings towards Pamela Morgan but Tiffany had referred to her as *Saint bloody Pamela*. It was clear Drake continued to venerate her. What wasn't clear was how that helped to find out who had killed Robert Morgan or where Suzie had gone. His gut told him that one of them knew something, probably Edith Stevenson, but he couldn't race across to Hull on the off chance of being allowed to try and wrest the information from her, and he had nothing solid to pass on to a nearer colleague.

The key would be in Tiffany Drake's emails. He'd listened to everything Drake had had to say to Davis on that score. The recordings sat open on the screen in front of him. The obvious liars were Joyce Yeatman about the note, Brad Tippet about the car and China Kowalski about the rocking horse. He wondered about Kowalski. Could she be tied into Tilly Brown's disappearance? But it had been talk of the horse that seemed to bug her, not the bits and pieces that had turned up in the grave. His instinct was to dismiss it as some childhood misdemeanour that still played on her conscience. She'd sought out the Tippets and gone to some trouble to talk to John Farrar's father. On impulse he looked out Tippet's number and clicked it into the phone.

It was Brad Tippet who answered. Webber recognised the voice. He toyed with asking to speak to Brad's son, but decided against it. He'd never met the son, and would rather their first encounter was face to face. Brad was startled to know who was calling then his tone brightened. Clearly he thought Webber had uncovered something to further one of his vendettas. Webber wondered which of them Tippet most wanted to topple, Drake or Farrar.

'It's just a bit of a loose end, Mr Tippet. All those years ago when your car was stolen you said you thought it was your brother-in-law.'

An irritable humph. 'No one ever fully convinced me it wasn't.'

'I was just looking back at the record. That car, the Ford Tempo, you bought it some years after your sister died.'

'I can't give you dates, Superintendent, not just off the top of my head at this hour on a Friday, you'd have to give me time to look out the documents.'

Webber felt his eyebrows rise a little. It fitted his image of Tippet that the man would hoard paperwork. 'It's not that,' he said. 'It's that Drake wouldn't have had keys. After all it was your sister who had keys, and those were for your previous car.'

'Yes, he had keys.' A note of triumph. 'Has he told you differently? He's lying.'

'He hasn't told me anything about it, Mr Tippet. I haven't asked him. Why did he have keys?'

'Oh … well … I gave him a set. Now if that's all …' Tippet tried to make it a casual throwaway remark, but Webber heard a sudden uncertainty beneath it – had Tippet only just now given this memory proper scrutiny?

'You gave him a set?' Webber spoke firmly, ignoring Tippet's aborted attempt to end the call. 'Why on earth would you do that? Did you want him driving your car?'

'No, of course not. It was … it was for Tina. She'd have wanted me to.'

Webber bit back a snort of incredulity. Tina Tippet was eight years dead before her brother changed cars. 'Oh, I see,' he said brightly, as though he'd swallowed the lie whole. 'That explains it.' The ghost of a sigh signalled Tippet releasing a held breath. This wasn't one to take any further without Tippet face to face and officially on record. He cast about for a red-herring to toss into the mix. 'And that insurance policy,' he said. 'Why did your sister go with you to the broker rather than going with her husband?'

'That's far too long ago, Superintendent. I've no idea who went where with who. It'll have been some story Michael Drake told the police at the time. If you don't know from your files then we'll never know.' A poor attempt at a laugh. 'It was 40 years ago. Who keeps records for that long?'

You do, thought Webber, you've just told me so, and so do we; it's all on file. But he said nothing. The change of tack to the insurance policy was just to plant something other than the car in Tippet's mind. He didn't want the man working to create a more credible scenario around the Ford Tempo's spare keys because his answer had come without hesitation and with the ring of truth.

Could Suzie have gone after Tippet? It was on the tip of his tongue to ask if he'd seen her, but he held back. There couldn't have been anything in the current Mrs Drake's emails that would have set Suzie onto Tippet.

He ended the call with no loose ends snipped off and even more flapping around him. Drake cut ties with the Tippets two years after Tina's death. Had Tippet presented his ex-brother-in-law with a set of keys to his brand new car six years later? If so, it could only have been to set him up for the theft.

He thought about the overlapping tight-knit groups each riven with its own fights and jealousies. The splits when they'd happened had been deep and acrimonious; Brad from his father, Drake from the Tippets, Kowalski from the other quintets. Maybe Gary Yeatman too. In everything he'd read and heard it was Pamela Morgan, in person or in memory, who had held them together. Everyone loved Pamela. The only person he'd heard speak against her was Tiffany Drake who had never known her.

He glanced at the time. It crept closer to the mystery man's alleged target for traffic chaos. Vehicles criss-crossed these cases as randomly as that makeshift game with Sam's toy cars; a van concertinaed at a junction, shocked motorists babbling about green lights ...Tippet's Ford Tempo speeding away from the post office so soon after it had carried Robert Morgan's body... a lorry, fat belly revolving to keep its concrete load from setting, reversing down the track to the walkway foundation, driven by Trent who would die later in his own car with tiny traces of the elaborate mechanism which had propelled it on its final journey ... Gary Yeatman and the crash that had been flagged as driver suicide ...

He thought about putting someone, already dead, behind the wheel of a car and sending them into a stream of fast-moving traffic. If traffic lights were being tampered with across the city, everyone would look the wrong way for the culprits and assume the wrong cause of death. It was fanciful. It wasn't the way to do murder, even for a psychopath.

A knock at the door interrupted his thoughts.

'This came through about the schoolgirl who went missing in Dorset.'

Webber took the scrap of paper, skimmed it, then stopped to pull in a breath before reading it through again. It had been a simple enough query – had any of Tilly Brown's family returned to the York area – and it had generated a simple enough answer, but not the one he'd expected.

What had florid-face said? *We have a tiger by the tail ...* Interesting he should have chosen that metaphor.

Then there'd been Davis about Michael Drake. *If he's guilty of anything it's loyalty to a friend ... whatever it is, I can't prise it out of him.*

Picking up the headphones, he switched to Kowalski's recording ... dragging the slider until he heard the break in her voice as she talked about Pamela's overdose.

As it played, he clicked open the internet browser and typed in *Charlie Sheen*. More than 30 million hits ... famous quotes ... a list of films... The Execution of Private Slovik had been Sheen's first big screen appearance, just as the obsessive Mr Tippet had told him. Kowalski's words swam about his head as trivia from the world of celluloid stardom scrolled down the screen.

Tiger blood...

Webber was up out of his seat, tearing off the headphones, his stare raking the big office. Everyone was busy ... it didn't matter. He hadn't a shred of evidence anyway, all he had was a sudden solid certainty that Suzie had been right.

Clamping his phone to his ear, he raced to the desk demanding either the keys to a car or someone to drive him.

chapter fifty

Ahmed glanced at Michael Drake dozing in the passenger seat. He looked old and drawn trapped in a second marriage that was sucking the life out of him. Tiffany was no better off. They'd forged this strange alliance for all the wrong reasons. Ahmed wondered why they hadn't simply called it a day and parted company, but perhaps there was a financial angle. Michael had needed an injection of cash to break free from the Tippets. Tiffany had married him for financial security but maybe divorce would not provide enough for either of them. One way or another they would have to sort it out between them. His priority was to get his hands on the email that had sent Suzie to her next appointment.

It would have been quicker for him to mine Tiffany's PC in situ, rather than cart it back to the station. But Drake was shattered. He hoped Tiffany would stay away at least until her husband had had a good night's sleep.

As he pulled up outside the house he said, 'I'll be in and out as quick as I can … leave you to get some sleep, you look all in.'

'I'm going to sit in my shed and relax,' Drake said with a note of stubbornness. 'I'm out of reach there and I've turned off my mobile. I'm not sure I could cope with the sound of a phone ringing again tonight … Your boss won't be wanting to speak to me again today, will he?'

Ahmed noted the small catch in Drake's voice. He was more upset than he'd let on. As he climbed out of the car he clicked his own phone to silent. 'No, no. Don't worry. I'll be in and out in two minutes.'

Once inside, Drake ushered him into the sitting room. 'I'll go up and get everything for you.'

'Let me come upstairs and help.'

'No, I'd rather you didn't. I've had people all over Tiff's stuff. I feel bad about it. Sergeant Harmer meant well, I know, but it's a matter of trust. You wait here.' As Ahmed hesitated, Drake added firmly, 'Really, Mr Ahmed, I appreciate your concern but I was very uncomfortable having Sergeant Harmer going through Tiff's things.'

'I didn't think she had,' said Ahmed. 'I thought you'd done it.'

'She insisted on trying to help. I'm afraid I got her making tea to get her out of the way. It isn't that Tiff has anything to hide, well not that I know about.' His face clouded. 'But I know she'd hate it. She won't let me near her stuff, so if she finds out that I let a stranger … Speaking of tea, maybe you could put the kettle on for me, it takes a while to heat up, and I'll go and get what you need. At any rate, you won't need me to search out that notebook again. I gave the passwords to Sergeant Harmer.'

'It would be useful if you can put your hand on it.' Ahmed kept his tone casual, his reassuring smile in place. Lack of passwords wouldn't be an insurmountable problem, but would mean a delay.

He heard Michael's footsteps plod up the stairs as he headed for the kitchen, keen to get a glimpse of the potting shed.

A tatty bit of a lean-to, that was how Davis had described it, and he couldn't better the description. The door that led into it from the kitchen wasn't robust. He suspected that Michael's claim not to be able to hear the phone was a fabrication made up earlier in his marriage. He paused to make sure Michael wasn't on his way down the stairs and then stepped inside the ramshackle add-on and eased open one of the cupboard doors. A half bottle of blended malt glinted at him from behind a plastic cup.

He returned to the kitchen where an old-style kettle with a whistle stood on the hob. He checked it for water and turned on the ring under it. It explained how Suzie had strung out the tea-making so long. So both she and Drake had used it as an excuse to keep out of each other's way. With one ear trained on the muffled sounds from upstairs, he eased open the kitchen units one by one peering inside. All the usual things, a cutlery tray, stacks of plates and bowls, some tinned food and a few packets, the open ones sporting clothes pegs to keep them closed. There was nothing that Drake could turn into a quick snack, but maybe a hot drink was all he needed. He supposed the tea would be supplemented by the liquor in the lean-to. He clicked open the fridge, feeling his nose pinch in disgust at the sweetish smell that wafted out. Suzie had mentioned a bowl of meat on the top shelf. It was an unappetizing mass of raw liver.

The kettle gave a lacklustre rattle as though noticing the ring of heat beneath it for the first time. Ahmed walked to the foot of the stairs. 'Everything OK, Michael?'

He heard a grunt and the padding of footsteps. Drake's face peered down at him. 'I've just mislaid the printout,' he said. 'I wonder if I put it back on the printer. Would you have a look, room behind you?'

Ahmed strode through, his gaze raking the printer and surrounding table on which rested a laptop. 'No, there's nothing here,' he called back, 'but isn't this her computer?'

Drake managed a tired laugh. 'That's what Sergeant Harmer thought, but no, Tiff keeps hers upstairs.'

'Michael, let me come up and help you. You're exhausted.'

Drake's raised hand signalled no. 'Don't worry. I'll find it. I'll have it for you in a moment. It has to be in here.'

Ahmed blew out a sigh and went back to the kitchen where the muted rattle from the kettle gave the promise of properly boiling water within the next ten minutes or so. Why on earth didn't they get an electric one? He'd clicked on the light, but its anaemic bulb did little to dispel the gloom. Through the uncurtained windows he could see the edge of the lean-to, dark, gloomy and far too cold for an unwell man to sit in drinking alcohol. If he dozed he might succumb to hypothermia.

Footsteps from above and a muffled shout. 'Got it!'

Spinning on his heel to head back through, all Ahmed's attention was on the bend of the stairs. He was unprepared for the sudden raucous buzz of the doorbell which made him jump. He hurried out into the hallway as Drake made his way down the stairs, a bulky laptop computer in his arms, an A4 page lying on top.

Ahmed took it from him as Drake took a step towards the door saying, 'Tiff's got a key.' He shot Ahmed a worried glance.

Ahmed took the point. If it was Tiffany she was about to walk in and see her computer in his arms. That would not only mean hell to pay for Michael Drake, it would put a block on finding the all-important email. He'd met Tiffany Drake. His mind raced to dredge up reasons to make her cooperate.

He tensed as Drake turned the lock and swung open the door, then felt his eyes widen in surprise. Outside, slightly breathless and with a uniformed officer at this shoulder, stood Martyn Webber.

Webber gave no apology or explanation for his sudden appearance. He pointed to the heap of leads, machinery and paper in Ahmed's arms. 'That the printout?' Without waiting for an answer he reached forward to pluck it from the tangle of wires and ran his gaze down it, before passing it to the officer behind him. He indicated the computer. 'Take that too and get them back to DI Davis. I'll come back with Ayaan.'

'I was just leaving,' Ahmed said, nettled at Webber's offhand tone.

Drake stood to one side clearly wanting to close the door against the cold evening air, but unable to while the two officers blocked the way. Webber signalled with a curt nod of his head that Ahmed was to hand over the machine.

As the computer was taken away Webber stepped into the

hallway. Drake pushed the door closed murmuring, 'Do come in, Superintendent,' an edge to his voice, the comment aimed at Webber's back.

It took a moment for Ahmed to catch on. Melinda Webber's race to Hull. Of course, Webber wanted the full story from him before he went home and for some reason hadn't wanted to wait until he returned to the station. That didn't make it fair on Drake.

The three of them stood at the foot of the stairs. Webber looked appraisingly at Drake but spoke to Ahmed. 'Your phone's off, Ayaan.'

'Yeah, sorry. I had it on silent.' Ahmed pulled it out of his pocket and unmuted it, noting a missed call.

'Was there anything else you wanted me for?' Drake's voice had lost much of its accommodating tone. Ahmed watched as the man's stare bored into the side of Webber's head. 'It's been a long day.'

'Yes, a couple of things,' said Webber still not looking at him.

Drake's eye briefly caught Ahmed's with a look of annoyance. 'Well, I'm sorry but I've had enough for today. I must insist that you leave unless you're going to arrest me for something.'

Webber glanced briefly at Ahmed, then turned a speculative eye on Drake. 'Sorry Mr Drake, that's exactly what I'm going to do.'

Drake gave an uncertain laugh. 'What do you mean? What for?'

Ahmed felt the tension like electricity across his skin. He felt as shocked as Drake looked, yet it didn't seem real. It looked to him as though Webber was toying with the man, but why?

'I intend to arrest you for murder, Mr Drake,' Webber said, his tone mild.

Drake's laugh this time held incredulity. He looked at Ahmed with a shake of his head as though to signal that Webber had gone mad. Then he raised his hands, a gesture of mock surrender and exasperation. 'Well, go on,' he said. 'Surprise me. Whose murder?'

'Mrs Pamela Morgan,' said Webber. '21st of October, 2001.'

chapter fifty-one

Webber had expected a reaction but its intensity took him aback. The shock was real. Drake's face drained of colour, making his skin translucent. In the gloom of the hallway he might have been a ghost about to dissolve to nothing. It was Ahmed who leapt forward to catch his arm as he stumbled. Webber knew he'd misjudged something ... no time to puzzle it out ... couldn't let this turn into a total collapse. He moved forward to take the man's other arm. Between them they steered Drake to an armchair. He slumped into it and put his head in his hands.

An eerie background shriek rose in volume to fill the air. 'What the hell's that?'

'The kettle,' said Ahmed. 'I put it on so Michael could get himself a hot drink.'

'That sounds like a good idea,' said Webber. 'Plenty of sugar.'

'One sugar, thank you,' snapped Drake glaring up at him.

'OK, Mr Drake, just stay there and get your breath.' Webber ushered Ahmed back towards the hallway. 'For God's sake shut that noise off and get him some tea.'

Ahmed leant close and lowered his voice. 'Did he really kill her?'

Webber nodded.

'How? Why?'

'I don't have all the answers,' Webber murmured. 'But he did it.'

'Kowalski was right then?'

'I don't know that either yet. Now go and get that tea and get that blasted noise shut off.'

When Webber returned to sit on the settee, Drake's head was back in his hands. Webber leant forward to hear what he was muttering to himself. As far as he could tell, Drake kept repeating the single word, 'Pammy.'

He said nothing and waited for Ahmed to return with a steaming mug which he put into Drake's hands. Drake gave Ahmed a brief glance and then raised the tea to his lips and sipped at it.

'Feeling better, Mr Drake?' Webber asked. 'Up to answering a couple of questions?'

Ahmed, standing behind Drake's chair looked disapproving.

Drake glared. 'I thought I was under arrest.'

'No,' Webber said. 'I'm going to arrest you but I haven't yet.'

'I have plenty of questions to *ask*, Superintendent, but I think I've done enough answering.'

'Fair enough.' Webber said. 'But if you answer my questions I'll think about answering yours.'

'That doesn't sound like a fair balance.'

'It's all that's on offer.' Webber let his voice harden, saw both Drake and Ahmed tense at the change in tone. 'Off the record. You answer my questions and I'll think about answering yours.'

Drake hesitated, glanced round at Ahmed, clearly found no help there and turned his gaze back to Webber. 'You'll tell me about Pammy?'

Webber was silent for a moment and then said. 'Probably.'

'OK,' said Drake. 'Deal.'

Webber heaved an inward sigh of relief. Listening to the recording of Drake talking to Davis he'd been struck by an overwhelming impression of a man with secrets that he was desperate to offload. He thought it more than likely Drake could lead them to the long-ago murderers, the ones who buried the bodies or fed them to tigers, but that wasn't his focus. There was a more recent nugget that Drake probably didn't know he held. Suzie had found something that had set her on a collision course with the contemporary killers,

427

the ones who left bodies inadequately covered by concrete or out in plain sight in their crumpled cars.

Gary Yeatman was the link that bridged the cases, somehow involved long ago and apparently killed in what became a rehearsal for the more recent crimes. He would have to tease the information out bit by painful bit and this might be the only opportunity he had. His opening gambit was to close the door on any more lies. 'The John Brown you knew years ago,' he said. 'You told DI Davis about him.' Drake nodded. 'You didn't remember him when you were here, you remembered the name when you were talking to DI Davis afterwards.'

'It's a common name,' Drake said. 'And it's years ago.'

Webber could see Ahmed holding back a flood of questions. If his ploy worked, Ahmed would get all the answers he wanted.

Suzie had been right about this man's wife. He didn't know how or why but it hadn't been a natural death any more than Gary Yeatman's had been a suicide.

An image floated in front of him of the second Mrs Drake marching unawares in the footsteps of Tom Jenkinson and Arthur Trent. He had no idea how long she'd been a part of the grisly pageant, but now for reasons no one had begun to fathom she had Suzie right beside her. And Drake knew something that would lead them to both women ... two women and one child ... his child. There wasn't time to process Drake properly, nor to work out just who he was protecting or why. All he had to play on was the man's guilty secret from years ago. Saint-bloody-Pamela would be his ally softening him up and then squeezing him dry. On the far wall an old-fashioned clock ticked loudly marking down time to the intended sabotage at three junctions across the city.

'But once you remembered this John Brown, you recalled the way he signed off his ... letters would they have been back then? JB, just the initials.'

'That's right. It's funny what pops out of your head. Though I suppose it's not relevant to anything.'

'No, I suppose not.' Webber spoke mildly, aware of Ahmed's intense scrutiny. 'So you remembered the way JB signed his letters years ago but you didn't think to say that Sergeant Harmer had left a printout behind earlier today.'

'Didn't I? I'm sure I did.'

'To me and DC Ahmed, yes, but not to DI Davis.' He turned to Ahmed. 'I'm not saying it happened this way but has Mr Drake had the opportunity to create that so-called email from scratch since you got back here?' Ahmed became very still for a second and then gave Webber a brief nod. Webber turned back to Drake. 'So what else can you tell me about Tilly Brown's brother?'

Webber kept his gaze on the curtained window, Ahmed stood in his peripheral vision, his stare bouncing from Drake to Webber and back again. Webber concentrated on Drake's voice.

Ignoring the accusation about the email, Drake said, 'It's all a very long time ago, Superintendent. What sort of things are you looking for?'

'Was he at the same school with you?'

'Uh … no, I don't think so. It's a long time ago,' he repeated. 'I didn't know the family that well.'

'Didn't know them, Mr Drake? What about Tilly and the quintets? You were one of them.'

Webber saw Ahmed's stare snap to Drake who responded with an angry snort. 'I don't know what you're talking about. Tilly Brown and her family left the area long before …'

'Long before what?'

'The whole quintets thing. And that was all childish nonsense anyway.'

The childhood injustices still stung. Webber could hear it in Drake's tone. He turned to face him. 'Tilly Brown was an only child. There was no brother.' As Drake sat forward to speak, Webber held up his hand. 'I'm sure you can concoct a story to fit, Mr Drake, but don't. I'm going to suggest something and you tell me if you think it's a good idea.'

He speared Ahmed with a look, wanting him to understand that explanations would be forthcoming in due course and he must keep a lid on it for now.

'Let's make this genuinely off the record,' he said. 'Ayaan here can go and find you a change of clothes. I assume you'd prefer to wear something better than those rags when we take you in again.'

Drake smiled. 'You're almost tempting me, Superintendent, but I have a problem in that I can't trust you. What guarantees do I have that it would be genuinely off the record?'

Webber surveyed Drake with some irritation as he sat in his ridiculously tatty suit. He imagined Melinda's reaction if he should take to wearing rags, even if it was confined to their own garden. Annoyingly, although Drake had taken the bait, he had a point. 'Nothing you tell me in these circumstances can be used in evidence,' he said. 'And nothing's being recorded. I can give Ayaan my phone if you want to make sure.' Drake still looked at him with suspicion. The clock ticked on into the silence. 'You can frisk me for electronic devices if you want.'

Ahmed looked aghast, but Drake was weighing the offer. 'OK,' he said, suddenly business-like as he pulled himself to his feet. Ahmed took half a step forward as though to offer Drake his arm, but Drake steadied himself.

Webber handed his phone to a clearly appalled Ahmed who stood open-mouthed as Drake subjected Webber to a thorough frisking, even getting down on his knees to check for hidden pockets and wires. Webber offered him his arm to get back to his feet.

'Satisfied, Mr Drake?' Drake nodded. Webber turned to Ahmed. 'Make yourself scarce. Look out some decent clothes for Mr Drake. We won't be long.'

Drake watched the door close behind Ahmed then moved to the

table in the window. 'Over here, Superintendent, just in case your monkey's listening at the door.'

Webber shrugged and moved to sit the other side of the table. Drake had spoken loud enough for Ahmed to hear if he was in earshot. It seemed a needless insult. Up to now he'd had an ally in Ahmed.

'The JB thing,' Webber said. 'You made that up, manufactured the email. Suzie Harmer didn't leave anything on the printer. Why did you do that?'

Drake smiled. 'I wanted a lift home. Anyway you deserved it for the way you've messed me about today. Sergeant Harmer was all over those emails. No warrant or anything.'

Webber felt the thump of his heart. Don't let it be as simple as wanting a lift, he prayed. He surely hadn't got it that wrong.

'No warrant needed when you give permission. You could have refused her.' He reflected that Drake might not be so prickly if he knew Suzie had gone missing. He wasn't to know that she'd been in touch with Ahmed after she'd left his house. Webber squirreled it away as a potential angle to use if needed, adding, 'Think yourself lucky you're not in worse trouble.'

Drake gave a laugh. 'You say you're going to arrest me for murder. How much more trouble can I be in? And by the way I didn't do it. I want to know …'

Webber held up his hand. 'All in good time, Mr Drake. We're not going to find anything on that laptop, are we?'

'No, I wiped it after she'd gone.'

Webber suppressed a smile. That was what he wanted to hear. The alternative was that Drake had swapped machines on them. The man was no techie. He wouldn't have cleaned the PC effectively enough. 'Your wife won't be too pleased that you've deleted all her stuff.'

'She's two choices.'

The words were offhand in a way that surprised Webber. The

power balance in this marriage wasn't the way Ahmed had read it. Yet he didn't doubt Drake's reaction to his wife's suicide attempt. The shock had hospitalised him. He veered away from his intended questions to say, 'I don't get the impression there's a great deal of affection between you and your wife.'

'There isn't any,' Drake said. 'Never was.'

'Then why did you marry?'

'She's greedy. If I die before her, she'll inherit a tidy sum. Good odds with the age difference.'

That was honest enough. 'That doesn't explain why *you* married *her.*'

'Oh, much the same reason. I'll be in for a small fortune if she dies first. Insurance. Longer odds, better pay out.'

Webber remembered Ahmed's report of Drake after his wife's suicide attempt – shocked and angry. 'But it wouldn't pay out for suicide,' he guessed.

'Yes, it'll pay,' said Drake. 'I made sure of that, the way she is. There was always a chance she'd do herself in before she drove me into doing it for her.'

Webber stared at Drake whose gaze was unfocused, voice hard. His tone said he was speaking figuratively but did he realise how it had sounded? 'Then why were you so upset?'

Drake looked up to meet his eye and gave a cold laugh. 'It has to be two years. She knows that. She timed it so she'd die one day short and I wouldn't get a penny. God, it was close!' The anger was unmistakeable now. Webber prayed that the raised voice wouldn't bring Ahmed crashing in. Drake was breathing hard. 'Can you imagine …?' He stopped suddenly as though remembering the context of the conversation. With a glance towards the door, he made a visible effort to calm himself, lowered his voice and leant forward, eyes hard. 'Can you imagine having that happen twice?'

Webber felt a frisson of shock stand up the hairs at the back of his neck. He hadn't expected this. 'Tina Tippet?' he said.

'Tina lied to me,' Drake said. 'Told me the policies were identical. Turned out hers was dated differently. That was Brad's work.'

'Brad was right,' Webber said. 'You killed her.'

Drake laughed. 'I do hope you're not looking for a confession.'

Webber felt shaken. This wasn't what he'd been digging for. He had to keep going because of Suzie and Tiffany Drake. Thank God Suzie had made it out of this man's clutches, but whose had she walked into? Somewhere along the way, this bunch had become entangled with the people responsible for Jenkinson, Trent and probably Will Jones and Gary Yeatman all those years ago. Drake was not only covering for them, he had been nursing darker secrets than Webber had anticipated.

'About Pamela,' Drake said. 'I need you to tell me ...'

'I'm not finished yet, Mr Drake,' Webber snapped, his strategy derailed. Drake was toying with him. He'd intended it the other way round. There was nothing to do but track a path from the past and hope that he was right about Pamela Morgan. 'Tell me about Will Jones,' he said.

'Who? Oh him. What about him? He was sweet on Edie and off his head about the animal cruelty thing. He killed Pammy's husband.'

Drake's speech started out in genuine puzzlement. He hadn't immediately remembered Will Jones.

'How did he kill him?' Webber asked.

Drake gave him a withering look. 'I'm sure you keep records of these things. Jones went to gaol.'

'Manslaughter,' said Webber. 'He didn't know Morgan was in the warehouse ... did he?'

Drake shrugged. 'He released the tigers. Ergo he killed him.'

'Yes, but Morgan was already dead. All the tigers did was fight over his body.'

'Well, well,' said Drake with a smile. 'It's taken you three decades to figure that out.'

Webber fought to retain his indifferent demeanour. He'd been right! He'd known this man was desperate to unburden himself. Not entirely right. He'd thought Drake a man with secrets that weighed on his conscience, not a man bursting to get his light out from under a bushel.

'The car I suppose,' Drake went on. 'I spent years wondering if it would turn up and I'd forgotten all about it by the time it did. So what was still in there that gave you all that?'

Webber ignored the question. 'It must have been a nasty shock when it was stolen. It disappeared in Dorset, didn't it, and I'm guessing it was just chance that the guy spotted it. I don't believe he followed you down there.'

Drake nodded. 'I had to hitch a lift. It was touch and go getting back in time. I'm sure we left a trail a mile wide for anyone who had the gumption to look. There'll be nothing to find now.'

We left a trail? 'Do you mean you and Edith Stevenson?' Webber regretted the question as soon as it was out. None of this was relevant. He'd been caught by a sudden curiosity to know the details of the 30-year-old crime but it wasn't what mattered.

'No, Edie was here creating our alibi,' Drake said. 'I was ...'

'Never mind about that, Mr Drake,' Webber interrupted. 'I want to know ...'

'Isn't it my turn to ask the questions?' Drake spoke over him.

'Not yet,' said Webber firmly. 'Once you've told me ...'

'No, no, Superintendent. You don't call all the shots. I'm answering your questions. I'm being very frank with you. And I've decided to tell you about that night in Dorset. If you can't be bothered to listen then let's call it a day. Get your gofer back in here and be done.'

'OK, OK. If that's what you want, tell me about Dorset.'

'Interesting logistics,' Drake began, 'getting Robert to the right place and ...'

Webber set his gaze somewhere above Drake's left shoulder.

He could see the clock. He'd shown his impatience, shown there was something specific he was after. Drake was going to delay and obfuscate, tell him things from the past but not the present. He would have to let him talk the Dorset thing out. Drake was enjoying telling the tale. This was what he'd heard in the interview with Davis; not so much a secret to be unburdened than a desire to boast about the so-called perfect crime. He'd had few enough people to tell over the years, fewer still as the quintets disappeared. Webber wondered how many of them had known about it. More of the pieces clicked into place. Will Jones's part in the killing wasn't as he'd envisaged and the story Drake wove around Gary Yeatman didn't quite fit with what he knew. Drake knew the score, knew there was no hard evidence left to find. Webber's best chance was to concentrate on taking in every detail and writing it all down as soon as they finished. That way he'd still be without evidence but would know which track to follow to build a case. The problem was that as soon as he got what he needed all focus would be on finding Suzie. By the time he got to writing out a full account, the finer detail would have disappeared from his memory. He had to move things on and the Pamela card was all he had left.

'Why did you do it to Pamela?' he said into Drake's next pause. 'She'd been a good friend to you.'

'I told you,' Drake's eyes narrowed. 'I didn't do anything to Pammy, but I want to know …'

'I didn't mean that. I meant what you did to Robert Morgan. Why did you do that to her? She never got over it.'

'Nonsense! Pammy should never have married him. They were going to split up. You didn't know that, did you?'

'I heard something to that effect.'

'I saved her a very expensive divorce.'

Drake leant forward, his stare intense. Webber wondered which one of them Drake was trying to convince. He too leant forward reducing the distance between them. Let's see who blinks first, he thought. 'You should have given her the choice,' he said quietly. 'She would have chosen the divorce. It cut her life in two when Robert died, especially after that botch of a coroner's court and all the publicity. She had to live with thinking her husband had been eaten alive.'

Webber could see that Drake was boiling inside. His jaw worked but no words emerged. He looked on the point of striking out. Webber half hoped he would. It might tip the balance. When the words finally came, Drake's voice was husky and his gaze dropped. 'That's not true,' he said. 'And Pammy knew who was to blame for what happened. That idiot who was sweet on Edie. And now I need to know ...'

Again Webber interrupted but his tone was kind. 'Just one more thing, Mr Drake, then I'll tell you what you want to know.' That was a lie but time was running out. 'I want to talk about what Sergeant Harmer found when she was here.'

Drake sat back and laughed, his mood switching from overcast to sunny in a heartbeat. 'He was greedy, you know, that dirty little car thief.'

By dirty little car thief Webber assumed Drake meant big brother post office, the eldest of the trio who had disappeared after the raid. 'Came to you wanting money, did he?' he guessed.

'Hadn't had enough from his sordid little theft apparently.'

'Blackmail?' said Webber. 'So I take it you hit him and buried him.'

Drake laughed again. 'Like I said, no confessions. Well, are you going to come out with it? Sergeant Harmer's disappeared. You don't know where she is.'

Webber froze. No one had told Drake that Suzie was missing. He couldn't have overheard anything. He'd left the station before they knew themselves. But she'd left this house before she went missing ... hadn't she? 'What are you saying, Michael?'

'Don't worry about her ending up in the ground lost for years.

I'm not up to digging deep holes these days. Far better sport to leave them out in plain sight. Now wouldn't it be ironic,' Drake glanced at the clock, 'if Sergeant Harmer gave my wife a lift and then crashed her car and killed them both? I might get compensation from you as well as the insurance.'

chapter fifty-two

Webber sat at his desk head in his hands until a knock at the door made him realise he must look like Michael Drake hunched in that armchair. He snapped upright. 'Anything?'

'No, but you said to tell you when the search team was on the go.'

He nodded. It had taken time to get the right expertise on the spot. He suspected poison, something subtle; didn't want any accidents or anything missed. Drake wouldn't have said as much as he had if he thought there was anything to find.

Webber had formally arrested Drake for the murder of Pamela Morgan and sent him away, then he'd waited at the house, resisting the urge to get started before the initial search team arrived. It had been following brief discussion with the woman in charge that they'd decided to send for specialists.

'Christ! It's cold,' she'd said. 'Can we turn on the heating if there is any?'

'Sure.' He had no compunction about running up Drake's energy bills, but he'd left them still shivering because the central heating turned out to be solid fuel and there could be no light put to it before everything was raked out and checked.

As for tracing Suzie, it had become needle in haystack territory. Nothing they tried bore fruit. And the clock crept on … two minutes to eight … just over an hour … what was going to happen at nine o'clock? No traffic light scams, that was for sure, not without Jenkinson's sleight of hand. It was a smokescreen, some sort of cover for something else altogether.

Michael Drake was in a cell. Webber had sent a team to question him but Drake was all injured innocence and no comment. He looked very different in the smart suit Ahmed had dug out for him. The last he'd heard from the custody suite was that Drake had settled himself in 'like one of the regulars' and fallen asleep.

Ahmed was raking through files and notes. Webber could see him now, three quarter face, bowed down with guilt. 'I've forgotten something,' he'd kept saying. 'Something she said. It all got tangled up in chasing after Mrs Webber.'

As Webber watched, Ahmed suddenly shot upright, mouth half open, his gaze darting about but not focussed on anything nearby. He strode through.

'What have you got, Ayaan?'

Ahmed's stare turned to Webber, his expression puzzled. 'Edith Stevenson. She knew we were there. Outside that supermarket when we filmed her.'

'Go on.'

'It's not what … it just popped into my head. We saw her car, thought she was coming our way out of that crescent, but then she swung the car left, last minute, made a meal of turning the corner. She must have seen us. She wasn't going to the supermarket at all. Suzie had just been banging on her door. She'd pretended to be out. As soon as we left she raced off.'

'So where do you think she was going?'

Ahmed spread his hands in a helpless gesture and shook his head. 'I don't know, but I'm certain she was one step ahead of us. And if she knew we were watching her when she came out of the shop, maybe she put on that weird walk deliberately. Why would she do that?'

'To cover for using the disabled parking.' Webber voiced the obvious. 'Are you saying that wherever she was heading might be where Suzie's gone?'

'Maybe, but …' Ahmed shook his head, frustration clear on his face. 'That's not what I was trying to remember. It's something Suzie said to me today. I don't think it's anything to do with Stevenson.'

Webber returned to his office. Experience told him that the stress of the situation had Ahmed building up some scrap of memory that wouldn't in the end be worth the angst, but he'd have to work through it in his own way.

The phone on his desk sprang to life simultaneously with his mobile. The former identified itself as Farrar but the latter showed his own home number. He cursed inwardly; should have rung Melinda before now. He'd managed a brief call earlier but had had to cut it short, promising to ring back. The last time he'd red-buttoned Melinda she'd vanished. Farrar was out at a black tie do. He'd be ringing for a progress report during some kind of interval. Mel was safe now. She would understand … he hoped.

Farrar's voice was low, the background sounds loud. 'I don't have long, Martyn. Have you found Suzie? What the hell's going on?'

Webber could only give a negative and admit, 'I misjudged it, John. I took Michael Drake for the patsy. I thought Edith Stevenson was the brains. Maybe it's a case of equal partners. They were responsible for Robert Morgan and the first Mrs Drake and he knows something about Suzie but he's not talking. It's tied in with the second Mrs Drake. He more or less confessed but not in any way I can use. I've got him locked up but I'll be letting him back on to the streets tomorrow evening. I haven't a shred of evidence that'll stand up.'

'Slow down. You're saying he was planning to kill his current wife?'

'Yes, for the insurance. We're turning his house upside down. If he poisoned the first Mrs Drake and got away with it, chances are he's pulling the same trick with the second. But we got the warrant because of Suzie. That's the last place she was known to have been.'

'It's not though, is it? She contacted Ayaan after she left. And where's her car?'

'OK, I'm chancing my arm a bit, but we need to find whatever's there before we have to let Drake out again to destroy more evidence. And wherever Suzie went, it was because of something she found there.'

'If we go after Drake for his first wife,' said Farrar, a measure of distaste in his tone, 'we'll need Brad Tippet.'

'Yes,' agreed Webber. 'Loose cannon of a witness but he'll remember it all like it was yesterday the second he knows Drake's in the frame.'

'And the traffic business?'

'Still no idea how it links to them. We're going through what they managed to recover from the stuff Stevenson threw off the Humber Bridge. But she picked her spot. She knew what she was doing.'

'And what was the whole media circus thing?'

'That was Mel working old contacts. She knows just what buttons to press to bring them out, though they'll not trust her again after this.'

'But why did she do it?'

'It was her way of making sure she had witnesses on the spot, though apparently they didn't go where she'd told them.' PC Melinda Bryant's old contacts network knew that her tip-offs came with baggage. 'It might have stopped Stevenson throwing herself off the bridge. She'd have done it quietly but not with an audience. That fits with what I had from the teacher, Meyer, and Mel had something similar from Joyce Yeatman.'

It wasn't the only thing Melinda had had from Joyce. There was the issue of loyalty to her husband that had apparently been the motivation behind concealing the last page of Pamela's note. He felt a burst of anger at the officialdom that had missed the fact it had been incomplete. What had Pamela revealed? Presumably Gary Yeatman's part in Robert's death. Not that Webber was convinced Yeatman had been involved. Drake's version had woven a tale attributing the master plan to Yeatman, but then Drake would say that. He intended going back yet again to listen to Kowalski's version of Morgan's funeral. There had been something in it that chimed with the story he'd had from Drake.

'We know Jenkinson was approached in Hull by Streetwise's henchman,' Farrar said. 'And later Streetwise went to some trouble to track down Stevenson in York. So even if they didn't kill Jenkinson, could they be behind this traffic business – some planned disruption for another purpose? It's all very well saying they do their own dirty work, but that applies to murder not to road traffic accidents. Is that what Suzie found, some link to Streetwise or Boots Boy?'

'I don't know.' Webber had nursed a similar idea but found nothing to add weight to it.

Farrar rapped out orders. Webber was to make contact again with their Norwegian counterparts, to see what else might be unearthed from the undercover operative. 'Let them know about Suzie if you haven't already. I want them pulling out all the stops. Get on to them right away.'

They didn't give a fuck about Tom Jenkinson, Webber thought sourly. He didn't think a Detective Sergeant from York would feature much higher up their list.

As soon as the call ended he picked up his mobile and punched in his home number. 'Sorry Mel,' he said. 'I was on the other line to John. Are you OK?'

'Never mind that,' she said. 'Tell me about Michael Drake. You'd got up to where he'd confessed to killing his first wife.'

He glanced around and hunched over the phone, lowering his voice. Of course he shouldn't be telling her any of this. It was his *quid pro quo* for not coming home, for staying to direct the search for Suzie. 'I'll have to stop if anyone comes in,' he said.

'Then get on with it,' she snapped. 'Did he confess to Pamela Morgan?'

'No. Not even close. It was barely a confession about his wives, nothing I can use anyway.' Webber told himself that talking it through with Melinda gave him a better chance of remembering the detail for later, for when they'd found Suzie and had time to concentrate on the old crimes again. 'He spun it that the three of them, him, Gary Yeatman and Robert Morgan, went to Dorset to stop Will Jones doing the tiger stunt. Jones had told Stevenson all about it. Supposedly they were going to keep Jones out of trouble. He gave me a patchwork of a story but he let a few things slip that he didn't mean to.'

Webber glanced round to make sure no one was in earshot. Ahmed looked like he was going to start tearing at his hair. He would have to go and have another word. 'I haven't had time to check,' he went on, 'but Drake talked about hitching a lift after the car was stolen. There's a reference to it in the case files from the time. Someone came forward to say they'd picked up a hitchhiker. It wasn't followed up but it was in the area of the warehouse. The thing is ...'

He paused as someone strode down the corridor past his open door. The hands of the clock would soon be nearer to nine than eight. 'The thing is,' he repeated, 'the timing would fit one of them dumping Morgan's body which of course was before the tiger lorry arrived. And it was a single hitchhiker.'

'So the three of them drove to Dorset, but why did they go in Brad Tippet's car?' Melinda said. 'And anyway how? We know that's not the car Michael Drake had keys to.'

'Presumably they didn't use one of their own cars because they knew they were going to put a body in the boot,' said Webber, 'and as to the keys, I have a theory about that now I've seen how Drake operates.'

He thought back to what Ahmed had told him from when he'd spoken to Suzie. She'd offered to make tea in Drake's house in order to get out of Drake's way. Ahmed had teased her about it. Suzie

Harmer didn't make tea for anyone. What were the chances that Drake had made comments about hot drinks as he needled Suzie with his frustratingly painstaking search for Tiffany's password book? He thought back to his own request to Drake,

Would you let us have a look at your wife's computer? DC Ahmed here could bring it away with him …

He'd done the asking but Drake had prompted it with his comments about Suzie's search. And what had Tippet said about giving his ex-brother-in-law a set of keys to the new car?

It was … it was for Tina. She'd have wanted me to …

His tone had turned to hastily smothered surprise as though he'd only just realised how stupid a reason it sounded. Drake had finessed the keys out of him, the car had disappeared … and Tippet did what he'd always done, pretended not to notice, except that when it was still gone by morning, he'd reported it.

'We can take it that he had keys,' he told Melinda. 'The way I see it, the three of them were in the pub before they went to the warehouse. Drake told me Gary Yeatman went off with Robert Morgan and came back alone with the tale of some kind of fracas, Morgan in a fight with Will Jones. He was lying. He was the one who went off with Morgan, took him to the warehouse. Yeatman must have stayed in the pub.'

Drake had blurred the edges in the telling, wary probably of what secrets the car had revealed.

'None of them recognised the man who used to be at school with them – the eldest brother from the post office raid. But he recognised them, and he recognised that they were in Tippet's car. He knew the deal, he knew the players, he knew Drake would have taken the car without Tippet's permission. He followed them and he lifted the car.'

'Followed them? He didn't take it from the pub?'

'No, that doesn't fit with the hitchhiker. From the pub it's a short walk to the station. And anyway Robert Morgan was alive when he left the pub. He was dead by the time they got to the warehouse. The hitchhiker fits with someone stranded at the warehouse.'

Webber's hand reached for a pen. He scrawled the words he'd heard from Drake.

I had to hitch a lift. It was touch and go getting back in time.

He had to hitch a lift, not Yeatman. Webber smiled. For someone who'd had decades to polish his cover story, that had been careless.

'I think the car was taken from the back of the warehouse,' he told Melinda. 'Drake wouldn't have locked it while he went in to dump the body. Must have been a hell of a shock to come out and find it gone.'

'But does that mean ...?' Melinda's voice tailed off into a half question.

'Exactly,' said Webber. 'For big brother post office to know where they'd gone, he must have followed. And you know what that means. He witnessed the murder; he saw Drake stop the car, hit Morgan on the head and bundle him in the boot, before driving on to the warehouse. After the post office raid, after they'd dumped the car, he tried to blackmail Drake about it.'

'So he drove the car back, did the raid the next day, dumped it in the gravel pit and then ...'

As she paused he finished the sentence for her. 'He went to Drake and tried a bit of blackmail. And he ended up in the grave where someone had put Tilly Brown 15 years earlier.'

She gasped. 'Tilly Brown?' He'd forgotten she didn't know that bit.

'It's not a 100 percent confirmed yet but that's who it's going to be.'

'But why? Why Tilly Brown?' She sounded shocked but before he could respond she changed tack as though remembering they were on borrowed time for this call. 'Did Will Jones know or not?'

'I don't think so, not at the time. I think he put the pieces together while he was inside. And I want to know what Joyce Yeatman's been hiding; what was in the rest of that note.'

'I can go and confront her about that. She'll tell me now. It's way too late to be protecting anyone.'

'No, Mel, you mustn't …' He paused to soften his tone. Barking orders at her was the worst thing he could do. She was safe at home and couldn't go off anywhere because of Sam. 'We'll get to her in good time. I guess there was some allegation about Gary, but I'm yet to be convinced he was in on the murder.'

'Really? You're not just saying that for Joyce's sake?'

'Of course not,' he snapped, irritated. He would happily slap Joyce Yeatman for what she'd put them all through.

'But Martyn, about the car and everything. The warehouse was out of the way … middle of nowhere back then.'

'That's right.'

'So if it happened the way you said, big brother post office wasn't alone. He must have followed in a vehicle. I mean he wouldn't have left his own car behind, not if he'd just witnessed a murder.'

She was right. He felt a surge of something like triumph. 'That's good, Mel. That's bloody brilliant.'

'No need to go over the top,' she grumbled at him. 'It doesn't help you find Farrar's golden girl.'

He felt his mouth curve to a smile. She was pleased he'd been so easily distracted from Suzie's plight. He could have pointed out that Suzie had well and truly lost her golden girl status, but said only, 'You should switch to CID.'

A snort of derision. 'Not a chance. I'd die of boredom.'

He hadn't been over the top. With all that was in his head, in everyone's heads at the moment, that small insight could have lain hidden for a long time. With a feeling of satisfaction he clicked together the links. Ahmed's scatty witness, Larry Scott, the one who'd been in the pub with the post office brother when he'd spotted the Ford Tempo … Scott's wariness around all mention of the car … why would those tiny details have stuck? Why hadn't Scott mentioned the car 30 years ago when he'd tried to grab his piece of the limelight? Some trivia about seeing a car should have been swamped and forgotten in all the furore over the tigers … unless it was linked … the car … the tigers … the killing. Had Scott been the accomplice? Had he and big brother post office followed the Tempo and then stolen it? Everything hung by a thread from this distance in time, but it was possible. He wanted to be there when Michael Drake was told that there was a living witness to Morgan's murder.

A shout from across the corridor snapped his attention to a sudden flurry of activity.

'Hang on. I have to go, looks like something's kicking off.'

'But wait, what about Pamela?'

'I don't have anything, Mel. I still don't know. I'll ring you later, soon as I can.'

He clicked off the call and leapt from behind his desk, stopping as he remembered Farrar. He'd told the Chief Super that he'd ring the guy in Norway before it got too late. 'What have you got?' he shouted across.

'Suzie's phone's just gone live.'

Florid-features could wait. He strode over to join the huddle round the screen. A shiver went through him to see that symmetrical grid again.

Another phone rang. A hand reached out to pluck the handset from its rest.

Webber glanced up to see Ahmed standing by his desk. He'd obviously just got to his feet, but something had frozen him to the spot, eyes glazed, expression puzzled …

His attention veered back to the phone call which was from the search team.

'They've just found it at Drake's house. They turned it on.'

The words punctured the momentary elation that had been in the air. 'They want confirmation that it's Suzie's.'

'Call her number,' someone urged.

As the man beside him clicked Suzie's number into a handset,

Webber glanced again at Ahmed who had his own phone in his hand and was staring at it as though it was a ticking bomb.

He turned back to the officer taking the call. 'Where in the house did they find it?'

It was no surprise to hear it had been down the back of the table that held the printer, as though it had slipped from her pocket as she leant across to get the pages from the tray. Nice try, Michael, Webber thought, and was it supposed to have turned itself off in the fall?

'Fucking! Hell! Fire!'

The curse was loud enough to reach everyone's ears, but it wasn't the profanity that made Webber stare dumbfounded, it was the source. Ahmed, who rarely swore and never in such strident tones, stood horror-struck staring at the phone in his hand.

'Ayaan!' Webber called sharply to jerk Ahmed out of his trance. 'What is it?'

Ahmed's gaze rose to meet his, despair written into his expression. 'I didn't talk to her. She didn't ring me. It was a text. It was a fucking text! And just look at it. It's not her. Suzie didn't write that.'

chapter fifty-three

Webber watched as things wound down. It was time to admit defeat and go home. He'd caught up with florid-features who had surprised him by having already done some more digging.

'I have new information for you,' he'd said. They now thought that Streetwise's meeting in York had been with the go-between, not the target; the target was a man.

By the time the information reached him, it wasn't news. Just like Ahmed recalling that text message. It reinforced the theory that Suzie hadn't left Drake's house to go off after someone else. Drake had done something to her … taken her somewhere. The problem was that by the time anyone was back in Drake's face wanting answers, he'd had time to move about, to hide things, and they'd been asking the wrong questions. It might help keep Drake behind bars, but said nothing about where Suzie was now.

The search for Suzie would continue from across town until he was back at his desk tomorrow. Ahmed was still in the big office in animated conversation with two colleagues but the place was closing around them, lights going off. If anything happened overnight he'd hear about it. He'd have a clearer head for having a break. But he still couldn't quite make the move to shut down the systems, pick up his coat. There had to be just one more thing he could do before he left. Again he looked across to where the trio of officers stood in a huddle. Something stopped him walking across to join them despite a growing need within him to talk things through.

As he reached for his phone to call Melinda to tell her he was finally on his way, he paused, then sat back down. It struck him that it was Mel he wanted to talk to. It felt like a revelation, though why it should be such a surprise he didn't know. These last few weeks, talking through cases without holding back, discussing ideas with her had become more than a distraction from Suzie Harmer. And now that Suzie was centre stage once more for very different reasons, it was Mel he wanted to turn to.

The only light outside was the dim glow from the car park. His thoughts meandered to Drake, tucked up in a cell, maybe sleeping – was he really so laid back about it all? Was it just an elaborate act? He'd watched him on the CCTV walking across the carpark next to Davis; those weird flapping rags. Did he wear them just to annoy Tiffany? Was Drake as indifferent as he seemed? Before he'd been taken away from his house he'd asked if they would light the stove for the central heating in case his wife came back; that same central heating system the woman in charge of the search team had later wanted to light to warm the house. In saying yes, Webber had annoyed her by telling her to do what she was trained to do, stressing the need to empty it out and search it first because Drake's apparent concern for his wife's well-being jarred with the snide remarks about her that he'd tossed into the mix as he'd pulled off the ragged trousers.

He clicked his home number into the handset. The phone rang only once before it was picked up. His smile and greeting stalled. It wasn't Melinda's voice that answered him. In the second it took to identify who it was – the female half of the middle-aged couple who lived two doors away – he failed to remember a name. 'Hello, it's Martyn. Is Mel there?'

'Melinda's just popped out,' she told him. 'I'm minding Sam.'

It annoyed him that she wasn't there, but it wasn't unusual for this woman to pop in so Mel could nip down to the shop. 'Tell her I'm on my way back. Is Sam OK?'

'I've not heard a murmur from him.'

As he turned, pocketing his phone, Ahmed was in the doorway, coat in hand. 'I'm off now …' His body language said that he too was reluctant to make the move. 'I … uh … I'm sorry about that CCTV. I was certain it was Edith Stevenson.'

Webber shrugged. 'Even the analyst noted the similarities. Michael Drake told me everything and nothing, you know. He wanted to boast but he's not ready to confess. He told me it was Stevenson who stayed behind in York fabricating the alibi the night Robert Morgan died. I suspect that's true.'

Webber felt frustration at how unprepared he'd been. He'd known Drake was in the middle of it but had been so fixated on getting to the house he hadn't thought about hidden recording devices. Even if he had, he'd never have kitted himself out with anything sophisticated enough to withstand the frisking Drake had given him. And if Ahmed had left the house before he arrived, Drake would have disappeared.

'I'd like to listen to Drake again,' he said.

Ahmed looked taken aback. 'What, now?'

'No, not Davis's interview. I meant my off the record chat.'

'So did I.'

Webber stared. 'But …'

'I … uh … I recorded it.' Ahmed looked worried. 'I thought that's what you wanted me to do. I left my phone in the room. I haven't had time to upload it yet and I don't know how clear it'll be. I shoved it down the side of the armchair.'

Webber felt a grin spread across his face. 'Ayaan, you just wiped the slate clean for that CCTV.' As he said the words, an atom of doubt crept in. But no, the analyst knew her job. With sudden decision he tossed his coat over the chair, pointed at the computer screen and said, 'Get me those images up on here, the images we had analysed.'

It was clear to Webber that Ahmed was watching him as much as the footage that he must know backwards by now; the mystery figure caught fleetingly on camera meeting Jenkinson.

'Just look at that,' Webber said, a sense of astonishment creeping over him. He glanced at Ahmed to share the moment of triumph but Ahmed's brow was furrowed. He hadn't clocked it yet. Ah, but he hadn't seen the rest of it. 'Now look at this.'

He led Ahmed to the big office, clicked on the overhead lights and retrieved the car park camera images.

'He didn't know there was a camera round the back,' he said as they watched Drake and Davis stride side by side towards the corner of the building. 'The moment he thinks he's under surveillance, he slows to a hobble. Doesn't want us to see what he's wearing.'

'He's wearing rags,' said Ahmed.

'No, he isn't,' Webber said. 'It's some kind of theatrical stunt, a costume made to be seen in motion – acrobats use them and dancers. The dusk exaggerates the effect but look how his legs vanish. Imagine if he didn't have that big coat on, he'd be more a ghost than a man. That's why he crept at snail's pace along the front. He didn't want the effect showing on our cameras.'

Ahmed's jaw dropped. Then he raced back to Webber's office to rerun the sequence of the mystery man. Webber followed. 'Is it him?'

'It … it must be … mustn't it? I don't know. That same effect. It's not just a fuzzy image. It looks too small, but he's bent over. It must be him.'

'Go carefully. I think all we can say just now is that it's someone wearing that same stuff. Maybe Drake learned the trick from someone else. Or he's been teaching someone else.' Despite his words of caution he felt a mounting excitement. 'They've been alibiing each other. They've been at it for years. Remember those scraps from the old files. Alibis confirmed by chance bits of CCTV. One of them out doing the dirty work; the other flitting about on the periphery of someone's security camera.'

'Why the walk …?' Ahmed's words died away and he answered his own question. 'They always stood out in a crowd.' Webber realised Ahmed was quoting Jack Meyer. 'The way they dressed, the way they walked ... anything as long as it's memorable. And if it's a memorable something that doesn't match, then it lets them off the hook.

It was as Webber saw his satisfaction mirrored in Ahmed's face that a thought crept in, a sudden doubt that mushroomed to near-panic.

The ragged clothes! Drake's snide asides about Tiffany clashing with his apparent concern for her welfare; Webber's own concern that the search team be comfortable so they didn't skimp anything. That central heating stove. 'Search it first,' he'd told them. Then he'd pointed to the heap of ragged clothes that lay where Drake had thrown them down as he'd changed. 'Check those for pockets,' he'd said, 'and if you want to do his wife a favour put them in the stove before you light it.'

'Are the search team still at the house?' He saw Ahmed react to the undertone of alarm. 'Get on to them,' he ordered. 'I want those clothes in for forensics. No ...' as Ahmed reached for the phone. 'Call from in there.'

Ahmed rushed back to the main office. Webber watched him go then picked up the handset. He needed the reassurance of Melinda's voice. I won't be back yet, he would tell her, and if Ahmed remained out of earshot he'd tell her he'd acted like a bloody fool; that Michael Drake was running rings round them.

Again it was snatched up on the first ring. His heart sank. She wasn't back. It was the nervy neighbour worried that a ringing phone might wake Sam.

'Is Mel not back yet?' he said. 'Just tell her ...'

A deliberate throat clearing cut across his words. 'Um ... yes ... she ... She told me that if you rang twice I was to tell you ...'

'Tell me what!' He felt a constriction at his chest.

'That ... that there's nothing to worry about but I'm to tell you where she's gone if you ring twice. She said you'll know who these people are. Someone called Fiona was in touch with her ...'

'Mel's gone to Fiona's?' Webber's head spun with the implications of Suzie returning home to find Melinda there.

'No, no,' said the voice in his ear. 'She said to tell you she's gone to get some information from Joyce.'

The world rocked under him. She'd done it again. He stared at the clock. Five to nine. How long had she been gone? Was she still on the road? What if she was on her way back as the hour struck? Where was Joyce Yeatman's house in relation to those three junctions?

Ahmed was back in the doorway, his expression bright. 'It's OK, they've got them. But listen Martyn, he was wearing them. It–'

Webber stared at him, aware it was his own expression that had cut off the words. What was Ahmed saying? Where was Mel? What did he do now?

He raised his hand. 'Just a moment, Ayaan.' He paused to pull in a deep breath, to keep the panic out of his voice.

Ring Melinda on her mobile. That was the obvious next move. She knew the score ... she wouldn't have forgotten about the traffic business ... would she? Why couldn't she have rung him? What had Fiona said to set her off? He should ring Fiona, too. Ahmed jigged impatiently in the doorway.

'What were you saying, Ayaan?'

'Michael Drake. Why was he wearing those clothes when DI Davis brought him in?'

'Because I wouldn't allow the time for him to change.'

'Oh ... well, I didn't mean that. I meant why was he wearing them at all? It was nothing to do with that potting shed, was it?'

Webber fought to get his mind to follow Ahmed's line of reasoning. Worry about Melinda had made him sluggish. Potting shed? Clearly just a tale to explain the rags, because ... because they weren't rags. A sudden burst of adrenaline snapped him back to alertness.

'You're right,' he said. 'Mr Drake must have been on the point of heading off out when Davis collared him. And he didn't plan to be distinct on any cameras he happened to pass. He talked to me about his wife and Suzie.' His glance strayed to the mobile phone that lay in Ahmed's hand. It was too late to replay it now. It couldn't give them the concrete detail they needed. 'He talked about irony,' Webber said, 'and the possibility of his wife dying without him having to do it. He talked about Suzie killing them both in a car crash.'

'But where is she?' Ahmed's voice was heavy with despair. 'We've looked everywhere.'

Ahmed was right. Every possible hideaway had been sought out and checked; Drake's house and Stevenson's ... garages, cellars ... Everyone remotely connected to them, to the Yeatman's, even the Tippets had been shaken out until they spilt all they knew. Brad Tippet had fallen over himself to cooperate when he knew they were asking about Drake, but that had led nowhere. Had Drake hidden Suzie's car or spirited it away from the city before they'd begun to look for it? There was no CCTV usefully near his house and nothing had shown up further afield.

The time! His gaze snapped to the wall clock. Ahmed was staring at it too. They stood frozen in the gloom of the empty building and watched the last few seconds tick down to nine o'clock.

chapter fifty-four

'It won't happen,' Webber said. 'If it's Drake, it won't happen because there's no one to make it happen.'

'But if it isn't Drake ...' Ahmed's eyes lost focus. Webber's mind completed the thought. If it isn't Drake, then it might happen, and Melinda's out there somewhere.

The phone rang from Webber's desk. He reached for it without checking the number.

'Wasn't expecting to catch you.' The voice sounded surprised. It was the DI from across town. 'It's Edith Stevenson, she's demanding to talk to you.'

His head spun. 'Stevenson? To me? Why?'

'She says it's about – and I quote – "the policewoman". She must mean Suzie but she reckoned not to have a name. She said for her information to be of any use, we'd need to be quick. It has to be worth a try.'

Webber's glance strayed to the clock. 'What were you going to do if you'd missed me?'

'Oh ... uh ... get you on your mobile.' That was a lie. They'd have had someone get in touch pretending to be him. He and Stevenson had never met so there was probably no reason why not.

'Stevenson doesn't know we have Drake in custody, does she?' he asked.

'No, she shouldn't. Why?'

It occurred to Webber that a lot of people knew things they shouldn't. 'It might mean the time pressure's not as tight as she thinks,' he said. 'And where is she? Last I heard she was in hospital in Hull. We can't do this stuff by phone.'

'She's still there, can't be moved. And there's no time to get you and her in the same city, never mind face to face. We talked about it, maybe sending in someone who's on the spot, but I suppose she knows what you look like.'

'I've never met her but I wouldn't want to take the risk, not if she's going to talk.'

'Yes, so I want to do it as a conference call so we can listen in. Is that ok? It's pretty certain Stevenson was set to jump. She's vulnerable ... nothing to lose. We want to play on that.'

It was clear they'd discussed strategy and hadn't expected Webber in the loop at all. The phone call across here had been so they could say they'd tried to get him. Maybe he should leave them to it. His focus should be to get after Melinda. But what if Stevenson knew his voice?

'Let's get on with it,' he said. He covered the mouthpiece while connections were established and gave Ahmed the bare bones of this latest development, adding, 'I called home. Melinda's gone off after Joyce Yeatman. She's out there somewhere right now.'

He wasn't sure what had made him tell Ahmed, other than a need to unburden himself. Ahmed looked aghast. 'Your wife?' he said. 'She's gone and ...' He tripped on his words.

'Yes,' Webber finished for him. 'She's gone and done it again.' He wanted to tell Ahmed to get after her ... to contact her ... but it wasn't the right thing to do. And if she was driving, he wanted all her concentration on the road ... on the junctions. 'OK,' he said. 'I'll put it on speaker. Stevenson knows your voice, doesn't she, so keep quiet. Let's see what she has to say.'

Webber felt the tension rise as they listened to his officers talking to Hull ... the whirrs and clicks of connections being made ... the clock ticked on ... and Melinda was with Joyce Yeatman.

The tone from the handset changed, became clear and echoey

as they made the final connection. It would be like talking in a vast cavern knowing that listeners were hidden in the shadows. Edith Stevenson's voice came through low and gravelly, as though in the aftermath of a long shouting match. 'Is that Webber?' she asked without preamble. Webber glanced at Ahmed to see his expression harden. He'd recognised her.

'Yes. You wanted to talk to me, Miss Stevenson.'

'Do you want the golden girl back safe and sound?'

The turn of phrase threw him. It wasn't something that should come out of Edith Stevenson's mouth. 'What do you know?' he said.

'Oh, not so fast. I need an answer. Do you want her back safe and sound?'

'Yes, of course I do. Where is she?'

'You know that you need to be quick, don't you? You know what time it is.'

Webber couldn't stop himself looking up at the clock. Almost ten past nine. He reached forward to scrawl, *Traffic – find out*, on a scrap of paper and looked round for Ahmed, but Ahmed had returned to the big office. Webber could see him raking through a heap of papers. Hadn't he told him to stay and listen?

'Maybe it's already too late,' he said into the phone.

'No, it's not.' He heard a tiny note of panic in her voice. With a feeling of floundering in the dark he pushed a little further. 'How would you know from where you are?'

'Window dressing,' she said. 'Distractions. The real one won't happen yet, but it won't be long. You don't have forever to find them.'

'What real one and where?' He barked out the question as an order to spark against her growing anxiety.

'I know exactly where they are, but you don't have long. And I'm not telling you for nothing.'

Now they were getting to it. 'What do you want?'

'I want a cast-iron guarantee that I won't get a custodial sentence.'

He felt his eyebrows rise a fraction. 'You must know I can't do deals like that.'

'I know that deals get done. Deals just like that.'

'Not by me,' he said, though he knew she was right. What she didn't seem to have thought of was that no deals like that were done for people like her and not over an open phone line with this many witnesses.

He heard her sigh. 'You don't want her back, do you? Solves a lot of problems for you if she dies, doesn't it?' There was no triumph in her voice, just defeat. He felt uncomfortable that this was being recorded. Stevenson clearly knew all there was to know, the expression 'golden girl' had given that away. He wondered who she'd talked to.

'Miss Stevenson.' He kept his voice level. 'Tell me what you know. It won't go against you to be honest, not even this late in the day, but I'm not promising you anything I can't deliver.'

She laughed without mirth. 'I hope you don't think I was going to rely on your word. I'm not that stupid. It'll be a cast-iron guarantee or nothing.'

His gaze strayed again to the hands of the wall clock. 'You need to start talking Edith, before it's too late.'

'I didn't think you'd bite, but it was worth a shot.' Her tone had flattened, the anxiety he'd heard before had gone. 'Maybe you're right … maybe it's too late already.'

'It's not too late to tell me what you know, Edith.'

'No, it isn't, but I'm not going to. You don't get anything for nothing in this life, Webber.'

He sensed she was about to cut the call and grabbed at a memory. 'You had something for nothing once, Edith, a generous gift from your friend, Pamela. You can't return the favour to her, but you could repay something by talking to me now.'

There were a few seconds silence. He wished they had a video connection. He wanted to see her face. Eventually she murmured, 'Dear Quinny,' her voice soft, reminding him of the change in

Drake's voice when he'd talked about Pamela Morgan. 'She should have been pleased.'

Before he could shape a response, there was a click. The echoey cavern was gone and the DI's voice was in his ear.

'She's cut the call. I'll talk to Hull, see if they can push her face to face, but if this means that Suzie Harmer was with Stevenson's friend, Drake, then she's safe while he's in custody.'

Webber wondered if the upbeat tone was an act by this DI to keep up the energy in his team. 'Bear in mind,' he said, 'that Streetwise met Stevenson, not Drake. I'm not saying you're wrong but we still don't know where Suzie is.'

'I'll keep you posted, Guv, and sorry, that was a bit of a waste of time.'

As the call ended, Webber looked round for Ahmed who was standing in the big office, a sheaf of papers in his hand, his stare aimed at one of the evidence boards. Not entirely a waste of time, he thought. Edith Stevenson might have given them a key piece of the jigsaw. He couldn't quite catch the significance but had an idea that Ahmed was working along the same lines.

'What are you doing?' he said as he went through. 'Did you hear any of that?'

'Yes, I'm trying to figure out if they're right; was it Drake or was it one of Streetwise's gofers.'

Curiosity fought with the need to chase Melinda. 'What have you got?'

'I'm looking at the chronology … Tom was first approached by Boots Boy when he was in Hull. It makes sense that they'd have wanted a closer look at him. On paper he was a perfect recruit. It's the link with Drake and Stevenson that's the puzzle. Why did Streetwise target Stevenson? I'm looking at the traffic lights thing. Someone was scouting for someone to mess with traffic lights and Tom took the bait because there was good money on offer. He had some family loyalty but …' Ahmed looked troubled.

'There's a good chance he would have turned a corner, done OK,' Webber prompted. 'But what are you saying?'

'I can't see where Boots Boy fits in. He and Streetwise have shown no interest in anything round here apart from when they came to see Stevenson. It was Hull they were focused on, the port and all that. They approached Tom but they didn't keep up the contact ... well, not as far as we know.'

'That makes sense. They'd have checked him out but Tom Jenkinson wasn't anywhere near reliable enough for their sort of operation.'

'So if the traffic scam was nothing to do with Streetwise ...' Ahmed paused for a moment. 'I'm thinking that Tom knew there was big money to be made when Boots Boy first approached him in Hull, but somehow he'd blown his chance. Then this traffic light thing pops up in York. Maybe Tom saw the chance of a quick buck by passing it on. If you were Streetwise wouldn't you be curious about someone doing a job on a city's junctions like that?'

'You mean Tom Jenkinson gave them the mystery man.'

'Or woman,' said Ahmed. 'It was Stevenson they went for.'

'Apparently as the go-between. It wasn't her on that footage.'

Ahmed spread his hands in a gesture of helplessness.

'You're saying Jenkinson was the link.' Webber mused. 'Streetwise and Stevenson. Remind me, those old enquiries; Tilly Brown, Robert Morgan ... the quintets were interviewed, weren't they?'

'Yes, but never as suspects. They came forward as acquaintances of Will Jones, so there was a bit of interest in them, were they involved in the animal rights stuff, all that ... but they had their alibis ready.'

'And if I remember rightly, some random CCTV footage firmed up some of the stories.'

The pieces floated about, Jenkinson ... Streetwise ... Michael Drake. It had begun to look like it could coalesce into a coherent whole. Jenkinson gave Drake or Stevenson or both to Streetwise. Maybe Drake told Jenkinson too much about the traffic scam before he realised that the boy was a liability. Jenkinson had followed a man and a woman up towards the gravel pits. The scant description fitted Edith Stevenson's car.

'Jenkinson gave Streetwise enough to track them down,' he said. 'That must have hit Drake and Stevenson like a bombshell, having someone like Streetwise materialize knowing their secrets. And it'll have flagged up that Tom knew who they were. That's why they had to get rid of him. He must have known the identity of his mystery man all along. If only he'd come clean with you. He was on the verge of it.'

'It was Drake.' Ahmed breathed the words, his tone incredulous. 'It was Drake.'

Webber looked at him, momentarily fazed by his look of horror, but of course if Drake was as embroiled in this as he seemed to be, then who else but Drake had killed Jenkinson? And Ahmed had spent time with the man, felt sympathy with him over his rocky marriage, his unstable wife.

'It might be Drake,' Webber amended, 'but that doesn't mean we can prove it and it doesn't mean Suzie's safe.'

chapter fifty-five

Head hunched against the rain and cutting wind, Webber sprinted down the street and across to his car. He climbed in, slammed the door against the drizzle and pulled out his phone to ring Melinda.

Disbelief! He stared transfixed at the screen, finger frozen in the act of calling up the number. It showed a missed call from her. It must have rung as he hurried across to his car, the sound drowned out by the weather. He couldn't believe it had happened again. He jabbed in the number and clamped the handset to his ear. It went straight to voicemail.

It didn't mean anything sinister … she was probably trying the office phone … she'd ring back.

He had to fight to stop his mind going into overdrive with thoughts of grids and trackers … of not knowing where she was.

He drove away from the station concentrating to distinguish car lights from reflections in the damp and mist. In his head he tracked his route, knowing that in a few minutes he'd be at a T-junction where he had to decide … left or right … head for home or for Joyce Yeatman's. It wasn't a decision he could make with the information he had. He must pull over and call Mel, find out where she was … call home too maybe. If he ended up heading for Yeatman's the neighbour would be on duty for longer than expected.

The need to know she was safe was a constriction in his throat. He moved forward with the flow of traffic slowing for the red lights as the junction approached. Left or right? Indicators flickered from the cars in front, orange pinpricks winking on and off. He reached forward to slot the phone in its cradle. One more try to get Melinda before he gave in and pulled over, didn't want to lose his place in the queue. Plenty of time ... these lights took an age to change.

Relief hit him in a wave of elation as her voice filled the car, her tones irritated, 'God, Martyn you're impossible to get today.'

The audacity was breath-taking. 'You can talk!'

'Have you spoken to Ayaan? He said he'd try to catch you.'

'I've just left him at the station. He'll be on his way home now. And no, I don't have the full story. There hasn't been time.'

'Full story? Oh you mean Edith Stevenson.' Her tone was dismissive. 'I didn't mean that. I spoke to Ayaan not five minutes ago. He answered your office phone.'

Webber became aware of a low moaning sound. It was coming from the phone.

'Mel, where are you? Who's with you?'

He still didn't know which way to turn. Ahead of him the sea of orange pulsing lights flashed left and right as the traffic began to move ... in a few more metres he would have to make up his mind one way or the other. He'd wanted a few more seconds to decide ...

'Oh, it's just Joyce,' Melinda said. 'Ignore her. I had to get her to talk.'

'Christ, Mel, what have you done to her?'

A bolt of shock coursed through him. Yeatman and Melinda vanished from his mind. He'd forgotten where he was ... had wanted a few more seconds ... expected a few more seconds ... the lights had changed too soon. No! He wanted to leap out and scream at the cars ahead, but it was too late, they were pulling out into the main road blinded by the high wall and poor visibility, impatient to be home, beckoned on by the luminescent green disk.

He held his breath, every muscle tensed as he saw the cars at the head of the queue surge confidently forward.

No smash. One car at least had snaked round the corner and out of sight. No sickening crunch of metal on metal.

It was late, the main road might be clear.

That didn't mean safety. A heavy goods vehicle could be thundering down the hill right now seeing only a green light clearing its way.

His turn now at the head of the queue. Slowing to a crawl, he edged the car out straining to see through the gloom and beyond the wall that blocked his view of the main carriageway, desperate for a glimpse of the opposing lights ... ready to slew his car sideways and block the road. The motorists behind him signalled their impatience in a blare of horns.

It was OK. The cars on the main road were stopped, their lights on red. He breathed again and speeded up. Paranoia ... misjudgement over the timing ...

'Sorry Mel, what did you say?' He pulled his mind back on track. His heart thumped hard as he tried to force his breathing to slow.

'The lock-up.' She sounded impatient. 'I told Ayaan. He's going to get on to it.'

'Lock-up? What lock-up?' They'd chased down every lock-up, every garage they could find that had any link to Drake or Stevenson ... found nothing.

He couldn't stop. It was a clearway, visibility was bad. His need to check the lights had forced him to turn across the traffic, not the way home.

'Wait, Mel. Give me a minute. I'm driving. There's a layby up ahead.'

'I need to get home. I've left Sam with ...'

'I know, I know but just give me a minute.' That was it ... the low moaning ... that throwaway comment. 'What have you done to Joyce Yeatman?'

She laughed. 'I woke her up, that's all. Did you think I'd hit her?' A level of defensiveness behind her words left him unsure. 'She's drunk ... barely coherent. And by the way ...' Her voice took on a grim tone. 'She's got the note, Pamela's note.'

'Have you seen it?' The layby appeared. He signalled and pulled in. A dark mass filled the parking space. As he closed on it, his headlights revealed a giant cattle truck that rocked gently as he watched, though whether from a live cargo or the strength of the wind he couldn't be sure. Wisps of straw flew free and skittered away into the darkness. The bulk of the vehicle wasn't unlike the old photographs of the tiger cage that had been taken to that warehouse 30 years ago.

'No, I haven't,' Melinda answered him, 'But I know she's got it from what she said when I finally got her to talk. It's obvious she's read it recently but she must have stashed it before she got wasted. Thank God she doesn't have open fires and I can't see any sign she's tried to burn anything anywhere.'

'If she's kept it this long, she'll find it hard to destroy,' Webber said.

'I've looked through the bins anyway. And it's not in her handbag or anywhere obvious.'

'Mel! Stop. You can't go searching her house. If need be we'll get a warrant. Let the woman sleep it off. We'll get someone to her first thing.' It occurred to him that if Yeatman was as bad as she sounded then Mel must have broken in to get to her; he pushed the thought aside. 'But what was it about a lock-up?'

She sounded triumphant. 'Something Gary told her. He mentioned it the last time she saw him alive. I knew she'd know something. She didn't react to Edith Stevenson the way she did for nothing. The Browns, Tilly Brown's parents presumably, had a lock-up. They kept it on after they moved away. They rented it to Michael Drake's parents.'

Electricity prickled across his skin. They hadn't had a sniff of this in their hours of searching. A lock-up that might still be in the name, Brown. 'Where? Does she know where it is?'

He heard her sigh. 'I think so, but I couldn't get it out of her and she's past saying anything now. It's not my thing, Martyn. I needed you here.'

He felt a disproportionate surge of pleasure to hear her say she'd needed him. She'd broken into Yeatman's house, conducted an illicit search, possibly assaulted the woman to get what she'd got out of her. He shouldn't be pleased at all. She was right. It wasn't her thing. She could subdue a crowd of unruly drunks in the blink of an eye but the subtleties of chipping out information from a witness bored her.

'You say you told Ayaan Ahmed all this?'

'Yes, and he'll pass it on before he goes. You can come home. I'm just setting off now. I should be back before you.'

You can come home …

He could hear the enticement in her voice and swallowed against a suddenly dry throat. She was all fired up by the adrenaline of battle even if it had only been Joyce Yeatman and not a rowdy football crowd. 'Are you sure she's OK, Mel? Should you call her an ambulance?'

'She'll be fine.' He could tell from the way she raised the volume that she intended Joyce Yeatman to hear her couldn't-care-less tone. A pause. 'In fact it looks like she's asleep again, stupid cow.'

Webber toyed with the idea of driving straight to Joyce Yeatman's. He was uneasy about the woman. He wanted Melinda away from her but wasn't sure she should be on her own. If she was really that far out of it she might not be safe, and if she was putting on an act she might be waiting for Mel to leave so she could destroy evidence or get away … but what evidence and away to where? If she was going to destroy the suicide note, she'd have done it by now.

'Don't leave her on her back, Mel. We don't want a corpse on our hands come morning.' What he meant was that if Joyce died there would be no hiding that Melinda had been there. 'I'll see you at home.'

He pulled out on to the main road. The layby didn't allow for a U-turn so he had to continue in the wrong direction through the dusk and drizzle.

The road was clear now. He reached for the phone and clicked in the number of the station across town. Ahmed would have been in touch but he wanted to be sure.

They got the DI on the line when they knew it was him. Yes, Ahmed had updated them on Mrs Webber's information from Mrs Yeatman. Webber smiled coldly at the formality and phrasing. Melinda had blurred the detail of just how and when she'd had the information from Joyce and they were plainly curious. He wondered what the reaction would be if he were to say that she'd broken into the woman's house and beaten it out of her.

'The records are so old,' the DI told him in despairing tones. 'We're getting people out of their beds and all sorts but it's needle in haystack stuff. Shame they were called Brown. We've found an allotment they had …' Webber felt a burst of anticipation immediately damped by the words that followed '… but they gave it up when they left, and anyway it's a housing estate now. But it's looking like the best lead we have. We'll find it.'

Headlights shimmered towards him, reflecting off the slick road surface, but it was hardly heavy traffic, not enough to justify missing another chance to turn back, but he carried on anyway. Where was he going? He wondered if Ahmed too was trapped in this no man's land. Going home would be going to Melinda; but it would also be pressing a pause button on his part in what was happening and he wasn't sure he could do that. He imagined trying to say to Mel that it was nothing to do with Suzie, that it would be the same whoever it was.

There was a right turn up ahead. It was a circuitous route but he could go that way, swing round a long looping detour and head for home. He flicked on the indicator and listened to it ticking as the car left the main road. There was no need to loop so far round. He could slash a couple of miles off the journey by simply cutting back.

He continued on the longer route. In about half a mile there was a turn that would take him off on another tangent. He knew now exactly where his gut was leading him. He reached forward to make another call.

The DI's voice in his ear held suppressed impatience that he wouldn't leave them to get on with it.

'That dive team,' Webber said. 'The group who lease the fishing lakes and all that land, have you been on to them?'

'Well … no. What for?'

'Aren't there some old allotments up there, right at the far end of the site? Possibly lock-ups too. Get pictures of Drake and Stevenson in front of them. See if they know them. Let me know what you get. Ring me.'

By the time the call ended, Webber could see the scrubland that fringed the site, its outline melting into the dusk. He swung the car to face the gates, flicking the headlights to main beam, lighting up the track that led down to the lakes, the hut, the half-built walkway. There were garages and storage areas attached to the hut; not rented out, but part of the commercial fishing operation. He climbed out of the car, pulling his collar high to shield him from the rain, and went to inspect the padlock securing the gates. It was large and chunky but not the last word in security. He could undo it with a penknife.

The night closed in around him, the wind biting through his jacket. There was enough light from somewhere to paint a gleam across the surface of the fishing lakes. And off to one side would be the dark expanse of the water in the gravel pit but that wasn't visible from here, not even in the day time.

He strained to see as far as the low building but the path curved and his headlights were at the wrong angle to light the bottom of the slope. There would be nothing down there.

He returned to the car, backed off and drove slowly around the boundary as far as the road would take him. When it turned at right angles to head back to town, he eased it off the tarmac and on to the dirt track that traced the perimeter of the old site. He wouldn't get far in a vehicle but it was the closest he could get to the far end of the site. As the car bounced in and out of giant ruts, the headlights flashed glimpses of the deserted scrubland up ahead, even showing a scrap of tape still flapping in the wind from where it had been cordoned off.

When he came to a pothole that was more of a cliff edge spanning the track, he had to stop. This time when he climbed out, he clicked the key fob to lock the car, zipped his jacket to the top and set off on foot trying to see by the inadequate light from his torch.

When he'd walked in with Suzie and the woman from the lab, they'd come through the main site, down the hill. He was approaching from a new angle. It was as he neared the tangle of brush that edged the makeshift graveyard, that his phone rang. He used the thick vegetation as a temporary shelter as he answered it.

The DI again, his voice animated. 'Yes, they didn't recognise anyone but the name Brown is on their paperwork. They inherited sitting tenants when they leased the plot. There are odd parcels of rented-out land the other side of the dual carriageway, no longer physically attached to the fishing site. The only paperwork they can dredge up is invoices which don't show addresses or locations. The one person who might know detail is out and not answering his phone, but they think there are records in the office at the fishing lakes. I've sent someone up there.'

'What about the scrubland at the back,' said Webber, 'where we found the bodies, up beyond that? That used to be allotments or something, didn't it?'

'The people we've found just don't know. They're focused on the fishing lakes and the business. We're hoping to get chapter and verse from the records.'

'I'm up there now, the scrubland round the back I mean. I took a detour on the way home.'

'Have you found anything?' The sudden excitement in the man's tone irritated Webber. As if he wouldn't have said something straight away.

'No, nothing, but I'll have a bit of a walk round.'

'What made you home in on that bit?'

'Because there were three bodies buried up here.'

He ended the call and peered forwards into the gloom trying to make sense of the topography. With the pitiful torch beam and dancing shadows he could walk right past something as big as a car without seeing it. There was no point in exploring further, but he carried on, placing his feet carefully on the bumpy ground, feeling suction from the cloying mud. The curve of the land took the ferocity out of the wind, but he could hear it whistling across the higher ground somewhere up ahead. He tried to track a straight path across the boggy expanse but it wasn't easy with no solid landmarks and dusk swallowing the horizon.

An involuntary shudder rippled through him as memories leaked in of the early documentation on Robert Morgan's death. A man trapped as night closed in, hearing the pad of giant paws on concrete ... or hearing nothing until the striped death machines exploded out of the air.

Of course that was all garbage. He tried to shake the images out of his head. It hadn't happened like that.

The squelch of his footsteps seemed to echo.

Sudden realisation ... he wasn't alone. In his mind, big cats crouched in the dark. He spun round with a gasp, torch beam scouring the vegetation behind him.

The blaze of a heavy-duty flashlight seared an iridescent blindfold across his vision.

chapter fifty-six

'Martyn, is that you?'

The light veered away leaving a splash of colour dancing at the centre of Webber's field of vision.

'Ayaan? What are you doing here?' He struggled to hide the wobble that lay just behind his words as he drew in a deep breath to slow the beating of his heart.

'I came up here with the dive crew to get the records,' Ahmed announced, breathless. 'Then they said that you were round this side so I thought I'd come across.'

'I thought you were on your way home,' Webber said.

Ahmed spread his hands. 'Yeah, but ...'

Webber let it go. He too should have been on his way home. And as the momentary blindness from Ahmed's powerful torch faded he became aware of a background glow, pulsing blue. It was coming from the direction of the main site, the area he'd decided not to check. 'What's happened? What have you found?'

Ahmed paused a moment catching his breath. 'It's Drake's car ... it was right there ... round the side of the office building.'

A chill speared through Webber. 'Suzie?'

Ahmed shook his head. 'Nothing, no sign of anyone. But what's his car doing up here? It's supposed to be in for repairs. There are footsteps in the mud around it.'

'Going where?'

Ahmed gulped before answering, 'Across the path towards the

grass, no clear trail, but it's on a line towards the gravel pit. They're waking Drake, going to get an explanation out of him.'

'He'll just say it was stolen.' Webber dismissed the interrogation of Drake as a waste of time.

'They've sent for proper lights. They're going to look at the pit again.'

Webber stared across into the inky blackness of the encroaching night, pushing away the thought of anyone in that freezing water in the dark, and shook his head. 'No,' he said. 'They won't be there. That's not how he does it.'

'What do you mean?'

'Drake never intended to dump Tippet's car all those years ago.' As he spoke he set off again, traipsing through the mud, aware of Ahmed stumbling to keep close enough to pick up his words over the rush of the wind through the scrub. 'After he'd finished with Morgan, he was going to give it a cursory clean and return it to Tippet. He wasn't expecting anyone to focus on the car, not in relation to Morgan's death. That was all going to be done and dusted with none of the quintets within miles of the crime scene. If it was spotted, it would be Tippet in the firing line, except that he happened to have a cast-iron alibi. It was that hapless eldest brother spotting it and stealing it for his post office job that put a spoke in the works.'

He sensed Ahmed's puzzlement in a semi-articulated query, but he wasn't looking for questions or formulating answers. He was thinking aloud.

'Drake doesn't dump people in lakes,' he said, raising his voice to counter the weather. 'Dumping Jenkinson was as near as he got to that and it went pear-shaped.' He paused for a moment as he played out the scene in his head. 'I bet he thought it would be child's play, shove him under a bit of rubble, get Trent in with his concrete lorry. But it wouldn't cover that jacket. That must have been a panicked few minutes.'

He thought of the heavy Scandinavian inflection he'd listened to on the phone barely a couple of hours ago. *You have a tiger on your patch ...*

In his mind's eye Webber imagined the unflappable Mr Drake in a fury when the bright-coloured jacket wouldn't stay hidden under the inadequate layer of concrete that would have been drying out fast as he wrestled with it. He wondered why his mind imagined fury. The overwhelming impression of Drake was that he'd never experienced a strong emotion in his life. Then he recalled that comment about Tina Tippet. Rage, almost instantly smothered, had blazed to such fire in Drake's eyes, the imprint remained burnt on his memory.

'Must have been touch and go to get it off the boy at all and get him covered over,' he said, setting off again. 'And it was all for nothing. No, he'll go back to his tried and tested ways.'

'But why leave his car there?' Ahmed said, hurrying in his wake. 'It'd have been found in the morning anyway.'

'Then he must have expected to move it tonight. I'd guess he wanted a quick route home. Was he going to walk up here, do whatever he was going to do and then get the car so he could be back home before the shit hit the fan?'

'But what was he going to do?'

'Back to basics,' said Webber. 'Something a bit more sophisticated than a blunt instrument ...' Involuntarily he crossed his fingers as he said the words. Please God, let Drake have gone for the clever route and not the bludgeon or they might already be too late. 'He'll do something that's worked before.'

'You think he was going to bury Suzie and Tiffany up here?'

'No. He can't bury anyone any more. We've found the grave. But he doesn't know that we know about Trent or Gary Yeatman.'

'Do we know that he killed Gary Yeatman?'

Ahmed was thinking about the lack of evidence, but Webber was sure, even if it could never be proved.

'The point is,' he said. 'It was the method that worked, the method that was still working as far as he knew. Whatever he did to his wife … wives … it was far too slow for the likes of Jenkinson and Trent. That talk about Suzie crashing her car and killing them both. That's what he had in mind, but where in hell are they?'

It was slow going across the uneven scrubland. Even with torches, the shadows played tricks, disguising the shapes that reared up from the grass hillocks.

'There must have been another way in,' Ahmed said suddenly.

'What do you mean?'

'Those old workings when they had a go at a bypass and had to abandon it. They didn't get vehicles in from this side. This stretch must have been boggy like this forever.'

Webber tried to visualise the map of the area, trying to pull detail from the dead area that was this useless scrub. 'Where?' he said. 'Where would they get a road in?'

'Old farm track I think. It must come in from right across the other way if it's still passable.'

'It'll still be passable,' Webber growled as he stumbled on a briar. He wished he'd thought of it sooner. Too late now to think about going back and getting the car. They were almost across the low marshy stretch and set to climb the slope to higher ground. 'Call in, let them know.'

'But we don't know if there's anything to find,' Ahmed objected.

'Call it in,' Webber repeated. 'This is it.'

He stopped to catch his breath at the foot of the sharp upward incline and then caught hold of the tough grasses to pull himself up. Drake and Stevenson had had access to this site since Tilly Brown's family lived here. He wondered again, was it just Drake and Stevenson? They'd had Gary Yeatman in their clutches somehow, probably no more than the unwitting dupe. China Kowalski? Pamela Morgan? Those huge cash gifts. Had Pamela been using her money to keep certain of her old school friends at a distance?

As Ahmed floundered with the steep slope his phone rang. Webber watched as the DC grabbed at a sturdy root for balance and pulled the handset from his pocket, pressing it to his ear against the whistle of the wind.

'There's a turn-up,' he told Webber as he ended the call. 'Drake swore blind he'd taken his car to the garage, said it must have been stolen from there.'

Webber rolled his eyes. 'It doesn't surprise me in the least, and you forgot to ask for backup.'

'Yes, but get this,' Ahmed said. 'The garage says the same. It was on their forecourt ready to be worked on tomorrow morning.'

'Garbage! Sleight of bloody hand. Drake whipped it off the forecourt and he'd have put it back there. Everyone's ready to rush in with alibis for Mr Drake. They always have been. Hell, he almost had me at it with those sodding clothes. Come on. We must be nearly there.'

'But Tilly Brown,' Ahmed called after him. 'Why would she walk out of her own home and sneak 250 miles north? And how? She was only 16.'

'I'm sure she thought she was going back home again,' Webber called back. 'And what's the betting she thought it was all her own idea from the off? Tilly Brown was the first one. Maybe she was an accident, but Mr Drake had scores to settle.'

Even through the gloom he could see that Ahmed was far from convinced, still on a see-saw of emotion about Drake, unable to mesh a cold killer to the man with whom he'd interacted on a very human level, but it was no longer speculation to Webber.

The pieces were falling into place. The tangential close shave with organised crime in the persons of Streetwise and Boots Boy had been an unfortunate distraction. In fact Streetwise and Boots Boy had been smarter than any of them in recognising what they were dealing with. They'd backed off smartly and left Tom Jenkinson to his fate.

Drake had been a cancer that had both held the quintets together and then driven them apart. China Kowalski had run a long way away, putting real distance between herself and her old school gang. He didn't feel he'd yet got the measure of Robert Morgan's murder or Pamela's – Drake's throwaway comment about saving Pamela an expensive divorce was a poor excuse – but the answer was in one of those taped conversations, he was sure of it.

They scrambled to the top of the rise and out from the shelter of lower ground. Webber turned his head to avoid the full brunt of the wind. It was a firmer gravel surface beneath his feet, a track, useable and with some evidence of use. They played their torches all around and there ahead stood a row of four ramshackle garages.

Webber let the thin beam of light run back and forth as they approached. He leant into the wind as he peered through the gloom. One end of the row had succumbed to the ravages of time, its roof caved in. The other three doors sported padlocks but two of them looked ancient and rusted, their doors only held upright by the embrace of tangled brambles whose long barbed stalks lashed out in a frenzy at the gale that tore round the structure.

One door was clear of vegetation. One garage still in use. The lights of the city lit the distant horizon but everything nearby had melted into the night. He imagined how it would look on a sunlit day. Worn, deserted, uninteresting and with a clear path to the makeshift grave.

The padlock was conventional but heavy duty, it wouldn't succumb to a penknife. He pointed at the abandoned buildings. 'Find a jemmy or something,' he shouted against the squall. 'We need to get this open.'

Ahmed gave him an unsure glance but then pulled back a rusted hinge, heaved the rotten wood aside and squeezed through the gap. After a moment's muffled banging and scraping, he re-emerged with a sturdy metal bar which he jammed behind the secure padlock, before jerking it in a swift downward sweep and snapping the hasp with a loud crack.

'Now ring in and get some back up,' Webber yelled as he dragged one of the doors open.

The smell that blossomed out hit him like a physical force. He staggered back, gasping. As he did so, his torch beam caught the sparkle of a reflective surface; the silver rim around a car headlight.

chapter fifty-seven

Ahmed was aware of Webber's stumble, but his stare had locked on to the front fender of the vehicle as shock flooded him. It was Suzie's car. Webber had been right. He'd been telling him to ring it in. He grabbed for his phone as he pushed through the gap into the garage.

The stench hit him like he'd walked into a wall.

Sickly ... sweet ... suffusing his airways, stinging his eyes ... the honeyed aroma of fresh cut flesh ... the festering reek of ancient decomposition ... Notes of decay and putrefaction seared the back of his throat.

Bile rose. The phone slipped from his grasp as his hands instinctively clamped a barrier across his nose and mouth. He leapt round, juggling to grab the handset, to stop it landing in the mud, as he dived for the open air.

Webber had spun away from the open doorway, gagging as the force of the wind hit him, his face puckered as he gasped for breath. Their eyes met. At once Ahmed punched the numbers into the phone and clamped it to his ear.

As he did so, Webber pulled out a handkerchief, fighting the storm that tried to snatch it, and tied it across his face. They had to go in there. Whatever this hell-hole was, Suzie might be lying injured in the middle of it.

Ahmed rapped out as concise an account as he could manage into the phone, and tried to get an image of the map in his head to describe where he thought they would find vehicle access to this remote site. He wrestled one-handed to retrieve gloves from his back pocket, and hoped that he too had a hanky large enough to tie round his face.

Webber's gloved hand reached out to take his flashlight. He surrendered it, taking the tiny pocket torch in return – the bad end of the bargain. He watched Webber, face scrunched in anticipation, ease his way through the gap and disappear into the darkness.

Call ended, Ahmed took in a deep breath before stepping close to the entrance, where he began to pull the wooden doors wider in hopes of dissipating the foul odour.

'Careful,' Webber called, voice muffled. 'Don't let anything blow about.'

He compromised on half-open and went inside.

Webber's mind raced. The car sat motionless and silent, its windows fogged. What the hell had been going on in this place? The floor felt spongy and uneven beneath his feet, the air still, the whistle of the storm muted by the walls. The flashlight bounced its beam right back at him from the vehicle's windows. He squeezed down the side, conscious of his clothes sweeping against the metal, compromising the scene. Standing the flashlight on the roof, he pressed his face to the side window, cupping his hands to focus.

And there was Suzie. She looked relaxed … just dozing, sprawled half across the seats. The thoughts reared up … this woman was corroding his marriage, destabilising Sam's secure future. All he need do was fail to find her in time and she'd be gone from his life.

That's what Michael Drake had hinted, confident it was what Webber wanted. But what he actually wanted was that the whole Suzie thing had never happened; it wasn't the same as wanting her dead. Drake wouldn't appreciate the nuance. As he shifted his gaze he realised she wasn't alone in the car. Someone lay curled up on the back seat.

He grabbed at the door handle. It wouldn't shift. The windows were reinforced glass. There was no room to swing anything with enough force to break them.

His eyes had adjusted now. He could see the glistening strands, the details of the mechanism that would send this car to wherever Drake had planned its end to be. But even without seeing the detail it was clear how delicate it was. They couldn't get to either woman without shattering the whole contraption, collapsing it to a bundle of meaningless wire strands. He wanted a record. If he could preserve the scene, he'd have an ace to play. Surely this whole set-up should provide aces enough, but even now he didn't trust that Drake couldn't slither out of the trap.

There would be no clear photographs until the doors were open, and once open the priority had to be the women inside. He wanted to wait for specialist teams, but he couldn't, even if he could see that she was breathing – and he couldn't see any movement at all – he couldn't neglect the woman who was carrying his child in order to preserve a crime scene.

A sudden flash of light made Ahmed jump. He fought to keep his breathing shallow. What was Webber doing? He had his phone pressed to the car window and was taking photographs. There wasn't much room. He squeezed down the other side of the vehicle, trying to see inside. The windows were misted over. Webber was leaning in close, using his cupped hands to focus his gaze before pulling back and again aiming the camera. But if Suzie was in there – and as his eyes adjusted he could see the indistinct form of a figure leaning across half behind the wheel – they had to get her out, not piss about with photographs.

He grabbed the door handle and yanked at it but it wouldn't budge. The keys would be at Michael Drake's house or even in the custody suite with the man's other belongings.

No time to speculate. They had to get into the car.

'Is it Suzie?' He held the cloth tight to his face as he spoke, trying to avoid the taste of the foul air as he peered in.

'Yes.' Webber's camera phone flashed again. 'In the front. Tiffany Drake … I assume it's Tiffany Drake … is curled up on the back seat.'

'But … but are they all right?'

'God knows. I hope so.'

'They're drugged, that's all,' said Ahmed buoyed by sudden certainty. 'He doesn't kill them till just before the crash.'

'That was true for Trent,' said Webber, 'but who knows about Yeatman? Most of the victims were bludgeoned then buried … or left for wild animals to find. Get that jemmy thing. See if we can force one of the doors.'

Ahmed pushed his face on to the windscreen, cupping his hands the way Webber had, and stared into the car's interior. At first it seemed that the whole space had been filled with silky cobwebs, the delicate strands looped this way and that around the controls, anchored to the seat backs. His mind fogged with the scene in front of him … she hadn't been missing long enough for insects to weave this complexity. Then the figure focused out of the haze and he could see it was Suzie, lolling sideways, hands in her lap, head tipped forward. The strands looked less like cobwebs and more like fishing line. He strained to see movement, a rise and fall of her chest. The shadows and the filmy strands wouldn't allow a clear view.

He peered again to see between the seats to where Tiffany lay on her side, legs drawn up. The tableau felt surreal, as though he was staring at two plastic mannequins … another sleight of hand … not the real Suzie or the real Tiffany at all.

'It needs specialist photographers to get the real complexity of it.' Webber's voice cut into his thoughts.

What was he saying? The strands … the silky web that threaded its way all over Suzie … wrapped around the wheel … the controls

… disappearing down into the foot well. He understood. This was the mechanism designed to operate the car for a short distance. No chance of understanding it from here but even his restricted view showed the care that had been taken with the loops and ties. It could be yanked free leaving no more than a few scraps of anonymous thread secured to the anchor points – just the way they'd been in Trent's smashed vehicle.

Specialist photographers? Then leave it to them, he wanted to shout. We have to get them out of there.

He shuddered. The sudden surge of annoyance with Webber raised his heartrate; forced him into a deeper breath. What in hell had been rotting in this place and how long for? He couldn't hold back a cough as he fought the nausea.

He dived back outside, gulped in a mouthful of sweet-tasting air and grabbed at the cloth round his face as it flapped madly in the wind. His gaze raked the ground and with a crow of triumph he caught the metallic gleam of the jemmy.

Webber clamped one hand over the top of the handkerchief to try to keep the stench at bay. In the car Suzie sat immobile.

Footsteps. Ahmed was back with the metal bar. Webber saw the DC's face pucker as he stepped back into the garage. 'What's been going on in here?' he gasped.

'God knows,' Webber said. 'Bring that thing round here.'

Ahmed worked the iron bar into the gap between door and frame. Webber crowded close to help give weight to the improvised lever. It needed too much effort for shallow breathing. An aura of decay seeped into every inch of his being.

The door frame buckled … a scream of tortured metal became a crack as the door gave way. At once the car's alarm shrieked into the darkness.

Webber pulled the door as wide as the cramped space would allow. Head throbbing with the deafening noise, he squeezed in sideways and reached forward, feeling the soft skin at Suzie's neck under his gloved fingers. Her strong steady pulse lifted a weight from him. He kept his hand pressed into her flesh, savouring the relief, then realising that it must look to Ahmed as though he was searching for a pulse. He twisted round, seeing Ahmed's face still furrowed from the odour of death all around them, and gave him a nod. Then he turned and reached for the figure in the back, resting his hand against her for long enough to feel the rise and fall of her chest.

'Are they OK?' Ahmed shouted over the pulsing scream of the alarm.

'Alive and breathing,' Webber shouted back as he eased out of the car. 'They can stay where they are until the medics get here.'

He saw Ahmed's slump of relief and heard him mutter, 'There's enough here to keep him behind bars forever.'

Webber aimed his camera phone again although much of the delicate mechanism had sprung free. He flapped his hand to signal they should get out of the tight space and away from the deafening echo of the alarm as it bounced off the walls.

His ears rang with the sound even as the weather damped its intensity. 'Trent's car was clean,' he said. 'And Jenkinson's flat. Who's to say this car's going to give us anyone other than Suzie and the current Mrs Drake?'

'But it's his lock-up, isn't it?'

'It's in the name of Brown. They didn't recognise his photograph. We've got our tiger by the tail, Ayaan, but that's not the same as having him caged.'

chapter fifty-eight

Noise and lights overran the area, proper vehicles, proper kit. After he'd directed the new arrivals, warned them to preserve the scene as far as possible, Webber could only stand and watch from the side-lines as the medics eased their way into the tight space, their priority Suzie and Tiffany Drake's safety. They wanted the car out in the open so they could get at the unconscious women. He wanted to say no, they're not injured just drugged, haul them out with the car in situ, but it wasn't going to happen so he kept quiet and watched the evidence take a beating from the weather before anyone could step in with specialist equipment. Then the ambulance doors were shut, its light revolving lazily, washing shades of blue across the bright spotlights that opened up every corner of the gruesome garage.

And at last the CSI team was in there and all over the car. He envied them their suits and masks.

'The traffic lights business was a diversion, wasn't it?'

Ahmed spoke from close behind him. Webber gave him a glance and a nod, remembering the thoughts he'd had when mulling over Gary Yeatman's death. 'If you put someone already dead behind the wheel of a car,' he said, 'and send them into a stream of fast-moving traffic, and if traffic lights are being tampered with across the city, then we'll be looking in all the wrong directions and cause of death isn't going to be in the spotlight like it should be.'

'Gary Yeatman and Arthur Trent died on deserted stretches of road in the early hours.'

Webber nodded again but he'd already followed the line of thought. 'Yeatman was the first and I don't think he dared do Trent out in the open. He needed to know if the trick still worked. But yes, I know what you're thinking.'

Drake hadn't been working on the traffic charade in order to cover the killing of Arthur Trent. Trent had been collateral damage after Tom Jenkinson's death. Suzie hadn't been on his radar then either, nor had Tiffany. But Drake didn't dispose of his wives that way.

'He was planning to kill someone else,' Ahmed said, 'before Trent, before Tom, before Suzie.'

'I think he'd decided it was safe to get rid of Joyce Yeatman.' Webber imagined Drake's years of worry about Pamela Morgan's suicide note, the one that neither he nor Edith Stevenson had ever managed to prise out of Joyce.

There was a flurry of activity that turned their attention to the car. 'When I first saw them in there,' Ahmed said, 'Suzie and Tiffany Drake, they didn't look real.'

Even now with the vehicle empty, Webber felt a surreal air over the scene. He wondered why the ambulance wasn't moving off, which of the women was considered serious enough to need treatment on the spot. Michael Drake had said he wasn't up to digging holes these days. So who or what had he been butchering in this garage? Now that it was lit up, it was obvious this place hadn't housed a vehicle for a long time. The garage contents had been shoved aside to make room for the car.

He supposed they'd never know if this lock-up had been used years ago to set up the stunt that killed Gary Yeatman, but it was plain it had been used for very different purposes since then.

'What's the betting there'll be human remains once we've sifted it?' someone speculated, but Webber didn't think so. He'd had no hint of uncontrolled carnage as the driving force behind Drake or Stevenson. This was something else altogether.

He moved towards the entrance to try for a clearer view of the rest of the space, but had to turn his head away as the putrefaction wafted over him.

A suited figure stood upright from inspecting something on the ground, an evidence bag in hand.

'Can you tell what's been going on in there?' Webber asked.

'It's animal remains by the looks of it.'

'What sort of animals?'

'Dogs and cats, I'd say. Hard to tell with the older stuff.'

'They found animal bones over that way.' Webber pointed back towards the scrubland. 'Illegal disposal of cattle decades ago.'

'I've not seen anything that looks like cattle bones.'

Webber nodded. 'Any sign of anything bigger than dogs and cats ... more exotic?' He wanted to ask if any of the bones could be big cats, tigers say, but that was foolish.

Whatever this was, it was the work of Michael Drake and Edith Stevenson. Stevenson knew the game was up. Her escape plan had been suicide. He wondered why she hadn't done something simpler like take pills and burn the artefacts she'd wanted to destroy, rather than heading for the sea. Joyce Yeatman had clearly been in touch with the woman over the years, but something about that last summons had spooked her enough to draw in Melinda. He'd bet that Stevenson had wanted one last try to get Pamela Morgan's suicide note ... must get on to that and see if Mel was right. If the note still existed he wanted to see it.

Out of nowhere he remembered the film that Ahmed and Suzie had shot outside that supermarket; Ahmed's certainty that Stevenson had known they were there. She'd moved just like a man, she must have known they had it on tape. Was she dropping hints about the way they got in the path of random security cameras, either bolstering alibis for each other or disguising their real identities? Maybe she'd been trying to reveal their secrets for years.

It hadn't all been paperwork that she'd thrown off the bridge, and because of the press and their cameras there was detailed footage to study.

He and Ahmed were trapped here until someone had the time to drive them round the track to the road and to the far side of the site where their cars were parked. The direct route across the marshy scrubland wasn't a tempting prospect now the light had gone altogether.

He said to Ahmed. 'What did Stevenson chuck off the bridge? Why did she do it?'

'Evidence I suppose,' said Ahmed, his stare like Webber's glued to the gaping mouth of the garage. 'Or maybe trophies. Going back years. They recovered a toy bridle that I'm guessing will match that piece from Tilly Brown's rocking horse saddle.'

It had been Melinda who identified that, putting together the clues she'd picked up from talking to Jack Meyer. Webber thought back to Kowalski. Something had bugged her about that horse.

'It'll wash up, won't it, the rest of it? We can't drag the bloody Humber.'

Ahmed's gaze dropped. 'It's not that simple. She'd practiced that move, maybe thrown stuff off before. Get the right spot and the right tide and things can be swept for miles, that is if they aren't torn to shreds in the currents. Me and Mrs Webber were talking about it on the way back, wondering why she'd done it the way she had.'

Webber indicated that they should move into the shelter of the far end of the row of buildings. 'Go on.'

'Joyce Yeatman thought her husband had been part of the crimes years ago. Either Stevenson convinced her or it was something in Pamela Morgan's note. It gave Stevenson a hold over her.'

Webber nodded. He didn't believe Gary Yeatman was guilty of much, but he believed in Edith Stevenson's hold over Yeatman's wife.

'Stevenson knew the game was up. I guess she called on Yeatman because ... well, we couldn't work out what she wanted exactly.'

'Pamela Morgan's suicide note, I should think,' said Webber.

Ahmed seemed to weigh this and then nodded. 'She knew exactly where to go. She even had the diversion planned to shake a follower. By the time she got to Hull, she had about 20 … 30 minutes to catch the right tide.'

'How did they end up swapping cars?'

'They went to Stevenson's house in Joyce Yeatman's car. While they were there, Stevenson slipped out. Mrs Webber says she thinks Yeatman helped her, diverting attention and that, but she didn't know why. I mean why take her along at all if she's going to help Stevenson get away?'

'I suppose she wanted Stevenson to dispose of any evidence against her husband, but she didn't want to go with her. You were saying about the cars.'

'Yes, Stevenson took off in Yeatman's car, leaving her own out front hoping Mrs Webber wouldn't spot that she'd gone. She did though. She said she realised quite quickly that Stevenson wasn't coming back from making tea.'

'Making tea …?' Webber murmured, watching the activity in the garage. After Melinda had raced off in pursuit, Joyce Yeatman called a cab and returned to her own house to pour alcohol down her throat. The officers Davis had sent for Stevenson hadn't missed them by much. Something nudged at him but he couldn't catch it.

'No, nothing,' he said to Ahmed's puzzled glance. 'Go on.'

'She got it out of Yeatman that Stevenson was heading for Hull, for the Humber Country Park.'

'But she wasn't, was she?' Webber felt his eyes narrow. Mel really needed some better training in questioning witnesses, she was too impatient, thought she could bounce people into blurting out the truth. It might work on Saturday night drunks but in cases like this all she would get were half-truths and false confessions.

'It's a straightforward route,' Ahmed went on. 'She clocked her quite quickly and stayed with her, hoping that she hadn't been spotted. But she must have been and that's why Stevenson led her round the park. I've traced it through from what Mrs Webber told me. Stevenson cut through and back, then parked up in the open, so Mrs Webber almost met the car head on. When she saw that Stevenson wasn't in it, she parked out of the way and went to follow on foot, assuming she was heading up towards the cutting. Stevenson was probably just standing in the trees with her head down. You know she was wearing rags when they found her? Just like Michael Drake. It was blowing a gale. She'd have been invisible as long as she didn't show her face.'

Webber shook his head. 'Melinda didn't say anything about rags.'

'She'd have had something on over the top of the outfit, but she must have been dressed and ready to go.'

'Joyce Yeatman turned up without Pamela's note and with a police officer,' Webber mused. 'I guess Stevenson decided to cut her losses and run.'

'Mrs Webber climbed up to the top path,' Ahmed went on. 'She caught a glimpse of someone up there but it must have just been walkers. Then as soon as she was well away from her car Stevenson made her move. That's when Mrs Webber saw her, but she had to get back down and drive right round from the top, where Stevenson could drive right out. She said she was on the phone to you when she saw Stevenson.'

Webber nodded. 'She dropped the phone then?'

'Yes, she said she stumbled when she saw Stevenson getting into the car and the phone flew right out of her hands and bounced down the hill.'

'Even so, Stevenson can't have gained much.'

'Just a few minutes, but that was all she needed to get herself to the exact spot and have time to throw things over.'

'Was she going to jump?'

Ahmed shook his head. 'I don't know.'

Webber thought back to the account he'd had from the teacher, Jack Meyer, of Stevenson's paranoid hatred of being the centre of attention. Melinda's actions had brought people to the bridge ahead of Stevenson. Maybe they'd prevented her leaping into oblivion, though no one had stopped a wealth of evidence hitting the water.

The sound of an engine revving grabbed his attention. It was the ambulance moving off. They seemed to have stayed a long time; he wondered suddenly if anyone had thought to tell them that Suzie was pregnant. It hadn't occurred to him. It was something that everyone knew but no one mentioned.

Ahmed watched Webber's gaze track the path of the ambulance as it bumped its way out along the track. It went slowly over the uneven ground. He wondered what was happening inside, what had been used to knock out the two women ... why had Webber fastened on to that comment about Stevenson making tea?

Webber suddenly spun on his heel and marched towards the front of the buildings. Ahmed hurried after him.

The voices of the team were close by, they'd moved from the first garage to the one he had scoured for a jemmy to break into the car. He saw people lifting wire cages, took in their puzzled expressions, listened to half theories tossed about as they searched and bagged the artefacts.

'... must have been years ... but ...'

Webber stepped forward to peer at the materials now being unearthed. 'How far back do those remains go?' Ahmed heard him ask. 'Best guess.'

An overalled woman tipped her head in an indeterminate gesture. 'A year ... 18 months ... but don't quote me.'

'I thought they were a lot older than that.' Webber sounded surprised.

'Oh yeah, there's some desiccated stuff from way back, must be decades old.'

He saw Webber's eyes narrow and wondered what the woman had thought he was asking. Her response was disjointed from the question. A year ... 18 months ... decades ...?

'So they actually go back ...' Webber was snappish but he stopped abruptly. Ahmed tried to read his expression. 'The really old stuff ...' The annoyance was gone. Webber's tone was speculative as he asked, 'Could we be talking four decades?'

The woman gave a shrug and spread her gloved hands. 'I suppose so, but really don't quote me on that one.'

'But there's a gap, isn't there? It's relatively new or very old. Nothing in between.'

'It looks that way.' She nodded and went back to her evidence bags. Webber turned to him. 'When Suzie was at Drake's house ... she phoned you ... she was making tea. Tell me what she said.'

Making tea ...? What was Webber chasing? Ahmed struggled to get the memories in order. 'She'd left him upstairs with some excuse about ...'

'Don't summarise,' Webber said. 'Tell me what she said.'

He stepped aside to be out of the way of the team as they tracked back and forth to their vehicle, then itemised his conversation with Suzie as best he could, Suzie making tea ... her derogatory comments about the Drake's kitchen ... her giving him the addresses of Tiffany's friends ... Drake upstairs searching for the password book; a book that probably never existed at all he thought now. Webber's stare was intense but Ahmed had the impression his thoughts were racing beyond the words he was listening to.

'What is it, Martyn?' he had to ask. 'What have you got?'

'Not sure,' Webber murmured. 'Something and nothing. I'm wondering if I've caught another of Drake's red-herrings or if ...' Ahmed watched Webber pull out his phone. 'I need to ring Mel, tell her I'm on my way back.'

That didn't shed any light on what had caught Webber's attention about making tea. Ahmed felt a frustrating sense of a lack of substance … like the gossamer strands that had shrouded the car interior.

'It might be another misdirection,' Webber went on, pausing in the act of clicking a number into his phone. 'But we can at least test this one.' His eye met Ahmed's. 'Go and get us some transport. I'm going home. I want to talk to China Kowalski and I want a landline to do it from. But first off, find out where they took Tiffany Drake. I need to talk to the medics. I think I know what he's been up to.'

chapter fifty-nine

Melinda was waiting for him, bright, alert, ready to talk. Her evidence boards stood against the blank TV screen. Half an hour in front of some mind-numbing programme while he ate would be good, but she wasn't going to allow that without a fight and he didn't have the energy. He needed space to get his thoughts in line for talking to China Kowalski.

As he'd climbed into his own car the other side of the gravel pits, he'd sent her an email labelled *Pamela Morgan*. He'd expected his name and the subject to push it to the top of her priority list and he was right. The reply had beeped into his inbox before he was half way home.

'Says she's in a meeting,' he told Melinda, 'but she'll be free in thirty minutes. She keeps some long hours, it can't be more than seven a.m. where she is.'

'I'll bet she's not had a good night's sleep since Pamela Morgan died,' Melinda said, walking across to the boards. 'I can cross her off, can't I?'

Webber nodded, finished the mouthful he was chewing and added, 'You can cross them all off bar one.'

She applied the eraser. He watched as each name disappeared until only Michael Drake was left. 'Have you enough to charge him?'

'For Pamela Morgan, no. Though I'd rather have him behind bars for her than all the rest together.'

She gave him a speculative look. 'So what can you pin on him?'

'Attempted murder of his wife. At least I hope we don't have to fight to upgrade that from GBH. It's looking good for Trent and Jenkinson, too. I think Jenkinson will be the jewel in the crown. That'll please Ayaan. We'll have a good look at Will Jones but … unlikely … and I doubt we'll get a sniff at the post office brother or Tilly Brown.'

'The first Mrs Drake?' Melinda asked.

'Maybe … maybe not. She's a long-shot.'

'Brad Tippet won't like seeing his ex-brother-in-law in the dock without Tina on the charge sheet.'

Webber grunted, indifferent to Brad Tippet's likes and dislikes. 'And of course we'll have another look at Gary Yeatman,' he added, 'but we've zilch on him for that.'

'Other than you know he did it,' Melinda said sharply.

He shrugged, conceding the point. Neither of them had mentioned Suzie's name. He'd simply said, 'They're OK,' when he'd rung her. She'd get to know the detail from Fiona. He wasn't going to be the one to tell her that the rest of Suzie's pregnancy would be shadowed by the knowledge that the baby could have been damaged by what Drake had done to her. If he said anything, Mel would want to talk about it and he'd yet to work out what his feelings were, other than murderous towards Michael Drake.

'What's so important about Pamela Morgan,' she said suddenly. 'Why would you rather do him for her than all the others?'

'Because she's the one he minds about … the one he regrets. If he were to end up in court on eight counts of murder …'

'Eight? Is that right?'

'I mean apart from Pamela.' He counted them off on his fingers. 'Tilly Brown bashed over the head and buried, his first wife poisoned, Pamela Morgan's husband hit over the head and fed to tigers, big brother post office bludgeoned and buried, Will Jones likewise, Gary Yeatman the car stunt, Tom Jenkinson bludgeoned and Arthur Trent the car thing again. Yes, eight. He'd be fine with that. He'd love it as long as Pamela wasn't in the list. He wants to boast about how clever he's been.'

'Not so clever that he hasn't been caught.'

'We haven't got him yet. But if the charge sheet's heavy enough that he knows he's looking at life, he'll probably tell all so he can have his day in the limelight.'

'But he'll not confess to Pamela,' she murmured.

'No, he regrets killing Pamela. Regrets it to the point of denial. I wonder why he did it. Maybe she found out about Robert and was going to shop him.'

'How did he kill her, Martyn?'

Webber blew out a breath. 'Fed her an overdose somehow … got her to write that note … I don't know. I've a feeling we already have the answer, all the pieces anyway, in the various interviews. Just haven't put them together yet, and until we do I've no idea if they'll turn into hard evidence or not.'

'Why are you so sure it was him who did it?'

'Because of the way he minds about it.'

Melinda glanced at the clock. 'Half an hour you said?'

He sighed and pulled himself upright. Maybe if he hadn't put Pamela's name in the subject line China Kowalski wouldn't have replied so promptly, but she had, so he supposed he'd better get it done.

'Will you take notes for me?' he asked, adding, 'The line might not be good enough for speakerphone.'

He knew that curiosity would make her agree. It would mean sitting close, leaning together so they could both hear. It would be a struggle not to get too comfortable, not to give in to the temptation to doze off on her shoulder.

China Kowalski's voice was alert and eager. 'Have you found out about Pamela?'

'We're close,' said Webber. 'But I need some more detail. I'd like you to tell me about Michael Drake's first marriage, it seemed to take everyone by surprise.'

'Yes, it did. Tina Tippet. Does that mean that …?'

'Please, Dr Kowalski, could you answer my questions first. I need to fill the holes in the background before I can give you any definitive answers.' He twisted his head to share a brief raised-eyebrows look with Mel.

'Yes, of course. And yes it was a surprise. Tina had been running after him but no one thought … then she was pregnant and they had to get married.'

'Yes, you told me that before. She miscarried, didn't she?'

'Yes, she was very ill. It was a late miscarriage. I don't know if it … uh … damaged her in any way. They didn't have children and of course she died not so long after.'

'Would they have married if she hadn't been pregnant?'

'Oh no. Michael was livid. He thought she'd trapped him. Still, he made the best of it. He always did make the best of things.'

'Dr Kowalski … China … uh, can I call you China? You told me – I think it was the first time you emailed me – you told me it was nothing to do with the quintets.'

'It wasn't,' she said. 'It was Michael. It was always Michael. I'm just so glad you've got there.'

He shared a look of surprise with Melinda.

'China, I get the feeling you're being more open with me than when we spoke face to face.'

'Well, yes,' she said. 'I'm out of your reach here. I had to be careful when I was in York. I didn't know if I might get dragged in.'

'Why would you have been dragged in? Were you involved?'

'In what!' She sounded shocked. 'No, I wasn't involved in anything, but they might have drawn me in the way they did Tilly and Pamela.'

He mouthed the name Tilly at Melinda, indicating that she should make a note. He wanted to explore that little outburst further. But for now … 'So Michael didn't want to marry Tina Tippet. Did he want to marry Pamela?'

'I thought so at the time, but I hadn't realised how much he hated her ... how much he hated us all. Except Edith.'

Webber's mind flew across memories of the various accounts he'd had. Something didn't fit. Was China Kowalski wrong, was he wrong ... were they all falling victim to Michael Drake's misdirections?

'You were such a close-knit group,' he said. 'Everyone says so.'

'Yes, but he was using us. We couldn't get away. I made it but only because I realised what would happen if I didn't.'

'Robert Morgan's funeral,' he said, changing tack, feeling Mel's irritation, she'd wanted him to explore that line to the end. 'There was some kind of rift. Tell me about it.'

There was a long enough silence that he'd begun to wonder if the line had cut, but when she spoke, her tone was quieter, firmer, as though she'd made up her mind about something.

'That's a good guess, Superintendent Webber.'

'Martyn,' he murmured.

'Martyn ... yes, I think that's when I knew ... really knew ...'

'Knew what?' he prompted.

'That they hated Pamela as much they hated us. I hadn't ... it was horrible to think of. It's hard to look back.'

'Who's they, China?'

'Michael Drake and Edie Stevenson.'

'Talk to me about what went on ... who said what to who ... whatever you can remember.'

It was a disjointed story. He was pretty sure she was mixing different events ... Robert Morgan's funeral, Gary Yeatman's, Tina Drake's ... and even a couple of school reunions. She told of feeling apart from the group, of drawing closer to Gary Yeatman in mutual repugnance at Michael Drake and Edith Stevenson.

'It was as though they were trying to jolly her out of it,' she said. 'At the funeral, for heaven's sake. Edith even told me that Pamela's grief was put on, that she was pleased really because she'd been going to divorce Robert.'

'Had she been going to divorce him?'

'I don't know. They had their ups and downs. Winning all that money made it easier for them. People say it drives you apart, that sort of windfall, well it didn't them. I don't think Robert liked the way she gave so much away but that was just Quinny.'

It had occurred to him before that Robert Morgan might have been less than pleased at his wife's generous gifts to her old school friends. 'Were they just gifts, China, or was Pamela paying them to leave her alone?'

She gave an uncertain laugh. Webber had the feeling this was a new idea to her. 'Well … no … I don't know … That was Quinny. It's just how she was.'

Tiredness was creeping up on him now. He wanted to keep the conversation going more to feel Melinda leaning up against him than that he wanted to unravel all China Kowalski's stories. He was too tired to be properly on point for this. And if he thought Mel would stay here beside him, he would end the call right now.

'So you know that Pamela gave a large sum of money to Michael Drake … also to Edith Stevenson. I don't know whether Robert knew or not.'

'Oh, he'd have known. Quinny didn't keep secrets from anyone.' He noticed she'd lapsed into the old nickname. He glanced at Melinda's notes. There'd been a couple of things he wanted to go back to, but before he could speak, she said, 'Oh, just a moment. There's someone here that I need a word with … can I ring you back?'

'How long will you be?'

'No more than a couple of minutes.'

'I'll stay on the line.'

He smiled at Melinda. Easing the handset from between them and covering the mouthpiece he said, 'This way she'll hurry,' letting his head rest into her shoulder, and turning to nuzzle her neck.

She didn't respond, but she didn't pull away.

'When you rang, you told me you had to get on to the hospital, that you knew how he'd been poisoning his wife.'

'Yes, possibly.' He hadn't envisaged using this break to discuss rotten meat. 'I remembered something about rank meat in the Drakes' fridge. Offal of some kind. A couple of people commented on it, Ayaan and … uh … anyway, I just put two and two together, might have made five.'

He felt her stiffen. 'You mean Harmer. You can say her name, you know.' The words were ice-coated and she sat upright away from him.

'Well anyway … you can do nasty things with contaminated meat, and then we found all that stuff. Of course it hangs on the age of it, but it looked like a trail of newish carcasses or the remnants of decades-old stuff. I thought maybe he'd poisoned his first wife with it and he was doing the same with the new one.'

'What sort of remains?'

'Dogs and cats mainly.'

'Eww! Offal from dogs and cats? That's gross.' Her face pinched in disgust. It reminded him of the way Ahmed had looked. 'How could you possibly poison someone with that? Who'd go near it?'

'Like I said, I hadn't really thought it through, but the timing … it fitted too well. I spoke to the medics. They got quite excited, thought there might be something in it.'

'Martyn … Martyn … are you still there?'

He clamped the phone back to his ear. 'Hello, China, yes.' He gave Melinda a quick smile as he returned to the call. She picked up her pen and pad. 'Just a couple more things. You said they drew in Tilly and Pamela. By *they* you mean Edith and Michael, don't you? What do you mean by drew in?'

He reached across and hugged Melinda to him so that they were close again and she could hear the call.

'He was jealous … they were both jealous of Tilly. She was a lovely girl, she'd have done so well. They'd no need to be like they were. Gary wasn't jealous of her and she teased him just as much.'

'When her parents moved away, didn't she stay with Edith to finish out the school year?'

'Yes, with her stupid rocking horse ...' Out of nowhere, China Kowalski's voice cracked. They heard her gulp in a couple of breaths. He shared a look of surprise with Melinda as Kowalski pulled herself together and added, 'They persuaded her to come back that summer, in secret.'

'You didn't say anything at the time,' he said gently, 'and I know you were questioned.'

'I didn't know then. I didn't know how much they hated her ... hated all three of us. It was Gary who told me to keep my distance. I was talking to him and his wife, saying we needed to keep an eye on Quinny. Edie and Michael were being so obnoxious, acting like it was a celebration after Robert died. Gary said, "Keep your distance from Michael Drake, I'm going to." And I have. I don't think I saw him again until Gary's funeral. I had to come back for that. Gary was the first of us to die. The first of us to have a funeral anyway. The first to die was poor Tilly. She ... she was lying dead nearby when the police were round asking questions all those years ago.'

He'd hoped to get at that nebulous something that would clarify things around Pamela Morgan's death, but wasn't sure now that she was the link he needed.

'Yes, probably.' He answered her question. 'Not that we can date her remains that accurately after all this time.'

'Remains?' she said. 'You've found her!'

Alarm bells clanged in his head.

... she was lying dead nearby ...

She hadn't been speculating, she'd been certain ... but she couldn't know anything about when or where Tilly had been found ... they didn't have final confirmation themselves yet. And she shouldn't know anything about when or where Tilly had died. He jerked upright gripping tight to the phone. 'Um ... buried up on scrubland behind the fishing lakes,' he told her.

'Oh! Well that's wonderful, that means she can have a funeral and a proper burial. I'll contact her aunt. I'll help with the arrangements. But how awful that it's too late for her parents.'

'Hang on … you couldn't have known we'd found Tilly's body. Why were you so certain that she'd be round here and not in Dorset?'

'Well, I always sort of knew she must be dead … when she never turned up, but …'

Shit, thought Webber looking across at Melinda's evidence boards, the ghost of Kowalski's name shimmering from behind the work of the eraser. Had he got it all upside down?

'… that's how I knew about Quinny,' Kowalski was saying. 'Once I knew Tilly went back to York because of them, I knew they'd killed her, so they must have killed Quinny too. I wonder if she confronted them. That's why I didn't want my name anywhere near it. They'll come after me. I might be out of your jurisdiction but I'd never be safe from them.' Her voice had lost its calm veneer.

Webber struggled to make sense from the jumble of words. It had been madness to start this tonight. 'What do you mean?'

'Bradley Tippet promised to keep my name out of it. He thought he was just causing trouble for some policeman or other, getting us into that club and pretending to bump into him by accident. I'd have let it lie if I'd known I couldn't trust him.'

'Too late for that, China. And it wasn't Bradley Tippet who gave you away.'

He gave Melinda a quick glance. She'd been the one to find Dr China but he wasn't going to drop her name into the mix.

'China, you were all interviewed when Tilly went missing. There was no hint that she'd come back to York. When did you find out? Who told you?'

'No one told me,' she said, her tone defensive. 'Well … Tilly told me I suppose. It was last summer after her mother died.'

'So you stayed in touch with Tilly's parents?'

'No, no, it was a firm of solicitors about her will. She left me Tilly's rocking horse.'

'Why would she do that?' He could tell from Melinda's sharp intake of breath that she was itching to shout her own questions down the phone, but it would only take a fraction of a second for China Kowalski to cut the call and go to ground.

'Tilly wanted me to have it. If only she'd … oh, I suppose she couldn't have known the significance. Apparently Tilly said I was to have the rocking horse if anything happened to her.'

'Really? I don't remember anything like that from the original case.'

'I don't think she left a note or anything. It'll have been something she'd said. The thing is her mother knew Tilly wanted me to have the rocking horse and all its stuff but she didn't want to let it go. It had been so important to Tilly. I can understand that, but if they'd only told me at the time …'

'What? What difference would it have made?'

'I'd have found her stuff. Michael could have been stopped.'

'What stuff?'

'Her diaries. She wrote everything down. She always did. They'd planned for her to go back that summer. I don't know why she never told the rest of us. She shouldn't have trusted Edie … maybe she didn't … why else would she have told them to give me the horse? If her mother had only told me at the time, we could have had the paperwork out and … oh, I don't know … maybe nothing would have stopped him. I had it shipped out. It arrived in March. Customs made quite a mess of it, thought it had drugs inside.'

Webber felt his jaw drop as she talked. 'These diaries … they were inside the horse?'

'Yes. Tilly used to carry her things round in the saddlebags but the horse's body was hollow where the saddle fitted on. It was where she kept things secret from her mother.'

'What was in there? What does it say? Do you still have it?'

'It's not all there,' she said. 'It's a fraction of what she must have written over those years.'

'But why didn't you tell someone?'

'Tell them what? The plan for her to come back could have been taken as just another story, like the ones about the allotments.'

'The allotments?' he asked feeling a frisson of apprehension run across his skin.

He listened aghast, sharing a disbelieving look with Melinda, as Kowalski spoke. He already knew that the garage had been leased by the Browns. It became clear that all the children had played up there. Kowalski didn't seem to think the very old stories were relevant to anything, but he gave her a prompt.

'You said something about farmers. What was that about?'

'Some friends of the Browns. I told you Tilly wove stories around everyone she knew. I didn't know them.'

'A foot and mouth epidemic,' he queried.

'Yes, that was the story. How did you know?'

'Tell me that story, China.'

'I can't remember ... that's not what's important. Well, it was something about how the animals were saved. There was an outbreak of foot and mouth. They saved some of the animals, that was the story. It was just Tilly. It was just a story. It's the other bit, the bit about her coming back here, that's the part that's true.'

'Why are you so certain there's no truth in the earlier one?'

'Because it's all or nothing with foot and mouth. You don't save *some* animals.'

Not unless, thought Webber, you get someone to help you dig a deep pit to dispose of the carcasses of the ones you can't save. Not a fatal disease in most cases, just too contagious to allow an infected herd to live. Some of the quintets at least had known about that cattle pit, maybe even helped with the logistics of the cover-up.

'So why didn't you mention Tilly Brown to Donald Farrar? Why just Pamela Morgan?'

'It was too late for Tilly. It was 45 years ago and it was just a story. But I thought there might be a chance of getting them for Quinny if only someone would look properly.'

'What do you mean too late!' He had to make an effort not to shout. 'There's no statute of limitations on murder.'

'I was one of the quintets back then.' Her voice was quiet. 'I was part of the group.'

Webber pulled in a breath and felt Melinda react. But he knew that China Kowalski wasn't confessing to involvement in Tilly Brown's murder, she was saying … what was she saying?

'They'd have known,' she went on in that same quiet voice. 'They *will* know. After all this time it could only be me. But I wasn't around when they killed Quinny.'

So she was still frightened of them, despite the distance she'd put between them. 'Do you still have Tilly's diaries?' he asked. 'I need to have them. I'll arrange to have them securely shipped.'

After the call was over, Webber slumped back into the cushions, thoughts spinning. 'She should have been pleased,' he murmured as he slotted the handset back in its base.

'Who should? Pleased about what?' Melinda said, but went on before he could answer, 'Martyn, does this mean you can get him for Tilly Brown?'

He shrugged. 'I doubt it. Even if she's telling the truth … depends what state this evidence is in … whether we can tie it to him or not. I wonder if we can…'

'What? If you can what?'

'I wonder if we can get him for Tilly Brown,' he said. 'Come on, it's late. Let's get to bed.'

She should have been pleased.

Who had said that? Not China Kowalski. It meant something but tomorrow would be soon enough to figure it out. He'd known from the off that he'd arrested Michael Drake on a charge that couldn't go anywhere, but having Tilly Brown reach out from his past and get the better of him one last time wouldn't be a bad second best.

chapter sixty

Webber heard the phone ring the next morning while he was struggling to dress Sam.

'It's someone from the hospital.' Melinda's voice was frosty. 'Said you'd asked them to call.'

'About the poisoning,' he said as he took the handset from her. 'Not ...'

'Come on, Sam. Let's get breakfast.' Sam grabbed his father's trouser leg to pull himself to his feet and set off unsteadily after his mother. Webber watched them as he put the phone to his ear.

'It's about Mrs Drake.' The words were upbeat. He recognised the medic he'd spoken to the night before. 'Good shot, Superintendent, it's looking like you were on to something. There's no easy test but the symptoms fit. It's just so unusual ... not something we'd look for in the normal run of things.'

'Will she be OK?'

'Well ...' The buoyant tone deflated. 'It depends. Best case she'll recover naturally ... worst case she'll be on a transplant list, life on hold.'

When he finished the call, he rang Ahmed because Ahmed was up to date on the cold cases and would remember the detail.

It fitted. It all fitted. Surely they had Drake now for what he'd done to Tiffany, even if they couldn't prove he'd killed Tina. And he had to be inextricably linked to what had happened to Suzie. His makeshift slaughterhouse had easy access to the burial site where three bodies had been unearthed ... and to where Tom Jenkinson had been killed.

When he walked through to the kitchen, Sam was in his high chair, his cereal in front of him.

'Eat up those lovely vitamins,' Melinda was saying, 'so you grow big and strong.'

Webber smiled. 'It looks like that's what Drake fed his wives.' He nodded towards Sam's bowl, then had to leap forward, hand upraised to stop Melinda from grabbing Sam's breakfast. 'No, no. I didn't mean that. I meant vitamins. He's been overdosing them with vitamins.'

'What?' Melinda stared at him.

'Vitamin overdose. There's some fancy name for it. She had all the right symptoms, dizziness, nausea, sensitivity to sunlight, bone pain. Turns out it's very hard to diagnose ... there's no real test for it and no one thinks to try. But deadly. Depending on the dosage it can be quite quick. Drake was careful. Didn't go overboard. I've just spoken to Ayaan. He'll go back over everything but there was always a reason for when Tiffany's health got bad. She was just back from staying with a friend ... she'd been trying herbal remedies ... anything but Drake's home cooking.'

Melinda glanced at Sam and then out of the window to where the garden wore a hard frost, early light shimmering from the silver threads that adorned the bushes.

'Vitamins? But aren't vitamins good for you?'

'Well, recommended daily amounts and all that, but they can be nasty in quantity.'

'How is she?'

'They're keeping her in to see how bad she is, but the best treatment is Drake being behind bars and no longer in control of what she eats.'

She turned to Sam and made a pretence of straightening his bowl as she asked with apparent carelessness, 'And how's Harmer?'

The question hit him like a slap in the face. Of course he should have asked about Suzie. He'd forgotten her in his rush to chase up the details of the poisoning. 'Uh … I didn't think to ask. It was the medic who'd been treating Tiffany Drake.'

'For heaven's sake, Martyn! What were you thinking? She's one of your officers. Oh, never mind, I'll ring Fiona later.' She gave him a hard glare, then snapped, 'Watch Sam,' as the clack of the letter box signalled arrival of the post.

He watched her stalk out to the hallway, her rigid form radiating self-righteousness. She'd snapped at him but she'd been pleased.

She returned with half a dozen letters which she skimmed through, tossing a couple aside and handing him a thick ornate envelope. He was aware of her curious glance as he took in the intricate lettering that spelt out his name and address. It looked hand-written and yet too neat not to have originated from a machine. As he reached for a knife to slit the top, he saw that Melinda's attention had turned to a letter of her own. He caught a glimpse of unfamiliar handwriting as he slid out a stiff card with embossed edges from the fancy envelope. It was a formal invitation to Mr and Mrs Webber – brackets, *and Sam Webber*, close brackets – from someone he'd never heard of … what the hell? Then in amongst the ostentation of the decoration that wove its way around more of that perfect calligraphy, he spotted a familiar name.

'Ayaan's wedding,' he said. 'We're all invited, Sam too.'

She smiled. 'When is it?'

'April 15th.'

'Well, make sure you've got the day off. Don't go letting everyone else have time and you end up working. I want to go and I don't want to be on my own with Sam. It'll be a really big do, by all accounts.'

Webber wanted to say, poor Ayaan, but held the thought in.

Melinda took the card from him and studied it. 'How come they have our home address?'

'Their daughter's marrying a detective.'

'A good detective you've always said.'

'Yes, he is.'

'Then you shouldn't resent him.'

'I don't,' he said, surprised. Where had that come from?

'Good.' She speared him with a look, then lifted up the letter she'd been reading. 'We're in demand today. Don Farrar wants us to have lunch with him the Friday before Christmas.'

A cascade of potential complications flooded Webber's mind. What would John Farrar make of his father inviting them to lunch? It was clearly a pitch to find out how the whole Pamela Morgan thing had panned out, and he'd targeted Melinda because she'd find a way to go even if he tried to demur. But maybe there was a way out.

'We can't,' he said. 'We'll be with your parents.' His heart sank a little at the reminder that the ordeal of the Christmas visit was yet to come.

'No, it's not to his house here, it's to his club. We could go into London from Mum and Dad's. It's only an hour by train. They'll look after Sam.'

'OK.' He bowed to the inevitable. And a lunch invitation from retired Captain Donald Farrar who'd been something-or-other in the Foreign Office would help oil the wheels with Melinda's father, who was a crashing snob.

'Does he know we have Sam?' Melinda asked. 'He'd love London, wouldn't you, Sam? I could get in touch and ask if it'd be OK.'

Maybe she would end up refusing the invitation after all. 'No, it wouldn't,' he told her. 'I looked up Farrar's swanky club after the whole thing with China Kowalski. No children under fourteen and no women members.'

'You're kidding!' She spun round with a disbelieving stare.

'You'll be there on sufferance as a guest.' He didn't hide his amusement as he watched conflicting emotions cross her face. Curiosity would win out in the end, he thought, and a day's escape from the Bryants would be a bonus.

It was as she cleared away Sam's breakfast that she returned to the previous topic.

'Was it a particular vitamin, Tiffany Drake I mean, or was it just any old stuff?'

'They don't know for sure, but vitamin A is the lead contender, it fits her symptoms.'

'But Martyn, what did he do? How? He didn't force-feed her cornflakes. And what ...?' A look of horror swept across her features. 'Those animal remains ...'

'He could have been overdosing her on supplements, over the counter stuff, but he might have thought the purchases would be traceable. And preliminary analysis of that stuff in his fridge looks like canine liver.'

Melinda put her hand to her mouth. 'Yuk! But how on earth could he have persuaded her to eat it?'

'Plenty of people like liver.'

'Not dog's liver!'

'Who's to know once it's cooked? It probably all tastes much the same.'

'You said there were cats as well.'

'I daresay he was experimenting. It's something to do with animals that eat bones. The excess vitamin A gets stored in the liver; the older the dog, the greater the concentration. Apparently husky-type dogs were his best bet. Polar bear or seal liver would have been more toxic but they were out of his reach. At least I assume they were. God knows what we're going to find traces of in that garage.'

Melinda went to lift Sam from his highchair. Stray tales of other people's children crossed Webber's radar from time to time ... the faddy eaters, the children who spread destruction in their wake wherever they went, Mel's friends who wouldn't join in trips to the park because of the stress of keeping their offspring away from roads, ponds and anywhere they could hurl themselves into mortal danger. He thought of Sam sitting placidly at work in the middle of a mini grand prix. Someone had once said to him, 'You might not be so lucky with your second. They're all different.'

His second child would be Suzie's, maybe damaged by whatever Michael Drake had used to subdue her. How had Drake got Suzie Harmer of all people to ingest anything, let alone a strong barbiturate? Whatever it was, it would turn out that she'd thought it was her own idea.

'You know something?'

Her words made him jump. It was as though she'd sensed he'd been thinking of Suzie. He wanted to say, yes, I was thinking about her but not like that! The thought evaporated. She already knew Suzie was nothing to him, that wasn't the point. And dear though Mel was to him, she wasn't psychic. She'd been reacting to her own thoughts, not his.

'No, what?'

'I can't get it out of my head that China Kowalski was right. She was, wasn't she? Michael Drake killed Pamela Morgan but you're never going to be able to pin it on him.'

He nodded slowly. Her words floated about bumping into other people's stray pronouncements.

China Kowalski was right ... Not Quinny! ... She should have been pleased ...

No, China Kowalski wasn't right. She was wrong. They hadn't hated Pamela Morgan. They'd worshiped her. Hers was the one death that Michael Drake genuinely regretted. Maybe it was that simple. First thing in the morning, he'd be on to John Farrar.

chapter sixty-one

....

It was Webber's last day at work before Christmas. Tomorrow he, Mel and Sam would drive down to stay with the Bryants. He hadn't told her that this was anything other than a routine day for him, and he hadn't told Farrar about the lunch invitation that Melinda had accepted for both of them. After the event would be soon enough for that.

It wasn't by the book. He shouldn't be having anything to do with Michael Drake now, but Farrar had agreed to go along with it. The man's legal team hadn't seemed anything special; it had felt like a joke that they should try for bail, but they did and it had hung in the balance. Clearly a string of terrible crimes lay beneath the bland wording of the charge sheet but a compelling impression was built that the frail and kindly Mr Drake had been wrongly accused, so how could it hurt to allow him to stay in his own home over Christmas? Thankfully the public safety risk weighed heavily, but it had been too close for comfort.

'And what if he insists on contacting his brief?' Farrar had asked when Webber outlined what he wanted to do.

Webber thought it more than likely. 'Then we go ahead with Drake's legal team in the room.' Farrar hadn't looked at all convinced so Webber had borrowed a metaphor from their Norwegian colleagues. 'We have this tiger by the tail, John. We can't let him escape.'

No guarantee that Drake would see him; although the man's arrogant persona would think himself well able to get the better of Webber, and the cooperative façade would agree without question, only Webber didn't think the cooperative side of Michael Drake would see the light of day again until he was in front of the jury of his peers who had his future in their hands.

They'd barely started the drive when Farrar's mobile began to ring and he spent most of the journey issuing orders into the handset. As they neared the gaol, he clicked it off. 'Pull over here.'

Webber stopped the car and waited. After a moment, Farrar said, 'We could completely screw things up, Martyn.'

'We don't want him walking away from it.'

'How's that ever going to happen?'

'He'll shove it all on to Edith Stevenson. She'll fall apart in court.' He held back the detailed argument. Farrar knew the score. He'd seen emotion smother the most solid of evidence when the courtroom drama played out the wrong way.

'His defence team'll crucify you if they get their teeth in.'

'I know.'

'Not just you. Melinda … Suzie … young Ahmed.'

Webber pulled in a breath. 'If he walks free, John, it'll be like those tigers are loose again.'

'But are you sure?'

'I was there with him … that off-the-record chat, remember?'

'The recording Ayaan Ahmed made wasn't very distinct.'

'If there'd been video you wouldn't have any doubts.'

'It was quick thinking on his part that there's any record at all. He's a good officer, Martyn, you mustn't resent him.'

'I don't!' Webber felt his jaw clench. If one more person implored him not to resent Ahmed, he was going to start resenting him for that reason alone.

A memory popped up.

Farrar barking at him, *If you're thinking of lobbying me about Suzie's maternity leave, don't.*

Mel the next day, *John told me … said what you'd … it was a nice thing to do.*

He was gobsmacked. Farrar had thought he'd gone to lobby for Melinda to take on Suzie's maternity cover. And that's what he'd told Mel. That's why they thought he would resent Ahmed being brought in.

As if he'd have tried something like that … He bit back on a furious reply as he remembered Mel's smile, the first glimmer of a proper smile that he'd had since Harmer's bombshell. Had she stayed with him because he'd been prepared to throw out such a fundamental principle for her? He'd probably never know. If there was ever going to be a good time to ask that question, it wouldn't be any time soon.

He pushed Ahmed and Mel out of his mind. Any spare resentment he had was reserved for Drake for revelling in his moment in the limelight whilst still holding on to the hope that he would wriggle out of the way. He must have escaped many tight corners in the past.

Not this time, Michael.

'We know they have to put Drake on the stand,' he said to Farrar. 'If he just shows a courtroom a glimpse of what I saw in him, no jury'll want him walking the streets, but …' He stopped; he was repeating himself. They'd been through all this. So much of the case seemed damning but so much of it was circumstantial … smoke and mirrors …

There was a theoretical chance that Drake wouldn't take the stand, but in that case they were home and dry. The evidence was overwhelming. Drake's only chance was to paint himself as wrongly accused, misguided, the unwitting dupe of Edith Stevenson, and that of course played right to Drake's talents. If he could maintain the charade, he might just do it.

Farrar shrugged. 'Let's give it a go.'

Drake agreed to see him with an alacrity that in itself rang alarm bells. He would store this up for later hay making with claims of coercion and harassment.

It was an old-fashioned interview room that lay empty as Webber and Farrar looked into it from behind the glass. The space they were in was cramped, dusty, a makeshift storeroom. No one used the one-way glass these days. The interview suite was kitted out with recording equipment that currently lay comatose on the desk. They watched as Drake was brought in, saw his glance take in the recorders, the cameras, the fact that they were all switched off.

Webber pulled in a deep breath. He wanted to say, wish me luck, but Farrar wouldn't like that. He settled for, 'OK, here goes.'

He didn't look at Drake as he entered the room but was aware the man was watching him, his expression relaxed, mildly amused.

'Good morning, Michael,' he said as he sat down across the table.

Drake glanced again at the equipment, all its reflective screens blank, all its switches set to off.

'Another off-the-record chat, Mr Webber?'

'Is that a problem for you, Michael?'

Drake shrugged and smiled. 'All the usual questions, I suppose. Yes, I'm not doing too badly. The food in here ...'

'No, Michael, I've no interest in how you are. I'm here to read you Pamela Morgan's suicide note.'

Drake's eyes narrowed in a flare of suspicion and his hand reached forward to stroke the control panel, to feel round the edges as though to uncover a fake and reveal that they were being recorded after all. 'I heard it at the time of the inquest.'

'Did you? How well do you remember it?'

'As well as anyone would remember something like that.' Drake's tone took on a sharper edge. 'Pamela was a dear friend. I'm not sure I want or need to hear it again. And certainly not from you.' He began to push himself to his feet.

'Sit down, Michael,' Webber barked at him.

Another line crossed. Their stares locked for a second then Drake sat back down.

'The coroner remarked on the anomaly of it not being signed. Do you remember that, Michael? Turns out Joyce Yeatman held back the final page.'

'I know all about that.' There was a level of scorn in Drake's voice now. 'She told ... um, uh ... said so.'

Webber heard Drake's small trip as he veered away from saying 'told me' or 'told us'. He was relieved to hear 'told' and not 'showed', though he was fairly confident Joyce hadn't shown anyone that last page. Her problem had been the way the key phrases had etched themselves on to her memory. The sheaf of yellowed papers in his hand was something he'd constructed using descriptions of the original.

Joyce Yeatman had burnt that final page before the inquest and the rest afterwards. All he had were the phrases that had eventually been squeezed out of her and the quotes that had found their way into the coroner's report.

He was confident Drake didn't know the note had been destroyed. If he'd known then he and Stevenson wouldn't have invested time keeping an eye on Joyce over the years.

He looked down at the page in his hand and began to quote the extracts that Michael would recognise.

'... I've tried but I can't live with the way it happened ... now it plays out in front of me ...'

He looked up from the page and rested his gaze on Drake as he said, 'She couldn't take the news that autumn, could she? I wondered about the timing when I first read about her. People trapped, knowing that death was moments away.' He didn't have the exact quote for that. To minimise morbid press interest, mention of 9/11 had been omitted from the report, and as Joyce remembered it, Pamela hadn't referred to those events by name, but then they might not have acquired the label that early on. He went back to the page.

'... *we'd quarrelled, never made up ... it won't get better ...*'

'Poor woman,' he said. 'Having that to live with. Did you know they'd quarrelled when you put him in that warehouse?'

Drake sat motionless, his demeanour calm. Webber could see no sign he was getting under his skin.

'... *and now seeing the same horror multiplied ... I can't stop seeing it ... I'll never stop seeing it ...*'

Drake murmured, 'Poor Quinny.' Webber heard true regret in his tone.

He flicked through the papers. 'And then that final page,' he said. 'The one that Joyce Yeatman hid for all these years.'

'She told me about it.'

Webber wasn't convinced; he felt an underlying edginess.

'Joyce was frightened of you, Michael. I don't think she ever dared to tell you what she'd read.' He paused, let his gaze flick briefly over the page.

'... *I can't live with what happened to Robert ...*'

Drake remained still, too still, except for his right hand whose fingers rubbed together as though obsessively rolling a scrap of paper.

Webber moved only his eyes; a glance at Drake ... a glance at the page. Drake's gaze was unfocussed. Was he hearing Pamela's voice from across the years?

'... *I can't live with knowing it was deliberate ...*'

The spike in tension was tangible. Webber felt it as a bolt of lightning piercing suddenly and silently, immobilising everything living but making every hair on his body stand on end.

'... *and of all people ...*'

Drake's stillness sent a shiver through him. He hadn't meant to pause at this point. His mouth had dried. Drake was listening hard for the words that Joyce had told him were there, but at the same time seemed to be willing Webber to stop. Webber had a sudden flashback to a warehouse scene that had never happened; a man crouching in the dark realising that the silence was too solid, too complete, that it was a tiger poised within arm's reach. If he didn't get the words out now, he was going to bottle it.

'… and of all people … that it was Michael who did it …'

His gaze slid up to meet Drake's. 'Pamela knew it was you, Michael … she knew …'

He made to stand up.

'No!' The shriek was deafening.

The crash spun Webber almost off his feet. Something solid, unyielding, crunched into the side of his head. If he hadn't been half standing he'd have been on his knees.

A moment of realisation. He'd been right!

Murderous uncontrolled fury. The tiger unleashed.

Raising his hands … desperate to fend off the attack, knowing suddenly, viscerally, that Michael Drake could kill him in a fraction of a second … too quick for Farrar to summon help … too quick for Farrar to intervene.

Barely time to thank the heavens the man was unarmed when the claw raked his face … fire igniting an agony of pain. His hands scrabbled at the iron fist … immovable … blood dripped on to his arm.

And it was over almost as it began. The rabid tiger slumped forward, gasping for air, face draining of colour. Webber scrambled to his feet, flapping his hand towards the glass.

'Medics,' he gasped. 'Get the medics in here.'

A second, he thought. It can't be more than a second since I said it.

Drake's breath rasped. His eyes rolled. He was losing consciousness. Webber fought an urge to stamp hard on the man, to scream in his face, 'She knew! Your precious Pamela knew it was you all along.'

This wasn't the time or the place. He'd done what he needed to do and though his hands were shaking from the speed and ferocity of the attack, he had Drake's feet hauled up on to the chair before Farrar dived in, his expression horror-struck.

'Christ Martyn! Medics are on their way. What …?'

Webber shushed him with outspread palm, a finger to his lips. Say nothing. Don't give him anything to chew on. Leave him with the shock of it.

They stood over him, wary, until running footsteps sounded and the door burst open again.

Webber pressed his hand to the side of his face, keeping his head turned away, hiding the blood that seeped through his fingers.

'He's in shock,' Farrar told them. 'We've got his feet up.'

As the warders eased Drake to a more comfortable position, Webber's eye caught the glint of silver as something slipped from the man's hand. Making a pretence of brushing down his trouser leg, he picked it up, concealed it in his closed fist to dispose of later; didn't need the extra complications of this encounter coming under the spotlight.

'I've never seen anyone move so quick,' Farrar said as they headed out. The disbelief in his tone matched the shakiness that Webber was trying to suppress.

Drake's guard never dropped, he realised, not for a fraction of a second. He hadn't arrived with anything in his hand, the warders couldn't have been that careless. There must have been a weapon nestling in a groove beside the console, and Webber would bet that Drake had spotted it the second he'd walked through the door. He remembered watching Drake's fingers feel their way around the recording equipment. It hadn't been a surreptitious inspection, Drake had done it openly, and Webber had fallen for it. In his hand he could feel the shape of the roughly straightened paperclip, the claw that had raked the side of his face.

'They'll need security to be on the ball when he's in the dock,' he said.

He tried to feel satisfaction in having been right, but couldn't shake the suddenness and ferocity of the attack from the front of his mind.

'He'll be wearing his frail and ailing personality again by then.' Farrar spoke with a sneer. 'I hope he won't have had time to come to terms with it.'

'He won't. It's how many years since his first wife died? He could barely contain his fury when he told me how she'd lied about the policy. And that was only Tina. This is Pamela.' Webber spoke with conviction. He'd seen it from up close; too close.

And he'd had the conversation last night with Melinda. She'd asked, 'How did he do it, Martyn? It was barbiturates, the same as he used on Tiffany and Harmer, but how?'

'I think he might have been trying to repay that huge financial injection she'd given him,' he'd said. 'I think that's where it started. He'd have done anything for Pamela, so when she was fool enough to voice complaints against her husband he decided to get rid of him. It was bad luck that it all got entangled with Will Jones and his plan to release those tigers. The three of them, Drake, Yeatman and Morgan, were on a secret mission to Dorset to stop Jones. I think Drake told Yeatman it was a desperate plea from Edith Stevenson but she was in it up to her neck.'

Her brow had furrowed. 'I know how he killed Robert Morgan. I was asking about Pamela.'

He'd told her that in the end it had been the same murder. 'He killed her the moment he killed her husband the way he did … or rather the way that it came to be painted in her head. She couldn't live with the thought of Robert's last moments. If he'd told her what he'd done, that Robert was dead before the tigers reached him, then she might have got past it, but he couldn't bring himself to do that.'

Melinda's expression had been close to indignant. 'Are you saying he didn't feed her drugs and trick her into writing a note?'

'No, she did those bits herself. Drake murdered her husband in a way that killed her too. And it took her fifteen years to die.'

Drake could only cope with being responsible for Pamela's death as long as he could believe she'd never known that he was the one who had killed her husband. He'd seen her suspicions grow, must have suspected that she'd worked it out. It had festered in Drake's subconscious over the years but the man had never faced it. Except that now he'd had to. Webber had forced it on him.

There would be a long time to mull it over before it came to court. Long enough that there would be nothing left of that initial bolt of shock, there would be no dramatic collapse to be misinterpreted, just uncontrolled fury at whoever was going to voice the unthinkable.

'All those years ago,' Farrar said. 'Brad Tippet was right. When did you suss him, Martyn?'

Webber had formed a don't-know shrug before realising that there had been a moment of realisation. 'After he'd gone off with Ayaan,' he said. 'I was listening to China Kowalski on tape and looking up Charlie Sheen quotes. Something struck a chord.'

Farrar nodded. 'Well, you've done it, you've planted the seed that'll unship him in the dock. Why are you looking so pissed off?'

Webber wanted to growl that apart from having been within an inch of losing an eye, or maybe worse, and having blood dripping down his face he felt just fine, but realised that Farrar was right.

'I'm pissed off about Pamela Morgan.'

Joyce Yeatman had finally talked about Pamela's suicide note and spoken the words Webber had misquoted to Michael Drake, the words that she'd burnt to ashes but never forgotten.

... and of all people ... that it was Gary ...

'Pamela got as far as figuring that it was murder,' he said, 'but she thought Gary had done it. She never knew the truth. I wish she had.'

'I suppose Drake eased her into thinking it was Yeatman once he saw her getting close,' said Farrar.

'Yes, but he could at least have told her that the tigers hadn't done it. It was the manner of his death that she couldn't live with.'

'Psychopath,' Farrar said, 'and with an ego that size, he'd never have come clean, not even for his precious Pamela. Leave it be, Martyn. We've done our bit. You can't go back and change the past however much you want to, and if you let it fester you'll end up like Brad Tippet, holding on to old grudges. I wonder if he's learnt any lessons from all this.'

'I wonder if any of us have,' murmured Webber, knowing as he spoke that he'd learnt the biggest lesson of his life, and might have learnt it too late but for a woman called Pamela Morgan who had been his one solid connection with Mel when everything else threatened to crumble. Distortions of the truth were dangerous beasts, he thought, and yet we've all been at it over the past few weeks, even straitlaced Ahmed with his behind the scenes work on Tom Jenkinson. A mental image of the ornate invitation to the April wedding came to his mind. He smiled. It gave him a glimmer of the optimism that went with opening new chapters, building new alliances.

'I hope the weather's good in April,' he said, as they pushed their way out into the cold December air.

THE END

"I'm different. I have a different constitution. I have a different brain. I have a different heart. I got tiger blood, man. Dying's for fools. Dying's for amateurs."
Charlie Sheen

about the author

Penny Grubb is a scientist, a researcher and a teacher as well as a novelist. Writing techniques are her 'thing'. She wants everyone to know about the power of the written word and how it works in academic, creative, journalistic, reflective writing and indeed all contexts. She believes that once people understand the power of words, they are protected from exploitation by mendacious purveyors of half-truths and propaganda.

Penny is author of the Annie Raymond mysteries, a crime series published both sides of the Atlantic that morphed gently (or perhaps violently) into a series of police procedurals of which Tiger Blood is the second.

Penny is active on social media when she can find the time and loves to hear from readers. Come and join her:

Penny's blog: pennygrubb.blogspot.co.uk
Penny's website: pennygrubb.com
Penny is also on Facebook, Twitter and LinkedIn

THE ANNIE RAYMOND MYSTERIES
Like False Money
The Jawbone Gang
The Doll Makers
Where There's Smoke
Buried Deep

Available from Amazon, Harlequin Mystery and the
FantasticBooksStore.com

www.ingramcontent.com/pod-product-compliance
Lightning Source LLC
Chambersburg PA
CBHW072010020726
47501CB00006B/1757